D1261400

ON THE EDGE OF A LIFETIME

FRANK McGILLION

ON THE EDGE OF A LIFETIME

MAINSTREAM
PUBLISHING

EDINBURGH AND LONDON

First published in Great Britain in 2002 by
MAINSTREAM PUBLISHING COMPANY (EDINBURGH) LTD
7 Albany Street
Edinburgh EH1 3UG

ISBN 1 84018 573 2

A catalogue record for this book is available from the British Library

Typeset in Bembo and Lithos
Printed and bound in Great Britain by Butler and Tanner

For Al, Billy and every other child like them.

ACKNOWLEDGEMENTS

Specific acknowledgements are due to:

Albion Rovers FC, for permission to use the club's name.

HMV and EMI, for permission to cite the HMV trademark.

Glaxo Smith-Kline for permission to cite the Lucozade trademark.

International Music Publications for permission to include short lyrics from: 'Stranger in Paradise'. Words and Music by George Forrest and Robert Wright ©1953 Scheffel Music Corp, USA, Warner/Chappell Music Ltd, London, W6 8BS.

Viv McKennel and Patrick Roberts, for suggestions and comment, and John Carmichael (photography).

Bill Campbell and Deborah Kilpatrick of Mainstream: the former for his commitment to, and encouragement with, the project, the latter for her inspired editing of the manuscript.

A special acknowledgement is due to my wife, Eve, whose assistance, encouragement and support have been quite simply invaluable and greatly appreciated.

A special acknowledgement must also be given to many of the staff and pupils at Sandyford Special School, Paisley, between 1953 and 1964 and Saint Mirin's Academy, Paisley, particularly those in attendance between 1964 and 1966.

PREFACE

Over the past century studies into the nature of memory and recall have been many and complex, and they've produced considerable changes in how we view these processes.

The interrelationship between memory, recall and our use of language has been given careful consideration too, with some researchers suggesting the nature of our perceived reality is actually determined by language. Humour too is now viewed as a complex phenomenon linked to a number of intricate psychological processes.

Given the speculations and findings ensuing from such studies, the precise nature of what any biographical account really is, and what it actually portrays, has come under scrutiny. Accordingly there are grounds for assuming there may be an as yet unconventional, but perhaps more credible, method of presenting biographical material than the one traditionally used.

On the Edge of a Lifetime uses such an unconventional form, and it does so in an attempt to present the biographical material it portrays in an honest, accurate, informative and entertaining manner.

INTRODUCTION

They say it never rains but it pours, and they may well be right. For it didn't rain that morning – not a drop. But it poured down later all right, metaphorically speaking, precisely when everything should have been bright and sunny. For I was starting school that day, and that's supposed to be a sunny day in a child's life, even a child with a life as precarious as mine was. They also say you can never predict the weather in the west of Scotland – where I'd been born and bred, and clung on to life like a congenital loser hitting a lucky streak in a back-street casino – and they say the same about the people there, too. For, like the weather, those hardbitten Scots have a deserved reputation for unpredictability so that it makes you wonder how they managed to live together long enough to forge a national identity in the first place. But they have a reputation for kindness too, and that can also be dramatic at times; and it has a habit of appearing at moments when it's most needed, most unexpected and most welcome.

As for the people I was going to meet that day – children mainly, but people just the same – well, unpredictable isn't the word for it. I don't think we even had a word for it back then – not for those sorts of people and not for that degree of unpredictability. And what about that traditional Scots kindness? Had they that? That's something you'll have to judge for yourself. For kindness is a value-laden term, just as terms like horrid, hope or handicap are value-laden – endowed with qualities they don't possess, and with attributes they'd be better off without.

Given this, the best I can do is to tell you about those children, describe them and their strange world to you, tell you how *I* saw them, when they acted with what I'd term unpredictability and kindness. Then you can make up your own minds, and decide for yourself how kind and how unpredictable they were, as you're fully entitled to do.

After all, it was people like you who put them there in the first place, people laden with opinions and beliefs not tried, tested or tempered by lessons that can only be learned by first-hand experience. People like me too, now, I suppose, though, there is a difference between us – a difference that chills me at times in terms of its simplicity and permanence.

For I was being sent there to join them, that morning. I was being sent to mix with them, get to know them and share my life with them. I was being sent to become one of them, that day. And ironically, the decision to send me there was both unpredictable and unkind, as I see it now, sitting here alive and well forty-four and a half years later, thinking about them, and, most importantly, writing about them while they've been erased, shut out, and totally forgotten, as if they hadn't mattered one little bit – when, in fact, they mattered every bit as much as you do.

1

It was a dry, sunny morning in mid-August when I stood outside our home with my mother, waiting for the bus that was to take me to school. There was no sign of rain whatsoever, just a few fluffy clouds that looked like a smiley face, as we stood beside what has since become a very busy road. But this was back in the more relaxed days of the early 1950s, when you could still catch a few minutes of calm by the roadside, in which to compose your thoughts and reflect on your surroundings. As it turned out, these were the last calm times I was to see for quite a while, for I was about to go off to what they called a 'special school' and I didn't quite appreciate what that meant – at least, not then. Though I was to find out soon enough, as you'll see, and that's when it did start to pour. Cats and dogs it poured then, with all the energy and vindictiveness of a spurned domestic pet.

My mother and I stood close together that morning, each of us quiet with our own apprehensions. But if I'd had even the wildest of guesses at what the day held for me, if I'd had the slightest hint at what was in store, I would have stood a lot closer. So close, in fact, that it would have taken a surgeon specialising in separating Siamese twins to remove me. For it's bad enough being separated from your mother when they insist you have to start going to school for the whole day. But it's even worse when you're being sent to the place I was being sent to – much worse. And I was as unprepared as a jellyfish for drought. That's about as unprepared as you can be.

Like an unblooded soldier preparing for battle, I'd been up earlier than usual that morning. Everything seemed normal when I washed myself in the bathroom washbasin; in fact the whole house seemed normal, and I could hear the usual chitter-chatter in the background.

My father had gone to work early, as ever, but my eldest brother and two sisters were at home and my mother was in the kitchen preparing breakfast. I knew she'd be sorting out my school clothes too; I couldn't properly dress myself yet, but we didn't mention it much.

The younger of my two sisters was in bed, unwell with her dickey chest, and I could hear her coughing in the bedroom she shared with my big sister. It sounded bad, but then it always did, so that didn't seem abnormal either. Nor did the fact that an apparition of my great-grandmother appeared in the mirror, shook her head from side to side and mouthed, 'Don't go, son. Don't go.' I knew I was seeing things; I sometimes did see things, but I told no one about it. So I'd seen a vision of the dead; why should I worry about that?

When I'd finished washing, I went into the living-room. The radio was on and the smell of fresh toast drifted through the music from the adjacent kitchen. My brother and sister were there too, but they preferred the radio to me and simply smiled 'good morning'. There was no fire in the grate, I noted, and as it was fairly chilly, my mother called me through to the kitchen so I could warm myself in front of the grill, where the toast was browning.

My brother took a quick look into the kitchen to see how the toast was doing. Quick smile apart, he'd completely ignored me when I'd traipsed past his nose just a few minutes earlier, but now he took the opportunity to speak.

'So – are you looking forward to school, son?'

He sounded sincere at least, and he probably was. He'd just left school himself and started as an apprentice joiner. His bag of tools sat out in the hallway, and they were very impressive, at least to me. What was less impressive was the fact he'd never wanted to be a joiner in the first place. Ever since I could remember, he'd wanted to be a pop star. Though based on what I'd heard of his singing, I reckoned he stood a better chance of making a living if he stuck to his tools.

I looked up.

'Yes, I'm looking forward to school,' I said casually, as my mother pulled a small white vest over my head and I ducked into it as if it were a lifebelt. 'School's going to be great!' I added with a surge of optimism; he looked at me with concern, while I waited for the reassurance past experience had taught me followed that look.

'Yes, it's going to be just great. There's not a single, solitary, suspect thing to worry about,' he said on cue, as he pulled the grill-pan out and helped himself to a piece of underdone toast. 'You'll meet some good friends, too, and you'll have a fabulous time reading, writing, spelling new words and playing with all the other cheery, happy, healthy-ish kids,' he went on, as if he were Chief Salesman for Schools, or something similar – something important that is, and not just a brother with a kid like me to look out for; a kid with a very bad heart that wasn't expected to beat for much longer. 'Yes, you'll enjoy school,' he promised. And I began to wonder at that. For past experience had also taught me the disturbing fact that when he enthused so much about anything, there was usually something wrong with it.

'But you told me you were glad to leave school,' I said. 'You said you hated it, so how come you're suddenly saying it's the best thing since sliced bread?'

He inspected his own slice of bread carefully. He frowned, considered something, decided to take a bite, and spoke to me, improperly, with his mouth full.

'I didn't like it much towards the end, but it was fun in the beginning. I was glad to leave, but I enjoyed starting it. Lots of kids do, you know,' he finished, as if the decision to leave had rested entirely with him and not with the perilous state of our family finances. They'd needed the top-up he could provide by starting work, so he'd started.

By then my mum had fitted me into my new shirt and trousers and I was sitting on the floor, pulling on my socks. I heard the radio get louder, and the song 'Stranger in Paradise' suddenly dominated everything:

> Take my hand,
> I'm a stranger in paradise . . .

It was Tony Bennett singing, and when my brother stuck his head round the kitchen door again he was grinning evilly. For though he loved Tony Bennett, he thought I detested that sort of schmaltzy music. He'd become a fan of the fledgling rock 'n' roll, and he assumed – incorrectly – that was all I liked. Accordingly, he passed what he considered appropriate comment.

'You'll be a stranger in paradise later,' he grinned vacuously, as my sister, who was sitting near the fireplace sorting through her schoolbooks, went over to the radio and turned the sound down.

She looked into the kitchen, smiled at me, and pushed my brother aside to make way for herself.

'Pay no attention to his scaremongering,' she said sharply. 'School will be fine. Don't worry.' But she sounded uncertain too. This constant reassurance was unnecessary. Of course school would be fine; why shouldn't it be? There was no need to keep reassuring me about something I was certain of. Was there?

She spoke again.

'Mum says there's a bus collecting you.'

Her tone seemed severe, but it wasn't meant to be. She was practical and efficient, my big sister, and she certainly sounded it; but she was kind too, and very attractive – a dark-haired twelve-year-old, with eyes as dark blue and interesting as the convent school uniform she wore, complete with self-knitted cardigan.

My other sister, the sick one, was only nine. She went to the local primary school when she could, but she was usually in bed with coughs and colds and the like, so she missed school a lot.

I smiled at my big sister and nodded.

'Yes, there's a bus coming to get me,' I explained, as she studied me carefully, the way they all did at times. 'It's going to stop outside and take me to my school.' I began to form an image of the bus in my mind, and almost shook with the sounds of its powerful engine. I'd seen it once or twice when it had dropped other schoolchildren off, so I could picture it easily. I thought I'd tell my sister about it. She'd seemed interested, after all, and sharing my thoughts about exciting things helped me to keep calm about them.

'It's large, red and powerful,' I said, 'and it has bright, beaming lights that pierce the darkness like fiery lances.'

'Lucky you,' said my sister, frowning. 'You're fortunate to be getting any bus – fiery lances or not-so-fiery lances. The rest of us have to walk to school and we have to start at nine, though this morning I've been given pre-emptive compassionate leave. But you; you're different – privileged. It's all right for some,' she said, adding another bit of frown to her face and making me look up at my mother for reassurance.

'You'll be fine,' said my mum. Then she frowned too.

My mother asked my sister to bring my shoes through from the living-room. She came back into the kitchen carrying them by the heels, then eased my mother aside, bent down, slipped them onto my feet and did up the laces. That was another thing I couldn't quite manage, and it bothered me.

That done, my sister looked round.

'Are these your new school clothes?' she asked, looking at the clothes on the kitchen chair.

'Yes,' said my mother. 'He's got a new cap too,' she added, and I looked at the cap with the quaint badge on it. At first I'd thought it showed two crossed swords, but my brother had said they looked like two crossed crutches, not that I believed that. Highly imaginative I may have been, but not that imaginative, not then; not until a few hours later, when I'd have to reconsider all sorts of things, including the meaning of the badge on my Special School cap.

My mother was tying a knot in my tie.

'He's going to look very smart,' she said, as she pulled me up onto my feet and started to dust me down.

'He certainly is,' said my sister, giving me a final look over and heading back into the living-room to pack her briefcase.

My brother reappeared with his toolbag. He was smiling, but his eyes looked sad.

'So all's well?' he asked. 'And you're happy about school? You're not worried anything will happen?' he added, and I wondered what the heck he was talking about. What *could* 'happen', as he euphemistically put it, on the day a normal little boy started school?

'I'm fine!' I insisted.

'Good! All will be well. Yes, all will be well,' he repeated. 'With God's good grace,' he said quickly, sounding uncertain again before changing the subject rather obviously. 'We can listen to some rock 'n' roll this evening if you're *compos mentis*, fit, well enough, up and around, and able to do so. There's a half-hour on Radio Luxembourg at seven.'

'Good,' I said, as my mother whipped out her rosary beads from her apron pocket. I'd no idea why she was praying, but I hoped God would answer and make it work out anyway.

By now my brother was ready to leave.

'See you later, son. And don't worry. Nothing will happen. Trust me.' He sounded like an oracle with a difficult message; then off he went, whistling 'Stranger in Paradise'.

My sister came back into the kitchen to collect a breakfast tray. She took one to my sick sister every morning, and stayed in her bedroom until it was time to leave for school. My mother was still busy in the kitchen, so I was sitting alone in the living-room, where, the radio having been turned off, it was very quiet and still. Such silence was still a bit of a novelty because, until recently, we'd had seven people living in our flat. However, my other brother had gone off to become a priest some time ago, so it was a good bit quieter now, with one fewer there.

'Time to get you ready for the bus,' said my mum. I looked up at the clock on the mantelpiece: it was ten past nine; the bus came at half past. I'd be ready.

My mother joined me, picking up my jacket and coat. Like all my new clothes, they were presents from my grandparents, who topped up our finances, too – when they could, one way or another. As I pulled on my jacket, my sister returned from the bedroom and made her own final preparations. The next ten minutes were spent getting everything organised for our departure; then I went in to say goodbye to our invalid.

She looked OK, propped up on her pillow with her breakfast tray beside her. But her voice was weak and when she spoke, I had to bend down to hear her.

'Enjoy school,' she managed, before breaking into a cough that rattled in her chest like a skeleton with epilepsy. She composed herself, calmed down and breathed relatively deeply, before she spoke again.

'Nothing's going to happen,' she said, scaring the wits out of me before coughing again like a recidivist chain-smoker.

I rushed out of her room wondering what exactly I'd let myself in for, and who exactly knew about it. For it was pretty evident now that I didn't!

As I returned to the living-room, where I sat near the radio, my big sister was ready to leave. She looked neat, tidy and efficient in her blazer, scarf and hat, and she held her briefcase under her arm like a trophy. She headed for the door and I wondered what it felt like going off to an ordinary secondary school, when I hadn't even started my special primary one.

I glanced out of the living-room window and saw it was a clear, blue, sunny day.

'Goodbye, son,' said my sister, while I stared at the sky. 'And don't worry about anything. Your brother's right for once. Nothing will happen,' she added, as I saw a group of pigs fly past and felt my stomach tie in a reef knot of apprehension that prompted me, at long last, to air my concerns.

'What do you mean by "nothing will happen"?' I snapped, as the pigs sped off. 'Everyone else goes to school and nothing happens to them!' I added, generalising and sounding surer of myself than I was entitled to.

My sister stared at me. It was a grim, sad stare.

'They don't all go to that school.'

'And what's so different about that school?' I persisted, and my sister paused for a moment, thought about it carefully, then spoke.

'You'll see,' she said.

And I did.

2

By twenty-five past nine, my mother and I had walked down the path to the pavement outside. It was a lovely morning: crisp, sunny and seemingly predictable. I breathed in deeply and looked around to take in my surroundings. The block of four flats where we lived was the last one on the road. Behind, to our left, were the extensive, walled grounds of the convent school my sister went to. A few yards to our right was another mysterious structure, visible from our living-room window. It was a large mound of earth, surrounded by a wall too, but a small wall – one I could see over easily. I'd been told it was the burial mound of Marjorie Bruce, the daughter of King Robert the Bruce.

Though not really her grave, this 'burial mound' marked the spot where the heavily pregnant Marjorie had fallen from her horse and sustained a fatal injury. Although she'd died, her baby son survived to become King Robert II of Scotland, the founder of the Royal House of Stewart. My brother once explained to me how this had led to what he called 'religious problems' in our country. But I didn't pay much attention to that. Religion was something certain in life – like starting school. What problems could it cause for anyone?

As I stood ruminating on old Scottish kings, I noticed a boy and his mother walking towards us. They passed the burial mound and came over. The woman smiled the sort of smile that hints at tragedy, and she reinforced this impression by speaking in a nervous-sounding voice.

'Good morning. Are you waiting for the Special School bus?'

'Yes,' said my mum, 'we are.'

'Good!' she said, glancing down at the weird-looking boy she'd brought with her, then at me, as if to compare us.

She spoke.

'My son starts school this morning. I'm glad we're not late. First-day nerves,' she smiled, and my mum and I both smiled back.

My mother nodded.

'Yes, it makes you nervous when you're not sure what's going to happen,' she said, 'and you just don't know what's going to happen on your first day at school. Especially that school,' she added as I blinked once, felt a flash of déjà vu, and tried to contain my wildest fears and my even wilder imagination. 'It's pretty nerve-racking all round,' she went on. 'Perhaps you should have taken something to calm you down a bit.'

'Oh, I didn't mean *I* was nervous,' said the woman, while I felt like taking one of the sedatives I had in my pocket – the ones I was taking to school so they could dish them out ad lib. 'I meant my son was nervous. Weren't you, son?'

The strange-looking boy studiously ignored her and examined his surroundings cautiously, like a mild-mannered herbivore at a feast for wolves.

'Of course!' said my mum. 'My son's a wee bit nervy too. His name's Francis,' she added, as I smiled politely, the way you're obliged to. 'But he's looking forward to school,' she went on, and they both looked down at me dubiously.

'My boy's called Martin,' said the woman in a flatter voice. 'He's a bit shy, aren't you Martin?' We all turned our attention to him now and he turned his to the ground. 'Yes, he's a shy boy,' she repeated, as if trying to convince herself that was all he was. 'But he'll be fine when he gets there. He'll be fine,' she repeated, as if trying to convince herself of that too.

Our mothers continued to talk, but in technical phrases and with lowered voices. This meant they were talking about health, or, more precisely, its absence. I was used to that sort of thing, as you might expect, but I still didn't like it. That said, it gave me the opportunity to look more closely at the boy, who, unlike me, was clinging onto his mother's hand. He didn't return my interest, however – just kept his eyes fixed studiously on the pavement and didn't budge them by a blink when my mother stooped down towards him.

'Well, Martin, are you looking forward to school?' she asked. He glanced up for a moment like a startled ape, but turned away again and stared off into the distance.

His mother had another go.

'Francis is pleased he's starting school, Martin,' she said slowly, as if she were starting a fairytale. 'It's good you're going together, isn't it?' He glanced up at her briefly, shot a look at me, and turned away again. 'Oh, he's just very shy today,' she said. But I suspected it was more than that. 'He'll be fine once he's there,' she added, reassuring herself but no one else. Then, in the same storytelling voice, she asked me what was by now a ridiculously stupid question.

'Are you looking forward to starting school, Francis?'

'Yes,' I said sweetly, lying my bad heart out.

'And do you know your teacher's name?'

I nodded.

'I did, but I can't remember it.'

My mother came rushing to the rescue. 'It's "Miss Goldenheart". They say she has lots of experience with difficult cases.'

I nodded again.

'Yes, Miss Goldenheart, that's it. Is she Martin's teacher too?' I asked, finally writing Martin off by asking his mother to speak for him.

'Oh no,' she said quickly. 'Martin has a different teacher. He's at the same school, but in a different class.'

Again I wondered what was going on. What was all the mystery, and what sort of 'difficult cases' did Miss Goldenheart have experience of? I was confused. Her son and I were both starting school, so we should be going to the same class. As we were not, I concluded he was different, abnormal in some way, and I detected something unusual in his mother's behaviour towards him which seemed to confirm that. There was something in the way they interacted that wasn't quite normal, an exaggerated tone in her voice, the sort grown-ups use to speak to animals or babies. All things considered, I had no doubt this strange boy – who was, after all, the first school companion I'd ever met – was not quite the full shilling, and I sensed his mum was ashamed of that.

I turned away and looked down the road that led to my school. It was no more than half a mile away, but, like most things in life at that age, it seemed very distant indeed. Just like Martin.

The bus appeared. My heart missed a beat more than usual, and I was delighted to see the same large, red bus I'd anticipated earlier. It was shining with health and vigour, and its engine purred proudly as it headed speedily towards us. I felt reassured at last.

'There can't be much wrong with a school with a bus like that,' I said enthusiastically – just as it went roaring past and I felt my tummy turn a somersault when I saw what was behind it.

Another bus: a grey, noisy, sick one. Its engine coughed and spluttered like my sister on a bad morning.

Martin's mother visibly stiffened.

'That's the bus now,' she said primly. 'Pity it's not like the one that comes for the normal children, that red one that just passed.'

I gaped, and envied her son's diminished sense of reality.

As our bus approached it grew bigger and darker, in direct proportion to my sense of apprehension. Now it was my turn to take my mother's hand, as I turned round again to look at Martin. Surely the sight of this monstrosity would make him speak? It would have wrung screams of total horror out of a laid-back mute. Surely it would shake something out of him: a word, a curse, a screech, a scream, a retch of the stomach? Surely!

Zilch!

His mother was fussing over him, and my mother was doing the same: tugging at my coat, straightening my cap and making certain I looked the part of the novice schoolboy. We stood there like a couple of flyweight boxers being prepared by their seconds for their first professional bout.

The bus arrived, pulled up beside us and shuddered to a halt with what sounded suspiciously like a death rattle. The ensuing silence was soon broken as a door at the back creaked open and, seemingly by themselves, some short steps emerged and folded out onto the ground. A lady climbed down. I wondered if she were the conductress.

She spoke.

'Hello, I'm the school nurse,' she said brightly. She looked at each of us in turn. 'And you must be Martin and Francis.'

I was concerned. Judging by her looks, she'd placed the wrong name with the wrong boy.

I nodded my head anyway and tried to return her smile, but I found it difficult as I was preoccupied with the bus, not to mention whatever was trapped inside it. For there was something trapped inside it all right; I could see its shape through the dirty windows. And from this side at least, it didn't look particularly friendly.

Martin stared at the nurse as if she were an extension of the pavement. Then he jerked his head and turned away, while pulling aimlessly at his mother's hand.

'What's wrong? What's the matter?' she asked, as the nurse walked over towards them and I glanced at my mother, exchanging the sort of blank-page look that speaks volumes.

'You'll be fine. Nothing will happen,' she whispered, and I wished I could believe that. But I was beginning not to.

Martin clung to his mother like a nursing baby with lockjaw and after a struggle, in which no punches were thrown but much emotion was expressed, he was finally prised away by the nurse. With me following like a somnambulist, she led him silently to the steps, then stood to one side and helped us board. She spoke with our mothers as she did this, in the same low, serious-sickness-chat tone I'd heard earlier, only this time it was interspersed with louder, more general comments.

'They'll be fine,' she said. 'They usually are. Forget what you've heard – it's just like any other school . . . more or less. So don't worry.' Then the *coup de grâce*: 'Nothing will happen!'

That took me aback. So far aback I was now in danger of hanging onto my mother and begging her to take me back home, instead of sending me off on my own to God-only-knew-what, on that small, sinister, grey bus. But even as I considered bolting for it, the nurse was in the process of helping Martin up the steps with casual but powerful pushes and for some inexplicable reason I was clambering up behind him, like a lemming with a precocious death wish.

At the very top he turned to look for his mum, and at last there was some life there. His cheeks were wet with tears and his hands were pulled into tiny red fists. His mouth was tight and contorted, and I realised he was crying. But he didn't make a sound. And that seemed very strange to me, though I didn't reflect on it. After all, I'd more to contend with than this weirdo, whatever deeper sentiment he may have touched with that desperate silence. I'd more important things to deal with for the moment – like personal survival.

I nudged Martin forward and we entered the gloom. Despite my panic, I hoped no one would think I was with him. On a bus like this one a boy with a bad heart was invisible. Not so Martin, with his odd appearance and stony demeanour.

He moved in a bit and away from me, and the path in front was clear for the first time. Accordingly I got my first full view of the inside, causing me to let out a cry that was no more than a breath. The horror! The horror!

It was dark, moist and gloomy and there was a smell lurking in the shadows, reminiscent of toilets. There were seats on each side of a central aisle and as we crept in our feet scraped noisily on a hard, metal floor. Strange-looking people with strange-looking faces occupied the seats, and they had what appeared to be lethal weapons beside them, well within reach. My perfectly natural state of supernatural unease increased pro rata, therefore, when I realised I'd entered a world of walking sticks, crutches, built-up boots, folded wheelchairs, articulated and unarticulated knee-joints, and the ominous and ubiquitous glint of things ungodly, metallic and dangerous.

With these images accompanying us like time bombs, a small girl appeared from somewhere, presumably to lead us to an empty seat. She had bright red hair with three pigtails, and she limped slowly if not very surely towards us.

'MARTIN AND FRANCIS!' she called, louder than usual in a confined space. 'LET ME TAKE YOU TO YOUR SEATS!' I noticed a hearing aid trailing out of her ear, like an uncoiling serpent. 'WE'VE KEPT A SEAT FOR YOU HERE!' she yelled, holding one foot off the ground. 'IT'S OVER HERE – FOLLOW ME!' she urged. 'FOLLOW ME!' she repeated, as her foot touched the metal floor. 'SIT DOWN, SIT DOWN!' she screamed finally and we did so straightaway, to shut her up.

As she assisted us onto the seat, her left shoulder dipped down perilously close to the floor. I wondered whether this intermittent bump meant she repeated words spoken when her bad foot made contact with the ground or, conversely, when she lifted her other foot off it.

Martin was beside the window, and I was beside myself with terror. Our feet were dangling in mid-air like fish bait, which merely added to the uncertainty. Then the nurse climbed back on to the bus, pulled the door hard behind her and sealed us in.

Staring past Martin like an oyster with shell shock, I looked out through the window. I saw our mothers waving goodbye, so I gave mine a quick wave back. But Martin still ignored his and simply sank his head down towards the floor.

His mother was smiling bravely, but I knew she didn't really mean it. And I noticed that, when my mum said something to her, she turned away as if she were crying. Sensing what was around me, I could identify with that and I almost joined her. But before I could do so, the bus shuddered with that death rattle, the engine ticked over and, creaking like a rusted hinge with a terminal squeak, it slowly moved off.

With me praying to any god who would listen, Martin looking as dumb as a deaf-mute on communication strike, his mum looking as if she were never going to see him again, and mine looking as if she didn't ever want to, our companions around us gave a collective wail.

We were on our way.

3

After I'd composed myself and emulated Martin by contemplating the floor for a time, I looked up to see something more of my surroundings. I must have gasped like a ball with a slow puncture, for sitting opposite me was an extra-large-sized boy whose head was quite simply gigantic. His eyes were as massive as dinner-plates and he peered from behind the lenses of heavily bolted, steel-girder-rimmed spectacles. He twitched constantly and I twitched too, like an arrhythmic heart cell. Down each of his classically monumental legs ran two iron rods fixed into bore holes in the sides of his big, black boots. He was clutching two walking sticks the size of tree trunks as if his life depended on it, and he seemed to need them just to stay upright.

He caught my look and gave an incomprehensible beep. Then his cavernous mouth began to form a sort of smile shape, but he lost control halfway through and the result was a wide-open abyss, getting wider by the minute. There was a growing gathering of foam around it too, and it looked like a 3-D picture of an egg-white soufflé I'd seen in my grandmother's upmarket cookery book.

I turned to Martin for support, as if our brief spell waiting for the bus together had forged an intimacy of the sort I hadn't wanted to encourage when we'd got on it. 'Any port in a storm', they say, and this was a storm all right, though not exactly the port I'd have chosen to shelter in.

But there was neither port nor support from Martin, nor much of anything else for that matter. He was still as impassive as stone and every bit as helpful, and I was well beyond the petrified stage myself when, in near-despair, I found myself humming 'Stranger in Paradise'.

Having no other option, I returned my attention to the boy-thing. I thought it best to calm him if possible, make friendly overtures – talk him down. My brother told me once, when wolves attack, you calm them by speaking softly. That wolf attack hadn't happened yet, but as this was the closest I'd ever come to it, I tested his strategy.

'Hello,' I said to the boy-thing, and it gave another series of twitches and its eyes flickered with life for a moment before it replied.

'OOG-OOG-AH! OOG-AH AH! OOG-OOG AH HAH!' I almost jumped out of my skin. 'OOG-OOG-AHHH!' it screeched with conviction, as it snarled and jerked and trembled, moving up the back of the seat and the Richter scale simultaneously, until it finally shook itself into the most terrible, pregnant silence I have ever known.

I'd been shaken into silence myself and I shot a quick glance at Martin. He was *still* staring at the ground, for God's sake, and I realised just how ill he was. That settled it! I finally excluded him as a source of assistance, while a further involuntary shudder from the creature opposite flooded me with freshly cooked adrenaline. I tensed as tight as a bowstring as it gradually flopped into what seemed genuine inactivity. Its eyes still flickered with a primal malevolence however, just as mine did with a much more primal fear.

I sat perfectly still and didn't make a sound. I watched it carefully. I was tempted to touch it to see if it was active, but I didn't dare. Was it waiting to pounce? Was it lulling me into a false sense of critically misplaced security? I'd no idea.

After the most fraught few minutes of my short, eventful life, I calmed down and had time to reflect on things. At least it had seemed polite enough when it screeched, and it was perhaps safer to attempt to respond in some way, rather than keep quiet and risk – through inattention – sending it into another episode of atavistic tantrums. I briefly considered returning a spirited 'OOG-OOG-AH!' back – a howling wolf howling at a howling wolf, as it were. But I summoned what inner reserves I had left, restrained myself and again tried to smile.

'Hello,' I ventured.

Nothing!

'HELLO!' I repeated louder, then for some reason added a redundant and meaningless 'Yes?' There was nothing. Not a twitch.

Suddenly there was a flicker in its arm, followed by some more general movement. It shook all over for a few moments, then slowly froze into place. I watched, I listened; I sniffed at the air like a hunting-dog, and it sat there frozen solid, unmoving, rigid and corpse-like. Then it slowly drew itself upwards until it was perfectly straight in its seat and its blue eyes glistened like sharpened steel, appearing every bit as deadly. As I braced myself for a full-frontal attack, it gave out a great, loud sigh and flopped back down again like a glove puppet without a hand in it. It seemed to be fast asleep, but I waited on the edge of my seat until I was quite certain. When I felt it was safe to do so, I slowly settled back a bit.

My fists were now clenched as tight as Martin's had been when we boarded this bus to the Netherworld, and I solemnly prayed to Saint Jude – the patron saint of hopeless cases – for this most frightening and unpredictable of journeys to end. That would do fine: journey's end. If I could just reach there in safety that would be miracle enough.

But the journey continued, and to add to my confusion our first stop was not at our school at all, but at a large stone house where a few of the bus's inmates were escorted off by the ubiquitous nurse. Martin was among them. The little red-headed girl who'd shown us to our seats helped him off, and he left as vacant and silent as he'd arrived. As he went, I again acknowledged the fact that he was quite unfathomable.

The children who disembarked with him didn't seem the same. Certainly they had similar-looking faces, but they were more boisterous than him, less retiring, and they were obviously excited and happy to be going to wherever it was they were going. I noticed a number of them attempting to reassure him, but he was studiously ignoring them as if they were family, too. He wouldn't make friends easily that way, I thought. On the other hand, perhaps he didn't want to.

While I was taking all of this in, the redhead boarded again and limped over with her pigtails waving like kitecords.

She sat down beside me.

'So you're Francis!' Her voice was many decibels lower than the one she'd originally used, and I realised she'd turned up the volume control on her hearing aid. I knew she was just being friendly, but I avoided making eye contact. You never knew.

'Yes, I'm Francis.'

She stretched out her hand.

'I'm Moira.'

'Good!'

'Shake,' she said, and the boy-thing opposite gave a shudder. I wondered if it had taken her offer to me as a command to it. I flushed as I pressed my palm against hers. Our fingers curled together like pleated wool. She smiled again. It was a warm smile, I have to admit.

'Welcome to our school,' she said. 'Derek's difficult to understand,' she added, looking at the boy-thing with affection. 'But I understand him. He's simply trying to make you welcome and ask you how you are.'

I stared at the boy-thing again and he seemed slightly more human. Moira unpeeled my clenched hand from her own and headed back to her seat, limping wildly.

'See you later. See you later,' she said, as her bad foot hit the ground and I realised my theory was proven: bad foot on or just leaving ground meant a repetition in speech. Perhaps her more succinct conversations were held when she walked with one foot on the pavement and the other over the kerb, on the road.

Still flushing, I tried to respond but couldn't. Yet for the first time in what seemed like aeons, I felt a slight sense of tenderness creeping into me. It came from what small, red-headed Moira had done. She'd tried to make me welcome and though it was like trying to reassure a water-baby left at the gates of Hell without its feeding bottle, it was a genuine gesture of kindness. And I realised that was something I was going to need very badly indeed.

By the time we resumed our journey, the engine of the bus was growling and coughing like a TB ward on its first fag of the day. It finally cleared its throat and moved off, however, and I saw that all the implements of infirmity – the sticks, crutches, wheelchairs, and myriad other strange-looking objects that adorned the place with Gothic ambience – remained untouched and unmoved. They were all sitting precisely where they'd been before our stop. Evidently the children who'd gone to the house with Martin didn't need them. Perhaps that's why most of them seemed so happy with life.

Without further major incident we arrived at the school and disembarkation began. It was the first of the many I was to experience over the next ten years or so and they were all as regular as clockwork, if not quite as smooth and precise. First off were those who had walking sticks and crutches, and they made it with only the odd clatter or so. Then those of us who could, in theory, make it under our own steam followed. Even so, the nurse assisted everyone down the steps, as making it 'under your own steam' wasn't quite as easy as it sounds for all concerned. Callipers had to be straightened, heads manually turned and forced to look in the proper direction, hunched backs momentarily straightened and binocular spectacles adjusted as carefully as theodolites, so that their owners could sight the true lie of the doorway and the virtual horizon of the steps.

I managed to clamber off without incident, which surprised me, and stood uneasily in the playground waiting for the unloading of the wheelchairs followed by their imminent occupants. My fellow traveller, Derek, was one of this group, and as he was lowered into his wheelchair, shaking excitedly and uttering grunts that would have graced the soundtrack of a Tarzan film, I noticed the nurse smoothing his hair as if he were normal. As he was far from it, I looked on in quiet amazement.

'You're fine, Derek. Tidy up your tie, please,' she told him. And Derek, the boy-thing, forced his large, ungainly head round to consume her with his dinner-plate eyes, while he unsteadily steered his hands upwards towards his tie and pulled at it with some considerable difficulty.

I looked dubiously at the nurse and she looked right back.

'You too, Francis! Tidy up your tie too, please.'

I stood up straight.

'Yes, Nurse,' I said, and I felt something strange pass between us. I'd no idea what it was, but for some strange reason she suddenly seemed wonderful. I pulled at my tie, trying to convince her I knew what to do with it and as I tugged, an unmotherly slurping sound broke through my Oedipal reverie.

I looked to see what it was.

It was Derek! Instead of straightening his tie, he'd coiled it round his neck and was facing the very real danger of self-strangulation. He was manfully trying to recoup his position, however, and attempting to reassemble the limp piece of cloth into something approximating neatness.

The nurse smiled.

'Derek, Derek, Derek,' she said, her voice feigning frustration, but sounding very calm indeed as she began to uncoil him. 'What are we going to do with you?' she asked, not expecting an answer, but he gave one anyway, or at least tried to.

'Ug! Ug! Ug! Ug! Ug!' he grunted, and little red-headed Moira, who'd jumped unsteadily off the bus and was standing very close beside him, translated. 'He's no idea. He's no idea,' she repeated, as her bad foot hit the playground with a thump, stabilised, and corrected both her wobble and the frequency of her sentences. 'He's no idea. He just wants his tie done up properly.'

As the redness began to drain from Derek's face, the nurse proceeded to do the tie up for him. But I could tell from his gestures and his grunts that he didn't really want her to. She could tell that too, so she left him to it.

'OK, Derek, do it yourself if you must,' she said. 'But don't rush it – take your time, and do it as well as you can.'

As she said this, it occurred to me that while Derek probably couldn't really do or undo the knot on his tie at will, at least he knew how to. And it was then, I think, that I felt my first hint of admiration for him. I observed him with renewed interest, noticing once again how enormous his boots were, with those bars of metal prodding into them, and I wondered if he knew how to do up his laces too. I considered this and everything else I'd witnessed, and I reluctantly concluded that, unlike me, he probably did.

Once we'd been unloaded, our group of academia's finest were led *ensemble* through the stone archway that fronted the school. We were ushered through a door that led directly into the cloakroom, and once there the nurse left us under the supervision of a woman who was as tall as a story about the happy handicapped. She wore a long white overall and under her careful gaze the more able and older children hung up their coats, hats, caps, spare prostheses and whatever else they had for hanging, then did the same for those who were unable to do so. I followed by example and did what I could. As the others gradually drifted away to their classes, I realised I was the only child from this exodus of the small grey bus who was actually starting school that day. As I stood wondering what to do next, I heard a banging sound and turned towards the door.

With predictable unpredictability, Derek was racing into my field of vision in his wheelchair. He was coming towards me at speed, and as this registered I simultaneously saw his hands were still at his tie and therefore not pushing at the wheels. With resigned amazement I realised there had to be some mysterious force that bore boys like Derek along in the manner brooms bear witches; in a miraculous manner – a manner exclusive to the very odd, the grotesque and the marginal in our society. As my mouth gradually widened in terror – and admittedly in wonder too – I managed to discern a shape behind the wheelchair. It was of a miniature boy who, apparently headless, raced past pushing the wheelchair for all he was worth.

It was he who was speeding Derek to his classroom, or wherever people like him went, not some infernal force associated sympathetically with crooked crocks and crazy cripples. Nonetheless I ducked as Derek passed, with his arms flailing in wide arcs around him and his tie flapping loose in the slipstream like a streamer. He laughed loudly at my reaction and, as our eyes met properly for the first time on either side of his bridge-like spectacle frames, I saw that his were as wide with excitement as mine were with shock. And as he and his escort disappeared into the distance, I was pretty certain I heard the words of a familiar song coming from the escort's invisible mouth:

> Take my hand,
> I'm a stranger in Paradise . . .

I wondered at that and took another reflective look at the rapidly disappearing Derek. Perhaps there was more to him than I'd thought on first acquaintance. Perhaps I was jumping to conclusions as ill-formed inside my own head as he had the misfortune to be on the outside. For irrespective of what he was, and irrespective of where or to what he was heading, he was enjoying himself immensely.

I realised he had a sense of humour, Derek. And that, I thought, as he was powered into the distance of the inner school, is one luxury in life we can all do with. We all need an occasional laugh, I reflected, whether we're able-bodied or otherwise, whether we've been sent off to a normal school as normal kids or packed off to a special school, as we had been. The problem was, however, by attending a special school you were a 'special kid' too. And that made you socially 'special', or, not to put too fine a point on it, a misfit.

Me included.

4

I'd seen a number of doctors before I went to school, one of whom, a long time before, had made the diagnosis that was to direct the course of my life. Seeing him was perhaps my earliest complete memory, and as is the way with memories, particularly early ones, it has that warm, nostalgic feeling about it that bears no relationship whatsoever to reality.

That doctor had prodded me about a bit, pushed his stethoscope around my chest like an ice-pack and tightened a minimum-bore blood pressure cuff round my arm with an enthusiasm better directed to inflating a motorcar tyre. I remember he'd looked sombre as he did this – every bit as sombre as my parents. We exchanged a few glances while he took my pulse, and they weren't very cheerful either. In retrospect, I imagine the effort of squeezing the bulb on his tastefully named sphygmomanometer was taking its toll. For, by the time he'd considered his diagnosis and decided what it meant, his eyes were all misty with tears.

When we'd finished I stood beside my mother, and the doctor pointed to a jar of sweets on his desk and told me to help myself. I can still see my hand dipping into it and grabbing a few for appearance's sake, while he sat observing me closely, the way a privileged tomcat does some common queen's poorly kitten.

'Take as many as you want, young man,' he said, with a smile that spoke of some recent tragedy. 'Help yourself, my boy. Get stuck in,' he urged, as I dug my hand in deeper and tried to grab a few more.

My mum interrupted.

'Oh, not too many, doctor. We don't want him taking too many at his age.'

The doctor leaned over and gave her a cryptic look.

'Better now than never,' he said, being even more cryptic, and I grabbed a few more and returned to my parents, who looked ever so pale, as though they could have done with a chat with the doctor themselves.

After that session – so I was informed years later – my parents were told I had two years at best. The doctor prescribed me a sedative and told them to take me home and treat me well. So that was the consensus: two years at best. And I knew nothing of it as I munched my sweets on my way out of his consulting room. I was aware, certainly, that something important had happened, but unaware of precisely what it was.

Having more than survived the allotted two years, I had to see another doctor about my immediate and (possibly) future schooling. That had been a different type of experience and, despite the recent introduction of the National Health Service, there was a fee. It wasn't paid in monetary terms, however, but in the much more disabling ones of the denial of a decent education.

I'd gone to see this other doctor with my mother and we'd waited nervously outside his consulting room. There'd been a few other children waiting with their mothers, and they went in and out of Medical Headquarters with the regularity of children queuing to see Santa in a chain store during Advent.

Just one boy sat alone. He was dressed in a very posh school uniform and had two walking sticks beside him, both of which were painted glossy white.

'He must be bilaterally blind,' my mother whispered, as I observed the callipers on his legs and arms and the swathes of padded bandages wrapped round his head like loft insulation. The fact his mother was nowhere to be seen didn't surprise me. What self-respecting mother would turn up anywhere with a boy like that, when there were boys like me around with no obvious infirmity, though admittedly with no posh uniform to display in public either?

Still, like the other kids, with the exception of him of course, I had the yellow star I'd been given to pin on the lapel of my jacket when I'd arrived. And while it didn't bear comparison with the fancy badge on Bandage Boy's jacket, it added a certain *je ne sais quoi* to my appearance and I sported it proudly. After all, with one obvious exception, all the other kids had one, so it made me feel as if I belonged.

What I particularly remember about that occasion is that the doctor had a nurse to assist him. He also left the decision about my schooling to me, though admittedly after explaining matters in a comprehensive way to my mother.

' . . . so you see, the rough and tumble of an ordinary school would be best avoided by Francis,' the doctor said, nodding and winking, while my mum and I sat close together listening. 'The diagnosis seems clear and the prognosis equally so,' he added, as my mother nodded her agreement.

'In addition,' he went on, 'we must remember Francis needs lots of rest and has his pills to take. Then there's the sad fact he mustn't be pushed too hard, either in an academic or a physical sense. These facts mitigate for him going to a special school,' he concluded, stressing the word 'special', so that I flushed a bit, like a dozy cow proud of being first choice for the abattoir.

'Of course, they also militate against him going to a school of normal status,' he said, winking again, while my mother continued to nod, as if she liked the sound of his voice. I wondered if this were beginning to annoy the doctor, who then turned his attention solely to me.

'In a special environment such as the one I'm going to propose to you, Francis, the staff have more time to facilitate things. You fucking cripple,' he said swiftly, nodding his agreement with himself and assuming mine accordingly, as if mine were an informed one too. 'They'll ensure you get your medication on time, ensure you're rested, ensure you're not pushed too hard – or around too much – and ensure your education is an appropriate one. As if it matters,' he winked, stopping for a moment, and I noticed the nurse was nodding too, and I began to wonder if I shouldn't start to nod myself, to get into the spirit of things.

'Additionally,' he went on, with a further wink, 'you'll be in the company of children with similar needs, and that can only help matters for no-hopers like you. So too will the fact the staff are trained in emergency first aid. This is a minor consideration for normal boys, of course, but a highly important one for a terminal tragedy and born loser like you,' he smiled, winking again as I sat more stiffly in my seat. It was the first time I'd even heard that sort of thing mentioned.

'If you take suddenly ill for example, drop down dead on the spot, as kids like you tend to . . . well, they have all the technical gear to deal with that stat. Schools like that have everything you need for fatal crises,' he said jollily. 'Such as the paperwork – we must never forget the paperwork.' I started to find him convincing, if a little bit scary.

'They can supply you with a disabled car sticker if you ever need one, a prestamped death certificate, or – if you want to make out a will on your arrival – they can supply that for free, too,' he laughed; and my mum nodded her agreement again and started to laugh as well.

'Then, of course, there's another, much more important fact we have to take into account,' he confided. 'The sad and sorry one that the Education Authority has committed ratepayers' money to that paradise for cripples.

So we need bums on seats,' he said, then frowned, paused, took a very deep breath and stared at me like one of those constantly winking hunting birds, before completing his assessment.

'In the main, you're small, insignificant, powerless, incorrigibly Roman Catholic and terminally working class. You're completely unimportant and would never amount to anything, even if we gave you the opportunity – which we won't!' he added, as he used his elbow to nudge the nurse, who was sitting close enough for him to do so. 'You won't even be any use as a heart transplant donor, when they do that sort of thing for the rest of us,' he went on, sniggering, as I tried to take in what he was saying and found I couldn't. 'And you used to be a sort of darkish colour, too,' he said, 'though you're reasonably pinkish now, so we can't stick you on the margins by that route,' he conceded, and I remembered the tales I'd heard from my parents about how I'd been 'off-white' for a year or so after my birth.

'Yet despite this, you're highly precocious,' he said irritably. 'You're years ahead of your time, have ambitions way beyond your station, and stubbornly refuse to lie down and die, as we suggested you should years ago. So overall and all things considered, I think it best you go to this special school. And you'd better agree or else, you little shit. Don't you agree?' he asked mildly, in a verbal turnaround as fast as a switchblade and every bit as convincing.

I studied his face for a moment, to be certain he'd meant what he'd said. He winked again like a Belisha beacon: slowly and with a tired, dull light, and I knew then he'd meant every single word.

In the deep and solemn silence that followed, I heard a grunting sound. I turned; the nurse had nodded off to sleep. She had her chin on her chest, and although the doctor's nudge hadn't roused her, the silence did. She gave a jerk of surprise and looked around in a panic. 'Was I asleep?' she asked, as she sat up in her chair and the doctor continued to inspect me, the way a life-insurance salesman would a lung-cancer case with a lit cigarette in his mouth.

There was another moment of silence before he showed his true clinical acumen and moved in carefully to close the deal. He twiddled a cheap pen in his fingers as he did so, and I knew by the way he studied it that if I agreed to his proposal, he'd give me it. 'You do understand that a special school's best for you?' he smiled, reasonable and utterly convincing. 'It's your only option, son,' he added, with a slick turn of menace. 'So think carefully before you answer. Grub-bait! If you don't go there, you're screwed. Up the creek without as much as a crutch. So you might as well accept my offer, boyo – it won't be there for long. Just like you,' he grinned, as I continued to watch the pen. 'So don't you think it best, sonny? Well don't you, hole-in-the-heart boy? Eh?' he pushed, as hard as a sales rep from a concrete firm.

I hesitated. He continued to twirl the pen between his fingers like a small, slim merry-go-round.

'Yes,' I said finally, as I nodded too, and he breathed a sigh of relief and slipped the pen back into his pocket.

'Fair enough,' he mused, sitting back and resuming his winking. 'I'm glad you've made your decision, young man. But I hope it's the right one – I really do.' His tone had changed yet again, and I understood what it meant to be 'punch-drunk', though I'd never even heard of it then.

'It concerns me, though, that special education might not be the best thing for you,' he went on, as my eyes tried to follow him but my head simply couldn't. He shrugged. 'Still, you seem to know what you want and you're pretty insistent, for a small boy with a big heart condition. That makes it hard for a big softy like me to refuse. So, against my better judgement, and against all the principles I hold sacred by Hippocrates and his buddy Judas, I'll agree to bend the rules and send you to this special school place. But under duress,' he said sadly. 'Under duress. So! Be it on your own sad little head if it doesn't work out,' he warned. 'And don't blame me if it flops, even if you do last long enough to work the whole thing out, slimepiece. Got it?' he asked, as his tone changed yet again and I nudged my mother. She jerked into life, as if she'd been half-asleep too, or maybe just hypnotised by the cadences of the doctor's ever-changing voice.

'Yes,' I said, as my mother came to at last.

'Thanks, Doctor,' she said, as we rose to go. 'You've been very helpful and considerate.' The nurse stood up too and stretched a bit, yawning widely to help her wake more fully. 'Thanks again, Doctor,' said my mum, like a beggar getting alms from her betters. But I understood her response, for I knew, in my mother's mind, doctors were just like priests but without their dress sense.

As we made our way out of the consulting room, Bandage Boy rolled towards it on what seemed to be castors on the soles of his expensive leather shoes. He propelled himself efficiently with his white walking sticks, and as he arrived at the door with a thump, we heard the doctor's voice again as he made his own way there and gave him a wink, too.

'Hello, son. How you doin'?' he said, and Bandage Boy winked back.

'Fine, Dad,' he signed in ASL – the contraction used for 'American Sign Language', which was all the rage with deaf-mutes at the time.

'Aren't you at school today?' the doctor asked, moulding the words with his lips, as if they were made of plasticine; and Bandage Boy's fingers fairly flew by way of reply.

The doctor's face fell.

'A day off! Bloody Hell! Those private schools . . . ' he mouthed, with an incomprehensible curl of the lip. He was a diminutive man with a limp, I noticed, and that made me think, just as Bandage Boy's uniform had. 'You pay these bloody extortionate school fees,' said the doctor. 'You do the best for your kids, bring them up to look after their own self-centred little interests, and those quasi-professionals in what passes for private education these days give them all these blasted days off!'

When he complained, at least he sounded like a human being, rather than the superhuman being he'd appeared to me – at first, anyway – and to my mum.

He calmed down and curled his finger at Bandage Boy.

'Come on in, son. Sorry about the outburst. Pressure of work. Too many sickly kids!' he said. 'Just let me lace up my leg a bit, clean up the glass eye and I'll be right with you,' he added, as Bandage Boy rolled in and signed something to his father and the nurse I couldn't quite see. Whatever it was, it made them laugh and they looked at me wryly as they did so.

'His heart!' the nurse mouthed and Bandage Boy stared at her, then back at me again. He carried his sticks for some reason, I realised, but not because he was blind. It was probably just to propel himself on his rollerskate shoes. And I realised something else at that moment, for the very first time in my life.

I was an object of interest to others, and of course it wasn't because I was blind either. It was because I had a problem with my ticker. And that was going to set me apart from other children, even if they looked as disabled and dysfunctional as Bandage Boy. But then neither my mum nor dad were doctors or anything, and a special school uniform was presumably cheaper than its normal counterpart. It was certainly more selective in terms of who could wear it, though I wasn't certain that was something to be proud of.

5

I'd been almost six years old when I'd seen Doctor Wink, having been kept away from any school for as long as possible, for the selfsame reasons that had now sent me to a special one. And whatever the merits of my medical with the good doctor, I'd duly agreed that special schooling would be the most appropriate for me. So here I was, the solitary novice pupil in the special school cloakroom, waiting with a tall woman in a white coat to discover precisely what I'd signed up for. Like some unlikely character in a novel, the woman in white showed me how to hang up my coat and cap. She proceeded to tousle my hair the way my mum did sometimes, speaking as she did so.

'So it's your first day, Francis. You're in P.H. 1, aren't you?'

I looked up and shrugged as she continued to rub my head, and I tried to work out exactly what she meant by 'P.H. 1'.

'A "P.H." class is best,' she went on. 'Better than "M.H." for a smart boy like you.'

This aroused my curiosity even more, as she started to run her fingers through my hair.

'You seem OK up here, too,' she said, and now I began to wonder what 'up here' meant. 'I'll take you to Miss Goldenheart,' she said finally, leaving my head alone, but dusting a bit at my neck with her fingers.

'Thanks, Miss,' I said, as I turned my face up towards hers, and saw her eyes still combing my hair like a fine-tooth comb. Her hands were close to my face, and I could smell the odour of something medical and antiseptic.

'NITKILL!'

The word pounced into my head like a jumping flea, with an image of a bottle containing a creamy-white liquid. I realised immediately that my caring, fondling, white-coated lady had been casually screening me for head-lice! I tugged myself away and tidied up my hair with my own fingers, while she repeated, 'P.H. 1', curled up her fingers like an osteoarthritic and placed her hands together thumb-to-thumb. Biting her lower lip with concentration, she crushed something between her nails with a loud, spectacular crack. Then she proceeded to walk away, indicating I should follow her. Given the general state of things, that's exactly what I did.

She escorted me through the assembly hall, which was massive, shiny, impressive and smelt of furniture polish. It had four stone stairways leading up to a floor above, and a large, shiny, brass bell stood splendidly at the bottom of one of the banisters. It seemed like the largest indoor space I'd ever seen in my life and I thought it quite incredible. I noticed a few low beds outside a door at one of its corners and wondered why they were there. It seemed a silly place to spend the night, unless you worked the night-shift as my father did, and I wondered if special schools did a night shift for blind kids or something.

We arrived at the door the beds stood close to and the woman knocked. It opened after a few seconds, and an elegant-looking lady stood there, smiling. It was my teacher, Miss Goldenheart.

'Why hello, Francis. What a pleasure it is having you here. Why don't you come in, and we'll settle you down with the rest of the children?'

I thought about this and considered it carefully. No matter how I looked at it, I thought I had better do as she asked. After all, I was no longer the dozy cow I'd been when I'd seen Doctor Wink. I'd lived since then – seen life. So, like a lamb to the slaughter, I followed her in.

The class was full when I entered and I could sense the other children watching as I was led to my desk. I tried not to limp or shuffle but, glancing around, I discovered there was an assortment of the world's walking wounded here. At first glance most seemed passably normal, except for the obligatory callipers, walking sticks, crutches and similar miscellaneous accoutrements of the chronically indisposed. I immediately realised there was nothing here I hadn't already anticipated after meeting the assortment of similarly outrageous-looking kids I'd encountered on the bus.

I was taken to my desk, which had a proper lid on it. It had an inkwell, too, like a blot on the top right-hand corner. I reflected on the fact that I'd been there; seen it; done it. And I was certain there was nothing further they could throw at me. Anyway, Miss Goldenheart oozed confidence enough for both of us. So why worry myself sick when I was in the hands of someone as competent as she was?

'This is your desk, Francis,' she said, as I stood there feeling very proud of my status as a sophomore. 'It opens, and you can keep your school things in it.' She pulled the top up and I looked inside. There was a pencil and paper. I smiled. There was a reading book too, and I blinked my happiness and gazed up at her in appreciation. She smiled back and I thrilled to my toes. At very long last, life was looking good.

'And this is your chair,' she went on, as she pulled a small wooden chair from beneath the desk. 'It's comfortable, and you can reach the top of your desk without any trouble. Now settle yourself in – on you go!' she instructed, and without a second thought I sat down. Miss Goldenheart helped me pull myself into place by adjusting my desk and chair, ensuring I was at ease and fully established. I felt a sense of security I hadn't known since I'd floated around in the womb listening to my mum's heartbeat.

'At last,' I thought. 'Things are settled. Scholastic expectations are being met, my mum's at home baking teacakes, God's in His Heaven – all's well!'

Life was predictable and safe again. I was refreshed, reassured and growing more confident by the minute. I looked around a bit and took in the local scenery.

The boys on either side of me had dark-blue faces.

'This is Alastair,' said Miss Goldenheart, introducing me to the marginally lighter one. He was a sort of indigo colour, like one of the unused colours in my paint box. 'And this is Billy,' she continued, introducing the darker blue boy who, for his part, had a skin tone reminiscent of my sister's school uniform.

'This is Francis, boys,' said Miss Goldenheart. 'Make him welcome!'

Introductions completed, she left us and I assessed these strange boys. The lighter one, Alastair, spoke. It was like listening to a piece of lapis lazuli.

'I dreamt about my teeth last night. My mother says dreaming about teeth means you're going to die soon.'

'Welcome to my school,' said the deep-blue one, Billy. He proceeded to produce something from his pocket, and I tensed. I needn't have – it was a packet of sweets.

'Take one each,' he said. 'They're good. My dad brings them from the shop, when he collects my mum,' he added proudly, and I wished my dad did that sort of thing too.

We ate the sweets together in silence and, even before we'd settled down to our very first lesson, I reckoned I'd made two new friends.

Before the lesson began, our teacher mentioned that certain members of our class had to take things easy and told us that if these children ever felt tired or unwell, they must say so immediately. In such an event, she explained, they'd be given an immediate medical, while they rested on the beds outside our classroom door in the Assembly Hall. I glanced round at the other children to pick out those who'd qualify for this special attention. As I surveyed them to find these presumably terminal cases, I realised Miss Goldenheart and the rest of the class were looking at my two blue colleagues and me! The penny dropped with a thump. We were the ones who had to be watched. We were the ones who were – dare I say it – terminal!

A quick check confirmed that my skin still had its usual pinkish-white colour, so I assessed this unwelcome information and decided that, although the offer was there, I wouldn't be taking it up. I'd come to school like a normal boy and I certainly wasn't going to throw the towel in the first time I felt funny.

Miss Goldenheart began to expand on the theme of our school as an institution. As she did so, I slowly began to understand the rules governing our presence there and precisely why it was 'special', why it was that bit different from other schools.

'This is a school for children who have overly sensitive constitutions,' she said. 'A school for children not as normally distributed as others in terms of the usual indices of paediatric development.' She looked at us carefully for a moment and we looked right back. 'There are two main parts to the school,' she said casually, 'a part for children like you, and a part for children not like you. Different parts – different handicaps,' she added quickly, as we looked around in a general rush of approval and I became aware of the fact I was one of the few there with no evident handicap. I was untrussed, uncallipered and unhinged. That was something to approve of too, I thought, and I made a mental note of it for future reference.

'These other children have different sorts of developmental idiosyncrasies,' she said. 'Idiosyncrasies that prevent them from performing as well as they might do otherwise.'

I felt she was giving little away, but we all exchanged glances again and nodded in a collective show of sympathy and of liberal and dispassionate understanding.

'In this part of the school, the classes are designated "P.H.",' Miss Goldenheart said, and I remembered the head-louse woman. '"P.H." is an abbreviation for "physically handicapped", and you're all in P.H. 1,' she said, smiling grandly and clutching her hands together with enthusiasm.

Everyone grinned at that, and some of the less retiring kids began to applaud and thump their desks with callipers and walking sticks. Some even began to cheer, though one bad asthmatic spastic case, a sort of walking spillikin, collapsed gasping, ruining the ambience for the rest of us and having to be removed to the Emergency Room on a trolley they kept handy for spontaneous shows of respiratory failure. Overall, however, there was transcendental joy at it all, and that joy was totally justified.

Or so I thought.

Initially I, too, felt proud of the acidic designation 'P.H.' After all, it gave us a name we could be collectively known by, a feeling we belonged together. At first, this gave me a warm feeling inside and I wanted to shake hands with Billy and Alastair simply for being there beside me. But when I thought about it, I had my doubts. Did I really want to be designated 'handicapped?' Even 'P.H.' – physically handicapped – as our teacher had described it to scenes of uncontained delight? Did I really want that? Well, did I?

Miss Goldenheart continued.

'Just because of this designation, don't think you're marginalised for life socially, or doomed to die before you reach P.H. 2,' she said, and I decided I didn't want to be thus designated. Why play handicapped when you don't look it? Why associate with cripples when you can walk just fine?

Miss Goldenheart was speaking more quietly now. The cheering had died down, too.

'In the other part of the school the classes are designated "M.H.",' she said, and there was total silence. 'Once again, this is an abbreviation for "mentally handicapped", euphemistic for "less-than-with-us".' And that had a sobering effect on everyone – including me.

I looked around and saw that a small girl a few rows away had dropped her teeth on the floor. She was trying to recover them and a larger girl, who was sitting beside her, was trying to help. Unfortunately, the larger girl had a metal brace round her neck, with chains wrapped round her shoulders to hold it in place. And as all this tackle prevented her from looking down properly, she couldn't help much. She tried anyway, creaking as she did so, and I left them to sort it out and returned my attention to my teacher.

'There's a third part to the school, isolated in a lovely big house not far from here. It's for children who have what we call "mongolism"!' She drew this last word out like an elastic band, retaining the tension while we gave her our total attention. 'That's another kind of non-idiopathic indisposition. And these children look almost the same as the rest of us. Though you'd never know, if you didn't look,' she said. I started to add one and one. 'They're very gifted children in many ways. So they have their own part of the school where they can develop these gifts,' she went on, as my attention took a quantum leap.

'Mongoloid children don't have lessons with you, but they travel in the same school buses. You may even have had the privilege of meeting one or two this morning,' she added, and I added two and two and waited to hear the rest. 'They tend to be cheery, happy children. Light, bright and nimble-minded as a light wispy mist,' she said smiling. 'And we must always treat them as we treat one another.'

Four! The elastic band snapped back into place and an image of Martin came to mind. As I'd suspected, he had some form of handicap and it was called 'mongolism'.

Without a pause, Miss Goldenheart continued.

'We also have children who don't operate on optimal optical operands. They receive special teaching too,' she said carefully. There was a flurry of renewed interest and most heads nodded or shook sideways with approval. But not mine.

'You may notice these children have beautiful, whitish hair,' she added. 'They also have lovely blue eyes that become pastel pink at times.' There was a collective gasp of excitement. A gasp, however, I held my breath at. 'Like all the other infirm you'll come across, these children are just the same as we are,' she said with authority, and I considered that carefully and doubted it.

'Blind' I knew about – in adults. But blind children at my school were something else, and a wave of anticipation rippled round the classroom at the very mention of these kids. Few things attract the attention of even the disabled like the disabled, so this was of great interest to the majority present by way of nature, and nurture too. But I was feeling distinctly uneasy. For despite my pen-induced nods to Doctor Wink, I'd wanted to be at a 'normal' special school and this one was sounding far from it.

Initially the comment about white hair and pink eyes had made no particular impression on me, but Billy caught my eye and, puffing for breath, whispered to me.

'My brother's got three white mice at home. They've got white hair and pink eyes too. But they can see OK,' he shrugged, giving me a 'you're-fine-with-me-around' type of smile, just as Miss Goldenheart renewed her talk on the true meaning of 'specialness'.

'We also have children here termed "dumb" children. They can't speak, by word of mouth, but they do have a form of language that involves spelling words out with their hands and fingers.' She proceeded to demonstrate this with her own fingers, to even more shouts of candid approval. 'We call this sign language,' she said with a flourish of fingers, a fair parody of a two-fingered gesture I'd seen Dr Wink make as I'd left Medical Headquarters. I thought of ASL and Bandage Boy, and the fact I couldn't really read sign language, though I sometimes pretended I could.

'We also have children who go about their daily business with total concentration.' There were more nods of approval and, from somewhere, a satisfied grunt. 'They're not aloof, they're "deaf" children,' said Miss Goldenheart, pointing to her ears and enunciating the word 'deaf' clearly, so she was certain we could hear her.

For many in the class, this was sounding better and better, and they nodded approvingly and thrust out their chests with empathy and renewed pride. Some even whirled leads from hearing aids and one almost hit me on the chin; I had to pull my head back to avoid it. As I did, I almost bumped into a hunchbacked kid behind me. To my horror I saw he had only one eye, and it was winking at me just like the doctor had. But he had no nose, no mouth and no ears either. I wondered how Miss Goldenheart would describe him when his turn came, though perhaps she already had and I'd missed it. I became very concerned, until I realised he was facing the back of the class – not the front – which meant his hump was facing me, and *it* had the single eye, which reassured me immensely.

The teacher told him to sit back down and it upset him. A tear formed in his eye and dripped out slowly, ran over his hump and fell onto the floor with a cute splash. I avoided the spray and returned my attention to our teacher. This whole thing didn't sound good; it didn't sound good at all. I wondered what I'd got myself into as Miss Goldenheart summarised.

'So we have children who are deaf and children who are dumb. We have blind children and mongoloid children, children who have physical handicaps and children who have mental handicaps.'

She stopped for a bit to let it all sink in. All sink in it did, and I began to reflect on it. I was perfectly clear by now why it was designated 'special school'. Because it was special all right, but not in the way I'd thought!

'Nothing will happen,' had said my brother.

'Nothing will happen,' had said my sisters and my mum.

Well, something was happening and I wanted no part of it. I wanted no part of a place where you mixed with kids like these and had to distrust appearances. This was useless for a trusting little boy, with a sense that all is as it appears to be. For goodness' sake! Children who seemed well could be ill; those who seemed ill could be well. Deaf children could be blind, blind children dumb, dumb children deaf or blind, or blind children deaf and dumb. The only thing that was self-evident was the fact you couldn't tell what a child was like by looking at them. So how were you supposed to know — ask them? What if they were deaf, dumb, blind, mongoloid and mute, and could neither lip-read nor sign, nor see a capital letter at two small paces, nor a word at three? Yet despite everything, I'd been born an optimist and an inner voice whispered, 'It could be worse. It could be worse,' as that congenital optimism fought a battle against the forces of despondency and despair. 'It could be even weirder,' it said, as I shifted my feet smartly out of the way while a small girl hobbled past, her two identical twin-type heads level with my desktop. She winked at me too. Twice at once!

I felt a frown on my face as dark as deadly nightshade and a headache just as lethal directly above it. I closed my eyes and prayed for guidance. I knew there was something positive in everything. That God didn't test you beyond what you're capable of bearing.

So, it couldn't get any worse — not now, not after all this. It couldn't. I opened my eyes.

It did.

From the corner of my eye, I caught a blur of movement. I turned to see a tiny boy-like creature whose body seemed to have collapsed in on itself. He was spinning in place on a wheelchair, faster and faster, until I could smell rubber burning.

Near to this spectacle from Oz-land, and static with concentration, was a pretty little boy sitting at his desk in isolation. He was arranging buttercups in a jam-jar and wore a white frilly shirt and blue velvet shorts; he had a coy, angelic look about him, like those cherubim in overdone religious paintings.

Miss Goldenheart went over to the wheelchair and started to pull it to a halt. As there was a predictable transfer of momentum, however, she started spinning herself. Nonplussed, she addressed the boy at the desk.

'How are you, Jason?' she asked, as her torque force decreased a bit and her spinning diminished pro rata.

'I'm very well thank you, my dear Miss Goldenheart,' he said, tossing back his wavy, fair hair and curling his neat rosebud lips into a minuscule pout. I noticed he had the tiniest beginnings of a moustache under his pert little nose too. He suited it.

'You're very gifted at your flower arranging,' she said, as she began to shudder to a halt along with the wheelchair and its occupant.

'Oh, you are a one,' said Jason coyly, flashing his grey almond eyes and tugging at the shirt-frills that crept round his elegant neck like feather down. 'It's nothing really, and you really must know that. Any woman worth her salt would,' he simpered, while he blushed and I began to wonder. He had no obvious deformity either; perhaps he was a heart case too.

Miss Goldenheart smiled.

'No, the flowers are really very well arranged,' she insisted, as she started to spin the creature in the wheelchair in the proper direction to reorient it. Its eyes shone with an unholy joy as she did so and its satisfied smile smothered the rest of its unfinished face.

'Just keep up the flower arranging, Jason, and don't worry about proper lessons at present,' she said as she returned to her desk and Jason looked round at me coquettishly. He shrugged one shoulder, flushed, gave me a glowing smile and went back to his buttercups.

The wheelchair had stopped, but my head still spun as yet another voice assaulted me. It sounded just like Jason's, but it was the girl in front. 'I'm Melissa,' she said, and I nodded. She'd been giving me unrequited smiles for quite some time now, and was obviously appraising me for future use.

'Hello,' I replied carefully, less certain about acknowledging strangers since my experiences with Derek. She seemed very nice, but her head was ever-so-slightly larger than it should have been and it made the rest of her seem small and neat in comparison.

She made eye contact.

'We must talk at dinner-break.'

'Fine,' I said, 'if I can fit it in.'

I felt anxious, and that's an understatement. I needed something to calm me down a bit – some sedative-induced breathing space. I looked at the clock. It was more than two hours until my next sedative.

ON THE EDGE OF A LIFETIME

A thin, pockmarked boy with short, spiky hair and an insomniac's eye shadows eased back in his chair. He was older: six and a half, going on seven. Eight at best.

'I noticed your agitation, man,' he said, as he whipped out some pills from his pocket. 'Generic phenobarb,' he whispered, 'ten milligrams for sixpence.'

Billy leaned over.

'Disgraceful!' he snarled. 'Sixpence? Keep them! I've seen fifty milligrams trade pentobarb for tuppence at the Cardiac Clinic. Sod off!' he said, which didn't faze Spiky Hair one little bit.

'It's your head, man,' he said casually, addressing me and ignoring Billy completely. 'If you need it straightened out, you do the deal, man. Not him. And don't ever forget, man, I'm the boy to see.' He put the pills and himself away and Billy held up two fingers – alluding, I presumed, to the cost of the pentobarb at the Cardiac Clinic.

A bell rang, causing jumps, twitches and some much more generalised trauma. Our teacher told us it was the signal for milk break, when we'd all be served a small bottle of milk. She explained it helped build up bones, teeth and that sort of thing. I thought it a good idea we all had some.

As if on cue, the door pushed open and a fat, older boy, wearing thick-lensed glasses, zoomed in backwards carrying a crate of shuddering milk bottles. I was soon to get to know him and to anticipate his entrance. I was to get to know, too, the fact that his eyes spun like the planets in the firmament. For this reason we called him 'Fatty Spinner'.

On this first occasion however, I didn't notice his eyes at all, for all I could focus on was the small bottle of milk that was placed on my desk, complete with straw sticking out of its metal foil top. I glanced at Billy and Alastair who'd already started sipping, so I began to sip mine too.

A sort of strained, satisfied peace fell over the room, but as various and diverse sounds encroached on it, I decided it was probably best not to look around too much. Even at that age I knew there was some strange law of sympathy in the universe, which stated that unpleasant sounds were usually accompanied by unpleasant sights. Hearing what I could, therefore, I didn't want to see anything.

For the moment, relative silence reigned, broken only by the odd slurping sound, a satisfied grunt, or the squeak of an iron-clad polio boot hitting the leg of a chair. It was the first time I'd heard what I came to know later as an 'uneasy calm' – the sort that presages well for the next few hours or so, but never, as I was learning fast, for very much longer.

6

If milk break was indescribable, lunch was impossible to imagine. I'd been seated beside Alastair and Billy again, and I remember them very clearly; I think I'll always remember the way they were that day, before Old Father Chronos crept in with that sickle in his hand – the one he'll use to cut you down too one day, quite possibly unannounced.

Alastair had dark-brown eyes and jet-black hair that reflected light like a blackened mirror. And his physical darkness hinted at his nature. For it too was dark and reflective and he was as impossible to fathom as the lunar Sea of Tranquillity. He tried to please, but rarely succeeded. He tried to be direct, but had that quality of detachment that suggested his mind was always on other things. Even then, he seemed to worry too much, and worry seemed his constant companion. By the age of five he'd lost a number of his teeth, because of his illness. If he'd put them under his pillow and found them gone in the morning with nothing left in their place, it would simply have confirmed for him how life was. Al wouldn't have been surprised, I think, to discover even the tooth fairy couldn't be trusted.

Billy, on the other hand, was made of lighter stuff. He had browny-coloured hair and sparkling blue eyes that were at least paler than the deep cyanotic tone of his skin. He was fast when he spoke and moved, despite his constant shortness of breath, as if his life were going to be a short one, and he knew it. Though he was obviously never the most energetic of children, whatever energy he did have had decided to make itself into one vibrant bundle. It was soon evident he wasn't any genius. But in addition to his being born a blue baby, he was also a congenital raconteur. He had a touch of anarchy about him too and he made it appear he couldn't give a damn about anything, giving a shrug of his tiny shoulders to life and its vagaries. He was perhaps the opposite of Al; he didn't brood, he didn't reflect on things and he smiled a lot.

I realise now, of course, we'd been seated together because we had very similar illnesses. None of us was expected to live for long, and I suspect Alastair was more aware of this than Billy or me, and that, in consequence, whatever the demons were that haunted him they had decided to frown on life and he simply frowned along with them.

After lunch, we visited the school nurse for our small white sedative tablets. As she dished them out, a boy she referred to as 'Siggy' accompanied her. She spoke to him quietly, in confidential tones, and as far as I could make out he was being given our case histories. When she'd finished, he stood assessing us, arms crossed.

'It's classic sub-cyanotic, neurotic-repressive, acted out, orally fixated behaviour,' he said as he studied us carefully. He gave us a smile as wide as the earth too but when we responded, he turned sharply away and totally ignored us.

'And you conclude?' asked the nurse.

He shrugged.

'If they had private means, I could maybe do something. But if they did, they wouldn't be in a place like this, would they?'

After we'd swallowed our pills, we were taken by a different nurse for a rest-break in a small building in the middle of the playground, called the Rest Room. It contained a dozen or so low camp beds and we were left alone there to ruminate on life. It all seemed very strange as we lay looking at the ceiling, listening to the others playing outside. We could hear the sound of a radio coming from one of the two normal schools on either side of our own. That radio would be on every lunchtime, and I enjoyed the music immensely, distant as it was. As I lay listening, it was playing 'Don't Laugh At Me', sung by the comedian Norman Wisdom. I thought it apt to have a funny man trying to be serious accompanying our first rest-break. After all, we weren't what we seemed to be either. We didn't act like invalids, but here we were, playing the part convincingly.

On that first day Billy presented us with a handful of what looked like stamps, and I wondered if he collected them.

'What d'you think of these?' he asked, rolling over onto his side and handing me a fistful of the little square pieces of sticky paper.

'What are they, stamps?'

'Stickers,' he said precisely. I was none the wiser.

'Let me see,' said Alastair, taking one and studying it. 'They look like stamps to me too.'

Billy shook his head in frustration.

'In my day everyone would've known what they are. They're stickers!' he repeated, puffing. He was a variant on my sister, this blue boy, and obviously not well. 'My mum got them from work, before she opened her shop. I found them in the back seat of my dad's car. They stick, see!' he said, suddenly, as he stuck one onto the frame of his bed. I stuck one on the frame of mine too. Alastair considered it, noted the effect and then, grabbing a handful himself, began to decorate his own bed.

We went at it for the duration of our rest-break. And by the time the smaller version of the school nurse had returned to take us back to class, our beds and even bits of the walls were overrun with red stickers advertising reels of thread.

'Had a good rest?' she asked sharply. 'Sleep well?'

We looked at one another and nodded.

'Well, now you're rested you'll be fit for class this afternoon, won't you?'

We nodded again, as the realisation began to impinge on us we'd almost completely redecorated the place.

Her eyes took in every detail of the stickers.

'Right! Who did this?'

No one said a word.

'I take it one of you has a relative who works at the mill.'

Billy nodded.

'My mother used to.'

'So *she* gave them to you.'

'I took them from my father's car,' said Billy, looking worried and paler; a sort of sky-blue colour.

The nurse shook her head.

'This isn't any common-or-garden mill for manual workers.'

'No, nurse. It isn't,' said Billy, and his voice wavered a little, just like Al's body and my gut. There was trouble brewing here and we could do without it.

'Well, there's no need for it to look like one, is there?' she spat, and we all shook our heads in agreement as she led us back to our class.

At home time, as I stood in the cloakroom with Billy, I caught sight of Derek standing near the outside door, supported by his sticks and looking distressed. A dark stain was slowly forming at the front of his trousers. It spread down his legs, over his leg-irons, across his boots and onto the floor.

Billy took a deep breath.

'He's peed himself.'

'Oh!' I gasped, as I watched Derek get even more excited and produce more pee. A regular little rapid was flowing. Billy assessed the dynamics of it all. 'I bet he'll dirty his trousers,' he said. I was horrified at Derek's plight, yet had a mounting desire to burst out laughing. But I didn't. I said nothing and simply watched in silence as this large, strange boy wept and wet himself.

'I'll have to go,' said Billy. 'My dad's picking me up. Let me know what happens.' I nodded and he walked towards the outside door.

As he passed Derek, he gave him a smile and touched him gently on the hand. Derek calmed down immediately and returned the smile as best he could. And that simple, tactful gesture hit me like a hammer-blow. For I realised that little, mischievous, puffing Billy had a generosity of spirit I'd seen in few others in my short life. I would have found it difficult to touch

Derek, even before he'd wet himself. Not so Billy. He smiled at Derek once more and then left. I watched him go and felt a rare softness inside. I'd heard my mother use the term 'rough diamond' before and now I knew exactly what it meant.

'OOG-OO-AH, OH-AH, OH-AH!' I rapidly returned my attention to Derek. He was waving his hand in the air like a windmill, in even greater distress than he had been before. The pee was flowing out like a gusher – a big, flowing gusher – as I stared at him.

On the back of his hand was a line of red stickers, with the legend 'Hometown Mill Cottons: Threads for Everyday Use' printed on them. I managed to catch Billy's eye before he went casually out of the door. His face was blue and impassive, but he winked at me like the glass-eyed doctor.

When we boarded the bus to go home I kept well away from Derek, who was utterly crestfallen. He'd been cleaned up certainly, but he still gave off a distinctive aroma.

As we drew out of the school gate, I spotted Billy in the front seat of his father's car. His brother was with them, but I couldn't see what colour he was. Billy looked smug and I wondered what I really thought of him. More specifically, I wondered what I really thought of what he'd done to Derek.

The bus stopped for a few minutes to pick up the mongols. Martin was still with them, and still silent, inert and withdrawn. He sat beside me again and I made a few more attempts at communication. But although the other mongols made small talk, swapped stories of their day and generally socialised, he gave me no sign of recognition whatsoever.

Our mothers were waiting for us.

'Had a good day, son?' asked mine, and I nodded. Martin's mother asked him the same, but she received no answer. We said goodbye to them; they left, I was home, and my first day at school was over.

'So what was it like?' my mother asked when we were safely inside. I told her what I could, ending with a brief account of the day's highlight – Derek.

'So a boy wet himself, and possibly dirtied his trousers,' she said dismissively. 'Small children do that, so you'd better get used to it. Anyway, they're not all as advanced as you, for their age, so don't worry about it.'

I wondered at this, but felt I shouldn't mention that the 'small child' in question was at least twelve years old.

That evening, as my brother and I sat beside the radio, I finally forgot all about school. The rest of the family were through in my sick sister's bedroom speaking with our priest, who'd appeared out of the blue. They hadn't looked too happy when I'd last seen them and now my brother wasn't looking too happy either.

My elder sister came in.

'Time for some tea,' she said, and looked at my brother. 'What's wrong with you?'

'That!' he said, turning his thumb to the radio. 'There was supposed to be rock 'n' roll on, but they've dumped it!'

My sister looked at him, thought for a moment, then spoke again quietly.

'Things a great deal worse have happened. And they'll continue to happen,' she said, as I watched her: practical, composed – and undoubtedly correct. She usually was about such matters, though on that occasion she failed to say exactly what she meant. We found out later though. Not that much later, but later nonetheless.

When it was far too late to do anything about it.

7

Day one at school had surprised me. But day two was less surprising, and I used it to consolidate my transformation from homeboy to schoolboy.

Martin and his mum were already waiting as we made our way down the path that morning. She acknowledged us but seemed uneasy. Martin had on indoor clothes, too. Something had happened.

'I had a visit from the Education Department yesterday evening,' said the woman. 'So I've just come to tell the nurse Martin won't be going in today. They've decided your son's school isn't suitable for Martin. It's ridiculous! He's not as bad as he appears to be.'

My mum was shocked.

'Oh, I'm so sorry. He got on so well with Francis, too. You'll miss Martin, won't you, son?' she said, being creative, and I nodded.

My mother rarely lied, but on the rare occasions she did it was in the best interests of all concerned. I'd lied myself by nodding, of course, for it was hardly as if two silent trips on a school bus made us bosom buddies.

His mother hadn't finished.

'I was told from the beginning he'd be able to cope there and it would stimulate his gifts. Now they're not even giving him the chance to develop those. They're just ripping him out after one pathetic day and he'll never get the chance to make anything of his life.'

I wasn't quite sure what kids like Martin did make of their lives, but I took her point in a general sort of way and so did my mum, who was Sympathy itself.

'That's dreadful! You'd think they'd get it right in the first place. So what's going to happen now?' she asked, and the woman looked at her son rather strangely.

'Something . . . different,' she said quietly. 'There's another place – a slightly more . . . formal place. I'll have to send him there. It's all that's left.'

She faltered and my mother approached and took her hand.

'I am sorry,' she said, realising as I had that the phrase, 'I'll have to send him there . . .' probably meant something else that wasn't the best of news.

She confirmed our suspicions.

'My husband isn't around. He wasn't able to deal with the situation all that well,' she said, looking at 'the situation', who was contemplating the ground as usual. 'It's only a passing thing, I imagine, but it isn't the best of things to have happened, all considered.'

My mum squeezed her hand.

'It can't be all that easy,' she said, as Martin's mother composed herself and told us a bit more about his new school.

'It's called "Our Lady of Lost Hope",' she said quietly, 'and it's residential, though they get home weekends every fifty-second week.'

My student-priest brother – my 'Otherbrother', as I called him – was at a residential school too. It was called 'The Seminary', and he didn't get home much either. However, I was pretty certain the place Martin was going to wasn't quite the same somehow, though Our Lady of anything was surely a good sign.

The bus drew up noisily beside us and the children stared out from the windows. One or two simulated a wave to me, but I pretended I didn't see them. It wasn't as if I was ashamed at the attention I was getting from them – I was too young for that – or realised it's best not to be seen socialising with that sort in public; I was too young for that too. I just didn't want Martin's mother thinking I'd fitted into school or made some semi-human contact there. After all, her son's former part of the school was a league down from mine, if that were possible, and he'd been shunted out after a day, friendless. So it wasn't a state of affairs to draw attention to by any show of popularity on my part.

When the school nurse came out to greet us, Martin's mother made straight for her. They exchanged a few words and my mother joined them. Martin was left standing alone beside me.

'A right bunch of nutters they are,' he said, in a strange, croaky voice.

'If you ask me, I'm well out of it.'

I stared at him.

'You can speak! You can speak like me!'

'No point when no one listens,' he said casually, as he turned and looked at the ground again, back to mute control.

I was amazed. Had I heard a voice? Had it indeed come from that odd little boy? I was beginning to doubt it already, as his mother came back and took his hand. I started walking towards the bus, still reeling. I stopped for a moment and looked back. His mother was fussing over him. I wondered if she knew he could speak.

I reached the door, went in and inhaled the characteristic odour. I made a quick check – Derek was there. He was dozing. I sat down. I wanted to tell someone about Martin. But who was going to believe me? 'Forget it!' I thought. 'They'll find out for themselves.'

And they did.

8

This time the journey was uneventful. The children and their implements were already less daunting and my second morning in class seemed almost normal. I was less conscious than I had been the previous day of my schoolmates' disabilities. Already I was becoming more aware of their personalities and idiosyncrasies, rather than the handicaps that had brought them here.

By the time Fatty Spinner appeared with the milk crate halfway through the morning, I was feeling much more comfortable. I'd got to know some of my fellow pupils' names too.

The girl with the problem teeth was called Jean, I'd discovered, and her teeth seemed fine to me today, whether lying on the floor or resting unsteadily in her mouth. The restricted plane of movement of Una – the girl with the neck-brace – now seemed a proper and precise one, and my admirer, Melissa, had a head that looked normal sized. Alastair and Billy had stayed blue overnight, but this didn't strike me as particularly odd either; on the contrary, it was a bonus and enabled them to stand out immediately in any group of otherwise monochrome people.

So by the time we'd eaten school dinner, had our fix of sedative, been inspected silently by Siggy and taken to our Rest Room by the irascible little nurse, I was feeling relaxed, self-assured and affable. The radio was playing Frankie Laine's 'My Friend', and like yesterday's song, it seemed apposite.

As the small nurse closed the door behind her, we lay down with heavy sighs. Frankie Laine's voice became much more distant and Billy's slightly higher one took precedence.

'It's a good school, this. My dad says it's the best of its type in the country.'

That surprised me.

'What does that mean?'

'It means it's the best, for children like us.'

Al thought about it.

'I wanted to go to a normal school, but my mum said this would be better.'

'Me too,' I agreed. 'The doctor said this would be best. He made that very clear,' I added, thinking fleetingly of twirling pens and sleepy nurses, and bandaged boys with white sticks who rolled around on castors.

'What else did he say?' quizzed Al.

'What do you mean, "what else"?' I asked, wondering what else Dr Wink could have said.

'Did he say why you had to come here?' Al went on, drumming his chest with his short, blue fingers where I knew the heart was located. 'You know . . .' he urged, 'what's really wrong?'

I touched my chest.

'The same as you. I've got a bad heart. There's a hole in it,' I explained, as he pushed his hand under his shirt and rubbed a bit more.

Billy snorted.

'Then why aren't you the same colour as us? You're not blue like we are, so your heart can't be that bad.'

'I suppose not,' I said, though I thought one hole in the heart was much the same as any other, until I saw Alastair's fingers disappear *into* his chest and scratch in there. He pulled up his shirt and vest and looked. I saw the hole was plainly visible in the dead centre of his chest – his fingertips were dipped into it! I looked away, as I didn't want to appear too inquisitive.

I turned to answer Billy.

'It's still pretty bad,' I explained, as Al stared at me.

'You might have a bad heart, but it's not as if you're going to die soon, is it?'

He moved his hand to his mouth and licked drops of blood from his fingers. Noticing my astonishment, he explained.

'It's leaking. You have to put as much back as you can.' He rubbed hard once more at his breastbone.

I gaped.

'No, I don't suppose I am going to die very soon,' I said, re-evaluating the degree of my disability. 'It's just a precaution,' I added, as Al finally licked his lips. There wasn't a speck of blood to be seen.

'What's a precaution?' asked Billy. I looked at him side-on. *His* hand now disappeared down the front of his shirt and came out at his back in a bump! He wiggled his fingers and the back of his shirt rippled.

I hid my astonishment and replied.

'Coming here – it's a precaution,' I said, pulling my things up and searching my own chest, checking it for subsidence and finding none.

Billy took his hand back out again. He licked it just like Alastair had.

'A precaution against what?' he asked.

'I don't know. It's what my mum says.'

Billy nodded.

'And what does your father say?'

'He doesn't really talk about it,' I said, feeling defensive. 'I suppose he thinks the same as everyone else.'

'Which is?'

'I should be here; Doctor knows best.'

Billy considered this.

'My father's putting me into a normal school soon – a private one.'

I was shocked.

'But you just said your father thought this was the best school in the country!'

'It is, if you need it. I won't need it for long, so I'll be going to a normal, private school.'

Al snapped at him.

'Rubbish! They wouldn't take you! If they would, you'd be there already. You're too blue to go,' he said, touching the skin on his knee with his fingers and pressing it hard to push his point home.

Billy looked determined.

'They'll take me after my operation,' he said. Al flinched at the mention of the word. 'I'll be fit for a normal school then,' said Billy. 'And when I leave, I'll work in my father's factory.'

I was impressed, but a look at Al told me he was less so.

'That might work, but I doubt it. They're dangerous things anyway, operations. They don't always work,' he said, as Billy turned on him.

'So what? They work sometimes!'

Al's eyes were dark and wide and haunted.

'Operation or no operation, you won't be able to go even if they would take you, which they won't.'

'My dad says they will!' said Billy. 'So does my brother.'

'Liar,' said Al quietly, as Billy stared at him.

I looked from one to the other and decided to intervene to prevent a full-scale, blue-blooded war breaking out.

'What age is your brother?' I asked, as Al lay down and stewed for a time. I noticed stains on the back of his shirt – fingertip stains. Obviously his hole, though smaller than Billy's, went right the way through as well.

'My brother's eight and a half now, nearly nine.'

'And what colour is he?'

I'd seen his brother the previous day in their car, but couldn't tell what he looked like. I suspected from Billy's reaction that his brother was unwell too, for he turned slowly to face me, obviously rattled.

'Well he isn't blue, if that's what you mean.'

'I didn't mean that!' I lied, for that's exactly what I *had* meant.

'He's normal – as white as you,' said Billy, looking to Al for confirmation.

Al sat up, frowned, looked at me and nodded slowly.

'He wasn't blue, last time I saw him. He was the same colour as you,' he said, and I believed him.

'So you know his brother?' I asked, feeling a twinge of jealousy.

Al twitched.

'I've met him at the clinic once or twice,' he said cautiously. 'Billy and I see the same doctor. Last time I went, he was there with his brother and mother. His brother wasn't blue then, so I doubt he's blue now.'

'He isn't!' said Billy emphatically. 'He isn't!'

'I'm sorry,' I said. 'I didn't mean to pry.'

He looked very angry.

'Forget it!' he said and glared at Alastair again, as if Al knew something about his brother that Billy didn't want me to know. I reckoned his brother *was* blue, and the family had the misfortune of having two boys who were very unwell.

We lay quietly for a time, but Al looked very worried about something. I decided to try and cheer him up. I'd overheard Miss Goldenheart tell him he was a bright boy. That was praise – intellectual praise, the best sort for a boy like him, a boy with no chance of ever doing a physical job. So I thought I'd mention it, remind him of just how good he was at school and take his mind off things.

'Miss Goldenheart says you're very bright, Alastair. I have two very bright sisters at home. I've got an Otherbrother who's bright too. He's gone off to be a priest. Would you like to do something like that?'

He looked interested.

'I'm certainly a lot brighter than I used to be,' he said cautiously. 'If I were bright enough I'd be a test pilot. But I'm not, so I doubt I'll ever manage it.'

'That's just your age,' I reassured him. 'You get brighter as you get older. My sisters did. They give you a test when you're eleven – an "IQ test". You'll be even brighter then.'

Al glanced at Billy, then back at me.

'I mean I'm a brighter colour, stupid.' He rubbed his skin, which lightened a bit. 'I'm less blue,' he continued, 'I'm becoming lighter.'

'Then watch you don't float away,' said Billy, who was looking at the skin on his fingers and pressing them as white as possible. I pondered this, looked at my own fingers and turned to find both boys staring at me.

'Oh, I used to be blue too,' I said quickly. 'I was a very blue baby, but I changed colour later, when I was about two.'

'And d'you think you might change back?' asked Al.

I noticed a pulsing movement under the front of his shirt.

'Back to being blue?'

'Well I don't mean back to being a baby, stupid! Back to being blue, yes.'

'Don't *you* be stupid!' cried Billy. 'It doesn't work like that. It isn't that simple. You don't change back when you've become white. When all this blueness goes, it goes for good!'

'Not when you die,' said Al slowly. 'When you stop breathing you turn blue, white or not.'

Billy studied him.

'You don't if you're blue already.'

'But he isn't!' said Al, pointing at me.

'But I used to be!' I pleaded, desperate to fit in.

'Then you don't want to die too soon,' said Al carefully, 'or you'll be back to blue again.'

I had to agree, but not completely.

'You can turn white, too, when you die.'

Billy gave me a sharp look.

'White?'

'That's later,' said Al. 'That only happens later when you're *really* dead.'

'Still, it's a thought,' said Billy wistfully. Then he cheered up. 'I'll be white after my operation anyway.'

'When is your operation?' I asked, and Al shuddered again.

'Soon – not long. In a few weeks, I think,' he said as he lay down again, face up and staring at the ceiling, as if reflecting on the lights above an operating table.

Al made scalpel-like movements across his chest with his forefinger. At least it was on the outside this time.

'I wouldn't want them cutting my chest open.'

I looked at him.

'Why not?'

'I'd rather get better on my own.'

'Can that happen?' I asked, reassessing his colour and wondering where it came from and if it could really go back there.

He gave me a look.

'You said it happened to you.'

'I suppose it did,' I agreed cautiously, knowing somehow that it wasn't quite the same.

'Well, then . . . '

'Well, maybe you will,' I said diplomatically as I lay back and listened to the noise of our schoolmates playing.

From the radio I could hear Winifred Atwell rattling something out on her piano. I wondered about these two boys, about our school and about the fact it was apparently so very different from other schools.

Time passed lazily. Winifred was replaced by Doris Day singing 'Secret Love'. Suddenly there was a loud bang at the door and a girl who sounded like my classmate, Una, shouted:

'Stop smashing that damned arm of yours against the door, Woody! There are very sick kids in there trying to sleep.'

Woody, whoever he was, replied 'OK, OK! Keep your brace on! It's a sad state of affairs if a boy can't smash his deformed arm in frustration and rage against a Rest Room door.'

'You can kill kids like them if you give them a fright. You should know that!'

They finally left and the three of us were alone again.

'I am going to get better, and without any operation.'

It was Al. He obviously wasn't one to let things drop. My mother would have called him a 'worrier'. He was sitting up, looking very concerned indeed.

'How can you know that?' asked Billy, who was lying face down, tracing shapes on the floor with his small, blue fingers.

'My mother knows,' said Al. 'She saw a gipsy who told her my fortune.'

I turned to face him.

'A gipsy?'

'Yes, a gipsy. They live in caravans, with horses that pull them around the country.'

Billy was amazed.

'They live in caravans with horses?'

'Don't be so stupid,' sneered Al. 'They live in the caravans and the horses live outside and pull them around from place to place.'

I looked at him carefully.

'Your mother went to a gipsy's caravan to be told her fortune?'

'Well no, not really.'

'Where did she go then?'

'To a gipsy woman who lives across the road,' he said, as Billy shook his head in total amazement.

'There's a caravan of gipsies across the road from you, with a horse outside?'

'Well, not exactly a caravan,' said Al. His voice dropped. 'But there's a gipsy woman, though she lives in a house like ours.'

Billy smirked.

'So you live in a caravan! Your parents can't afford a proper house,' he sniped.

Al became very animated.

'You know we have a house! And she did have a caravan! But she gave it up a long time ago when her horse died of equine fever. And she *can* tell the future,' he insisted. 'She told my mum my problems would go for good in a few years' time. And they will!'

'How can she possibly know that?' sneered Billy, lying on his front again. 'How can she know the future? I don't believe it!'

'Believe what you want, but she can! She looks into a crystal ball, at cards or into a teacup and finds out what's going to happen.'

Billy gave a tight smile.

'Teacups as in tea?'

Al clenched his fists. The atmosphere was becoming tense, so I intervened.

'What's a crystal ball, Al?'

'It's a glass ball that shows pictures of the future.'

'What, like a television?'

'No, like one of those balls you get at Christmas with snow in it. Only it doesn't have any snow and it tells you what's going to happen. If you're a gipsy.'

'A glass ball . . . ' I mused. It sounded incredible and I wasn't sure I believed it.

'That's plain daft,' said Billy. 'My brother says no one can tell the future. It hasn't happened yet.'

'Not true!' snapped Al. 'The gipsy told my mum once my gran would die and she did.'

'It can't work,' insisted Billy. 'How can they know that sort of thing?'

'They just do,' said Al.

'Rubbish!'

I wasn't too sure.

'Maybe they do. Who are we to know anything? Maybe they *can* see what's going to happen, in their crystal balls.'

'And in the cards, too,' said Al. 'The Ace of Spades means death, you know. I hate that card.'

I felt funny. I knew the Ace of Spades from the card games I played with my sick sister. She didn't like it either and tossed it aside whenever she turned it over.

'It's still plain daft,' repeated Billy. 'You can't tell the future. It hasn't even been here yet to happen.'

'Well, the gipsy said my gran would die horribly and she did die horribly,' said Al emphatically.

Billy shook his head.

'She would have died anyway.'

'How do you know?' Al asked.

'I don't, but I bet she would have.'

'You can't be sure,' said Al quietly. 'Anyway, she died exactly when the gipsy woman said she would. On a Sunday –'

'Luck,' interrupted Billy, as Alastair finished.

' – at twelve minutes past two in the afternoon.'

And Billy was finally quiet.

There was total silence, until I eventually broke it.

'If you could see the future and didn't like it, you'd change it.'

'You would, wouldn't you?' said Billy.

Al gave him a strange look.

'You can't! Not if you're going to die,' he said.

'You could always get an operation and save yourself,' said Billy, reviving a bit.

Now Al became dismissive.

'They couldn't operate on my gran. She'd something wrong that couldn't be cut out. Her only hope was Lourdes.'

Billy looked startled.

'Lourdes? What do they have at Lourdes? A gigantic camp of gipsies?'

Al shook his head in disgust.

'It's a religious shrine – a huge park for poorly Catholics. The Virgin Mary appeared to Saint Bernadette there and my mum's been and says miracles happen all the time.'

Billy was electrified.

'What kind of miracles?'

'Cripples walk, the deaf hear, the dumb speak and the incurable are cured,' said Al comprehensively.

'Ah, but do the blue become white?' asked Billy.

Al thought about it.

'They could, I suppose, if they immersed themselves in the sacred pool. If they said a few prayers, repented and came back out again cleansed then I suppose they could, yes.'

Billy frowned.

'Is the pool filled with bleach?'

'No, just water,' said Al. 'Very strong holy water.'

'Then maybe we should all go there,' suggested Billy sensibly. I was sorry to have to disappoint him.

'It doesn't work every time,' I said. 'Miracles only happen to a few people and anyway, it's probably expensive to get to. Most parents couldn't afford it,' I said, though I was generalising while thinking about my own parents, who could afford very little.

Billy gritted his teeth.

'I'd get the money from mine, OK. If it works.'

'You can only go after you've made your First Communion,' said Al, though he didn't sound certain.

'Then I'll go in two years' time,' said Billy. 'I'll go then,' he repeated – subject closed. He became silent, lost in thought, and was obviously considering the matter deeply.

We fell into another spell of silence. I reflected on what Al had said about the gipsy woman, and decided that being able to tell the future didn't really make sense from the point of view of the religious teaching I'd had so far.

'My Otherbrother says God makes everything happen.'

Al was looking at me oddly now, as if ready to tackle me on the whole matter, instead of Billy.

'He does.'

'Then if these gipsy women can tell what's going to happen, does it mean they can see Heaven in these crystal balls of theirs?'

Al was solemn.

'I don't know about Heaven, but they might see Hell. The Devil can tell the future too,' he said, and that really caused the silence to drop. We began to look around at the shadowy corners of the Rest Room. A piece of music I knew as 'The Creep' was playing across the way and that didn't help matters either.

Despite the sounds outside it seemed very quiet and still. The three of us lay on our backs and let it all tumble through our heads.

After a time Billy began to giggle infectiously at something. We'd no idea what, but we joined in anyway. We were still giggling when the nurse arrived.

'Hope there's nothing going on in here there shouldn't be,' she said as we got up from our beds and stood looking at her innocently. 'Nothing that causes problems like yesterday's,' she added, ushering us out of the door.

As we left she stuck her head back inside, as if she might have left another blue boy behind – missed one who'd hidden in the shadows.

We made our way back to class, with all thoughts of the future gone for the present, but we still gave the occasional laugh. The nurse shook her head in disapproval, as if laughter wasn't something she thought our due.

9

Later that afternoon the lady in white arrived in our classroom. She spoke to my teacher and they both looked in my direction. Miss Goldenheart came over and, bending down, explained what they'd been discussing.

'I'd like you to go with Miss O'Hare here, Francis. We have a teacher called Mrs Schiklgruber, who deals with school enrolment, ideological status of inmates and the like, and she needs to ask you some questions. Don't worry about getting tongue-tied or anything, for she has ways of making you talk. She'll simply give you a very hard time, which you've not to pay any attention to, then she'll give you a letter to take home to your parents. Is that OK?'

'Yes, Miss,' I managed, through a mouth as dry as a snow-free crystal ball. I thought of Martin. Were they going to shunt me off to a residential school too?

I left my desk and walked over to my escort.

'Come on, Francis,' she said, as if I had any choice in the matter.

Mrs Schiklgruber's class lay on the other side of the assembly hall, at the top of the stairs. I managed to climb these on my own, despite an offer of help from Miss O'Hare, who insisted we took them slowly.

When we finally reached the top we proceeded to a large door marked 'M.H.0'. My escort knocked, the door creaked open, and a voice emerged that was commanding, terse and strident.

'Enter!'

So we did.

Unlike my own class, which was unpredictable but happy, this one was like the army barracks I'd seen in a photograph from World War Two. Most of the pupils were sitting ramrod straight, and they were totally still and completely silent.

An atmosphere of fear pervaded the room and here and there were odd-looking stains on the floor, the sorts of stains I'd heard you found in torture chambers. I heard a groan coming from somewhere, but I didn't look. Instead I fixed my attention on the teacher. After all, she was the person I'd come to see.

Mrs Schiklgruber sat grandly at her desk, presiding magisterially over her charges. She was a short, squat woman, dressed in an army fatigue jacket with five golden stars on its shoulders. She wore a camouflage cap with a badge on the front, and held a long, tapering stick in her hand: the kind you point at blackboards or gouge eyes out with, if that's *your* preference. It was pointed at her class like a rapier, and I'd no doubt she knew how to use it as one.

She turned and faced me.

'You must be the hole-in-the-heart boy. Come! Stand by my desk!'

As I made to do so, I recognised one of the boys who travelled on my bus. He smiled.

'Attention!' she ordered, as if a smile constituted rebellion. The boy looked away, bit his bottom lip and became vacant. I approached her desk and stood to attention.

'So you're Francis, the heart case, are you?' she said, in a tone that sent shivers through her class – and me too, though I was determined not to show it.

'Yes, Miss, I am.'

'And you're a good Catholic?'

'I hope so, Miss.'

'And you go to mass as you're supposed to?'

'Yes, Miss. Every Sunday.'

'So you went last Sunday?'

I was taken aback at this and, sensing something amiss, one of the boys in the front row broke down, wailed and began to nibble the back of his hand.

'STOPPIT!' ordered Schiklgruber. He fell motionless immediately, though he continued to sob.

'So you went last Sunday?' she asked again, sounding impatient.

I nodded.

'Yes, Miss. To twelve o'clock mass as usual, with my mum and dad.'

'And what colour were the priest's vestments?' she asked, like an Inquisitor.

'Colour?' I asked, dropping the 'Miss' and turning respect to disrespect in one missed word.

'Yes, little Badheart. What colour of clothes did the priest have on?'

I looked at her hard.

'I've no idea.'

'Why not,' she barked, 'if you were really there?'

'Because I couldn't see him. We were sitting at the very back and I couldn't see a thing.'

'Ah!'

'But it was the Feast of the Assumption and priests wear white on that day, if that helps you with your problem.'

'Problem? PROBLEM? I have no PROBLEM!!'

'You do if you don't know the colour of the priest's vestments, given you want to know it now.'

'*I* know that!' she fumed and her pupils crouched at their desks, some even crawling under them and lying down flat with their hands covering their heads as if anticipating mortar fire.

'Then why are you asking me?' I asked, quietly.

She breathed in hard.

'To see if you'd really gone,' she spat and the class ducked down as one.

'I told you I had,' I said, and she looked at me as if I were the demon Astaroth, the cuddly one with the spiky hair and the smile that looks almost beatific.

My comment shut her up for a time, so I took the chance to look in the direction of the groaning. A half-naked boy lay face down, stretched out and tied by tight-looking cords to four nails hammered into the floor. There were weals on his bare back: they looked like lash marks and he was begging for water, but there was a sign displayed between his shoulderblades; 'Nil By Mouth' it said clinically, and I turned away.

'Just so,' said Schiklgruber evenly, inspecting me very carefully. 'You're very much older than your years, I'd say.'

'I'm nearly six years. I've been called a late starter.'

'You're a precocious little runt, aren't you?'

I'd been called 'precocious' before and I was reasonably sure what it meant, but I didn't want her to know that.

'I'm not sure what you mean,' I said. 'My mother calls me "precious" sometimes, if that's the same thing.'

'It is NOT the same and it's not a compliment either,' she snapped. 'So don't dare take it as such!' Her voice altered yet again and became as inquisitive as an agony aunt's. 'By the way, what does your father do?'

'At mass?'

'Of course not! For a living, you cretin.'

'He works in an explosives factory. He makes bombs, bullets, cannon shells and torpedo heads. Most of the men there wear overalls,' I said, 'but

I don't think they change colours on special Sundays, the way priests do vestments.'

She gave me a look that could have killed – and probably had.

I continued.

'Priests do that in honour of special saints or occasions,' I said, 'and I don't suppose they have many of those in an explosives factory, though they might fast now and then.'

'And how would a mobile cripple like you know anything about that?' she snapped.

'Because I have a brother who's training to be a priest,' I said gently, 'and he keeps me informed of such things. He says it's part of his calling.'

'You've a brother off to be a priest?'

'I do,' I said, and a few of the braver pupils began to clap, but the heart of the class wasn't in it and it never made outright applause.

'Well, that's almost something in your favour,' she said, her tone gentler, more accommodating: a drill sergeant's on parade, rather than a general's at the front.

'I want to be something like a scientist, a doctor or a lawyer myself,' I told her, non-committally.

'Fat chance of that,' said Schiklgruber, eyes dull and hard, peering into mine as if I had the soul she was searching for.

'We'll see,' I replied.

'We shall indeed. We shall *certainly* see,' she said, then fell silent again for a few moments and took the opportunity to stare at her class to maintain a state of terror.

There was a quiet whimpering coming from somewhere near the back of the room, but she ignored it. I looked, however, and was surprised to see the little boy Jason sitting in a corner on his own. He'd been in my class yesterday, yet now he was here. I couldn't understand it. He didn't have a jam jar of buttercups this time, just a piece of old plasticine with what looked like bits of broken razorblades embedded in it. He was cautiously trying to mould it into some shape or other and he looked unhappy and ashamed.

Schiklgruber fumbled in her desk drawer and a couple of her pupils bent down reflexively, as if she were about to pull out a gun and shoot.

'Take this to your parents,' she said, handing me a closed envelope. 'You can go now,' she commanded, and in general protest I refused to return her salute. I turned away and made my way to the door, where Miss O'Hare was still standing frozen to the spot. When she finally became animated enough to pull the door open, I heard Schiklgruber's military tones again.

'Oh, and just to let you know, boys like you don't become professional

ON THE EDGE OF A LIFETIME

people – doctors, lawyers, teachers, scientists – even if they are well enough to do so, unlike you.'

I turned to face her.

'You must have misunderstood me. I wouldn't want to be a teacher.'

'No? Well, I'd set my sights on something more apposite anyway. A minor civil servant in Hell, perhaps,' she suggested, 'with some demented slut from limbo as a secretary.'

'I don't think you'd like working for me, Miss,' I said, restoring her title as her eyes glowed like burning sulphur.

As we left, we heard the sound of a whip cracking, a howl of pain, a scream of fear, and a noise like thunder. There was a sudden screech. It sounded like some poor creature caught in a trap.

And we were probably all caught in a trap, when you considered it, having been stuck away out of sight in a school for the socially and medically abnormal. The trap Mrs Schiklgruber's pupils were caught in was simply less humane.

As we turned away, Miss O'Hare spoke quietly.

'You wouldn't normally deal with her,' she said. 'There's another teacher who'll look after your religious education. She's off at present trying to come to terms with her vocation, but she'll be back soon.'

'Her vocation? She wants to be a nun?'

'No. A teacher.'

'I thought you said she was a teacher?'

'She is. Officially . . . '

I thought about that.

'And she's . . . well, better, than Mrs Schiklgruber?'

'Not really. But she's a bit . . . younger. Prettier.'

'I see,' I said. Then I remembered the buttercup boy, Jason. 'Why's that boy Jason in there?' I asked. 'I thought he was in our class.'

She smiled.

'You mean that queer little fellow?'

'Yes.'

'We don't know exactly what to do with him yet. Oh, he is a queer little fellow, that one,' she repeated, as we walked towards the stairs.

She looked back at the door of M.H.0, from where strange sounds still emerged, though they were less distinct and – like most dreadful things – made much less upsetting by distance.

When we'd moved far enough away not to hear them at all, I began to wonder if what I'd just witnessed had actually happened.

Miss O'Hare interrupted my thoughts.

'They're mentally handicapped back there, you know.'

64

'Yes,' I responded. 'I could see that. All of them,' I said grimly, before she reverted to type and started picking at my head again. I looked up at her and I could see, from the look on her face, that she understood precisely what I meant.

10

When I arrived home that afternoon I gave the letter to my mother. She read it and handed it back.

'What do you make of that?' she asked.

I looked at her, hurt, and handed it straight back again. 'I can't read real writing yet,' I told her, 'and I didn't want to ask her to do it in print.'

'Sorry, son, I forgot. One of your teachers, a Mrs Schiklgruber, says she needs proof you attend mass every Sunday. Apparently all the other Catholic parents have been contacted about this. She says we've obviously chosen to ignore her "first, former and final communication", as she puts it.'

I could tell she was angry and I didn't want to make things worse by going into detail about my meeting with Schiklgruber.

'Yes, I know, I saw her this afternoon.'

'And?'

'And . . . well, she's not very nice.'

She stared down at me.

'Did she upset you?'

'I think I upset her,' I said tactfully. Then I briefly mentioned the interrogation on the colour of the vestments.

My mum was raging.

'I'll deal with this! I'll speak to the priest!'

The priest had been with my parents the previous evening. I still wondered why they'd been closeted in the bedroom and felt this was the perfect opportunity to find out.

'You could have spoken about it last night.'

'About what?'

'About the letter.'

Her face crinkled into a smile.

'How? You've only just given it to me!'

'Oh!'

She shook her head in mock pity.

'And Father Ireland says you're so very clever. He even said it again last night.'

'So what were you talking about?'

My mum took a deep breath.

'The possibility of a trip to Lourdes.'

I couldn't believe my luck.

'Lourdes!'

'Yes, it's where the Virgin Mary appeared to —'

'Saint Bernadette,' I interrupted. 'We were talking about it in school today.'

'Well, she can't be all that bad then.'

'Who? Saint Bernadette?'

'No, this Mrs Schiklgruber. She can't be all that bad, if she's discussing Lourdes.'

I shook my head.

'It wasn't her.'

'I see,' she said, looking at the letter darkly again.

'It will be great if I can go.'

'Go where?'

'To Lourdes. It might cure me once and for all.'

She looked upset.

'Oh, it isn't you we're trying to send, son. We were hoping to send your sister. She's pretty ill, you know. It wouldn't be just for religious reasons either. There's a famous chest clinic near a forest there, and a visit to that might do some good, too. We couldn't afford to take both of you, it's —'

'Expensive,' I said, and she gave me a frown.

'Yes, it is, and you —'

'Need to have made your First Communion.'

'Well, it's certainly better if you have,' she agreed. 'So where did you learn all this from?'

'A gipsy told me,' I said blandly. 'She saw it in a crystal ball.'

With my mother looking on in amazement, I went to my room, feeling very disappointed and just a little bit jealous. But I was well aware that my sister was ill far too often. So if Lourdes could help, well and good.

I usually brought her in a cup of tea around this time. I decided that today I'd spend some time keeping her company, too. After all, at one level I realised it wasn't her fault she'd been chosen to go to Lourdes, despite the fact we were both ill. At another level, however, I realised if something happened to her, I'd be the one to go. Everything has a positive side, I supposed — even that sort of thing.

When I went into her room, she was sitting up in bed, propped up by pillows and reading a book. She put it down when she saw me and tapped the side of the bed. It was my invitation to sit down and talk to her.

'Are you enjoying your book?' I asked.

'Yes,' she managed, before she began to cough. I picked up the basin from the bedside table, removed the tea towel we used to cover it and held it under her chin. She spat some thick, greeny stuff into it and lay back on the pillow exhausted.

When she seemed to have finished I placed the basin carefully back on the table, avoiding the bottle of Lucozade that seemed to sit there permanently, beside a brown bottle of cough medicine, her tablets, her pack of playing cards and an unopened tin box of catarrh pastilles.

'I'll talk,' I said, 'don't you bother.'

She stretched out her hand and squeezed mine. She was very pale and when she breathed she made rasping sounds.

'Tell me what you did today at school,' she said suddenly, and I grabbed the basin by reflex and stuck it under her chin. It was a long sentence for her in that state.

She shook her head and smiled.

'It's OK. I'm fine. Now tell me about school.'

I told her about Mrs Schiklgruber, about queer little Jason, and about Alastair and Billy and the gipsies. I was careful, however, not to mention Lourdes once and the subject of the Ace of Spades was certainly never referred to. I must have spoken for twenty minutes and in all that time she only coughed something up three or four times. That was good by any standards and as I watched her sitting there, exhausted but delighted I was with her, I felt ashamed of the thoughts I'd had earlier.

While I'd been speaking, I'd heard my big sister come in from school and not long afterwards she came and joined us. She had her knitting needles and some wool with her, but she didn't use them.

'Hello, how are you two?' she asked, walking over to the basin and checking its contents with a practised eye.

'Fine.' I replied for both of us. She took the basin to the bathroom to empty and replenish it with Zal disinfectant. When she came back in again I could smell it.

She looked at me.

'Mum says you had some problems with a teacher today. She showed me the letter,' she said, and her face was as still as a failed heart.

'It's nothing – it doesn't matter,' I responded, feeling a bit sheepish, especially as I knew how she could be at times. She was protective, to put it mildly, and liable to storm the school and take out Schiklgruber on her own.

'It does matter,' she said, and our invalid nodded her head in agreement. 'What kind of people are in that place anyway?' I shot a quick glance at her, but she'd anticipated my concern. 'Oh, I know it's for disabled, underprivileged, disadvantaged, mutilated, incurable and handicapped children,' she said inclusively, 'and the people who teach them must be near saintly to put up with it; but what sort of person takes a child – even that sort – and cross-examines them about their churchgoing habits? It's not as if they've any control over them,' she pointed out, as I heard the doorbell ring and my mother rush downstairs to answer it. It was my brother's early day and he'd forgotten his key.

My elder sister continued her sermon.

'Children aren't intrinsically bad or twisted, you know. They become that way when they're older, because of base adult influences. The abnormalities, perversions and vices of adulthood shouldn't be projected onto innocent little children, nor should they be accused of them.'

She was in her preaching mode, and I was used to it. I didn't understand half the words she used, but I repeated them word for word at times, which impressed some folk, especially those who thought having a physical disability made you a little bit 'slow'.

'I'm not overly religious, whatever you all think,' she went on, 'but I firmly believe God created innocent little children with innocent little souls. Admittedly they may be stained by original sin until the hour of their baptism, but they're quite incapable of sinning themselves until they're . . . well, older than you are, anyway.'

I cleared my throat and she made eye contact.

'I suppose I'm starting to bore you,' she said, giving me a look I knew well. It was her pious look and it moved over her face like the sign of the cross whenever she went on like this. I heard a rattling sound and looked at the bed. Our sister had gone to sleep.

The door creaked open, and my mum looked in.

'It's for you,' she said. 'There's someone downstairs waiting.' I waited for my sister to go and see who it was. 'No, it's for you, son!' she stressed, looking uneasy. 'It's a boy on a toy scooter. He wants to talk to you. I think he's from school.'

I raced out of the room and down the stairs. I wasn't used to informal social calls, let alone from boys on scooters. My sister followed me, ever protective. When I reached the door I saw Jason, smooth and soft as a tube of my mother's lipstick.

He smiled.

'Hi, Frankie, I was just cruising round the neighbourhood on my scooter and thought I'd pay you a quick call.' I heard my sister gasp behind me as Jason turned his wide, seductive eyes towards her. 'I see you have a sister,' he said, looking shy now. 'I bet she's got lots of pretty dresses.' My sister gasped again, and I wondered how Jason had managed to find out where we lived. After all, we were a long way from school, as these things went.

'I live just a few streets away,' he said, as if he were reading my mind. 'I don't get the school bus, because my father drops me off in the morning. Martin's mum told me where you live – they're neighbours of ours and we get on quite well. So I decided to pop round, just to say hello. We boys should really keep pre-tt-y close,' he said slowly. 'You never know what could happen, if we don't.'

My sister gasped again. Though she seemed ambivalent about Jason's visit, I was delighted to see him. By the way she was perched over me watching him, however, she obviously wasn't very impressed at all.

My mother was standing at the top of the stairs, trying to work out who my personal caller was. She asked him in, 'for a cup of tea or something'. He smiled and declined the offer politely.

'Thanks all the same, dear, but I'll have to run soon. If I don't my mummy will be ever so worried. She frets so – at times I really could kill her. Only joking,' he added hurriedly, and I began to wonder what I was dealing with here.

My sister finally spoke.

'So you go to the same school as Francis?' she inquired coolly.

'Yes. It's not exactly the greatest of fun, nor an oasis of liberal understanding, but I quite like it anyway.'

'And you're both in the same class?'

'Yes!' I said.

'No!' said Jason, making funny, shrugging movements with his shoulders.

'Well, are you or aren't you?' asked my sister, directing the question at me while looking directly at Jason.

'Well, sort of,' I said, uncertain myself of Jason's status. 'We were in the same class yesterday, but not today. I suppose Jason's . . . well, different from the rest of us.'

My sister's eyes widened.

'And what does that mean exactly?'

'He's not really one thing or the other,' I said clumsily.

'What do you mean by that?'

'Well, I'm a bit M.H. – P.H.,' said Jason, hand on hip and answering for me, just as I'd done the other day for Martin.

'"M.H. – P.H."?' repeated my sister. She wasn't privy to the special school's peculiar turns of phrase yet.

'Well, you see, they can't really decide whether I'm physically or mentally handicapped,' he explained. 'Though personally – if you ask me – I don't really think I'm either, though I could be a bit, well, bi – '

' "Bi . . . "?' repeated my sister, breathing in deeply and looking like a terrified goldfish.

' – polar,' finished Jason, and my sister breathed out.

'Oh, so you're just a run-of-the-mill manic-depressive,' she said. She wanted to be a nurse at that time and knew most of the medical words, as well as the religious ones.

'No, not really,' said Jason. 'Just a bit, well . . . uncertain at times,' he added coyly.

My sister kept at him.

'Well, presumably there's some reason you're going to a special school?'

Jason sighed.

'Well, if you must really, honestly, absolutely know, while I prefer playing with little boys' things,' he said – and my sister inhaled deeply again – 'I prefer dressing in little girls' clothes.' She exhaled again, like a blast from a wind tunnel.

'But the powers that be don't really think that's quite right, you see, since I'm a proper little boy – if you get my drift.'

My sister fairly stared at him.

'I think I do,' she said, as I rushed to Jason's defence.

'So he wears the occasional blouse! Big deal!'

'Shut your mouth!' she snapped. I wondered what had got into her.

'So they don't really know what to do with me,' continued Jason. 'And here I am,' he said, glancing at his fingernails, puffing at them softly and smiling with an up-and-under look at my sister.

'Why don't they just send you to a normal school?'

'They tried, but it didn't work out. Not really.'

'Why not?'

'Because the boys punched lumps out of me if I played with girls; and the girls absolutely tore lumps out of me if I . . . well, played with the boys.'

I felt angry at that – the bullies!

'And what did the teachers do about it?' asked my sister, and I could see she was truly concerned.

'They sent me to the special school,' said Jason.

She seemed to soften towards him.

'And now *they* don't know what to do with you?'

'No. Not yet, anyway,' he said. 'But I imagine they'll work something out. They usually do, don't they?' he added, and my sister smiled.

'And what do your parents say about it all?'

'Oh them! Well, they're really quite dumb,' he said casually. 'I don't listen to a word they say – not a word!' I felt less sympathetic towards him now and my sister looked positively angry.

'That's no way to talk about your parents!' she snapped. 'They brought you into the world and gave of their bodies and purse for you. Through the grace of God they – '

Jason shook his head.

'They can't speak,' he said. 'They've both been mute from birth. I love them lots and wouldn't hurt them for the world, but I don't listen to them, because they can't make even the tiniest, teeniest-weeniest little comprehensible sound.'

'Oh!' I said.

'That's sad,' said my sister.

'Why is that?' asked Jason. 'What's so sad about it?'

My sister seemed uncertain.

'Well, it's such a handicap,' she reasoned. 'There must be so many things they can't do properly.'

'Well, they managed to have me,' said Jason quietly, and my sister shut *her* mouth.

'Anyway,' he continued, 'I've learnt signing, so we communicate OK.'

He tossed his head to the side and tugged at his neatly creased, velvet short trousers.

'I'll have to go,' he said. 'It's been nice meeting you.'

He shook my sister's hand, bowed to me, walked down the outside stairs to his scooter and was gone.

We looked at one another.

'You wanted to know what the children in my school were like.'

My sister frowned.

'Forget it!' she said as we climbed back up the stairs. 'I don't think I fully understood the range of disabilities you had there.'

We heard footsteps behind us. It was my brother, returning home from work.

'Well, well, well!' he said, grinning like an ape. 'I've just seen a right little poofter out there. He almost took my foot off, flashing past on a scooter of all things. You should have seen the look he gave me, too,' he grinned wider. 'They're getting younger and younger, these perfumed – '

'Keep your mouth tightly shut,' snapped my sister, 'until it's had a good clean-out with disinfectant, or preferably something a great deal more corrosive.'

'Come on, sis,' he reasoned, 'I was only joking. It was just a kid dressed up in a frilly shirt and velvet shorts. Anyway we see all sorts in the music business; we're your archetypal liberals.'

'I thought you were an apprentice joiner,' she snapped. 'A strange bag of tools you're carrying for the "music business", as you put it. A trumpet might be more appropriate than a chisel, a saw, a claw hammer and a mouth the size of a carpenter's bench!'

He didn't respond, but I could tell he was hurt and angry. So he deflected it all onto me.

'What were you doing downstairs anyway?' he asked, sharp himself – still smarting, but trying to re-establish his credibility and I was the easiest option.

'I had a visit from a boy at my school,' I said.

'Nice,' said my brother. 'A little friend?'

My sister spoke.

'Yes, a little friend,' she said. 'A little boy called Jason. He had on a frilly shirt, velvet trousers and he travelled here by scooter. You may have caught sight of him when you were struggling to find your way home.'

My brother's eyes widened and he stared at me.

'She's kidding!'

'No, she's not. It must have been Jason who nearly bumped into you,' I said.

He was totally and utterly shocked.

'Well, I'll be damned,' he said, looking stunned.

'Most probably,' said my sister, as we walked into the sanctuary of the living-room.

11

The following year was an unbroken succession of school, popular music sessions, good times and bad times and some events that, if nothing else, at least sowed the first seeds of maturity in me. My sister had said long before that worse things had happened than my brother missing some rock 'n' roll on the radio. She'd also said they would happen again.

They did, just as she said they would. And they started to happen that year.

My brother had joined a professional rock band by this time. During the week, therefore, in addition to spending lots of time in the bathroom howling like a lone wolf with haemorrhoids, he kept his repertoire up to date by tuning in to all the radio programmes that broadcast popular music. I listened with him and, accordingly, I was becoming quite an authority on popular music and what some folks these days call 'kitsch culture'. So I became a sort of home-grown, blue-baby reference source on this emerging genre, or more precisely on its music. It was perhaps fitting, therefore, that popular music provided a prelude to the events that unfolded one particular Sunday; events that were to make such an impact on me that I'll never, ever forget them.

For me, it began in the afternoon, though, like most beginnings, picking any set time is an arbitrary matter. My sick sister was in bed with yet another chest infection. She'd been ill for some weeks and the doctor had come to see her the previous night. I'd heard the comings and goings, but our doctor often called to see her at strange times, so I thought little of it.

I looked into her room to say goodbye before we went to mass that morning. She was lying on her side and if she were awake she didn't hear me. I didn't try to speak to her either. To be honest, I couldn't be bothered; anyway, she was probably sleeping. I glanced round the room to make sure her bedside table was as it should be, with her medicines, the playing cards, the pastilles, the basin and the Lucozade all in place. It was fine, so I closed the door without saying a word.

When we came back from church, I went out for a walk with my brother, who'd volunteered to miss mass in order to look after my sister. He'd spent his time singing in the bathroom, I suppose, keeping her passively occupied and himself up to scratch with his music. The two of us often went for a walk on Sundays when the weather made it possible, and my mother made us sandwiches as a special Sunday lunch. As usual, I began to eat mine as soon as we left the house, but my brother didn't, which was unusual for him.

Not far from where we lived was a small wood that led onto open countryside. He often took me there for a couple of hours or so, as we both liked it a lot. It usually made him joke so much I went back home feeling sore in the face from protracted spells of feigned laughter. But not that day. He wasn't his usual chirpy self, for some reason, though we still walked a fair distance, which didn't tax me one bit as, in deference to my medical condition, he let me ride piggyback on his shoulders whenever I felt tired. I was still a small, light child then, so I don't imagine it was too much effort.

During this particular walk, he took the opportunity to tell me a bit about the historical background to rock music. I'd asked him to tell me more about it anyway and he was happy enough to oblige. That particular day, though, he spoke without his usual enthusiasm. I attributed this to the fact he'd been in quite late the previous night and had sat up chatting with the rest of the family until even later. His late nights usually accounted for this sort of lassitude. It certainly seemed to be the case that day, anyway, and I reckoned a bear with a sore head and tummy-ache would have been far better company to walk about in a wood with.

But tired or not, he was willing enough to speak about what he liked to call his 'musical influences' and, to be honest, I liked to hear about them. I was sitting on his shoulders when he started and I could feel them vibrating when he spoke.

'A few years ago a radio broadcaster called Alan Freed began to broadcast black music over the radio.'

We'd entered the wood by now and the branches of the trees hung over us like sunshades.

'Black music?' I queried as, holding onto his neck with one arm and freeing up the other, I pulled at a branch and let it bounce back.

He bent to avoid it.

'Yes, black music. It's music written and performed mainly by black, Negro musicians.'

I shook my head in confusion and leant over.

'What's a "Negro"?'

'You probably call them "Darkies",' he said, 'but they're supposed to be called "Negroes".'

Ever since the day my sister had ticked him off about his comments on Jason, he'd been very precise in his use of language when it came to describing people.

'Ah,' I thought. I knew what a Darkie was all right; I'd read about one called Sambo in a second-hand book I'd been given, and I'd seen a few in school, in the photographs of black children we'd been shown during our religious education classes. They were little ones though; 'piccaninnies', they were called. But we called them 'Black Babies', and you could buy one, name it and own it for half-a-crown.

It was a good system, that one. You bought them on hire purchase, a penny or so a week, until an official-looking book was filled with black baby stamps to that half-crown value. Then, when you owned a baby, you gave it a name. Some of these names were quite imaginative and they gave me a fair idea – as names always do – of what these fluffy little creatures were like. 'Sambo' was a favourite, as I've indicated. So were 'Erasmus', 'Uncle Tom' and 'Eliza'. However, 'Blackboy Winston' was my favourite. I'd chosen it myself from a storybook. But though all this Black Baby stuff gave me some idea of what these dark-skinned people were like and how they liked to be addressed, I'd never actually seen a real one. I suppose the nearest I'd come was through my everyday exposure to Billy and Alastair. Billy in particular looked like a genuine

Darkie. He hadn't had his operation yet, though time was passing, and he'd become an even darker blue. So he was a sort of honorary Darkie, I supposed, but I was keen to see the real thing sometime, preferably some time soon.

The images of small, black, loincloth-clad children in bare feet running around after a missionary priest receded and slowly my thoughts returned to my brother.

'This music was mainly rhythm-and-blues, preceded by something called "stompin' jive",' he said, as I kept a sharp eye out for toadstools. If I saw any on these trips, I picked them for Alastair's mum. It was said she used them to make tinctures, though no one in school could tell me what a tincture was.

My brother was still talking.

'You know what I mean: Fats Domino, Jimmy Turner – people like that,' he said, and I recognised the names. Then he whistled some of their music and, though it wasn't familiar, I liked it, it was good; 'dark and rhythmic' was how he described it, just like the Darkies themselves, I imagined, and I began to like them too.

'So what happened next?' I asked, looking around at the trees and recognising the few I was familiar with.

'Well, Alan Freed called himself "Moondog".'

'"Moondog"?'

He sounded angry.

'Yes, Moondog! What's wrong with that? It wasn't his real name, it was a nickname.'

'A nickname?'

'Yes – a nickname! I suppose he reminded people of a dog howling at the moon, or something,' he said, still angry.

He stooped, helped me off his back and placed me on the ground.

'So he was a bit like a wolf?' I asked, thinking of Derek.

'A bit, yes. A bit like a wolf. Wolves howl at the moon, you know,' he said, looking as if the idea appealed to him, 'and there's a great blues singer called Howlin' Wolf too, whose main influences were Charlie Patton, Tommy Johnson and – '

I interrupted.

'Howlin' Wolf? A singer?'

That didn't go down too well either, but he ignored it.

'Anyway, Alan Freed broadcast a programme on the radio one evening from a sports stadium.'

'So his job was to describe sport being played?'

My brother stopped.

'For God's sake, listen!' he said sharply, his temper quickening. 'Now let me finish or I'll shut up!'

I felt myself redden in embarrassment.

'OK,' I said quickly.

'OK, fine, right. Well, I think there was some other event on at the stadium too – a concert of some sort.'

'I see,' I said, kicking my feet in the grass.

'And Freed called it his "Moondog Coronation Ball".'

I said nothing and let him continue.

'Anyway, thousands of people turned up and caused complete and utter chaos.'

'Oh!' I said, genuinely impressed, but making a bit more of it than I normally would to make him feel wanted.

'Yes, well, the concert had to be cancelled, but Freed just happened to call it a "rock concert", and he referred to the music as "rock 'n' roll".'

'I see. And what made it so special?' I asked, as I stared back at a thrush that was sitting on a tree, cocking its head and looking at us. I wondered what it thought we were.

My brother stopped and bent down to pick up a pine cone.

'Well, before then, this style of music was mainly played to black audiences.'

'To Darkies?'

'Negroes! Negroes! Call them Negroes, for God's sake, not Darkies!'

He threw the pine cone in the direction of the tree and the thrush flew off.

'Where was I? Yes! Well, Freed's concerts and radio shows attracted lots of white teenagers too, and that wasn't all that common back then.'

That seemed odd.

'White teenagers didn't go to concerts?'

'Jeez-us! You're not yourself today, are you?'

Again I said nothing and just let him talk.

'They didn't mix with Negroes,' he said, pointing to a large bird flying far above us. 'That's a hawk,' he said quickly and I saw it floating gracefully above us like a sailboat, or a feather: something light and unfettered. It swooped downwards and I heard an almighty screeching sound. I immediately knew it had killed something, perhaps the thrush that had been staring at us.

I felt odd.

'What did the hawk just do?' I asked.

'It's feeding time,' said my brother. 'It has to hunt for its food. It probably killed another bird.'

'That's sad,' I said, feeling as upset as I ever had.

'Why?'

'It's killed something.'

'If it didn't, it would starve.'

'Couldn't someone give it birdfood?'

'Other animals are its birdfood,' he said, as I became quiet and considered this. I felt a shadow forming inside me somewhere. In retrospect, I think this was the first stirring of my sense of my own mortality. I tried to put it aside, but it stayed in the background. I think it's been there ever since.

'Why didn't the white teenagers mix with the Dark – with the Negroes?' I asked.

'I don't really know, they just didn't.'

He started walking again and I followed, leaving the hawk to its meal, whatever it was.

My brother was totally silent, but as ever he didn't stay that way for long.

'You know, son, in many places Negroes can't even travel on the same buses as white people.'

'Oh.'

'They can't go to the same cinemas, eat in the same places, get treatment in the same hospitals, or even go to the same churches. They can't marry white people, either; they even have to go to different schools.'

I thought about that.

'Just like me,' I said.

He looked down.

'No! Not just like you.'

'Why not?'

'Well, for a start, you wouldn't get hung up on a tree simply for doing the wrong thing.'

'Hung up on a tree? For what?'

'There was a Negro hung on a tree just for talking to a white girl.'

I thought about now.

'Why did they hang him up for that?'

'I don't know. They just did. They hang them up to break their necks.'

'Oh! Do they die?'

'Yes, they die all right. But not always quickly.'

'I see,' I said, wondering what that felt like – wondering why speaking to a white girl was a problem. After all, I did it every day.

We walked in silence for a time. I still couldn't quite grasp the significance of what he was telling me. It seemed that Negroes and Whites were at each other's throats for some reason. The Negroes were a different colour from us certainly, but then so were Alastair and Billy. And I wasn't at their throats. So why were people literally at the throats of the Negroes?

'It's called "racial discrimination",' said my brother, reading my mind as he often did.

'"Racial discrimination",' I repeated carefully. It was all very strange. 'Do they mix more now than they used to?'

'Sometimes.'

'But not always?'

'No, not always.'

'And that's why rock 'n' roll causes all this fuss,' I said, 'because it brings people of different colours together?'

My brother nodded.

'In part. There are other deeper, more fundamental reasons too.'

'What are they?'

He paused for a moment, considering it all very carefully.

'I don't know,' he said, flatly. 'But there are. Trust me.'

I'd trusted him the morning I started school . . .

I shrugged.

'I do,' I said, as we left the wood and started walking across a wide, open meadow. It was fresh and green with longer, lusher grass, and my feet swished through it as I looked around at the view. There were a few hills at one end and they formed a small, sheltered area – a sort of valley. In the grass there were buttercups and daisies. I'd gone up onto my brother's back again and as I bumped up and down, I reflected on what he'd said. I still couldn't understand it, but I certainly appreciated the main bit. Some white folk hated Negroes.

So what? They probably hated us back.

There was a bird singing somewhere. It was a terse, solitary sound and I wondered if it were the mate of one the hawk had killed some time. Another sound followed: almost the same, but much more hollow; it was the bird's echo. It touched me somewhere inside, lighting that shadow like stray sunlight. But it lasted only a moment, as if the shadow had darkened again and, for some reason I couldn't understand, I felt very strange indeed.

But I spoke normally.

'So why did Alan Freed call it rock 'n' roll?' I asked, as the echo faded for good. 'Why "rock 'n' roll", and not just "roll", say, like "jazz"?'

My brother paused again and tried to look at me, but he couldn't as I was still hanging onto his back.

'I don't really know,' he said again, lamely, as I let go once more and dropped back onto the grass. 'Maybe the large crowd rocked back and forth to the music,' he suggested.

'And the roll?'

'Maybe they rolled about on the floor,' he said. Then his mood changed abruptly and I realised all still wasn't well. 'Oh, I don't know. Why should *I* know everything?' he snapped, sounding worried and irritable.

'That's probably it,' I said. Then I spoke especially quietly. 'Do you want to go home?'

'Yes,' he said, turning and looking back the way we'd come. 'We might have some relatives visiting, so it's time we went back. We've been away far too long.'

As we arrived back at the house, I saw a car outside. My brother had said we might have relatives visiting, so I wondered if it belonged to one of them. We went in and made our way to the living-room. It was filled with my relatives, but they were all sitting quietly. Uncle Joe was there; he had a bit of a reputation for 'the bottle', as they called it. He also pretended he knew things, like what was what in popular music. I liked him a lot. So did my brother.

He smiled. I went over. I thought I'd test him out.

'Uncle Joe?'

'Yes, Francie?'

'Do you know the lyrics of "Gilly-Gilly-Ossenfeffer-Kaztenellen-Bogen-By-The Sea"?'

Before Uncle Joe had time to hear the whole of the title, let alone have a go at the lyrics, my brother leapt over, grabbed me and bustled me out of the room. He dragged me along the hall to our bedroom and sat me down hard on my bed. I looked up at him, angry and a little scared, wondering what was happening – what was causing his strange, unpredictable behaviour.

He caught my look.

'Your sister's dying,' he said quickly. 'The doctor's with her. He arrived while we were out. Mum and Dad are in the bedroom with them now. The priest's coming to give her the last rites later.'

I stared at him.

Thump!

I was truly and deeply shocked.

'Dying?' I asked incredulously.

'Dying, as in dead!' he repeated, thumping the top of the bed with his fist.

'Oh!'

'She's got pneumonia,' he said, pointing his forefinger to his chest and tapping it. My own chest stopped moving and my heart seemed to as well.

'I thought she just had another chest infection.'

'No, she's had tuberculosis and now it's pneumonia.' He was quieter now; more like the brother I knew and could rely on. 'She's not fit to be moved to hospital, but the doctor's trying out some new medicine. It might do the job and save her, but if it doesn't, and soon, we'll lose her.'

I could see he was close to tears.

'What about Lourdes?' I said, and I felt a twinge of what I think was guilt.

'Lourdes? What about it?'

'Can't she still go there?'

'It's too late,' he replied. 'Maybe last year when we tried to arrange it, but it was too –'

'Expensive,' I finished quietly.

He nodded again.

'Yes,' he said, ashamed, I think, that he hadn't been able to provide the money himself to enable our sister to go, and that was the first time I realised just how important money was for survival.

I took it all in slowly and it began to make sense.

'So that's why everyone's here. They've come because of my sister. And that's why you lost your temper when we were out, because you were worried about her.' Images of Doctor Wink and Bandage Boy and posh school uniforms and middle-class affluence flitted almost unconsciously through my mind, along with images of Lourdes and private clinics set in forests, for those who could afford them.

'Yes, I'm sorry, son. I was worried; I get that way. It's my artistic temp –'

I interrupted.

'So the car outside belongs to the doctor?'

He smiled.

'Yes,' he said gently. 'Who did you think it belonged to? Us?'

'I just wondered,' I said, feeling a touch of disappointment. 'So what's going to happen now?'

'We'll just have to wait and see,' he said.

And we did.

We waited in the bedroom until we heard the doctor and my parents come out of my sister's bedroom. Then we heard my big sister come out of the living-room, whisper, 'How is she?', and join them. They walked down the hall, speaking in low voices. When we heard the outside door being pulled shut, we went to ask what the news was.

'It's not good,' said my father. 'She's not well at all.'

He was very upset and I thought it best to remain silent. I realised that for the first time I was aware of, they were treating me like an adult – I was being included in serious family matters and I didn't want to disappoint anyone by being childish.

My brother, sister and I went back into the living-room, and two of my relatives went to the kitchen to prepare tea, with slices of a cake someone had brought. My mother and father remained with my sick sister, while we sat around for the rest of that afternoon, with my sister knitting to pass the time. We were just waiting, as my brother had said we would. Waiting to see if the new drug would work, if my sister would live or die.

She died that evening, just before the priest arrived, but he gave her the last rites anyway and someone told me she'd go straight to Heaven. The doctor came back too, and when he'd finished whatever it was he had to do, I was allowed in to see her. She was lying in her bed, wearing her best white nightdress with a pink cardigan on top. Her favourite ribbon was tied in a bow in her hair and the bedcovers came up to her waist. She seemed at rest and at peace, and very snug. I took her hand and said 'goodbye' and was assured by my mum she was fine and in a far better place. I looked at her bedside table and saw the same things I'd seen that morning. I picked up the bottle of Lucozade and stroked its fine yellow wrapping. I unwrapped it and put the paper to my eyes. When I looked through it everything was yellow. I touched the pack of cards we used to play Rummy with, and Old Maid, and Snap when she was up to it. The Ace of Spades had been dealt now all right and she hadn't been able to toss it aside this time.

Still peering through the wrapping, I picked up and looked at the old tin of catarrh pastilles. They were the same ones she'd had ages ago – the day Jason had visited. Everything looked just as it had when I'd looked in that morning, before mass, to say goodbye. I pulled the paper away and saw everything as it really was. And it hurt.

My relatives went in one at a time to say goodbye, then returned to the living-room. I sat there with them and everyone was very quiet, as if they might disturb my dead sister by speaking. My grandparents arrived and stayed until very late. They didn't have much to say either, but they went back and forth to the bedroom, and sat drinking tea and talking quietly with my mother. She looked very pale, but that wasn't surprising. At one point that evening, when everything was still and silent, Uncle Joe took me up onto his lap. I could smell whisky from his breath when he began to sing. But I didn't mind. No one did. His voice was very hoarse when he started to sing 'Gilly-Gilly-Ossenfeffer . . .', the song I'd tried to taunt him with. It's about a girl who had a dream that came true. He broke down and started to cry halfway through it. So did everyone else, including me.

<hr>

12

It was considered best I went to school the following morning. I was allowed to meet the bus myself by now, though my mother always watched from the living-room window. When it arrived, I smiled up at her and gave a quick wave as usual. She didn't respond, but I understood.

Derek wasn't on the bus that morning, and the trip to school was a solemn one. Every single person on the bus seemed quiet, as if somehow they knew something had happened. When we arrived I made my way to my classroom, went in, and said 'good morning' to my teacher. Most of us had moved up to P.H. 2 by now and we had a new teacher called Miss Trulygood. She was as endearing and kind as Miss Goldenheart had been. We were all very fond of her and considered ourselves lucky to have her. Billy and Alastair had arrived before me as usual, but Billy's spark seemed dimmer today and Alastair's face looked as if it had finally collapsed in on itself. I could tell immediately, somehow, they knew what had happened and I wondered if they all did.

Miss Trulygood came over and spoke to me.

'We heard about your sister, Francis,' she said quietly. 'I've told the class and we're all very sorry.'

I looked up.

'How did you know, Miss?'

'Your aunt telephoned on behalf of your parents. They thought it best we know.'

'Why?'

'In case you were very upset.'

'I see.'

'Are you?'

'A bit. Not too much. The main thing is, she didn't suffer,' I said, and Miss Trulygood blinked.

I was repeating something I'd heard from one of my relatives, and it seemed the grown-up thing to say. It certainly put people at their ease, but not me. I didn't know if my sister had suffered or not.

'If you want to speak to me about anything at any time, just do so,' said Miss Trulygood, but I didn't feel I wanted to speak to anyone, so I thanked her and got down to our lesson – working out how many sharp bits a five-pointed star had.

It was soon very evident I was being treated gently. Both Billy and Al remained subdued and didn't say much, except to discuss an electric train set Billy's brother had been given for his birthday. Apparently it had taken them hours to get it running properly, and Billy said he'd ask his father to pick me up from home some time, to bring me back to their house and let me play with it. He said his brother had offered to do that for any child at our school. It was a very kind thought from a boy who knew nothing about us except what he'd heard from Billy, though, given the nature of the offer, I wondered again if his brother had a heart problem too, one so bad it kept him from school. I also wondered if, given Billy's puffing, that was why they owned a car. For his part, Al said I could go home with him some time and his mother would read some chapters from a book called *Afterlife –What's Beyond?* I declined this offer politely, however – said it would cause them far too much trouble, but thanked him for the thought and told him to thank his mother as well.

At school dinner, even the mentally handicapped girls who served us seemed more tactful than usual and there seemed to be an area of complete quiet around me in the dinner hall. That made me wonder if every child in the school knew about my sister. Perhaps they did; or maybe they were just more sensitive than most to other people's troubles. After all, they had every reason to be.

After we'd been given our sedatives, again in the presence of the Siggy boy, who still appeared from time to time to watch us, the three of us were taken by the small nurse for our after-dinner rest. We lay down on our usual three beds, while the radio in the school opposite played 'Three Coins In The Fountain'.

Billy spoke first. His voice was quiet.

'We were told you lost your sister.'

'Yes, I did.'

He smiled.

'I wouldn't worry about it. We lost my brother in the airport once, when we were about to fly to America on holiday. It took us ages to find him and we almost missed the next flight too. We found him in the end – in the bank, cashing traveller's cheques. So you might still find her. Take it from me – don't worry.'

I gaped and Al turned away in embarrassment, but Billy, oblivious to the more subtle exchanges of social communication and possibly, I was beginning to think, to reality itself, continued. 'So where did you lose her?'

Al dealt with it.

'He didn't lose her that way; she died.'

'Died?'

'Yes, she died from pneumonia, yesterday,' I said.

Billy gave it some thought.

'What was it like?'

I knew he was looking at me, but I didn't return his look quite yet.

'What was what like?'

'Your sister. What was she like? Did you see her?'

'I saw her every day,' I said, 'and I brought her in a cup of tea every evening.'

'I don't mean that!' said Billy, flustered. 'Did you see her after she'd gone?'

'Gone?'

'You know . . . ' he said.

'He means *post mortem*,' said Alastair precisely.

I ignored this and finally looked at Billy.

'You mean after she'd died?'

'Yes. What was it like?'

'What was *what* like?' I asked, now genuinely wondering what he was referring to.

'Her dead body,' he said, quietly, as Al whispered 'corpse', and I paused for a moment and looked at them.

'It looked fine to me,' I said, finally. 'It was as if she were asleep and just not breathing. Her eyes were closed. She looked peaceful.'

Billy tensed.

'Was she stiff?'

'Stiff! How the heck should I know? I touched her hand, but I didn't try to bend her fingers back or break them off or anything.'

'You go stiff when you die,' he confided. 'Like a statue.'

Alastair spoke and his voice was different somehow.

'It's called rigor mortis. It loosens up before you start to rot,' he said, sounding very upset.

I caught his attention.

'Are you OK?'

'He's fine,' said Billy. 'He's just afraid to die. Aren't you, Al? You're afraid to die, aren't you?'

Alastair frowned.

'It's not that,' he said weakly.

'Then what is it?' asked Billy, animated and very angry for some reason.

'I just –' Al lowered his eyes. He couldn't look at us.

'You're afraid to die,' repeated Billy, 'I know you are. I heard your mother telling one of the nurses at the clinic.'

Outside, the sound of the other children playing seemed louder. The radio played. Inside it was perfectly still; the anguish on Alastair's face was dreadful.

I'd had enough.

'Don't speak about it any more,' I said.

Billy pointed at Al.

'See! Now you've upset Francis!'

Al gasped and lay down flat. I thought he might be crying.

'Speak about something else,' I said.

Billy turned towards me now.

'About what?' he asked, still very agitated, and I wondered if he would soon need two sedatives after lunch to keep him in check.

'Something else,' I said. 'Anything. Tell us again about your brother's train set. I'd love to come and see it, if the offer's still open.'

Billy looked away. He had a defiant look about him. He turned towards Al.

Al spoke.

'He doesn't have a brother,' he said quietly. 'He doesn't have any of the things he boasts about. He doesn't have a mother, a father, a brother or a train set. His aunt looks after him; he only calls her his mother. He's got nothing, not even a mum.'

If my dead sister had walked through the door with a clear chest and a smile on her face, I wouldn't have been any more astounded. I knew so much about Billy's family by that time, they were completely real to me. His mother was a caring, generous woman who used to work at the mill and now ran her own sweet shop. His father was a foreman at an engineering firm and owned a sleek grey car. His younger brother, whom Billy squabbled with on occasion, had just received an electric train set that had an engine with lights that shone. I sat up straight. Was all this really fiction?

Billy shrugged.

'So what? I had them once!'

'But your father never had a car!' screeched Alastair, still lying on his back with his small blue hands covering his eyes. 'And there's no train set, there never was and never will be!' he added, and again an eerie silence fell, and again the children just outside seemed miles away.

'Is this true?' I asked softly.

Billy sighed.

'They were killed in a plane crash when I was three.'

'They never were!' shouted Al, sitting up. 'They were killed in a fire at *his house*,' he shrieked. 'His father had been smoking in bed – but,' he pointed at Billy 'he really killed them! He was in hospital seeing if they could fix his heart. But they couldn't operate without killing him. So while he lay there waiting for the impossible to happen, they were burnt to a bloody cinder.'

'Oh!' I gasped, then no one spoke. Billy continued to avoid my eyes. He lay down; I did the same. Again I listened to the voices of the children outside. The occasional thumps of a ball hitting the door went unnoticed. The radio across the way no longer existed. So his family *were* dead. There was no mother, no father, no brother, no car – no train set. Just an aunt. I could barely believe it then, and even now it shocks me when I think of it.

'But I saw your father driving you home, the day we started school,' I said, ignoring reality because it didn't suit me. 'You were in the car with your father and your brother!'

Al's voice was tired.

'That was the man from the Rotary Club. He comes here sometimes with his son. They feel sorry for him and take him out for something decent to eat. He doesn't get much at home. His aunt can't afford it.'

I let this sink in. Billy kept quiet. I turned in on myself, lay down. I looked at the walls and the ceiling, focusing on the glow of the light bulb. I had a strange thought; I wondered how all those big things outside me fitted into my head. I felt like laughing. I almost did laugh. And I'd no idea why. I felt left out too, angry. How many people knew about this? If Alastair did and I didn't, what did that say about me? My thoughts were spinning. The shadow I'd felt the day before, when I'd been walking with my brother, grew more solid. I closed my eyes and waited for the nurse to come. She finally did. We shuffled out of the door like exhausted, miniature soldiers after a battle.

The nurse looked at us suspiciously.

'What's been going on in there? Something's been going on,' she said, sensing it. She looked at Billy. 'I hope your mother hasn't given you more of those stickers,' she snapped. 'I haven't forgotten, you know. It might seem a long time ago to you, but I haven't forgotten, and I never will.'

If we had been soldiers, I imagine we'd have shot her then. As it was, she received no reply from any of us and we trekked off back to our classroom in total silence.

13

When we got back we found the classroom half-empty and I checked over the children who were there to try and discover what they had in common. I knew they'd all paid their dinner-money; if they hadn't, they'd have either stood with Socratic wisdom in the mortifying queue for free dinners, which none of them had done, or brought the money in by now to avoid that unsavoury fate. Our usual teacher wasn't there either, just our religious education teacher, Mrs Darksole, who'd returned from her 'vocational break'. There was a fair spread of us: polio victims, encephalitics, spastics, the odd confused retard, a couple of interloping albino girls and an assortment of others. With our arrival, there were now three heart cases added to the list. 'Nature of handicap', it seemed, wasn't the common denominator. As we sat down, however, I immediately realised what was. For Father Littlegrace, the school priest, walked in accompanied by the Assistant Headmistress. Those of us in the classroom were all Catholics, and we were all about to receive a sermon.

'In a few weeks' time,' Father Littlegrace began, 'you'll make your First Confession. This is a sacrament,' he continued, 'and the second you have received. Your first was baptism and you had that as babies. Now, as I don't want to tire any of you out, any questions?'

He paused and smiled. He clearly felt compelled to take his time with us – not rush things, be normal. We occasionally found this trait in strangers and we didn't like it.

'Does the sacrament of confession remove the temporal punishment due to mortal sin, Father?'

It was one of the albino girls, whose eyes were pretty pathetic, really. She was directing her question to the wall, not the priest. At least she'd found a shape to talk to, which was something. I didn't know her well, but I did know that like me she had a brother who was going to be a priest.

Father Littlegrace looked worried.

'Temporal punishment. Ah! Well, ah, oh . . . ,' he said, taking his time about that too.

There was another voice.

'On the subject of temporal punishment, Father. Didn't the awarding of plenary indulgences by the Vatican diminish the role of confession? Don't they give remission of temporal punishment due for sin, *ipso facto*, without the need of a sacrament at all? Didn't all this assist the rise of Lutheranism, the emergence of Andreas Osiander, the ultimate vindic-ation of Nicolaus Copernicus and the eventual theological and philosophical fallacies that were adopted by the Church during the Counter-Reformation?'

I traced the voice to a small, shrivelled, lame boy whom I'd never even heard speak before. He was good when he did though, as we'd just discovered.

Before any considered reply was forthcoming from Father Littlegrace, the albino girl tossed back her head and her long, white-fair hair fluttered around her shoulders like some beautiful haze. She'd worked out the direction of the priest's voice by now and had turned her head to face it. Unfortunately he'd moved to one side by then, so she addressed yet another wall, albeit with articulation.

'What the learnéd lame boy says may be so,' she said. 'And indeed the effects of Counter-Reformation culture still dog *ex cathedra* epistemology today. However, I once heard it eschewed that baptism cleansed original sin, whereas other sacraments cleansed the temporal punishment due to unoriginal sin, as it were, in addition to the original sin – and by that I don't mean *original* sin – itself. I didn't think there was any temporal punishment due for original, *original* sin *per se*. Isn't that so, Father?'

Father Littlegrace's eyes widened. He drew himself up to his full height and opened his mouth as wide as the Great Dome in the Vatican.

'I . . . eh – ' he theologised and our teacher interrupted him.

'Let's not go into that at the moment, Iris,' said Mrs Darksole to the albino girl, who turned sharply and spoke to the door.

'My name's not Iris, Mrs Darksole,' she responded. 'You're confusing me with my friend,' she said, pointing vaguely in the direction of the other albino, who'd been sitting quietly swinging her head about like a radar machine.

'Yes,' she said. 'I'm Iris. Who is it?'

Mrs Darksole ignored her, returning her full attention to Father Littlegrace.

'Why don't we have questions later, Father? We could just run through the basics for now. Deal with more complex matters another time.'

He nodded.

'Fine by me,' he said, coughing and breathing in deeply. 'We, ah – yes. First Confession. Well . . . basically the priest hears your sins – the usual sort of thing: telling lies, eating too much or too little, complaining, wishing you had things you don't deserve, being happy too much, not being happy enough – you know, just about anything. Then he gives you a penance – a few prayers, a Hail Mary, a Glory Be – nothing hard. You then get a blessing, called 'absolution'. It gets rid of all the punishment coming your way for these sins. Your soul is cleansed, your life's brand new, and you're good and ready for Holy Communion.'

He looked around the class and smiled.

'Any more questions?' he asked, his smile welcoming but his eyes shrewd and cold like a hunter's.

A small girl in the front row was shaking. She seemed terrified. She didn't look bad to the untrained eye, but she had the sort of discrete brain damage that makes you look OK but shake like the clappers. Anyway, she'd be dead soon; we all knew that, including her, so it wasn't as if she'd have to put up with it for very long.

'What happens if you've been too happy and you die before you can get to confession?' she asked, still shaking hard.

Mrs Darksole pre-empted Father Littlegrace.

'You go straight to Hell,' she said and the priest didn't contradict her.

'Any more questions?' he asked, as the brain-damaged girl threw up into a paper bag she carried around with her for that very purpose.

'I have one, Father.'

It was Al.

'Yes, Alastair? What is it?' asked Mrs Darksole, pleased to hear a question now it was the normally passive Al who was going to ask it.

'Is it true you burn in Hell for eternity if you die and haven't received absolution?'

Father Littlegrace smiled again.

'Only if you die in a state of mortal sin, eh, Alastair.'

'And how do you know?' asked Al.

The priest sounded defensive.

'Well, I was educated at Saint Knowall's seminary in Holytown. And I studied theology at the University of Blessedsouls. Then I specialised in – '

'No. How do you know whether or not you're in a state of mortal sin?' asked Al.

Father Littlegrace looked furious.

'I'm not! The very thought!'

Al was clearer this time.

'No, Father. I meant how would any of us know?'

'Oh, I see. Well, it depends upon the, eh, sin . . . eh, Alastair. It's, eh, uncertain, but highly unlikely in your case.'

Al looked grim.

'Is lying a mortal sin?'

'Depends upon the nature of the lie.' The priest was quick, razor-sharp, Jesuitical. And I realised that, for a moment, he'd forgotten to whom he was speaking.

Al continued.

'So you could burn and sear eternally, have horrible images in your head forever. You could suffer fire, anguish, pain, grief and hopelessness, and the attentions of the Devil himself, if you told a certain kind of lie.'

'It would have to be a real whopper for that to happen,' the priest laughed.

No one else did.

'If it was a real whopper?' said Al very seriously, while turning slowly towards Billy, who looked as if he were haemorrhaging. 'If you said you had parents, for example, and you hadn't. If you'd indulged yourself by lying around waiting for a miracle, while your parents were burnt to death because they were so worried about you they were smoking in bed. If you no longer have them, but say you have. Is that the sort of lie that would count?' he asked. 'The sort that sends you to Hell for eternity – to suffer damnation for ever?' Al caught his breath at that, and I realised he was very close to tears.

Father Littlegrace sounded a little more serious this time.

'I don't think that would happen. Not to people like you.'

Al's voice was trembling.

'Why not?'

'Trust me. *Expertus dico*,' said the priest and a weird-looking little soul beside me woke up with a jerk and said: 'I speak as an expert,' though she didn't look it.

'*Experientia doce stultos*,' said the small, shrivelled lame boy, as Father Littlegrace shot him a glance, and weird little girl called:

'Experience teaches fools.'

'*Ex ore parvulorum veritas*,' said the older albino girl quietly, and he shot her a glance too, as the weirdo struggled to her feet and raised her voice. 'From the mouths of babes – truth!' We all shut up for a moment at that, until she sat down again and went back to sleep.

'Oh, I don't think that sort of thing concerns us here, really,' the priest countered defensively, still responding to Al, remembering where he was and no longer so classically minded. 'That's more for, eh, other people. Not for you, precisely. It shouldn't concern you.'

For once, Billy sounded terrified.

'It concerns me. I'm not too keen on burning. No bloody way!' he said, as Al and I looked at him.

Jean – the small girl with the loose teeth – spoke.

'He lost his mum and dad in a fire, Father. They were burned to a crisp. But he sometimes lets on they're still alive; understandable really, given the seriousness of his heart condition. So being untruthful's bound to worry him.'

The class became very quiet, and Father Littlegrace even quieter. I felt a rush of anger. I realised I'd probably been the only one of our class, and possibly our whole school, who hadn't known, until that very afternoon, about Billy's parents.

Father Littlegrace was studying Jean as if she were the Whore of Babylon. I was pretty certain she wasn't.

'Oh!' he said, 'I am sorry. I'm sure that –'

'– will be enough for today,' said Mrs Darksole, weaving in perfectly, like a Black Widow spider. 'I'm sure Father Littlegrace has lots of important things to do, children. Thank you, Father,' she spun, smooth as silk. 'Say "thank you" to your priest for wasting his time with you, children.'

A variety of sounds emerged, all well intentioned, if not exactly well intonated. Some of them were choked, of course, by the terror of the dreadful retribution they'd been told they faced after they died, if they transgressed the rules this man of God had casually mentioned in passing, adding further to the burden of terror many of them already faced. It's bad enough to know you might die any time, but to be told you might then suffer horrors for eternity . . .

I heard a sigh of boredom. It was the priest.

'Well, thank *you*,' he said, 'and goodbye.' He moved towards the door with the Assistant Headmistress in tow, like a waterskier. With a final flourish he gave us yet another smile, another wave, and another mouthed 'Goodbye'. I noticed he kept his eyes focused on Billy as he left, and even the sound of Jean's teeth chattering didn't distract him.

Billy turned to Al.

'I don't believe in Hell. How could a good God make a place like that?'

'I don't know, but He did. Oh, I believe in it OK,' he said with the well-worn lines of worry spreading with a dreadful familiarity across his face.

'Then you're mad,' said Billy fiercely. 'Madder than I ever thought you were,' he seethed, but Al said nothing back. Perhaps he'd said enough.

That comment worried me too, however, and I wondered if Billy knew something I didn't – something about Al this time, something that had prompted him to mention madness. Even worse, I wondered if everyone else knew about this putative madness of Al's, and if yet again I was being left out of it all.

Melissa touched my hand.

'Now don't get paranoid, Francis,' she said, observing me carefully with her big brown eyes. 'We don't know anything about this; it's the first we've heard of it too.'

'I'm not paranoid!' I snapped. 'Am I?'

'Of course you're not,' she reassured me, as everyone else gave knowing winks and nods. I watched them do so and wondered exactly what it took to become a real part of these kids, a proper part. Perhaps you had to look odd and stupid, and not just be treated as if you were.

When I arrived back home that afternoon, my mother was still at the window. I looked up and waved, touched by her loyalty in waiting for me. Once again, she didn't wave back, but my sister met me as I made my way up the path.

'Mum's not too well,' she said briskly. 'She'll have to go off to hospital for a few days. We're taking her there this evening. She's had too much,' she said, in response to my look of astonishment.

'Too much of what?' I asked.

'Of life,' said my sister, as she took me by the hand and led me inside.

14

Our First Confession was held in one of the classrooms. A section had been divided off with plywood to form two connecting cubicles. These had been curtained off from the rest of the room and a small square section of wire grille placed between them, through which you could speak to the priest. A row of chairs had been set up outside this DIY confessional, where we each waited our turn to unburden ourselves. There were nine of us for this very special occasion. Of the boys there was myself, Alastair, Billy and Jason. Of the girls, Jean, Melissa, Una and the two albinos. A few of the older children were to have their confession heard after we'd finished, but they weren't in the class yet. So we were the 'chosen few'.

Mrs Darksole oversaw us. She was a voluble and very pretty young woman, whose notoriously short temper had proven to me, beyond any shadow of a doubt, that beauty is only skin deep. Apparently a sort of locum priest had volunteered – or been instructed – to play the role of our confessor for this ecclesiastical *rite de passage*, and just before he arrived Mrs Darksole told us his name was Father Mortalsen. She stressed this was his first visit to our school. Apparently he'd been away for a time convalescing from overwork and a number of what she called 'mystical experiences'. Accordingly, she suggested we make him feel at ease and not ask any 'waste-of-time' questions; she eyeballed the elder albino girl as she pointed this out, then spat on the floor and rubbed it in with her foot. She also told us that as this was a very special occasion, there'd be a visiting missionary along that day, too. His name was Father Savage and he was a White Father missionary. This was the name given to a group of enterprising missionary priests who made converts to the Catholic faith in darkest Africa. Finally she asked us to make certain both priests were made very welcome – especially Father Mortalsen, as he was really quite cute.

There was a tentative knock at the door and Mrs Darksole opened it. It was Father Mortalsen. He was dressed all in black except for his white collar and light plastic raincoat. He carried a plastic bag, too, which presumably contained his pastoral needs. He shook Mrs Darksole by the hand and by the way he looked at her I could tell he thought she was pretty too. She motioned towards us and his hand moved in concert. He quickly let go; she smiled as he blushed.

He decided to give us his full attention. A smile formed on his face as he turned, but he must have had an acute attack of colic, I imagine, because he gasped, went very pale and became unsteady on his feet. Una, however, stood up and walked towards him to assist. Being unable to look upwards she gazed directly at his stomach. She prodded it and asked if he was OK.

'I'm fine,' he said, and looked down at her strangely. 'I've had a dizzy spell, that's all. I'll be better in a minute.'

Mrs Darksole opened the door to give him some air. He duly recovered, apologised and made his way in the direction of the confessional with an extremely determined look on his face. Pausing midway, he closed his eyes as if in prayer, then turned again and gave us his blessing. I noticed his hands were trembling with emotion as he did so and I found this touching. It wasn't everyone who could be confronted by a group of sick, infirm and sometimes odourful children and retain their total composure. After a few words about the importance of First Confession, Father Mortalsen took another look in Mrs Darksole's direction, then went into the confessional. He pulled the purple curtain over and we heard him arrange his religious items and murmur a few quick prayers. There was a period of silence, before a reverent and solicitous 'First, please!' echoed from the side of the cubicle where he'd now be kneeling. It came as a bit of a surprise and reminded me a little of going to the dentist.

The smaller of the two albino girls stood up. With her arms stretched out in front like a sleepwalker, she went over to the curtain, went in, and immediately came back out again on the other side. She proceeded to stroll over to the open classroom door and went outside, with her arms still outstretched. I wondered why she'd done this and where she'd gone. I thought perhaps she had nothing sinful to report and so she'd been sent outside to keep away from the rest of us sinners. It was only when Mrs

Darksole mentioned the Lord's first name I realised she'd indeed been heading for the confessional, but had miscalculated. With a snort of despair and a few more expletives, Mrs Darksole ran after her.

'And first once again, children, if you PLEASE!'

It was the priest's voice again. Someone had to go in, in place of the wayward albino. Her fellow albino, being equally badly sighted, was none the wiser concerning her friend's unplanned promenade, but she'd probably do the same thing if we sent her in, so we looked around anxiously for a volunteer. Always reliable in an emergency, Melissa stood up, tidied her hair, made her way to the curtain and entered. There was a sudden yelping sound from Father Mortalsen and she came back out again too. She looked dreadfully embarrassed as she headed for the other side of the cubicle.

'Wrong side,' I thought. 'Easily done.'

There was a murmur of voices, then some indistinct mumbling sounds, followed by total silence. Melissa reappeared, smiling beatifically, and I thought she looked like a saint. She walked back to her seat with her hands clasped in front of her and sat down. By the looks of it, all had gone very well indeed.

'And the next one, please!' said a slightly fainter-sounding Father Mortalsen.

Jean hobbled over, teeth held firmly in place, and went straight through the curtain into the confessional. It was the correct side this time, I noted, and we all kept our eyes fixed on it. Again a murmur of voices; it was becoming routine. Then, after what seemed like no time at all Jean came hobbling back out, teeth highly evident, but intact. She too gave us a smile, but kept her hand in front of her mouth as she did so. Like Melissa she looked beatific, but then she couldn't have had much to confess. I was looking at her fondly when the priest's head appeared from behind the curtain.

'Could you come back in, dear?' he said solemnly, his teeth tight together too. 'You haven't confessed yet. You just gave me your personal details.'

Jean spun round like a dancing doll and her teeth clattered onto the floor. She snatched them up and put them back into her mouth as Father Mortalsen came over and pointed to the correct side of the confessional. I noticed he avoided touching her hand as he did so, though I certainly couldn't blame him for that. A few minutes passed and she came out again, still looking beatific and obviously very pleased with herself.

The second albino girl went next – the one whose brother was a student priest. To avoid a repeat of her friend's exodus, Melissa guided her in. She was in there a long time, and there was the continuous drone of what sounded like a sermon. We couldn't hear what was being said, however – only that she was saying it.

Father Mortalsen appeared again, pulled the curtain from the confessant's side and dragged her out.

'Next!' he called, as she stood beside him looking even more disoriented than usual.

'I hadn't finished!' she protested. To the curtain.

'No, but I had!' said Father Mortalsen, giving her a quick absolution on the move before he turned to us, eyes closed and arms folded.

'Next! And make it snappy!'

He went back into the confessional as Melissa collected the albino girl and returned her to her seat. Her eyelids were flickering as if she were in REM sleep but, knowing her skills in debating theological matters, I imagined it was her confessor who'd just had the nightmare.

Mrs Darksole returned alone. She shrugged her shoulders and opened her arms wide, like Jesus did when he'd blessed the water and wine.

'She's gone,' she mouthed, referring to the first albino girl. 'No idea where,' she continued in mute.

Somehow the other albino sensed it.

'She'll have headed straight for our classroom,' she said. 'She can navigate by the magnetic field of the Earth. It's strong today, the solar wind being what it is. I'd like to go and feel if she's OK. Shall I bring her back?' she asked, thinking she was speaking to Mrs Darksole but actually, due to a continuing error of orientation, addressing a terrified Alastair instead.

'All right, dear,' said Mrs Darksole pleasantly and the albino's head swung round in her direction like a tracking dog's. 'Go and get her. But don't bother bringing her back. She can make her confession some other time, after we get one of the mentally handicapped children to tap out a prayer book in Braille, so she can say her penance properly. Just let us know she's there and hasn't tripped over a white stick, a guide dog or anything equally appropriate.'

Feeling at the wall to guide her, the girl went off to find her friend. When she'd gone, Mrs Darksole sat down and shook her head.

'The blind,' she said angrily, 'I've had them up to here!' She touched her brow with an elegant forefinger. 'I don't know why they ever let them in here in the first place. It's not as if they're really abnormal, just blind as bats with white fur on top.'

I wondered at that, but my thoughts were interrupted.

'Come on, move it, for God's sake!'

It was Father Mortalsen. He was still waiting for his next confessant – and it was my turn. So, putting my trust in God, I went over to the curtain, entered and pulled it closed behind me. I could vaguely see the priest's outline behind the grille. He seemed to be kneeling sideways. Beneath the grille was a small, padded box on which I'd been told I should kneel. As I did so, I heard the trickle of fluid and the rustle of paper. Father Mortalsen was using holy water to give me his blessing and checking my name from his list of confessants.

He spoke.

'Hello, Billy. Glad you could make it. You can begin whenever you want to, son. Why not start at the beginning?'

I was taken aback at the 'Billy', but I'd prepared my confession and had it approved by my family.

I went ahead.

'Bless me, Father, for I have sinned. This is my first confession.'

I heard the sound of more holy water being poured and Father Mortalsen gave a distinct gasp before he spoke again.

'Well, Billy? What have you to confess, son, eh?'

Again I ignored the 'Billy'.

'I've neglected my prayers, Father. I was cruel to my favourite pet and I've lied to the most beautiful person I've ever seen.'

He sounded disappointed. Perhaps I'd overdone it.

'Is that it?'

'Yes, that's it, Father. That's the lot,' I said.

He seemed to cheer up.

'So, you've neglected your prayers – you little devil! Well, that's between you and God, sunshine, but you've lied to your teacher too, Billy-boy, and that isn't good news at all.'

I felt it was time to clarify matters.

'I haven't lied to any teacher, Father, and anyway – it's Francis!'

'What's Francis?'

'Me – I'm Francis! Billy's still outside waiting to see you.'

I could hear the rustle of paper again; he was obviously rechecking his list. I heard him striking a match too. He must be lighting a candle for me.

The penny still didn't drop.

'Sorry, Billy, I thought you were Francis. Mrs Darksole told me all about you – your parents dying like that, burned horribly beyond recognition, your own uniquely terminal health problems, the tragic likelihood that you'll keel over and –'

I interrupted.

'No, Father, I'm Francis. Billy's outside, wearing a grey pullover.'

'They're all wearing grey pullovers.'

'I know, but Billy's the one with dark-blue skin – it goes better with the grey. He stands out from the rest of us; you can't miss him.'

'Blue skin?'

'Yes, Father, they say he's a perfect example of a fully developed blue baby.'

Father Mortalsen took his time. I could smell the smoke from his candle. It was harsh.

'Ah, yes, I noticed that one. So that's what it is . . . a blue baby, by God! Mmm. So, you say you haven't lied to Mrs Darksole?'

'I said I lied to the most beautiful person I've ever seen, Father.'

'Yes. Mrs Darksole.'

'No. My mum.'

He laughed.

'Of course, my mistake! Still, I think Mrs Darksole's pretty good-looking too, so it's an easy one to make.' He gave another shorter laugh. ' So you've told your mum little porkies, eh?'

'One porky, Father. I told her I wanted to see my sister's grave, but I didn't really. I was just saying it to please her.'

'Your sister's grave . . . Ah! Are you absolutely certain you're not Billy, Francis? Mrs Darksole said you'd – '

I'd had enough of this.

'No! I'm not! You're still confusing us, Father. Billy lost his brother in the fire that killed his parents.'

'Really?'

'Whereas my sister died of a chest condition. I'm Francis, Father, he's Billy. I lost a sister, but he lost the lot.'

That made an impact.

'I see,' he said, then paused. 'I've suffered a bit myself, you know. It tests the faith, doesn't it?'

'Yes Father, it does.'

'Yes. Quite. Now, about these lies . . . '

'One lie, Father.'

'About the one lie, then. We have to discuss it.'

'OK, I'm up for it.'

'Good.'

I heard some slurping sounds and a few more gasps. Father Mortalsen was obviously the sensitive sort and I wondered if he were getting weepy about Billy.

'We must avoid all lies, Francis. The divine spark within us darkens when we lie. We have to keep it glowing with brightness, free from stain, pure. We mustn't lie, my boy, it flies in the face of our Lord God Almighty.'

'Yes, Father,' I said, as I heard more pouring sounds.

'Still, you're not that bad, really, son. You're not that bad at all, my lad – all considered.'

'Thanks, Father. I don't suppose I am.'

'But you were cruel to your favourite pet?'

'Yes.'

'How cruel?'

This was a sensitive topic.

'I had to hard-comb his fleas out, Father. It must have hurt a lot.'

He hiccupped.

'Was it badly matted?'

'Was what badly matted?'

'His woolly coat – was it badly matted?'

'What woolly coat? Dogs don't have woolly coats; *sheep* have woolly coats! It's my pet dog I was cruel to, not a bloomin' sheep!'

He thought about that.

'You said your pet had a fleece!'

'I said I had to hard-comb his *fleas*! My dog didn't have any fleece, for God's sake; he had a decent, hairy coat, just like anyone else's dog!'

'OK, calm down, no need to go on about it, my mistake again – a slip of the tongue; fleas – tics – mites – sorry! I thought your dog had an exotic pedigree or something, that's all. Is he OK now? Coat as clean as a snowman's bum after bleaching?'

'Well, he's dead, if that's OK,' I said, and that surprised him.

'Dead! Killed by a few fleas?'

'No, Father. Killed by "The Poor People's Refuge for Sick and Unwanted Animals". He was put down because he had an ear infection.'

'Put down!'

'Yes. Put down, killed and disposed of.'

He was silent for a time. When he finally spoke, he sounded genuinely upset.

'Why didn't you simply have him treated? There's no need to put a good pet dog down just for a run-of-the-mill ear infection.'

'There is if you can't afford to get it treated, Father. We couldn't find the money for the injections he needed. They don't charge you to put dogs to sleep at the "People's Refuge", but injections are expensive, and we're not well off.'

I heard a clinking sound and the priest gasped again. His voice was very different, far away, when he spoke again.

'I've done bad things too, you know, pet things . . . cruel ones.'

A silence fell of such pregnancy that it must have been due to have triplets.

He spoke.

'I was cruel to Timmy once.'

'Timmy?'

'Yes. Timmy – my pet Doberman.'

'You can tell me about it if you want to, Father. I've lived a bit myself, you know; very little shocks me.'

'Thanks, son, it's much appreciated, but I'd better not.'

We had another protracted silence, and I noticed his shadow had slumped. Grief does strange things to people – affects them differently.

He spoke.

'We have to be good to our petsh, Franshish.'

'It's Francis, Father.'

'Yesh, Franshish. God made petsh to give us pleasure, you know, and He expects us to be good to them. They should be treated with conshideration, passhion and temperensh, Franshish. They have their place in the grand scheme of things, too. Your nameshake – Shaint Franshish – spoke to animalsh. Did you know that?'

'"Shaint Franshish"? No, Father.'

Father Mortalsen's hand crept through the grille and his fingers moved towards my face.

He clicked them.

'That'sh how closhe Shaint Franshish wash to thoshe animalsh, Franshish.'

He clicked them again.

'Thatsh how closhe he wash to reptilesh, inshects, mammalsh, fish and birdsh. Even shnakes were part of his domain – the shlimy, shlithery, shons of Shatan.'

I wondered if this were a part of confession I hadn't been told about. Then I heard tumbling sounds, grunts and some words it's probably better not to mention. There were a few more grunts and some huffing sounds I saw the priest's shape at the grille again and hoped he was all right.

'Are you OK, Father?'

'Yes! I'm fine! There's nothing like a good, old-fashioned tumble in the sanctity of the confessional to clear a fuzzy head, eh? Now where were we?'

'With Saint Franshish, Father.'

'It's Saint *Francis*, son – Saint Francis. Yes, that's it. He could speak with all animals, but little birds were his favourites: brown little sparrows, chirpy little chaffinches, little robin red –'

He paused.

'Do you ever think about girls, Francis?'

'Yes, Father. Quite a bit.'

'Right! You can tell me all about it in graphic detail, if you want to. It won't go much further. God and I are like – that!' he said, as both hands came through the curtain and clenched together in front of my face. They began to shake like terrified gelatine.

'I'd rather not tell anyone, Father.'

He composed himself.

'Well, you hear all sorts in my line of work – it's part of the job description. Are you quite certain you don't want to tell me all about it?'

'Yes, I'm certain, Father.'

'As you like. Anyway, you'd like a girlfriend one day, son. Eh?'

'Yes, Father, I would.'

There was the sound of glass chinking.

'Me too, son. Cheers!' he said, extending his hand through the grille again to shake mine. 'Best of luck to us both!' he added, and I shook his warmly.

'Before I give you your penance, is there anything else?'

'Just one thing, Father.'

'Yes?'

'What did Saint Francis say to the birds?'

'Ah! Saint Francis! Well a number of things,' he said quickly. 'But he said them in Italian, so we don't really know.'

'I see,' I said, as he murmured some phrases in Latin, then told me to say three Hail Marys for my penance.

I thanked him for his time, stood up, said goodbye and went back out into the classroom. My classmates were sitting in silence watching me. They started to applaud.

As I made my way back to my chair, Alastair passed by me; it was his turn now. He looked worried, but what was new? I felt a strange sensation in my chest, though, and suddenly wished I could go in with him to help. Still, I didn't suppose he'd much to confess. He wasn't the sort to be cruel to a dog – he wouldn't physically harm a thing. As far as I could see, the only harm in Alastair's life had come to him from life itself.

The rest of us heard Al's voice groan on for a full ten minutes. We caught the occasional snatch of conversation and I managed to make out the words 'lingering death', 'tombstone', 'infanticide', 'mortal sin', 'eternal damnation' and 'without a decent Christian burial'. It all seemed pretty normal for Al, and we didn't hear the priest speak at all. At one point, I thought I heard a low groaning sound, but it was probably just Jean's stomach churning. She'd confused First Confession with First Communion, and had fasted for twelve hours before it.

When Alastair came out, he was still looking pretty worried. Jason sauntered by, swinging his hips and heading in style towards the purple curtain. As he entered, he stroked the velvet between his fingers, gave us a coquettish look and was gone from sight in an instant. I wondered what the priest would make of him. We could just hear Jason's voice through the curtain. It was indistinct, but pleasant nonetheless. When it stopped, a gasp came from the priest's side of the box. The gasp was repeated, and I noted that sort of high-pitched tone I'd heard equated before with incredulity. Smoke rose from the priest's side. Had Jason made Father Mortalsen angry? Perhaps he was burning incense to cleanse the room? There was a complete and total silence until Jason sauntered out again.

'Good to speak with you, Father. You're truly a charming man,' he threw casually behind him. 'See you again some time, I hope,' he finished as he swaggered towards us, passing Billy who was next in line and saying, 'Good luck, Bill.'

Billy shook his head.

'I don't need it. I was born lucky.'

Jason smiled.

'Take some anyway.' But Billy shook his head in dismissal and went in to confess, smiling.

'Hello, Father Mortalsen,' he said, before the curtain was even closed. 'What d'you mean, close the grille? It's me, Billy!'

As Billy finally pulled the curtain closed, I heard a clatter followed by a laugh. There were some serious whisperings and I heard a laugh again. Then we heard Billy's voice; incredulous, loud and clear.

'A right prig you are, Father Mortalsen. What's so sinful about that?'

There were more whispers from the priest, but not from Billy.

He was almost shouting.

'Do I know Saint Francis? Of course I do, my grandfather was his first cousin on his mother's side.'

There were more murmurings, then, 'Animals? Come off it, Father. He never spoke to animals. You're having me on!'

There were a few strident murmurs from Father Mortalsen, then Billy's voice emerged again, its incredulity increasing by the moment.

'Birds? He spoke to birds? But birds *whistle*, Father. How could he speak to them?'

There was more laughter. The priest's voice took on an urgent ascendancy but, incorrigible as ever, Billy continued to laugh and speak simultaneously.

'Parrots! In Italian? Of course parrots can speak Italian. But you don't get parrots in Italy, Father. My elder brother's the right-hand man for the Pope in the Vatican, so I should know, shouldn't I? There are no parrots in Italy.'

There were feverish sounds from the priest, rising rapidly in pitch. Then Billy spoke again, his voice brimming with delight.

'A right one you are, Father Mortalsen. We're physically handicapped, by the way. The mentally handicapped are on the other side of the school!'

We exchanged glances and Billy's laughter began to spill out to us, to infect us. It gave us that funny feeling of loss of control when you feel you're floating dangerously near to madness and you can't do anything about it. We all began to giggle, except for Alastair.

Mrs Darksole frowned her pretty frown.

'Enough!' she hissed. 'Behave! This is your First Confession. Don't stain your soul so soon after attaining a modicum of God's grudged grace.'

We quickly shut up, but we continued to listen as Billy kept laughing and bantering with Father Mortalsen. Eventually he appeared from behind the curtain. It was a lighter shade of purple than he, and a fitting backdrop to the drama played out behind it. His coloured face was still lit up with a smile and his teeth were very white against his dark-blue lips. He raised a thumb, directing it back over his shoulder as he shook his head in approval.

'What a man that is! "Good value", as my stockbroker brother would say.'

He went back to his seat, still smiling and shaking his head in admiration as Mrs Darksole descended on him like the Nosferatu. She pulled him from his seat, across the room and out through the door, slamming it behind her. I wondered if he was going to feel her sharp little fists on his head, as I had once or twice already along with a few of the others. So much for a school where there was meant to be no corporal punishment. I wondered what *she* told her priest in the sanctity of the confessional.

A few moments later, the door opened again. The older pupils who were making their regular confession came in. There were perhaps a half dozen of them. And behind them, the very last to enter, was Derek. He floated serenely in on his wheelchair, pushed as ever by the Headless Boy. They headed straight for the confessional and Derek was wheeled in through the curtain. Melissa rushed over to retrieve the Headless Boy, who would have been happy to stay with Derek, though that was against the rules. But it was only as she did so that I realised Derek shouldn't be in there at all. Not only was he non-Catholic, but also he couldn't speak properly and there was no Moira to translate for him. As I wondered what to do, I could hear the familiar murmur of Father Mortalsen trying to put Derek at his ease. Presumably he was asking him how long it had been since his last confession. There was silence before he murmured again. Then a longer silence, some shuffling sounds, more urgent tones from the priest – and a further silence.

'OOG-OO-AH . . . ! OOG-OO-AH, O-HAH, O-AAH!'

Father Mortalsen rushed out with a look in his eye that would have redefined the meaning of 'feral'. A puddle of something was trickling around the confessional. Evidently he wasn't as experienced in the ways of the Dereks of this world as we were. Still wild-eyed, he gestured to Melissa and pointed at Derek's side of the confessional. As she made for it, he made for the door, whipping a number of items out from under his cassock. A prayer book, rosary beads, a crucifix or even an incense burner with bells on I'd have been prepared for – but not a packet of twenty cigarettes and a box of matches. He made off through the door, with his cassock streaming behind, as if all the hounds of Hell were after him.

Mrs Darksole, looking amazed as the priest rushed past her, came back in dragging Billy behind her. He looked pale and drained of what little blood he had. She bared her sharp, perfect teeth.

'What in the name of God's going on?' she screamed as a flustered Derek, retrieved by Melissa, was wheeled out from behind the curtain, trying to straighten his tie. The Headless Boy grabbed the wheelchair from Melissa and pushed it towards the door. Still screaming inanities, Mrs Darksole helped push Derek out. And I noticed he was totally dry. His trousers had no dark stain at the crotch, his leg-irons were pristine, and his boots were as dry as blotter dust. I wondered at this, until I noticed that the pool of liquid seemed to be trickling from the *priest's* side of the curtain.

Surely not! My imagination began to form a truly dreadful series of images. The others had spotted it too. Alastair looked shocked, Billy smiled and gave a grim little laugh, and the diminutive Jean was clicking her teeth as if they were castanets. Only Una looked composed, an attitude imposed more by her neck-brace than by any emotional sangfroid at such a perilous time for the Roman Catholic Church.

The classroom door flew open again. Instead of a returning priest, we now had Fatty Spinner. His eyes formed conjunction, square, trine, opposition and sextile aspects in a second, and it would have taken an astrologer to read them. He fell into the class with a bucket in lieu of his usual milk-crate. I was amazed: he'd brought sawdust for the stain as quickly as that? For a moment I wondered if Fatty were telepathic. Or perhaps it was a miracle – could Fatty be a saint? A prophet? A Doctor of the Church in the tradition of Saint Theresa of Avila?

Mrs Darksole hissed 'Bring that bucket here!' – and Fatty made towards her with it. She and Derek looked into it simultaneously – and simultaneously started back immediately.

'OOG-OO-AH . . . ! OOG-OO-AH, O-HAH, O-AAH!' they shouted together, as Fatty dropped it on the floor and I peered into it. Frogs! It was filled with frogs! The words plague and pestilence ran through my mind . . . the plagues of Egypt – frogs.

Mrs Darksole yelled at Fatty.

'They're for P.H.5, you obese cretin! They're for a biology lesson! We're having the sacrament of confession in here. Get out, you podgy imbecile! Get bloody out!'

Her screeching revitalised Fatty. He grabbed the bucket and ran out of the door. I returned my attention to the pool by the confessional. Still shaking with anger, Mrs Darksole was walking towards it. She pulled back the curtain.

On the floor lay a dripping bottle of something that most certainly wasn't holy water. Evidently, Derek's sudden and spirited confession had made Father Mortalsen jump and he'd knocked it over. That was distressing, but what was even more distressing was the fact there was a chair there too, and a newspaper, open at the racing page. Mrs Darksole picked up the bottle, smelt it and said it was cough medicine. My dead sister had taken plenty of cough medicine, but never anything like that stuff – it was the sort of thing my Uncle Joe preferred.

We were more upset at something else, however. We'd all assumed Father Mortalsen would be kneeling down just like we had. But he'd been sitting comfortably checking racing form, while we'd tried to kneel as best as we could and pour out all our sins. I felt a stab of disappointment, Billy shrugged and Alastair looked down at the floor with a sudden, desperate look. He was just seven or eight years old then, Al, and, in our eyes anyway, even his Church had let him down.

I was down on the floor beside Mrs Darksole, helping to clean up the mess, when Billy sidled over.

'It sthew hite fat herand hes abigbl ackdark ie,' he garbled and I wondered if he'd been at the 'cough medicine' himself.

Mrs Darksole turned.

'The what?' she snapped. Neither of us had understood him. 'Speak up!' she commanded, her eyes filled with the sort of hatred of life that some of those who taught us seemed to develop – or maybe had already, even before they joined us.

Not one to shrink from the controversial and being a boy who called a spade a spade, Billy did so.

'It's the White Father,' he said much louder. 'And he's a big, black Darkie!'

From our kneeling positions in the confessional, Mrs Darksole and I looked up to meet the widest smile I'd ever seen in my life. It was indeed the White Father – Father Savage. And, as Billy had tactlessly but honestly suggested, he was as black as the Ace of Spades, if not a good bit blacker.

'Well, you people sure do take confession seriously in dis dere country 'ere,' he said, his smile now so wide I thought his head might fall into it. 'What you two dun so wrong anyway, to git such a terrible penance?'

15

Father Savage was a revelation. The first thing on his agenda was to deal with his immediate predecessor. In due course Father Mortalsen came back to the classroom. His eyes were squinting like a hunted, paranoid fox searching for further signs of trouble and his hands were vibrating like a jellyfish getting shock therapy. Father Savage suggested that since he'd done such a good job with us, Father Mortalsen should get back to his church and get on with whatever pressing business he had there. He said he'd take over, look after our spiritual welfare and hear the confessions of the others who'd joined us himself. We didn't see Father Mortalsen for dust.

We soon discovered that the few sentences Father Savage had spoken initially had been in jest. He spoke with perfectly accented English, of a type better understood in the rest of the United Kingdom than our own west of Scotland version. He explained he'd been born in Lesotho in southern Africa and educated at a missionary school. He'd completed his religious training in Rome, then returned to Lesotho to become a parish priest. He was spending three months in our parish to see what he could learn. It was a sort of experiment, he told us, and we were part of it. He duly took the remaining confessions but this time it was carried out without incident. He then gave us a short but informative talk about the significance of confession and its place as one of the seven sacraments of the Church.

When finally he asked if we had any questions, the conversation turned quite naturally to his origins. Only Billy claimed he'd actually seen a black man before, his father apparently having brought one home from work once to join the family at dinner. Though I doubt any of us believed that, we continued to indulge him in his stories and accordingly it was Billy who began question time.

'So do you actually live in the jungle, Father, or just near it?'

'Nowhere near it actually,' replied Father Savage. 'I live in a small, residential town about two imperial miles from the centre of the city.'

'Are the houses made of mud?' asked Jean.

'No. Of good-quality brick.'

It was Una's turn and she was deadly serious.

'Do you have to hunt for your food, Father?'

Billy interrupted.

'Don't be silly! As a holy man, Father Savage will have slaves to do that. Pygmies probably.'

There was a hush of expectancy.

'We have no slaves, unfortunately,' said the priest. 'We do have a housekeeper, but she's neither a Pygmy nor a slave. Just a run-of-the-mill native lady.'

It was Woody next. He was one of the non-Catholics among us, and must have sneaked in with the older children, but that didn't really matter, not on a day like this.

'Do you see lots of lions and tigers?'

Father Savage nodded.

'Yes. At the cinema,' he said, 'or if we're lucky enough to visit one of the national game parks. Tigers tend to be a lot more common in India than in Africa, though we do see leopards sometimes in the game parks too.'

Alastair spoke next.

'Is there lots of cannibalism and torture?'

'Not too much,' said the priest enigmatically. 'But then, that sort of thing isn't all that obvious,' he added, and Al nodded slowly and gave me a sly, quiet smile.

'I knew it,' he whispered.

A new voice entered the conversation.

'They say Holy Communion is a form of cannibalism, Father.'

It was the older of the two albino girls. She'd ignored Mrs Darksole's orders and returned with her companion, who looked fine after her stroll. Father Savage must have been easy to detect, since her eyes were turned directly at him.

He sounded more wary.

'They do? And who are "they"?'

She took a deep breath.

'Analytical psychologists mainly, though I imagine some anthropologists would agree if they had a psychodynamic bent.'

She was a pretty little thing, this albino, and she was a girl and almost blind at that. Given this, it was hard to credit the things she knew about.

'Maybe, maybe,' said Father Savage. 'But we wouldn't share that view. Would we?'

She shook her head and her hair glinted in the light like spun golden threads.

'No, Father. Otherwise we'd be excommunicated *ipso facto*. But it's a thought, don't you think?'

'It is,' he said, looking slightly sad.

It was Billy again, his voice gruff and loud.

'Two questions, Father. Who picks the black babies we buy? What happens to the ones we don't pay for? And why do they cost two-and-six?'

Father Savage's fingers had counted three, I noticed, but he didn't say anything about that.

He answered.

'It's a sort of symbolic thing. The term "black babies" is really a general term used for poorer children. In many respects we're poorer in Africa, in a material sense, but we're richer in other ways that some people consider more important.'

He paused and looked at us.

'We collected money for White Babies during the War. We were told they were starving; did you know that?'

'Of course,' said Billy. 'That was all very clear, Father. Thank you.'

'So it's like transubstantiation?' said the older albino girl.

'What is?'

'You said the Black Babies Movement was symbolic. Surely that's like transubstantiation: the changing of bread and wine into the body and blood of Christ.'

Father Savage looked at her.

'No, young woman, we believe that to be literal.'

Father Savage walked over to her. Her head was shaking about wildly, as if she were trying to keep her eyes in one place by shaking it instead of them.

'What's your name?' he asked gently.

'Faith.'

'You have a questioning mind, Faith. That can give rise to problems, when it's applied to questions without rational answers.'

Al's face tightened and I felt that shadow grow cold again – the one inside me. I took his hand and squeezed it.

By now the albino girl was trying to sense Father Savage's exact location. She got close enough and spoke again.

'I have a brother who's going to be a priest,' she said. 'He doesn't question very much; so they say I make up for him.'

He smiled.

'What Order is he in?'

'The Society of Jesus,' she said, with evident pride.

'Why, that's marvellous; he must be very clever.'

'He is,' she paused. 'We hoped he might become a doctor – specialise in something practical. At one point he talked about ophthalmology.'

'Perhaps he will,' said Father Savage. 'Jesuits become doctors too, you know.'

'He won't,' she said quietly.

'Why ever not?'

'They want him to specialise in theology,' she said, with a strange tone to her voice. 'And that's exactly what he's decided to do.'

Father Savage spoke very quietly.

'We need good theologians too.'

'For what?'

'To understand the ways of God.'

Faith became very, very still. Except for her eyes, of course.

'You'd think God would understand His own ways.'

Father Savage jerked as if he'd been struck.

'I'm sure He does. But we have to also, and that isn't quite as easy.'

Faith leant forward.

'I suffer from albinism, Father Savage. My eyesight's almost completely gone.'

'I appreciate that.'

Faith's eyes were shaking very quickly; the rest of her was perfectly still.

'Some of the kids call me "Blind Faith",' she said. 'They're being literal too, and I don't like it.'

The priest bit his lower lip.

'That's pretty cruel.'

'It's also true,' Faith retorted.

He looked grim.

'The truth can be pretty cruel, then.'

'Not as cruel as lies and distortions, Father.'

'I'm not so sure,' he said, softly.

'Well, I am,' she said.

Her eyes were doing cartwheels by now and the rest of us looked at one another, trying to fathom what this strange exchange had meant. An embarrassed silence crept over us like a shroud.

It took Billy to lift it.

'What's a tar baby, Father?'

Father Savage looked startled.

'A tar baby? It's an unhelpful way to describe a Negro infant,' he said. 'It's best to simply use the term "child".'

'Tar child . . .' said Billy reflectively. He smiled. 'Yes, that does sound better.'

'Just "child",' said the priest quietly. 'Now, is there anything else?' he asked.

I wasn't the most confident of boys, but I did have experience in these matters and had something to say myself – so I said it.

'Is there much discrimination where you live, Father?' Everyone looked at me; you'd have thought they were surprised I'd even spoken.

I continued.

'I know it exists in some places. A young Negro was hanged recently for speaking to a white woman.'

They all stared at me now, including the priest. I would have stared at myself if I could have. Alastair was rubbing his neck nervously as I waited for my answer, and Father Savage soon supplied it.

'In God's eyes there's no segregation,' he said mildly. 'In his eyes we're all equal and have an equal chance of salvation, irrespective of who or what we are, or where we're from.'

That sounded good, but I hadn't mentioned 'segregation' and, though I could make a fair guess, I made a mental note to find out what it meant. I hadn't said anything about immortal souls being saved, either. I'd simply asked Father Savage, in an oblique manner admittedly, if there was discrimination against blacks by whites in his country. He hadn't answered my question, but he'd known exactly what I meant. So I drew my own conclusions.

Father Savage looked after our temporal as well as our spiritual welfare that day. When we'd finished speaking, he asked us to join him in a hymn. We looked at one another. Our school didn't exactly have a thriving choral society, and we'd never really sung collectively before – not in the strict sense of the word. A few of us had run through a sort of hymn with Mrs Darksole once or twice, as she had battered it out, and into us, on an old, geriatric piano. So when he asked what hymns we knew, all we could suggest was that one.

'It's called "Guardian Angel",' Melissa told him, somewhat defensively. She didn't like anyone to think she wasn't as informed as normal kids were in matters of the soul, not even a priest – and a black one at that.

'Ah, that's a new one to me,' said Father Savage, 'but let's have a go, anyway. If you start, I'll follow and join in when I can.'

We looked at one another again. Al hung his head and Billy looked angry. Woody tapped his bad arm rhythmically and Jean clicked her teeth nervously. None of us was really willing to start off. We were used to being led; initiative was not our forte. The silence went on for too long.

'Stuff this!' said Billy. 'I'll start!'

Whatever his other attributes, Billy's voice wasn't one of them. I'd stopped swapping the words of songs with him long ago, since his rendition of these in the Rest Room had been making me consider an increase in my phenobarbitone pills.

He took a very deep breath and his skin flushed a lighter blue. 'Guardian angel …' he began, making that deep throaty sound cats make before they attack.

'Guardian angel,' he repeated, in the sort of voice people make when they try to hit those cats with a boot.

He stopped.

'I've forgotten the words,' he said blandly. 'Let's try another one.'

'Another one?' asked Una.

Billy nodded.

'Another hymn.'

We looked at one another again.

'I don't think we know another one,' I said.

'I do!' said Alastair, with unusual enthusiasm.

Father Savage smiled.

'And what's that, young man?' he asked brightly.

Al looked uncertain.

'"*De profundis*".'

Melissa looked surprised.

'What does that mean?'

Al frowned.

'Out of the depths.'

'The depths of what?' asked Una.

'Despair,' said Al, with a face to match.

'Forget it!' snapped Billy. 'We want to keep Father Savage here happy, not send him back into the jungle heading for his tom-toms and ju-ju stick!'

Father Savage's face crinkled into that wide smile.

'There must be something you could all sing together.'

Melissa spoke.

'Francis can sing the blues, Father.'

She was looking at me proudly, but I went into immediate and total shock. I occasionally sang bits of songs to a select few of my classmates. They covered the populist spread, and the blues was just part of it. I'd no particular expertise in blues music or any other. Anyway, I didn't like performing live.

Father Savage's big brown eyes passed over my face with a look of surprise and delight.

'"The blues"?'

'I only listen,' I mumbled. 'My brother sings in a band and I listen to the blues on the radio, as well as rock 'n' roll and other stuff.'

Suddenly someone was looking at me as if I were something special, in a good way, for the first time in my life. 'Well,' he said. 'We have a young soul musician here. So, you like the blues?'

'Yes, Father, I do.'

'Does anyone else?' he asked, looking round our little group. With the exception of Una, heads nodded everywhere.

'Well, now,' he said, with a glance towards the door. 'Let's see what we can do about that.'

Father Savage began to click his finger and thumb. There was no similarity to Father Mortalsen's finger-click in the confessional. This one was rhythmic and well intentioned. He set the rhythm this way and kept it up by tapping his left foot. It was all kept in time by the regular movement of the tassel in front of his cassock and by his rosary, which swung back and forth on his shoulder-shrugging neck like a metronome. To our surprise and delight, he burst into a simple twelve-bar blues:

> Well ma name is Father Savage
> Ah'm a missionary of the soul,
> And ma mission's to find music,
> That will make you rock an' roll.

There were fingers clicking everywhere by now. Walking sticks and crutches were tapping time and the deep, dark bass of built-up boots and truly heavy metal shuddered through the floorboards. One of the older boys, who had a wooden leg with springs in it, tapped it in time too. He sounded just like a snare drum.

> Beads of prayer are on ma ros'ry,
> On my brow are beads of sweat,
> An' those sins that cause us mis'ry,
> Ah'll get rid of, man, you bet!

> For Ah know,
> Woh, woh, woh, .
> Ah'm a mission'ry of the soul!

The place was jumpin'. Callipers thudded on the floor, hunched backs bent and straightened, the chronically rigid swayed from side to side and the lame bounced in their seats like Michelin men. Woody used his unequal arms to good effect, by simulating a guitar solo on someone's crutch, and the albino girls' eyes were shaking like freshly struck cymbals, making me wonder if by any chance they'd received the gift of sight. I was ecstatic myself, as the priest went into the final verses with his rosary spinning round his neck like a blessed, beaded hula-hoop:

> An Ah'll give the holy water;
> That's the water in ma wine,
> To the faithful as I oughta
> As they hand the Lord their time.

> For Ah'm a messenger from Jesus;
> It's sweet Jesus that Ah choose,
> An' he lifts the veils of darkness
> When Ah sing the twelve-bar blues.

> For Ah know,
> Woh, woh, woh,
> Ah'm a mission'ry of the soul!

As he finished in a gripping, perfect pitch, Alastair jumped up and shouted, 'Oh yeah!' He immediately looked round in sudden, self-conscious terror, but he'd done it – he'd had a moment of forgetfulness. I hoped it might lead to more. We burst into spontaneous applause and the classroom rattled with delight. Father Savage bowed his head a few times, tidied his cassock, straightened himself up, pulled the rosary beads from behind his neck and generally calmed things down.

'That's truly music of the soul,' he said. 'A modern hymn. We're closer to our Maker now,' he smiled and we nodded our agreement. 'God wants us to enjoy life too,' he said, looking at Alastair in particular. 'He made this world for joy, not sorrow. And there's nothing wrong with good, wholesome music.'

We couldn't have agreed more.

The atmosphere was still electric when Mrs Darksole returned.

'Everything all right?' she asked, and I could tell she was treating this priest differently from the other one. The difference was in her tone of voice and general demeanour. It was because he was black.

'All's just fine, ma'am,' parodied Father Savage. 'We've just been singin' a few upliftin' hymns, that's all. That's about it, I'd say! Pity you couldn't have joined us.'

She smiled like a scorpion.

'How nice. If I'd known, we could have gone to the music room and I'd have accompanied you on the piano. Black-and-white keys it has – ebony and ivory. Beautifully positioned, too – each in its proper place.'

Father Savage gave her a big, toothy grin.

'Ah sure wish you had, ma'am. That would have been truly awesome. Perhaps another time, ma'am. Next time. Eh?'

'Perhaps,' she said, though I doubted it. If he'd sung the blues to Mrs Darksole, she'd have fallen down flat on the spot and requested another priest to administer the last rites. A white one.

After Father Savage had gone, I considered everything I'd heard about Negroes and their relationship with white people. That image of the black boy being hanged because he spoke to a white girl still haunted me. Oddly enough, it still does. We were too young then to be going around looking for girlfriends among our own type, let alone among the normal in society. But if Derek, or Woody, or Billy or Al had expressed an interest in someone's able-bodied daughter, I doubt anyone would have welcomed it. I was even beginning to doubt they'd welcome it if *I* expressed the interest. On the other hand, I also wondered if Negroes would hang one of us Whites for speaking to a black girl. I reckoned they would, if our roles were reversed, so to speak, and they ran the show as the white folks did. And do you know something? I reckoned if they could get away with it, some people, be they black, white, pink, yellow or tan-coloured, would have hanged us just for being infirm, disabled, handicapped, challenged, whatever you want to call it – just one word, 'different', suits me. For by now I'd noticed that some people had a strange look in their eyes when they watched us, and I didn't like it. It came over them when they thought we weren't looking; and it was as if we didn't belong here, didn't have the right to be placed alongside them.

And why shouldn't they think that? After all, we were herded into special schools like the characters in one of those freak shows that 'different' people joined years ago to enable them to keep body and soul together: or at least as much together as was possible, given what God had done to that supposedly natural relationship in the first place. I concluded that, in this respect, anyway, we, as a handicapped minority, were in some respects like Father Savage's race – outsiders, easily identifiable and picked upon simply because we looked different. Though in other respects, we were nothing like them at all.

And now I knew, from first-hand experience, something else I'd suspected for quite a while. Negroes could sing the blues a lot better than we could, whatever way you looked at it all.

<hr />

16

Soon after my First Confession, I thought I'd put my newly consolidated faith to the test so, when everyone was asleep one night, I slipped out of the house and headed for the burial mound. I'd been told the ghost of Marjorie Bruce had been seen around there on one famous occasion, by a handicapped boy called Robby, who, for some reason never explained to me, didn't attend our school. I felt that only if you actually saw a ghost would you be convinced they existed. Now I'd began to suspect I was going to feel that way about a number of things. While I couldn't hope to experience many of them, however, I could try to see for myself if ghosts existed. Bravery was never my most notable feature – it still isn't, but I had to find out if spectres of the dead really did wander around like some of the more directionally challenged pupils of my school. For I thought they would supply me with proof of an afterlife, and I felt I needed such proof. So, with much trepidation, and on a cold, dark night, I approached the burial mound with hesitation and with my bad heart thumping like a double bass at full blast.

When I reached the mound my heart seemed to stop, for behind it was a shape. I swallowed hard. My impulse to run back the way I'd come was so strong I'd already turned round when, for some strange reason, I stopped myself from doing so. Perhaps my desire for proof was stronger than my fear; perhaps I felt if someone like Robby – who spent his social life in a wheelchair and his nightlife in bed – could experience something like that and survive it, I could too. Whatever the reason, I stayed where I was – and nearly messed my underpants. The shape had come out from behind the mound and was moving in my direction. I was about to encounter Marjorie Bruce – not quite in the flesh perhaps, but in its afterlife equivalent.

The spectre spoke.

'Who are you?'

'My name's Fran –' I said, stopping when I realised I'd heard a man's voice, not Marjorie's. My mother, my father, my brother and my sister had all told me never to speak to strange men, but I stood my ground. What was the point of refusing to speak to them? Strange men could run faster than I could.

'So what are you doing here, Fran? What do you want here at this time of night?' It had occurred to me by now that this was no ghost at all, simply a run-of-the-mill strange man, and my heart approached normal sinus rhythm again as he continued.

'So what do you want here?'

I took a deep breath.

'I've come to check the mound's OK,' I said, in a sort of involuntary whining tone.

He nodded.

'I see. And what did you think might be wrong with it?'

'Nothing in particular. I just wanted to check it was still standing.'

He came a step closer, but was still hidden in the shadows. I shot a quick glance towards our living-room window, hoping to see my brother, my father or even my sister there, but they were all in bed and the window was dark. What had I expected at midnight?

'Seems a funny thing for a small boy to be doing at this time of night,' said the man. 'Do your parents know you're here?'

I didn't like the 'small boy' comment. I bristled.

'Who's asking?'

'I am,' he said, moving closer, and I could make him out a bit better now. He was tall and his hands were stuck deep inside his coat pockets.

'Well, maybe you shouldn't be asking. Maybe it's none of your business,' I snapped. 'Maybe I should be asking you what you're doing here, a grown man prowling around at all hours like some sort of vagabond.'

He stood perfectly still. I hoped I hadn't gone too far.

'I came here looking for the ghost of Marjorie Bruce,' he said.

'Marjorie Bruce!'

'Yes, she was the daughter of –'

'King Robert I of Scotland,' I interrupted.

'Oh, you know about that?' he said, sounding impressed.

I nodded.

'Of course I do, it's local history. Anyway, enough about me. Why are you here looking for a ghost, of all things?'

'I was told it was seen recently by some sort of disabled boy. So I wanted to see for myself. There's no sign of it yet.'

He moved forward again and I backed off a bit.

'You can't always take the word of a boy like that, you know.'

'Why not?'

'Because he can't speak,' I said, moving a bit further back. 'His mother translates for him, and you can't be sure she got it right. He might have made it up to get attention, or something.'

The man leaned over.

'Then why are you here?'

'Me? Like I said, I wanted to check the mound was still standing.'

'And that's it?'

I hesitated.

'If I happened to see a ghost while I was checking it, that would be fine by me.'

The man was well within reach now and he looked less threatening, tired – but safer, more human.

'Yes, it would be interesting.'

'That would be enough for me, the interest – the fact she was a great king's daughter.'

'You certainly know your history. What school d'you go to?' he asked suddenly and for the first time ever I was reluctant to answer.

'A local school.'

'Local?'

'Local, yes. One in the immediate vicinity.'

'There only are three schools that take boys in the immediate vicinity.'

'Yes, and I go to one of them.'

'Which one?'

'That's none of your business.'

'I don't suppose it is. So where do you live?'

He'd moved much closer now and I began to feel those hairs stand up: the fluffy ones on the back of your neck.

'I live just over there,' I said and pointed on the half-turn to my home. 'I live there with my brother, sister, mother and father and my dog. They're watching me right now,' I lied.

The man was completely still. Sinister.

'You have a dog?'

'A wolfhound,' I lied again. 'A big one. He's probably watching too.'

'I see,' he said. 'Then you'd better get back home right this moment. Or else . . .'

I bristled again.

'Or else what?'

'Or I'll drag you back by the scruff of your bloody neck.'

I was raging.

'Just try it!' I snapped angrily. 'My father will come straight down and break *your* bleeding neck.'

'I am your bloody father,' said the man.

'Oh!'

'I've been working night and day and you've probably forgotten all about me. I might not be around all that much, since I do double shifts and weekends to earn enough to keep us all, but I still have the right to sort you out,' he said and I felt myself blush like a shamed beetroot.

'Oh! Sorry, Dad,' I whimpered, recognising him at last. 'I haven't seen you for ages; I didn't recognise you.'

'That's OK, son. But next time you plan to take a walk at midnight, keep it to yourself. It might surprise you, but the fact you told your brother where you were going meant I found out too.'

I must have looked surprised.

'No need to puzzle over it,' he said. 'I came round the back way – it's quicker.'

Despite the adrenaline still pumping through me from this unexpected encounter, I felt betrayed.

'So he told you!'

'What do you think?' he said. 'Anyway, what are you really doing here? He mentioned this daft thing about the ghost, but that's not you. You're too sensible for that. So what were you doing out here at this time of night?'

'Checking the burial mound, like I said,' I repeated, my third lie in as many minutes, like Saint Peter before cockcrow. 'I was afraid it might be showing signs of subsidence. You told me about subsidence once, when Uncle Joe's bedroom wall fell over and trapped him in bed.'

'Ah, that explains it,' he said. 'That *is* you – practical and inquisitive, just like me.' He took my hand. 'Come on back now. At least you'll sleep well. Ghosts! Just as well you're not the imaginative sort.'

We returned home and I went back into my bedroom. My brother was in bed, snoring like a log with an internal combustion engine. I knew he was only pretending and I was tempted to confront him. But I reckoned he'd mentioned my midnight expedition to my father simply because he was being protective. So I let it be and went to bed, feeling rather excited about it all, but still not knowing what it was that waited for kids like Alastair when the bell finally tolled – nor me, for that matter. Though I did know at least one person in my family who would know the answer; the one who'd gone off to study such things professionally.

17

My Otherbrother arrived in a swanky taxi cab. He was met by all of us except my mother, who was still in hospital with her 'too much of life' problem. My father had taken a day off work for the occasion, the first time he'd done so in months. The driver came out and opened the passenger door of the taxi. He doffed his cap and assisted my Otherbrother out onto the red rug we'd placed on the pavement for his personal use. Then he opened the boot, inside which we saw two large, smart suitcases. As instructed by my sister, my brother ran over, lifted these out and carried them upstairs, while my father paid the taxi driver in freshly minted coin. My sister, who had a dark scarf over her head, opened her umbrella and held it over my Otherbrother's head. It wasn't raining, but it looked as if it might at any time.

It had been so long since I'd actually seen this Otherbrother that I wasn't sure how to welcome him. My father – uncertain what to do himself – had suggested I should shake his hand. I moved forward to do so, but he didn't respond. Instead, he stood very straight, stretched his arms out in front and twittered away in what I now recognise as standard Church Latin, giving us his personal blessing. I wasn't sure he was qualified to do this, but I stood to attention anyway, bowed my head and accepted it.

'*Dominus vobiscum*,' he finished, as my sister reverently whispered, '*Et cum spiritu tuo*.' For once I could contribute nothing; I didn't know the words.

When he'd managed to make it upstairs on his own, with us following behind in a sort of sombre procession, my Otherbrother went into the room that had once been shared by my two sisters. It was now used exclusively by my big sister, but from tonight until my Otherbrother went back to the Seminary, she'd sleep on a mattress between the two beds in the room I shared with my brother. None of us really minded this, though my brother had voiced some degree of dissent when first told about it. His concern wasn't about my sister sharing it *per se*; it had more to do with the fact she wouldn't tolerate his nocturnal forays into the living-room to listen to the radio. I shared this sentiment, because for the past few weeks I'd started nipping into the living-room with him, his threats of telling my parents on me going unheeded, since when faced with these I pointed out I could do the same to him. I suppose that sounds manipulative – but, don't forget, I was getting older.

So, despite the ill feeling between us that these forays could bring, they expanded my knowledge of the music industry no end, and I was becoming a regular connoisseur of popular music. However, the forays would stop from this day on, for we couldn't take the risk of disturbing our Otherbrother at night. We didn't want him losing any sleep and we

didn't want to interrupt his late-night or early-morning prayers either –
God forbid!

When I finally obtained an audience with my Otherbrother, I bent my
head and asked how I should formally address him.

'Call me Brother Peter,' he said sombrely. 'It has a nice ring to it and
after all, I am your brother and my name is Peter.'

Again this didn't seem particularly appropriate, but I did it anyway as it
seemed to please him. I also saw his two large suitcases, which pleased *me*,
for they had labels on them: 'Religious and Miscellaneous Books' on one
and 'Sacred Toys, Games, Novelties and Amusements' on the other. I was
desperate to see what was in them, but I'd learned discretion and control
since I'd last seen Brother Peter. So I kissed his ring, bowed low as I left
and bided my time.

He was tired after his long journey, but being essentially a holy youth
in transition to holy man, he was extremely charitable. Accordingly, after
he'd freshened up in the newly painted toilet, he came through to the
living-room to share a few wise words with us. As he preached he allowed
my sister to wash his feet in a basin, and sat on the newly upholstered stool
we'd borrowed from Uncle Joe and placed by the fire to keep his sacred
bottom warm while he addressed us. Initially he spoke in tongues but,
seeing our response, he soon began to speak normally. He had humility as
well as charity, Brother Peter, and didn't hesitate to demean himself by
switching from tongues to English. And of course, it was proper, formal
English, spoken with a proper accent and quite unlike our ill-educated,
colloquial, highly common form.

Brother Peter wasn't one to shirk manual labour either. Indeed, as he
spoke, he was happy enough to lift the poker hanging beside him on the
wall. We'd placed it level with his head to make it easy to reach, and he
dug into the flaming coals with an almost professional finesse and a
delicate, staccato prodding action. When he became too warm on one
side, we shifted the stool to the other side and he poked there. He
remained sitting on it while we did so and his eyes lit up brightly as he
was carried to and fro, so that for an unnerving moment they reminded
me of Alastair's eyes when he spoke about Hell. It was just a silly
coincidence.

My sister offered to dry Brother Peter's feet with her freshly
shampooed hair; he charitably declined, so instead she used the soft linen
towel we'd pawned my mother's wedding ring to buy. All done, she rose,
lifted the basin of scented water and went to fetch a tray of what Brother
Peter called 'venerable victuals' from the kitchen. When she returned, I
smiled proudly, seeing the crystal wineglass we'd borrowed from some

rich folks my aunt cleaned for. The tray also had a sterilised Lucozade bottle filled with fresh holy water, newly drawn from our local church font. It had our sole china side-plate on it, too, with some unleavened bread we'd obtained from an aunt in America.

Brother Peter quaintly referred to America as 'The New World'. Our aunt had sent the bread by registered post after my father had telegrammed her requesting it. We couldn't get it locally without going to a Jewish baker's and that wasn't really the done thing then – not by Catholics like us, or by Protestants either, for that matter. Anyway, this aunt was paying Brother Peter's seminary fees, so why keep the bread from his mouth, as it were, when she was willing to pay for him to become the token priest of the family?

Brother Peter took the unleavened bread and nibbled at it. Between nibbles, he told us that his other critical need food-wise was cornflakes. He took a full box every morning.

'And I take milk with them, too,' he said, 'goat's milk. But I take it from a separate bowl. It's a traditional custom, dating back to the days of Jesus himself.'

We already knew this. He'd forwarded a list of the various items required for his visit. It had been delivered by hand the previous week and cornflakes had featured prominently. He'd mentioned milk too, of course, but he hadn't stressed goat's milk, his mind being on far higher things. He wasn't fussy and didn't mind the brand we served, but he had to have cornflakes at least three times a day, and they had to be served in their own, separate dish and accompanied by a bowl of goat's milk. When he said this, my sister looked very concerned. I knew what was worrying her. Where in the name of goodness would she find goat's milk before morning? Her head turned to the window, in the general direction of the convent school. We'd both had the same thought. There was a nanny goat called Judy in there; she grazed in the convent grounds. She'd supply the milk, if we supplied the means to obtain it. My sister's gaze drifted off towards my brother. He was the least pious of us all and kept staring at Brother Peter with something like disbelief. When he caught my sister staring at *him*, however, it was more than disbelief I saw. He knew what she was thinking and his face turned red with anger at the very thought: him – a rock musician, used to playing a shiny guitar with a tremolo arm – playing around instead with a she-goat's dull, dried teats!

During his frugal meal, Brother Peter spoke to us about his favourite saints. He compared them all with himself and came out of it all quite favourably.

When we were certain he'd finished his first helping, my sister breathed out, her face quite radiant.

'Given all this coincidence of virtue, Brother Peter,' she said, 'don't you think you're possibly a saint yourself?'

He was horrified.

'Me? A saint! Oh goodness, no!' he said. 'It's much too soon for anyone to claim that.' He shrugged. 'But now you mention it . . . I suppose it's remotely possible I could be one some day – but not quite yet,' he said, as he surveyed us generously, his eyes warm and his smile even warmer. 'You see, to really be a saint,' he confided, 'you have to be able to levitate.'

'Levitate!' I parroted loudly, to the scandal of my family, who whispered harshly at me to tone it down a bit.

'Yes, levitate,' continued Brother Peter. 'To rise into the air unaided except by the hands of God. Like Saint Thomas Aquinas, Saint Teresa of Avila, Joseph of Cupertino, Sister Gemma Galgani and our contemporary ethereal flight master, Padre Peo,' he said, eyeballing us all and daring us to question this – which we didn't, though I briefly wondered if Fatty Spinner could levitate, but said nothing about it. 'And like Teresa Neumann too,' he went on. 'Teresa, a very sociable woman when you get to know her personally, has the stigmata, of course, but she levitates too, upwards and away.' His eyes fell closed at that and he was completely silent.

Apart from the crackling of the fire, you could have heard a pin drop. Instead, I heard a whining sound. It had come from somewhere outside and, as I looked around to see what was happening, I realised my brother must have slipped out unnoticed. The whining sounded like Judy the goat. He must have reached her by now and started work.

While we listened in total silence to Judy's whining, Brother Peter finally opened his eyes and finished off the remnants of his meal. He seemed to have moved upwards an inch or two, relative to the poker. I turned to my sister with a quizzical look on my face and saw she'd noticed this too.

'Don't say a word,' she whispered. 'You might negate it by the act of verbalising. Language dictates our reality. So say nothing and the reality we have will remain.'

I'd no idea what the heck she was talking about, but I didn't say a thing. Instead, I watched Brother Peter eating the second helping of his supper and decided all the effort we'd put into the meal was worth it. He was obviously enjoying it, so none of us minded having starved ourselves empty that day, the money we'd normally have spent on food being spent instead on the lavender water he preferred to wash in. As we collectively watched him finish his meal, my sister went through to the kitchen and brought back a fingerbowl and a warmed cloth. We were happy we'd taken the trouble to prepare these too. For it was a genuine and true pleasure, simply having someone as sacred and holy as he to attend to.

Brother Peter finally left us, with a grace and dignity in his movements that suggested he was indeed developing some sort of control over gravity, as I'd suspected but hadn't stated. We remained with our heads bowed for a few minutes more, ignoring the continued cries of Judy and contemplating all we'd just heard. At last we got off our knees, stood up and stretched a bit. We still didn't speak though, for that would have felt like sacrilege.

After a decent interval, I made my way to my room. As I passed Brother Peter's bedroom door, I heard a strange snapping sound and wondered what on earth it was. 'Snap! Snap! Snap!' it went, like a carpet-beater on linoleum. I stopped dead in my tracks, went onto my tiptoes and peered through the keyhole. I froze. Brother Peter was whipping himself. Snap! Snap! Snap! He was using the whip fairly gently, but it must have been pretty sore despite that. I wondered what the heck he was doing, but I didn't say a word to anyone. I didn't want to admit I'd been spying on my betters.

18

I slept well that night. My sister slept on the floor between my brother and me. He slept soundly too, as if he was absolutely done in after his struggles with Judy. I didn't ask what he'd done to her, but whatever it was, he'd returned earlier with a bucketful of goat's milk, which had been poured into the holy water font we kept in the kitchen for emergencies.

The next morning, to keep the bathroom free for Brother Peter, each of us took our turn washing in the kitchen sink and my brother and I hung around, staying clear of our bedroom, while my sister said her matins. After dressing, we drifted in procession into the living-room, where Brother Peter was sitting on his stool eating his cornflakes. I was delighted to see he had a bowl of fresh goat's milk beside him.

He looked up between mouthfuls.

'Good morning, brother, sister and younger brother.'

My brother fumed and said nothing, but my sister and I did.

'Good morning, Brother Peter,' we replied, as he licked at his spoon and brushed a cornflake away from his clerical collar.

His tone became solemn.

'I'm going to visit mother this morning. With a bit of help from God, I might be able to cure her. But don't build your hopes up. I haven't performed any really dramatic miracles for ages.'

'Don't worry, I won't,' I said, reaching for the cup of second-hand tea my sister had poured. We could only afford enough fresh tea for Brother Peter's use, so we drank what he left. It tasted foul, but I offered up the discomfort to God and I was certain Brother Peter would have lauded my act, had he known.

Later that morning, as I waited all alone for my school bus, with no one left to wave to me from the window, a small group of our neighbours gradually gathered behind me. I wondered what they were up to. Just before the bus arrived, another sleek taxi cab drew up and Brother Peter rushed out of the house past me, his long, dark, wool-and-mohair overcoat billowing out behind him in the chilly wind. I hoped he was warm enough, for it was freezing and I didn't want him catching a cold or anything. As he moved towards the car door, which the driver had opened, the neighbours applauded. Freezing myself, but proud of my Otherbrother's growing celebrity, I felt warm in my heart at least, and maybe just a little bit in my soul.

When I returned that afternoon my mother was home. She was sitting in a chair beside Brother Peter, who remained stoically on his stool beside the fire. I noticed he'd moved a little higher, as measured by the relative height of the poker against his skullcap, and thought I could discern a clear chink of light between his holy bottom and the top of Uncle Joe's stool. I didn't like to stare though, so I couldn't be certain. I was overjoyed to see my mum, and she me.

She hugged me.

'Hello, son, how are you?'

'I'm fine!' I cried, literally and figuratively.

'Oh, it's so good to see you again. Thank God! Yes, thank God . . . and Brother Peter,' she said, looking at her prodigal son. 'It might have been God's miracle that cured me, but it was Brother Peter's holiness that opened the channel through which it travelled.'

Brother Peter looked embarrassed.

'It was nothing! I've become a vehicle for God and I accept that humbly. Now, could I have another packet of cornflakes?' he asked, and I rushed off to get them, hoping there'd be enough goat's milk left until my brother could get another supply from the cantankerous Judy.

That evening after vespers, Brother Peter was taken for a night out by a group of notaries. They included the local bishop, the Lord Provost, a barrister from Uppertown and a representative from our relatively new Queen. This latter gentlemen had flown from somewhere down south in a jet plane of Her Majesty's fleet. He'd explained that while the Queen couldn't quite make it in person that evening, she would when Brother Peter was ordained, and it was appropriate for royalty to mix in public with the cream of Roman Catholic society.

These important men had arrived to pick up my Otherbrother in a limousine; the chauffeur, I noted, looked suspiciously like Bandage Boy from years ago. I wondered a bit at that, for if it really were him, why would he reappear after all these years? It was almost as if there were a limited number of people around to delegate jobs to.

With the exception of my brother, we were delighted to see my Otherbrother go off with such an elegant crowd of people, and as we watched – hiding behind a curtain in case they saw us – we felt very proud of him indeed.

The crowd outside had grown larger throughout the day. They bumped and jostled Brother Peter as he made his way out to be met by the Bishop himself. They'd obviously heard about my mother's cure and wanted a laying-on of hands of some sort, but when the Bishop extended his bejewelled hand to an old woman who had more than her fair share of head hair – 'overhead hirsutism', my sister called it – she shrank back.

Avoiding the pastoral hand, she made a bolt for Brother Peter. And as the Bishop looked on in amazement, Brother Peter touched her scalp and it changed immediately. The woman ran off praising the Lord to the skies and also, of course, Brother Peter. Watching from the window, I noticed her scalp was covered with eczema. I'd seen enough of that at school to diagnose it even if I'd been an albino.

When we'd made certain it was safe to emerge from our hiding place, my mother asked if I'd tidy up Brother Peter's room as a bit of extra penance in case I ever needed it. I agreed gladly and so, taking my shoes off and washing my hands very carefully, I made my way to his bedroom door and opened it. The room seemed neat enough, so I thought it might be a good idea if I tidied up his trunks a bit. I went to the one marked 'Religious and Miscellaneous Books' and raised the lid. It was full of books as it said, but the one on top didn't seem very religious. I'd made progress at school and could read well by now. The book was called *Onanism* and it was by a doctor called Samuel Tissot. I started to flick through it, and the time flew by.

By the time I'd finished, the entire house was quiet. Everyone – except

Brother Peter, who hadn't returned yet – had gone to bed, as they had an early rise for matins again. They'd obviously forgotten all about me, but I wasn't worried; the book was fascinating reading.

Doctor Tissot explained that an act he referred to as 'masturbation' was not to be recommended, saying it had ' . . . so great an influence upon corporeal powers and upon perfect digestion that the loss of an ounce of this humour would weaken more than that of forty ounces of blood . . . '

'Forty ounces of blood?' I thought. It seemed a heck of a lot.

Apparently one man had done this masturbation thing so frequently his brain had dried up and ended up rattling in his pericranium, whatever that was. Riveting as it was, I'd no idea whatsoever what all this stuff meant. I tried to think of someone who would know – and I thought immediately of Siggy. I'd come to know Siggy better by now and we'd have brief chats in the Emergency Room while I waited for my pills. A former patient of his – a mentally handicapped girl with a phobia about becoming normal – had told me he'd studied psychoanalysis as an infant, and knew all sorts of things the rest of us didn't.

'Don't worry, you can tell him anything. He's seen and heard it all,' she said, and I believed her. Though he still had little time for Al and Billy, for some reason. Once I'd moved to P.H. 5 he said he'd help me out if ever I needed advice. Well, I needed advice now OK, so I decided to ask him for it.

As I thought about this, I noticed that a few pages from an old copy of *The Boy Scout Handbook of 1925* had been slipped into my Otherbrother's bigger book. I read those avidly now, too: 'In the body of every boy who has reached his teens, the Creator of the Universe has sown . . . the most wonderful material in all the physical world. Some parts of it find their way into the blood, and through the blood give tone to the muscles, power to the brain and strength to the nerves.'

This was incredible! If I could get my hands on this stuff, I could distribute it throughout the school and treat all and sundry. In fact, if I could get my hands on lots and lots of it, I could distribute it all around the world and cure everybody of everything! I felt like shouting, 'COME AND GET IT! COME AND GET IT!' But I didn't. For I'd no idea how you got hold of it, what it was, or how you made it. That was the problem with stuff like that. Where did it come from? How could I get my sweaty little hands on it?

I continued reading. 'This fluid is the sex fluid . . . any habit . . . a boy has that causes this fluid to be discharged . . . tends to weaken his strength, to make him less able to resist disease.'

'Disease!' I almost shouted that out loud, so great was my excitement.

This fluid, whatever it was, could cure disease – the book virtually said so. I applied logic and reason. If losing the fluid made you ill, then getting it would make you well. Simple! Again I searched my mind. How could I get hold of the stuff? The book had said it was called 'sex fluid'. What in the name of goodness was sex fluid? I decided to ask Siggy outright. He'd know, and he was the only person I'd ever heard mention the word 'sex' before. Siggy was always going on about sex-this, sex-that and sex-the-next-thing. So I decided I'd speak to him first thing Monday morning. Meanwhile, I'd get on and tidy up my Otherbrother's trunks.

As I proceeded to do so, I discovered yet another piece of paper. This one was pasted inside a Scout Book, and it had a neatly written heading on it: 'Prophylaxis of Masturbatory Insanity'.

Under this, there was a list of foods recommended to prevent this insanity developing in the first place. And two items down, right after 'mealy flour', and 'graham crackers', were – would you believe? . . . 'goat's milk' and 'cornflakes'!

'CORNFLAKES,' it repeated, and written underneath in bold red ink: 'Any Brand'.

I slammed the lid of the trunk and looked around. I looked at the door, the bed, the wardrobe, at the room itself. I listened carefully for any sound. There was none. That list had provided me with food for thought, and I wanted to ruminate in solitude. First, however, I had to open the other trunk, the one labelled 'Sacred Toys, Games, Novelties and Amusements'. I just had to see what it contained, as I suspected that it, too, might hold a surprise. I leaned over, grabbed the handle and opened it.

On top lay the whip. It was lying on top of box after box of model aeroplane kits. Many of these were still in their original wrapped boxes, but those that were already assembled had been put together in the shape of crucifixes instead of aeroplanes and their little pilots had been nailed onto them with tiny metal nails! One of them had been assembled in the form of an 'X' shape; the shape of the cross of Saint Andrew, the not-very-intellectual patron saint of Scotland!

I made a mental note of it all. Then I gently closed the lid and slunk off to my bedroom. I went in and trod carefully above the face of my sleeping sister. She looked serene but tired out – emaciated, I imagined, by fasting.

I got into my bed, crept under the sheet and wondered what exactly I'd stumbled upon. As my head touched the pillow, I heard a noise outside; it sounded like a car door closing. Hearing voices, I got up again and crept under the closed curtain to look.

It was Brother Peter returning. He'd just emerged from the limousine that had taken him away earlier and the chauffeur was holding the car door open and saluting. Again I suspected it was Bandage Boy and, odd as it sounds, he didn't seem to have aged much. When Brother Peter stepped onto the pavement, shouts of joy went up as a large crowd flocked towards him. They'd been waiting in total silence outside our home, and now he'd arrived there was uproar.

My sister woke.

'Is it time for matins already?'

I shook my head.

'No, it's just Brother Peter being mobbed by a crowd,' I said as my brother woke too and joined me at the window.

'I've had enough of that wanker,' he said bitterly.

I looked at him.

'Why's that?'

'Because he's a phoney! Miracles, my bum! Look!' He was holding what looked like a bit of Judy's underside. 'It's a wig! I found it on the path earlier this evening. It fell off that old woman's head. She thought her chronic hairiness was cured, but it was just her wig all along. Chronic hairiness – crap! She's been a hypochondriac for years; she used to complain about baldness and eczema, then she got a wig and began to complain about being too hairy. Miracles my backside. He's a phoney!'

In Scotland, as in other action-directed places, when someone has attacked another person unexpectedly, we say they 'went for him'.

My sister went for him.

'He's no phoney! You pernicious heretic!' she yelled as she kneed my brother in the groin, then crushed it hard with her hand.

He fell.

'You're nothing but a piece of frustrated nunnery,' he cried. 'You should be wearing a crusty old nunnish habit!'

'And you won't indulge any more in *your* crusty habit!' she cried back. 'You'll never masturbate in this house again! You dirty, filthy sex-fluid generator. I've had enough of washing your seed from your sheets and pillowslips. You disgust me, you filthy, rotten Onanist!'

'Onanist!' 'Seed!' 'Sex fluid!' 'Masturbate!' The words trickled through me like an iron tonic. So *they* knew about it! Had I once again been left out of things, even within the bosom of my family? Was I once more being excluded from deep and solemn secrets? I wondered about this, as I saw my sister grab my brother's hair to keep him in place. He'd managed to kneel, but his eyes were shut, his face tense and he was cupping his private parts gently. If you'd missed the beginning, you'd have thought he was praying with his hands too far down.

'He's no phoney,' she snarled, as my brother continued to cup manfully what I'd once accidentally heard him call his 'balls'.

My sister was raging.

'He's developing the stigmata too,' she shouted. 'I found proof when I was washing his clothes. There were drops of blood on his gloves, his socks, in the rim of his hat and on the right side of his shirt. That's the side Our Lord had pierced by the spear of the centurion Longinus!'

My brother bravely managed a faint 'Crap!' and I stared at my sister in wonder as her voice hit a supernatural high.

'I watched him when he came out of his bath too!' she went on. 'Oh, it may be wrong, but I looked anyway. And I could see the marks on his brow, hands, feet and side!'

My brother was a sort of grey colour by now: pasty.

'Bollocks!' he grunted, and she tugged his hair harder.

'He's starting to levitate, too!' she cried, looking to me for agreement, but I didn't commit myself.

'He's still a wanker,' groaned my brother, as his eyes flooded with tears of hate, humiliation and pain.

'And so are you, you quasi-potent fornicator!' shouted my sister, looking wonderful to me – Saint Joan of Arc at the siege of Orleans. 'And I've seen plenty of proof of that, my boy, every time I've fed your autoerotically starched washing through the CheapStain wringer. Even Kleenitoff doesn't touch those disgusting, sinful stains you make. I'm amazed you're still able to walk at all with your underpants on, you pathetic mobile starch pad!'

As my brother let out his longest groan yet, I looked out of the window again. The crowd had formed into a conga line and were dancing off into the night, holding small, lighted candles and singing some hymn or other. As I took in this singular scene, I gasped at something I thought I saw there – something I wouldn't have imagined in my wildest dreams. I heard the noise of the downstairs door closing. It was Brother Peter coming back, stigmata and all. I thanked God I hadn't been discovered in his bedroom, and I rushed back to bed and under the sheets, while my brother still groaned quietly on the floor. As I lay there, I groaned too – inside, for I was shaken to the core.

I could have sworn I'd seen Alastair amongst the crowd; sworn I'd seen him turn his face towards Brother Peter in the glare of the lamplight. And that face had looked lighter to me – lighter than I'd ever seen it! I was certain it was him, and I was equally certain he'd been talking to another boy, a boy who seemed to be enchanting Al with his wit and volubility. It had been *Martin*, for God's sake. And he'd been rabbiting on like some witty, erudite and privately educated sage!

19

Having made an appointment with Siggy through some well-connected contacts in M.H. 2, and having sent him a brief family history by messenger, I spoke with him formally after lunch. Alastair had been absent from school that day and Billy had to leave early for a visit to the cardiac clinic. Accordingly, Siggy was allowed to keep me company in the Rest Room. The powers-that-be no longer pretended we went in there to sleep any more, and accepted that a rest was every bit as useful when we had a bit of company, and often much better.

The song playing on the neighbouring school's radio was 'Memories Are Made Of This' and Siggy, who didn't approve of things like radios, sat on a chair he'd placed at the top of my bed, where I couldn't see him. As I lay and spoke to him, I could hear him sucking at the liquorice he had permanently in his mouth while he took notes in an old school jotter and made appropriate noises to encourage me. I told him everything. About us borrowing things for Brother Peter's arrival, about my sister washing his feet and his clothes, about the miracles with my mother, Martin and Alastair, the levitation, the Airmake kits, the book on Onanism, the cornflakes, the Scout manual, my confusion about masturbation – everything! I held nothing back, except the fact I'd pretended I'd been drinking fresh tea, instead of the stuff I was really drinking. I'd lied about that by omission and I felt too guilty to even mention it. It all poured out in a haemorrhage of confusion, and Siggy carefully applied the psychological tourniquet. As I spoke, I began to feel I loved him. I wanted to buy him gifts – anything: a cigar perhaps, some personal trinket just from me he could keep as a memento of our session.

He listened until I was quite finished, then sat where I could see him. He spoke.

'I'm actually Jewish,' he began. 'I pretend to be a sort of Waspish Christian, which is better for my family and me as things now stand. As such, I don't believe a word of any of that mystical crap, but for the moment just you pretend I do. It's the way I work,' he said. 'Is that OK?'

I nodded.

'Fine by me,' I whispered, sobbing a bit, but calmer now.

'Good! Well, your mother may have had a catharsis.'

'A what?'

'A catharsis: a sudden and seemingly spontaneous resolution of her emotional problems. The fact your brother visited her in hospital possibly made her well, in and of itself. It was a necessary and sufficient condition for spontaneous and immediate cure.'

I thought about that and wondered what it meant. It certainly sounded good.

'How come?'

'She'd just lost her daughter – your dead sister. That's when she went totally thumb-suckin' crazy, you see. So she may have been worried she'd lose her favourite son too.'

That shocked me.

'Favourite son!'

'Symbolically, of course. He's clever, attractive, well-educated and healthy. These are all symbols of worthiness for life – socially sanctioned conditions, and preconditions for deserving being and existence. No wonder she felt that way; it's not as if she didn't love you perfectly equally. In her own way that is.'

'I see,' I said, feeling better about it. 'But he isn't ill. In fact he cures illnesses.'

'So you say, so you say,' intoned Siggy. 'But she may have worried about losing him to another woman.'

'Another woman!'

'To Mother Church,' he said, seeing my incredulity. 'Not consciously, mind you, but unconsciously.'

'But she was wide awake when – '

He interrupted.

'I don't mean she was literally unconscious. We can't be too literal here, and it's a waste of my time and yours if you think we can be. Just take my word for it – trust me.'

'I do,' I said quietly, and I think he smiled.

'Anyway,' he continued, 'in such an event, just seeing your Otherbrother could have cured her. I've seen it happen before, you know.'

'You have?'

'Yes, often. Now, let's take a fresh look at these so-called miracles. Martin I know about. Jason sees me on a regular basis about a problem he has. He's a neighbour of Martin's, as you know, and Martin has improved by leaps and bounds since he started his residential school and his father came back – loaded, as it happens – to live with him and his mother.'

'Oh good!' I cried, 'I must tell my mum!'

'Quite,' said Siggy. 'Anyway, that accounts for Martin, if he were indeed as voluble, animated and socially interactive as you say he was.'

'He was. I'm absolutely certain he was.'

Siggy brought his chair round and sat beside me.

'Of course he was; social mutes become garrulous all the time. So that's him dealt with; now there's Alastair. You said he'd become white or something.'

'He had! I saw the lamplight reflecting from his face.'

'Of course he had. He's been a blue baby from birth, has a chronic, inoperable cardiac condition causing irrevocable dermal cyanosis; there's never been a spontaneous case of reversal of his condition in the history of medicine, so of course he was white. And here's how it happened. His mother tried to conjure up the spirit of Doctor John Dee.'

'Was he from the cardiac clinic?'

'No. He was an eccentric polymath from Elizabethan England. He was a magician, an ambassador and an intellectual, and he had a fairly decent life until he got caught up with some Irish type called Kelley.'

'Oh.'

'Anyway, Al's mother thought he might be able to help out with Al's heart condition, which is refractory to conventional treatment as I've said – including, I might add, psychoanalysis.'

'I see,' I said, 'and . . .'

'Well, I'm an atheist myself,' admitted Siggy, 'a dyed-in-the-wool Marxist. But word on the street is she got her ritual wrong or something, and instead of Doctor Dee she conjured up the Devil.'

'Never!'

'Yes – daft, isn't it? Anyway, it seems Alastair turned white the moment he saw him.'

'I see . . .'

Siggy took a slow, deep breath and nibbled on his liquorice.

'Admittedly that doesn't explain why he was smiling. That *is* a problem, whatever dynamic I use. But a white face? It explains that,' he said. 'How do you think you would look if you suddenly came face to face with the Devil, eh?'

I nodded and said nothing.

'They've taken him to hospital to try and make him cyanosed again. Being white isn't good for that boy, apparently. It might mess up their textbooks and we can't have that.'

'Goodness me! Who'd believe it?'

'Quite. Now this Onanism business, the Boy Scout book and the cornflakes, I'd rather leave for the present; come back, if you want, in a few years' time when you're more . . . well, developed.

'But what I can say is that some young men have certain habits, and that twenty years ago it was believed by some doctors – including this Doctor Tissot – that graham biscuits and goat's milk could cure these habits. According to them cornflakes could too; indeed, that's why cornflakes were invented in the first place. Did you know that?'

'Never!' I said. 'Goodness me ...'

'Oh, it's absolutely true,' said Siggy. 'But very few cerealphiles actually know it. It's true, OK: cross my heart and hope to die,' he went on, crossing it, though he hadn't finished on that topic yet.

He spread his arms wide.

'Myself? I think these habits are healthy enough in frequent moderation. But that's not a general view, and certainly not one held by the Catholic Church. So be aware of that in a few years' time too. I'll say absolutely no more about it for now.' He looked at me carefully to see how I was reacting.

I was fine, but inquisitive.

'And the Airmake models?'

Siggy smiled.

'A classic paraphilia. An immediate, putative, post-war, guilt-driven obsessional neurosis, whereby sublimation of the Thanatos instinct finds erotic manifestation in a quasi-metaphysical earth-spirit symbol, namely the crucifix. That latter, of course, lies more in archetypal realms than I, as a Freudian, am comfortable with. But I think it explains it all, all right. I hope that's all right. All right?' he asked, and I nodded.

'You see, while the collective unconscious of the rest of us is still reeling from the material decimation of World War Two, Brother Peter is repressing these guilt-ridden feelings and projecting them onto Airmake models.'

I beamed at him.

'That's incredible, Sig! Incredible'.

'It's nothing – just a touch of modest brilliance. The main thing is: does that explanation help you?'

'Oh, yes! Of course it helps – especially that bit about Thanatos. I suspected it myself.'

'Of course you did.'

'But what about the levitation?' I asked.

Siggy sounded very pleased with himself.

'The answer to that one lies with your Uncle Joe.'

'Uncle Joe?'

'Yes. He has a drink problem, I believe, if I recall your family history correctly.'

That upset me.

'No, he hasn't! He enjoys the odd glass of beer now and then, mainly at Christmas or a wedding, that sort of thing. It isn't a *problem*. He has no *problem* with it.'

'Are you certain?'

'Of course I'm certain. He's my uncle! He's a social drinker: at the weekend, Friday, Saturday, Sunday, that's all. The odd Monday if it is or isn't a Bank Holiday, the rest of the week if it is, or isn't, snowing, and never before seven or eight in the evening.'

'"The weekend"? "Seven or eight in the evening"?'

I moved about a bit to loosen up.

'Well, he has one or two more than he should on occasion, before or after work, before he goes out or when he comes in. Then he'll have perhaps an aperitif at lunchtime, a digestif after breakfast and dinner . . . but who doesn't? I mean . . .'

Siggy picked up my case notes and read from them:

'According to your own account, he's a "raving dipso with a thirst a post-modernist would call hyperalcoholic".'

I nodded.

'Yes. He is.'

'Right. Anyway, I thought about it all this morning, after you'd spoken to me about the general history.'

'And?'

'And the stool he lent you was probably made from an old bucket. I bet he's covered it with half-decent material and put a cork top on it,' he said, to my astonishment. 'But inside,' he went on, 'I'll bet you a Scots pound to a shekel it contains an illicit brew of beer. He forgot to remove the beer when he lent the stool to your family, and it's now fermenting and pushing the top up. Brother Peter isn't levitating, Francis. He's being pushed hard on the bum by a giant cork which is itself being pushed up by a bucketload of gas under enormous pressure.'

I could barely believe it.

'Amazing!'

'Isn't it just?' said Siggy.

'You're a genius.'

'I know. Great, isn't it?'

'So what about the stigmata?'

He frowned.

'Does your Otherbrother shift the stool around from one side of the fireplace to the other?'

'Yes – well, we do it for him. If there's a draught from the door he'll sit on the other side, so we move it around to accommodate him.' I began to get the thrust of Siggy's logic. 'I see,' I said. 'So moving the stool about causes the redness somehow.' I thought about it. 'I know! He's allergic to beer vapour! When we move him the beer swills around and gives off a vapour that reddens the skin on his hands!'

Siggy looked amused.

'Nice try, but no. He gets the marks from using both hands to push the poker back and forth into the fire. It's classic bilateral masturbatory emulation. He pushes the poker in with his palms – it's more fun that way because it generates more heat – and that causes localised palmar redness.'

'Good grief,' I said. 'And the feet?'

'Kleenitoff soap powder in the water your sister uses to wash them in. It's a common additive for menial washing work amongst the lower classes, so that's consistent. But she doesn't know it causes localised erythema in the soles of the feet of a better class of person like your Otherbrother.'

'And the marks on his side?'

Siggy thought for a moment.

'You don't happen to have a CheapStain wringer at home, do you?'

'Yes, we do.'

'Then that's it!'

'What's it?'

'CheapStain wringers have a red manufacturer's motif on the front. It leaks a red dye that stains your right side if you put Catholic clerical shirts and collars through them immediately after a pair of striped pyjamas and a couple of overstarched handkerchiefs.'

'It does?'

'Yes.'

'Really?'

Sig seemed defensive.

'Can you think of something better?'

'No, of course not, it's just –'

'Well, then . . .'

'So that explains it,' I said.

'Except for the marks around his head,' said Siggy despondently. 'I can't get my own head around that one at all.'

I felt useful.

'Well, that's no problem.'

'Why not?'

'I thought I'd told you.'

'Told me what?'

'After he whips himself . . .'

'Yes?'

'Well, he sticks a crown of thorns on top of his pate and batters it down with a hammer.'

Siggy considered that carefully.

'Yes, that might explain it.'

'It does; it's all explained!' I smiled. 'So what's your conclusion? Be as detailed as you like – I'm used to it by now and can follow the technical stuff.'

'Fine, I shall be.'

'Good!'

'I think Brother Peter is a wanker,' said Siggy. 'He's suffering from masturbatory dementia.'

'"Masturbatory dementia"? The book called it "masturbatory insanity".'

'It's a variant; student priests get it,' he explained quickly.

'So what can we do for him?'

'That's quite another matter. I'm not a religious man, as I've said, but I'd recommend an exorcist.'

'An exorcist? One of those priests that cast out devils?'

'The very same, yes. Better safe than sorry, I always think. It's worth a try – anything's worth a try when there's a devil in your home, whether it's a real one, a symbolic one or a human copycat. Though given some of the people I see professionally, I sometimes fail to appreciate the distinction.'

I thought about it. An exorcism wasn't easy. There were formalities to be followed; official channels, that sort of thing. Could we really approach the bishop for permission to cast out a demon, if all that was wrong was masturbatory dementia?

Siggy saw my confusion.

'You get a suitably qualified priest to do a homer,' he said.

'A homer?'

'Yes – quietly done, off the record. Pay in cash, no more said.'

'Do you have someone in mind?' I asked.

He nodded.

'Ammabig.'

'"Ammabig"?'

'Yes. Nothing wrong with that, is there?'

'No, not really.'

'Ah, you want me to explain it. You've caught the bug – analysing everything: where did a name like that come from? Well, when this particular priest was born, he had acute postnatal Oedipal vocalisation syndrome. After taking first breath, he cried out "Big Mamma!". The name stuck, but for practical purposes on the domestic front, they decided to drop a letter and shake it all around a bit, like "Oh, Hokey Cokey Cokey!"'

Siggy spun in place as he sang this, and I wondered what had attracted him towards assisting the mentally ill, the deranged and the totally mad in the first place.

'Really?' I said.

'Yes, really. They were a cultured family too, all things considered, so they decided to call him after an eccentric, and what you might term "Jasonic", Irish writer also.'

'Oh?'

'Yes! The priest's full name is Ammabig Wilde Savage. He's a White Father and a friend of my uncle's – the one who's become Catholic to get on.'

This coincidence amazed and almost frightened me. Again, like the apparent reappearance of Bandage Boy, it was as if there were a limited number of people who kept reappearing in my life.

'We all have to escape our stereotypes at times,' Siggy went on, 'and we shall do until the never-to-come day when we all get along in a manner that celebrates our diversities. Anyway, Ammabig does a very good line in exorcisms, and he just happens to be visiting our town at present.'

'I know; I've met him,' I said wistfully, as Siggy stared hard at me.

'He's a first-rate and relatively inexpensive exorcist, but he's a very good blues singer too,' he said, and I nodded my agreement.

The small nurse appeared at the door of the Rest Room right on time. She came in and inspected us.

'No Alastair today,' she said. 'He's at the hospital: some accident or other, so I heard.'

She looked at Siggy.

'Well, at least *you're* looking better, Billy. A bit of proper colour in your cheeks for once. I don't know what you've done exactly, but you should do it more often.'

'Thanks,' said Siggy.

As they said, he'd seen and heard it all.

20

I was watching from my bedroom window when Father Savage arrived by cab. It stopped outside our house and he climbed out and closed the door himself. He had on a coat and hat and was carrying a small suitcase. His shadow fell long behind him in the lamplight and he hesitated a few moments, looking around and penetrating the darkness with his big white eyes. Then with a sudden surge of what may have been either confidence or resignation, he walked up our path. I heard him knock at the door and as he did so, a howl filled the night. It was Judy! She hadn't been milked for three consecutive days now and she was letting us know all about it.

My parents had gone off to make a novena at church, so my sister went to let Father Savage in. Siggy was already in the living-room making preparations, so I left him to it and raced through to Brother Peter's bedroom. My brother had strapped him to the bed in preparation for Father Savage's arrival and was currently stapling my Otherbrother's mouth shut with a staple-gun.

I intervened.

'Good grief! What are you doing?'

He had a crazy smile on his face.

'I'm closing the seven orifices on his head. That way no evil spirits can get in.'

'Don't be crazy! The idea is to get them out! Leave him alone!'

He considered this for a moment, then snapped a staple into Brother Peter's ear lobe, making him screech.

'Why did you do that?' I yelled.

'Because I hate the hypocritical sod and I wanted to hurt him!'

I took his point.

'Fair enough, but don't do it again.'

'Fine,' he said reluctantly, moving away and placing the stapler on the bedside table as Father Savage came into the room with my sister and Siggy.

Father Savage looked round.

'Please leave us alone,' he said, not recognising me from school, and engaging Brother Peter with his full attention. 'This should present no problem, but please leave and close the door firmly behind you.'

'Yes, Father,' we echoed as we went out, leaving him and Siggy to it.

We remained outside, listening. None of us wanted to sneak a look while there were others present, so none of us did. What we did do, however, was listen to Father Savage's voice intoning a special prayer. He did this in an odd, commanding tone, and it was pretty scary at the time. The prayer began in a mainstream populist vein – a sort of generic common prayer. There were some good two-point vocal harmonies, with Siggy hot on falsetto, and my brother and I began to tap our feet, to the disapproval of my sister. It was catchy, so why shouldn't we?

Anyway, it soon became evident that this was no common prayer after all. As they would say on the radio, it went like this:

> In obedience to the Immaculate Conception
> I command you,
> Every unclean spirit to depart
> Cease your attacks on me
> And upon all for whom I pray.
> And in the name of Jesus
> I command you into the deep pit.

There was total silence, followed by some further muttering by Father Savage. Then there was a loud shout, a crying sound and a sudden shriek, followed by yet another odd noise – one I'd never heard anything like before. It was similar to the sound raindrops make when they fall hard and fast against a window, but it was a great deal louder than that and a lot sharper too, like popcorn popping.

The door creaked slowly open and Father Savage's face emerged. He was wearing something round his neck that looked like a small, fancy scarf. When I looked closer however, I saw it was too thin to be a scarf. Whatever it was, he was using it to wipe the sweat from his wide, black brow.

'You can come in,' he said softly. 'It's over.'

We grinned at each other and shook hands briefly. I jumped with joy a bit and we followed him back into the bedroom.

Brother Peter was lying on the bed with the straps undone. He'd been crying and his face was red, but he looked composed enough, all considered. Siggy was standing at the foot of the bed stroking his chin and contemplating something in that abstract way of his. He was in the process of unwrapping a fresh liquorice stick. But what gripped my attention was the fact that the room was filled with something I didn't quite recognise. There were hundreds of pieces of a golden, leaf-like substance everywhere. They lay over the carpet, the bed, the trunks and the table. I picked one up and examined it. Cornflakes!

Father Savage spoke.

'He threw these up at the very end,' he said solemnly. 'You probably heard him. Cereals are no damned good for that sort of thing, anyway,' he added, in general terms, pointing towards my Otherbrother's private parts. 'So he doesn't have to eat them any more.'

Perhaps because I was the youngest, or perhaps because I'd seen my brother pick up the stapler again, I made my way protectively over to Brother Peter.

'How are you, Brother Peter?' I asked, and he looked up at me exhausted. His eyes were filled with the woes of the world, but he managed a weak smile.

'I'm fine,' he gasped. 'It's going to be all right. And, by the way . . .'

'Yes?'

'Call me Pete,' he said. 'After that lot, this Brother Peter lark's over for good.'

21

Perhaps because of all these mysterious goings on, I began to develop an interest in science; for it seemed to me that if any of us were to escape our genetic destinies, it might be through the application of scientific principles, rather than by accepting our fates were irrevocably determined by God's will and investing hope in ever-seductive miracles. 'God helps those who help themselves,' they say; and you can't expect Him to do all the work. I hadn't totally given up on religion, however, and the prospect of a visit to Lourdes to find an instant cure was still one I eagerly anticipated – if the money could be found. But I now saw science as an adjunct to miraculous intervention and decided to add it to my list of things to study, in addition to my continuing pursuits in the area of popular music. So, using an old, two-volume American dictionary – the only really serious books we could afford to have at home – I entered the world of microscopes, test tubes, electric generators and magnets. Though the only one of those I could actually get my hands on was a magnet.

I mentioned my interest in magnets to my godfather, who was an electrician. A few days later – and just two days before he was killed when an ambulance ploughed into him – he paid us a visit and brought along a bar magnet, a solid-state battery and a length of electrical wire. He gave me a demonstration of the principles of magnetism by putting a few pins, some paper clips and a couple of small nails onto the kitchen table and sliding the magnet towards them. They jumped across and stuck to it and I was delighted. I thought action at a distance like this was very exciting, though my brother said he'd seen it all before from centre stage and it didn't impress him. My godfather told us that if the wire were wrapped around the magnet and an electric current from the battery passed through it, it would become even stronger. He proceeded to show us how to do that too. With my brother's unenthusiastic assistance, I did what he'd suggested – and the magnet indeed became stronger. The nails, paper clips and pins fairly flew across to it, and I was mightily impressed both by the magnet and the methods of science.

When I was preparing for school next morning, I saw the magnet still lying on the kitchen table. It had been left there overnight, attached to the battery, and lying there in the morning light it looked very powerful indeed. I decided to show it to Alastair and Billy, so I put it in my pocket and brought it into school.

By then most of us had moved on a class or so and we had Miss Tartankilty as our teacher. She was an old-fashioned Highland Scot, of the type the Roman historian Tacitus despaired of because, as he said of their tribes, 'By fighting individually, they were collectively defeated.' So even back then the Scots found it difficult to get along with one another.

I was sitting behind a girl I didn't know yet, though I'd been told she was a northerner herself and had been in Miss Tartankilty's class for seven years. I'd smiled at her as I walked to my desk, but she'd ignored me completely. I must have bored her stiff, I felt, because I noticed her eyes dim as I passed and she flickered her eyelids in a very un-Christian way in an attempt to be dismissive. This girl was large by any standards; she wore two XXL callipers and had a small mobile crane beside her, to enable her to move around whenever she felt like it. Accordingly, her legs stuck out from beneath her reinforced desk, as straight as the freshly painted girders on the Forth Bridge. By the look of things, she was yet another run-of-the-mill polio victim, but one never quite knew with certainty what was wrong with some of these kids, as I'd discovered to my cost on a number of occasions.

As was traditional, Billy and Al sat on either side of me. Billy's eyes were glinting with mischief as usual. I'd already told him about the magnet, and as soon as I produced it he opened his desk and fished out a large iron nail. He'd told one of the newer boys his father had given it to him from his ironmonger's shop, so the myth that he had a living family persisted – in his own mind, if not in ours. Siggy, who had graduated by now to wearing pince-nez and affecting a well-trimmed goatee beard, had told me Billy needed this fantasy to function properly. Perhaps he did, and for our part we never said anything to dissuade him from it.

Alastair, as ever, looked very concerned indeed when Billy produced the nail. Billy explained it was one of those used by the Romans to hang Jesus and to keep him still on the cross while he was painfully and sadistically crucified.

While that in itself probably didn't concern Al a great deal – he'd heard worse from the clergy, I'm sure – he told me his mother had a part of each of those nails in a collection of relics she'd amassed over the years.

Accordingly, he'd sensibly reasoned that if she had parts of all four nails used to crucify Our Saviour, what in the name of God was Billy doing with a complete one?

When we'd all settled down, Miss Tartankilty went to the gramophone she kept on her desk. As we'd entered it had been playing as usual, but now that the lesson was about to commence she lifted up the sapphire-needle arm and turned the machine off. The drone of her scratchy, seventy-eight rpm recording of a lone piper playing 'Scotland the Brave' fell silent. I'd never actually seen the record at close quarters and I wasn't so sure it was on a commercial label. But Al assured me it had been recorded by HMV many years ago, though I wasn't sure about that either.

With the class silent, I removed the magnet from my pocket and stretched over to hand it to Billy. As I did so, the left leg of the big girl in front gave a slight jerk and I pulled the magnet back again. She stayed still and unresponsive and I tried again, moving the magnet carefully this time, holding it higher for clearance and easing it ever so slowly in Billy's direction.

There was another jerk, and the same left leg, of the same big girl, rose up into the air and bent slowly backwards towards the magnet. I panicked! I tried to pull it back before any further attraction took place, but her leg bent at right angles to her thigh, then, ever so slowly, followed the magnet. In full and complete shock, and wanting nothing further to do with it, I tossed it over to Billy, who caught it neatly. 'Good shot!' he whispered, fingering his iron nail, which I desperately hoped *had* come from the Cross, as I started to pray fervently to the warm, caring Jesus I'd so foolishly tried to edge out via the harsh, cold methods of science.

This time *both* of the big girl's legs shot out from the sides of her chair and she began to move back towards Billy and the magnet in a slow, precise motion. Her legs suddenly shot inwards and she was pulled under her desk and along the floor. He looked at her in amazement, and then at the magnet. Quickly realising what was happening, he stuck it into his desk and closed the lid hard to shield it. Meanwhile, Alastair – having duly meditated no doubt on the fact that the dog pictured on HMV labels was sitting on its master's coffin, listening with ear cocked to the old fellow's disembodied tones – had made the connection between the girl and the iron nail, but not with the magnet. His face was a picture of terror, and if that selfsame dog had suddenly jumped off his master's coffin and barked at him, he couldn't have been more scared.

Despite the magnet being shielded by Billy's desk lid, the big, heavy girl gradually slid towards Billy, rose up from the floor in the slowest of motions and fell on top of his desk. His legendary composure broke into fragments. In a panic, he began to shake the desk to break the magnetic attraction and get her off. She, in turn, began to shake with it, cradling it beneath her like a protective mother whale. With a shriek, he jumped back and his face paled to a sort of diluted magenta colour.

'What'll we do?' cried Billy, as Miss Tartankilty and everyone else looked over and took in the scene with surprised and excited eyes. 'She'll be dragged into the desk and smothered!' he yelled, as he pushed his small blue hands under the girl's bosom and tried to pull her further onto the top of the desk to keep it shut. I was wide-eyed with fear myself, and Alastair was openly praying to the person he now doubted had been crucified with the nails his mother had bits of.

In one of those flashes they call 'eureka moments', I suddenly realised magnets had a field that spread well beyond them. This, however, presented even worse possibilities! So I dropped under my desk and quickly looked at all the callipered legs I could find. There were loads of them and I made an instant appraisal of where they were in relation to Billy's desk and thus to the magnet. None of them was moving, however: it was obviously a local effect. I didn't know then magnetic forces followed an inverse-square law, so I needn't really have worried about a flurry of polio victims being dragged screaming towards Billy's desk and the offending magnet.

By now Miss Tartankilty was at the big girl's side. She put her arms round her neck and began to pull. Still the magnet held her and despite my continuing terror I was amazed at its power. It had certainly moved the paper clips and the small nails, but I'd never even suspected anything like this could happen. My face became grim. We should never have left it attached to the battery overnight! I'd noted that, despite my terror, there was a trace of objectivity in my assessment of the situation. Like Al, I may have been praying for it to end, but unlike him, I imagine, I knew it wouldn't until we got the magnet out of the desk, out of the class and away from the girl. The only other option I could see involved getting the girl off the desk, out of the class and away from the magnet.

Irrespective of all that was happening, I discovered a sense of delight somewhere inside me. It came from my realisation that the experiment with the wire and the battery had worked and, more or less alone, I'd made and applied a highly powerful and attractive magnet. I was very pleased with that, even as I contemplated the harsh certainty that I was going to get into serious trouble over the whole sorry business.

By now, one or two of the older pupils had joined Miss Tartankilty. They pulled hard, until the still-shaking girl was slowly dragged off the desk and onto the floor. Using their feet they rolled her onto her back and, working like the proverbial navvies, they heaved and pulled until they managed to throw one of her trunk-like legs over, in order to anchor her onto her side. In the ensuing mêlée her blouse and Liberty bodice fell open, exposing some of her ample abdomen. I noticed she had a tattoo around her middle – a strange-looking circle with a line through it. At first I wondered what it was, then I clocked it. I'd seen one or two before. They were Plimsoll lines, and they were imprinted on fat, crippled kids like her so they could swim in safety. I wondered what Samuel Plimsoll would have made of this innovative application of his invention. With the slow and gradual ease of a redwood falling to earth after being set about by a frenzied lumberjack, the girl's leg finally went over, as one of the tinier boys shouted 'T-I-M-BER' and stood smartly aside. When the leg fell at last, creaking and groaning like an arthritic joint during a rogue cold spell, it gradually pulled her with it. It held her safe in place on the floor like – a sort of makeshift anchor. The magnet wouldn't get her now.

Another team of children ran in, a team of First Aiders – these days we'd call them 'paramedics'. Working together like irritated ants, they pulled at her tongue and cautiously uncoiled it as if it were a boa constrictor with a temper and an appetite. They stuck a pencil sideways through her teeth too and I briefly wondered if they'd all reverted to some Palaeolithic form of dentistry.

Slightly more composed by now, but still very worried, I glanced round at my friends to gauge their reaction to this seminal and important event that would one day be entered in the annals of the history of science. But before I could really do so, I heard a lovely Scots accent.

It was Miss Tartankilty.

'Away and tell the nurse Catriona's had anither epileptic fit,' she said calmly, in her lovely, soft, poetic voice, which would have reminded my Uncle Joe of a good malt whisky. 'Dinna bide here,' she said, 'off wi' ye, please.'

She was speaking to one of the older boys called Rollup Boy and he nodded, though it came across as more of a bow, as he had a badly hunched back. He was a boy I knew did his equivalent of fifty sit-ups every lunchtime without ever breaking sweat. I'd thought he was a smoker at first when someone mentioned 'roll-ups', for my brother sometimes smoked these secretly in the bathroom. But I soon learned it was exercise this boy was taking, not cigarettes, and I admired him for it and for the evident fitness it had conferred on him. Taking notice of our teacher's instruction, he clicked an assortment of buckle-things on his knees, pulled a short wooden stick from his pocket and beckoned to another boy to follow him. This boy, who stood with his tongue hanging out and panting in eager anticipation, swung his head round rapidly in Rollup Boy's direction and wagged something behind him that could have been a vestigial tail. 'Throw me the baton,' he barked and Rollup Boy did so. Then he clicked his fingers, made a slurping sound with his tongue and they both ran off and headed for help.

By now the possibility began to infiltrate my brain that it wasn't magnetic attraction that was causing all this fuss, but epilepsy. I looked on, freshly astonished. 'Epilepsy!' It made sudden sense. It had been an epileptic seizure that Catriona had come down with; my magnet was totally innocent and possibly quite weak. At least now, I reflected, some sort of medical science would help the situation, so I stifled any lingering urge to pray, signalled to Alastair what had really happened by shaking my whole body around, and generally pulled myself down from a state of red alert, through amber to green. It had all been one great big misunderstanding, and I had proper science on my side now: medical science. So I knew that when the school nurse finally arrived, all would be well.

And it was.

Small and hunched Rollup Boy may have been, but he could move, despite his canny, semi-canine companion and the baton. Within ten minutes the school nurse had arrived, and Catriona was finally carried away to recover. I'd seen my first-ever epileptic fit in close-up and I was a wiser young man for it. For his part, Billy had stopped smiling for once and had realised life was a contingent thing: a thing that could change suddenly and unpredictably. But as I reflected on it, I realised he must already know that better than anyone.

Nonetheless, just like me, he'd genuinely believed the magnet had pulled the Catriona girl off her chair, under her desk, across the floor and onto his desk, and the very thought of it had stunned him into a rare sobriety of mood.

When the class finished, I gave him the magnet to keep and take home.

'You can give it to your brother if you want,' I said, within earshot of Miss Tartankilty.

'Thanks,' he enthused, 'he'll like that. He's training to be a pilot at the moment and the magnet should help him design the new gyro-compass for his fighter plane.'

Miss Tartankilty overheard him.

'I thought yer brother was only ten or so, Billy; he hasn't aged by seven years or more in one, has he?'

'Ah, my younger brother's only ten, Miss,' he explained, 'but my elder one – the former neurosurgeon – is going on seventeen now.'

'A neurosurgeon!' squealed Miss Tartankilty, delighted. 'A real neurosurgeon . . . ' she dreamed. 'Och, I wish we'd had someone jist like that around when big Catriona collapsed on us.'

'I'll tell him that,' said Billy. 'Next time he might be able to rush here in his new racing car and help us out.' He was happy now that, if not the hero of the piece, at least he was the centre of attention.

'Ah, yer a great braw, blue, brazen, boisterous, brilliant, bonnie wee boy, Billy,' said Miss Tartankilty, smiling at him as if he were normal. 'It's typical o' you tae try an' help in an emerge-in-say.'

'That's awe-fy good o' ye,' Billy responded, sticking the magnet into his pocket, along with a few dozen paper clips that had stuck to it. 'Any time at a', Miss Tartankilty. All ye have tae do is ask.'

She smiled at that and so did Billy. Though he didn't smile a great deal after that. For things were set to change in a number of ways – and by no means were they all good ones.

22

The following afternoon, Al, Billy and I sat around during our rest period and talked first about magnets, then about some of the things our schoolmate Faith had spoken to me about one afternoon. She'd told me about the discovery of something called DNA; she said it might change all our lives some day. She was very informed about all sorts of things despite her sight problems, and I loved listening to her.

I was becoming progressively more convinced that science had lots to offer youngsters like us and, though I really knew nothing about DNA, I mentioned it to my two blue chums. There was no radio playing that day and I missed the background music. Billy responded with a considered nod, as if he knew it all already, but Al ignored me. He couldn't tear himself away from a piece of paper he was scrutinising, which had funny symbols written all over it. I'd never seen anything like it, so I dropped scientific discussion for the time being and decided to find out exactly what he was looking at.

'What's that?' I asked, piqued he was staring at a sheet of paper, no matter how fancy-looking, instead of listening to me.

He looked up.

'It's a horoscope. My mother had it done for me, though she didn't tell me about it.'

Billy leaned forward.

'By a gipsy?'

'No. By an astrologer, who attends a group of faith healers she met through an allopathic pharmacist in her local coven.'

'What's a horoscope?' I asked, and Al turned towards me.

'It's a sort of map,' he said. 'It shows where the planets were when I was born, and it tells you what's going to happen in the future.'

Billy sighed.

'Not the future again!'

'It's not like a crystal ball,' said Al defensively. 'It's more . . . ' He couldn't find the word.

'Scientific?' I offered, trying to get back to territory I was happier with.

'Yes,' he said.

Billy simply commented, 'Crap!'

For once, Al didn't defend himself. He just handed the strange-looking paper over and I had a look myself. I couldn't make head nor tail of it. It had a large circle in the centre drawn in red and black ink, and all sorts of strange shapes in and around it that I'd never seen before.

He noticed my confusion.

'They're the signs of the zodiac,' he said, pointing to the marks on the outside of the circle. 'And these are the planets,' he added, pointing to the marks inside. 'These marks here are called "aspects",' he went on, pointing to small triangular, square, circular and asterisk shapes drawn in a box at the bottom of the circle.

I didn't quite know what to say.

'And what does it mean?' I tried, as Billy studied the horoscope too.

Al twitched.

'I'd rather not say,' he said, pulling it away from us. 'No one's meant to know except my mum and the astrologer.'

'You stole it!' shot Billy, and Al spoke in a voice that seemed filled with tired resignation.

'I didn't steal it. I found it in a drawer where my mum had hidden it, together with the notes the astrologer made. I read them, but put them back.'

'And?' I said, despite myself.

'And what?'

'What did they say?'

'They didn't make for very good reading,' said Al quietly.

Billy spoke.

'You don't still believe in that rubbish,' he said quietly, chastened by Alastair's tone of voice, I think. 'It's the same as faith healing; it might happen at Lourdes, but it doesn't happen here or anywhere else.'

Al grew angry.

'You know a lot about it, for someone who doesn't believe in it and has no family to leave behind if *you* die.'

'I didn't say I didn't believe in it!' snapped Billy. 'I only said it was rubbish and it didn't work.'

Al and I looked at him, puzzled.

He saw our confusion.

'What's the problem? D'you think what I've just said doesn't make any sense? Is that it?'

I answered.

'How can it? You can't believe in something that doesn't work.'

'You believed in the magnet,' he said, 'and don't try and tell me you didn't.'

I nodded.

'I did, yes, I admit it. But my belief was based on something the magnet *could* have done, not on something it couldn't.'

'Exactly!' said Billy, and I think it was at that point I started to see him in a clear new light.

'Exactly what?' I asked.

'Exactly as I've said,' he responded. 'You've got it in one.'

'Got what in one?'

He smiled.

'The answer!'

'The answer to what?' I asked, desperately.

'To your question,' he explained, looking at me as if I were hopelessly stupid.

I thought about that for a moment, considering our exchange, and a terrible thought crossed my mind. It was the first time that particular thought had done so, which was a miracle in itself. For I suddenly realised that for all his banter and conviction, for all his enthusiasm and despite his truly dreadful lot in the world, Billy was even less bright than I'd thought him to be.

'Of course,' I said, humouring him. 'You're right, of course,' I repeated, just as I would to a cretin with attitude.

He smiled again.

'I thought you'd get there in the end,' he said, as he stared off into the distance somewhere – and I felt as if I'd lost something precious.

After a few moments of silence, I turned my attention to Al again. He might be a misery at times, but at least he was intelligent.

'As we've said, you can't believe in that stuff – it's nonsense.'

He shook his head.

'It doesn't matter if you believe in it or not. It happens anyway.'

'And what do you think's going to happen?' I asked.

He gave me a strange, weary look.

'I'm going to die,' he said quietly.

Billy snorted.

'We're all going to die.'

'Yes, but not as soon as me,' said Al.

Billy fell silent. I studied Al's face. There was the usual grim acceptance of the fact that whatever life threw at him, there was nothing he could do about it. It was painful to see — a sort of helpless realisation that nothing could be done about anything. I may have known almost nothing about DNA, and I knew even less about horoscopes, but I did know this boy didn't need them or anything like them.

I smiled, tried to buck him up.

'It's only superstition. It isn't really true.'

'How do you know? You know nothing about it.'

'Perhaps I don't. But the planets are a long way away. They can't touch us.'

Al shook his head and gave a sigh. He looked very tired.

'God's far away, too,' he said. 'Are you telling me He can't touch us because He's got some sort of problem with distance?'

'No, I'm not saying that — but that's different. He *made* the planets and stars, and He didn't make them so bad things could happen because of them.'

Al frowned.

'So why did He make them?'

'To light up the sky,' I said, having nothing better to offer.

He looked unconvinced.

'He could have made lanterns for that,' he countered, 'electric lanterns, if He'd been that concerned about the darkness.'

Billy shook his head and took a deep breath of frustration.

'They didn't have electricity in God's day,' he said, but we ignored him. Al continued.

'The astrologer says God made planets to tell us about things: to indicate what the future holds.'

'Then the astrologer's wrong,' I said. 'No one can know that. No one can tell what's going to happen. We've told you this before; I wish you'd listen.'

He shrugged, looked at us and then lay flat on his back.

'We'll see,' he said.

And we did.

23

Al died ten days later. I sometimes wasn't certain how much I missed my dead sister, but I missed Alastair all right and I still do sometimes, even after all these years. He was a haunted little boy and nothing very special, I suppose, with his blue face and dark hair, and his equally dark eyes reflecting his even darker thoughts. But I missed him as much as I'd missed my sick sister, and sometimes I think I missed him even more; not an easy thing to say, but an honest one.

The Assistant Headmistress announced his death in class.

'Alastair won't be back,' she said. 'He was very unwell, God called for him and he went. He won't be back – ever.'

No one said a thing and even Billy had the wit not to ask where he'd gone. He seemed to take the news well enough, though I suppose he'd more experience of that sort of thing than the rest of us put together. That said, for a few days afterwards he misbehaved, something quite unlike him given his behaviour outside the class. At one point the incorrigible Mrs Darksole sent him out of a religious education session. It was cold that morning and I remember vividly what she called after him.

'You can stand out there till you're blue in the face, Billy. Boys like you are protected too much anyway.' There was no need for that, whether it was said tactlessly or vindictively.

Most painful of all, I think, was my knowledge that life hadn't been easy for Alastair, despite his dying so young. I doubt there was one whole day when he was happy or at peace with himself. I mentioned before how he wouldn't have been surprised by a dishonest tooth fairy and I honestly can't bear to make a similar comparison with Old Father Time. The best I can hope for Al is that he passed into infinity peacefully one night, while he was deeply asleep and dreaming of things so wonderful he'd want to be with them forever. I'd like to think that happened, but I doubt it did. He wasn't the sort to have peaceful dreams and anyway, no one ever told us about the circumstances of his death.

The internal shadow I'd noticed since the day my sister had died seemed to grow and become harder to ignore. I was fully aware of the fact that one day I'd go the way she and Al had gone. There seemed nothing I could do about it but wait for it to happen, so the shadow became even more painful, if that's the proper word for it, and if shadows can hurt you inside for the rest of your life simply because you've lost folks you loved.

I asked my parents if I could go to Al's funeral, but as with my sister's I wasn't allowed to. They said it wouldn't be good for me, though I felt it would have been. I'd have liked to say goodbye to him, for he was my buddy, my confidant and my companion. And he was also my very first and my very best friend.

However it happened, Al's death was a dreadful blow and my growing realisation that Billy wasn't quite as quick-witted as I'd previously thought wasn't the best thing to happen, either. That too was like a small death and it affected our friendship accordingly. We continued to be friends of course, but we were never as close as we had been. It was as if we'd frozen our past friendship forever, but acknowledged it would grow no further. So at virtually the same time I lost Al, I lost Billy too; in a way, though, I always remained very fond of him and, oddly enough, fiercely protective too, making certain nothing bad happened to him – nothing I could prevent, anyway.

I was also feeling removed from my other friends. I liked them all and on the surface nothing had changed, but I'd changed somehow, and it put a distance between us I never was quite able to bridge.

At the time, I thought we were all just getting that bit older; growing up. But as I was to realise later, the reality was (at least I thought it was) I'd been seduced by my first scientific endeavours and horrified by the loss of my closest friend. Farcical as the episode with the magnet had been, I could explain it in terms of forces and fields and such things – things that made sense. Al's death, on the other hand, was inexplicable. Oh, I knew he had a bad heart, it had faltered and he'd faltered with it and gone to God. The thing was, if God was good, and everywhere, and knew everything and could do anything He liked, how could He do that to someone like Alastair? So for me, knowledge was fast becoming what walking sticks, Zimmer frames and callipers were to my friends. It was a crutch, of sorts, but like my illness it was never a visible one unless I elected to make it so. And of all forms of knowledge the scientific is the most seductive. It enables you to test the results of your ruminations on life and when those tests work, you think you've found an answer and have some sort of control over things, even if, in reality, you haven't.

A week or so after Al's funeral, his mother came to the school. She appeared in our classroom with the Assistant Headmistress, who spoke to us during the first lesson of the afternoon.

'Alastair's mother would like to speak with Billy and Francis,' she said. 'Could they come outside for a moment, please, and join us?'

Billy and I looked at one another and did as she asked.

Outside, I was amazed to see that Al's mum looked completely normal. There was no witch's hat, no ritual sword and no magic wand. She was just an ordinary, lovely lady, and I realised the stories of her esoteric interests were simply symbolic expressions of her utter desperation to try everything and anything to help, cure and keep her son.

As we stood there, uncertain what to say, she took two small packages from her handbag and gave one to each of us. Billy tore his open immediately, but I didn't. I placed it in my pocket and thanked her.

She spoke.

'This is a small gift for each of you for being such wonderful friends to my Alastair. He appreciated your friendship very much, and his father and I appreciate it too, boys – especially now.'

When she'd finished, she gave each of us a peck on the cheek and I felt strange. I wasn't sure what the feeling was, but it seemed like yet another deepening of my internal shadow. I think it happened because I realised something difficult to fathom, for a youngster. Here we were, getting gifts from Al's mum while Al lay dead and buried in the ground. I felt that behind her expression of affection, there must have been a dreadful anger inside her that she was unaware of; so whatever it was she thought she felt for us, it wasn't what she really felt at all.

The Assistant Headmistress, who'd stood aside to give us some privacy, looked around casually. Seeing the gifts had been handed over, she moved closer again.

'Now go back into your class, boys,' she said pleasantly.

I went in and opened my gift. It was a fountain pen, the first I'd ever had. I was delighted with it, so it didn't bother me at all when I noticed my recent fears about Billy's brainpower were well and truly justified. For when I glanced over to see what he thought of his pen, he had it in his mouth. It looked to me as if he were trying to eat it. But perhaps I'm being uncharitable, and he was only trying to pull the top off with his teeth.

24

In 1929, a German medical student named Werner Forssmann decided to teach his mentors a thing or two. For many years medical and surgical opinion had held that performing corrective surgery on the heart – with the exception of the most basic procedures – was not a viable option. There were then a few drugs around that were beneficial in certain cardiac conditions, but in terms of medicine in general, and certainly when it came to surgery, as in true love, the heart was considered inviolate and most thoracic surgeons had decided to leave it untouched. Then along came Forssmann.

This inventive 25 year old wasn't someone to spend years debating in learned journals what he believed to be obviously true, so he cut open a vein in his arm, stuck a tube into it and pushed it up into his heart. That done, Werner trotted off to his local radiography department and had an X-ray taken of this first cardiac catheter *in situ*. As Paul Anka did some years later with the lyrical 'Diana', Werner became an overnight celebrity, and on that same night the treatment of cardiac disease took a gigantic leap, to enter new and heady realms hitherto undreamed of.

By 1940, the first proper cardiac catheterisations had been performed on patients, and just a few years before I entered the world myself, the first simple operations on what were then fondly called 'blue babies' were successfully carried out. By the time I was well established in early childhood, therefore, and had reverted from my blue period to my pinkish-white one, an American surgeon had devised a machine enabling cardiac surgery to be performed on appropriate cases of little sicklets like me – sicklets who'd been born incomplete with holes in their hearts. This heart-and-lung machine opened the door to much more complex cardiac surgery. So for the first time in recorded history, blue babies had something to hope for; something that in the right hands would bring some proper colour to their faces at long last.

Such elective surgical colour changing was first carried out successfully by the time Guy Mitchell hit the charts with 'Cloud Lucky Seven' in 1953. Until then, the whole field of cardiac surgery had been dominated by the Americans and the Germans, and despite the mutual genocide of the Second World War we British had joined in for a few years ourselves. So by the time Pat Boone had replaced Guy Mitchell, with his very successful London–American label recording of 'It's Too Soon To Know', I'd been whipped into hospital in order to enable a few Scots surgeons to get in on the act.

In addition to skill, knowledge and expertise, these aspirants to the kill-or-cure knife required practice. So, having been presented with a box of sweets from my headmistress and having received a kiss on each cheek from the school doctor, who whispered 'Omertà' as he delivered them, I left on a bus with my mother for the first stage of the long trip to our surgical Mecca.

This centre of Scots chirurgical excellence was a hospital some miles from the city of Glasgow. It had originally been a recovery centre for victims of war, but had since been converted into a pioneering teaching hospital. However, before you can teach anything, you first have to learn how to do it. Too bad then, if, when you're admitted for a procedure in heart correction, it's the pupil who's keen to get his hands on you rather than the experienced teacher. But then everyone has to start somewhere, I suppose – even thoracic surgeons.

I was still a small, thin and fairly placid little boy before I was sent off to be a guinea pig for someone to perform human vivisection on, but the sight of a hospital catering solely for patients with chronic cardiac and lung conditions soon jerked me into life. For a start it had no wards in it. Instead it had what they called 'pavilions', a term I'd heard before then only in association with holiday camps. It also contained something they called 'male nurses', an innovative and early exercise in cross-dressing and jobbing that made me nervous just to think of it. I wondered what was so wrong with me I couldn't have normal female nurses like everyone else.

So I lay there on my fresh, clean hospital bed in Pavilion Seven, feeling extremely healthy, and wondering why I was in hospital when I felt so well and why it was the fates had conspired to make nothing in life normal for me, not even modern hospitals. For a start, there was no blood anywhere. I had no pain, I could walk on my own, there'd been no need for any last rites and I felt better than I ever had – in excellent nick, all in all. I had books and my box of sweets, my mum was with me, the sun shone in the sky like a smiley face with gold paint on, and my eyes were clear, bright and shining with vigour. My resentment at being admitted to hospital in such a hale and hearty condition therefore had merely been exacerbated by my being placed in a pavilion, instead of a ward, and by being attended to by a male nurse rather than a proper female one.

I considered myself a fairly brave and resilient young man by now. However, when my mother left me alone in the small, two-bedded cubicle I was sharing with an older man – who just happened to look like Death personified on an unlucky day – while she went off on the long, multi-bus journey home, I felt just a tiny bit anxious.

To be honest, I was scared witless. And when the animated cadaver beside me decided to explain some of the finer points of pulmonary physiology to me, my terror went way beyond wherever wits are, remained there for a considerable time and didn't all come back.

'Your lungs look a bit like this,' wheezed the man, as he leant over in my general direction and held up a bunch of healthy, green grapes in his nicotine-browned fingers.

I nodded.

'I'd no idea lungs were green,' I said anxiously.

'They aren't,' he said quickly, before lying back and gasping like my dead sister used to.

He sat up.

'What I mean is, they have all these little round bits on them,' he rasped.

'The ends of your lungs have little round sacs – sort of grape-bits, where the oxygen goes in.' He sounded like a chesty greyhound after a hard race. Then he suddenly performed a sleight of hand. 'But this,' he strained like punctured bellows, 'is what my lungs look like now!'

He was holding up that brown, twig-like thing you're left with when you've bitten grapes off – the bit that looks like a defoliated Bonsai tree.

'I see,' I said, not really seeing anything except that this man was getting progressively more short of breath and I hoped he wasn't about to die on me.

'Is there anything you'd like?' I asked.

'I'd love a fag,' he grunted.

'I don't smoke, I'm afraid.'

'I didn't think you did,' he smiled, suppressing a cough. 'I couldn't take one anyway, even if I had one.'

I was quiet. There was something about the way this man spoke that – bizarre as it sounds – reminded me of Alastair.

'They're beginning to think cigarettes are bad for you.'

That surprised me.

'I thought they were meant to relax you?'

He turned towards me, giving me a good view of the two tubes that led out from his nose.

'Do I look relaxed?' he asked.

'No, you don't. But then you're not smoking at present, are you?'

He laughed again, rattling like a bagatelle game as he held the bunch of grapes out towards me.

'Want a grape?'

'No thanks,' I said, as the male nurse came into our room holding a massive, glass syringe in his hand. His name was Joe, and I could see he was in a deadly serious mood.

'Turn over please, Francis. Just a wee jab,' he said. I turned onto my front and he eased my pyjamas down. He stuck the needle in deep and I yelped.

'That's you done,' he told me as he removing the needle in one long, leisurely pull. 'That's you ready to go to the theatre tomorrow.'

The syringe may have contained some sort of hallucinogen, or perhaps I was in what Siggy would call 'denial'?

'The theatre!' I said. 'The theatre!'

Joe turned me back round and put me right.

'The operating theatre. You're going to have some surgery tomorrow morning. We'll call for you at nine sharp.'

'Call for me? Nine sharp?'

Joe looked surprised.

'Haven't you been told you're going for surgery?'

'Well, not exactly,' I said, remembering the box of sweets, the whispered 'Omertà' and the finality of the look my mother had given me as she'd left. A pattern was emerging here and it wasn't one you knitted by.

'I was told I was having some sort of test.'

'You are, so you weren't misinformed,' said Joe, as he left the room, casting me a final look of what passed for reassurance.

'Then I hope I pass it,' I muttered, wondering what the heck I was in for the following day.

'Do you want a grape now?'

It was the cadaver. His morgue-like pallor looked entirely appropriate.

'No, thanks. I don't feel hungry.'

He eyed me carefully: gamekeeper turned poacher.

'You have to keep your strength up, son.'

'Thanks, but I'm fine,' I lied.

'Then try and get some sleep,' he said, before another bout of coughing took his voice away and pummelled whatever bits of lung he had left into gravel.

25

In the early hours of the morning, a proper lady nurse brought me a pill to take with just a sip of water. 'This will relax you,' she said with conviction. But with equal conviction, I knew it would take more than some jumped-up little white pill to do that. It relaxed nothing, not even the bits meant to relax by themselves when you're panicking. So by the time they came for me with a trolley – at nine o'clock sharp, as promised – I felt like bolting for it. But I couldn't.

So with a deep breath of resignation, I rolled onto the trolley and, unseen by my room-mate, who was dosing noisily, I was wheeled off to the operating theatre.

This was the first act in a rather unsuccessful and unflattering drama: one, I think, that placed cardiology in Scotland precisely where it was then – well and truly behind the rest of them.

I was wheeled directly into the theatre and rolled off the trolley onto the operating table. It felt cold beneath me as four or five people, dressed in a variety of outfits, moved into action like irascible plumbers at a blocked drain. I was asked to turn my face to the left, then my right arm was pulled to one side and punctured with what seemed a diversity of needles. If I'd known anything about Chinese medicine, I'd have suspected emergency acupuncture.

'We won't be sending you to sleep for this procedure; it won't hurt a bit,' a voice had told me as I'd entered. So I lay there wondering what having my chest cut open and my heart prodded about was going to feel like while I was still wide-awake. They weren't going to do that at all, of course, but no one had said what they were going to do; at least, they hadn't said so to me.

At some point in the procedure, in between the sounds of machines being switched on, knives being sharpened and disinfectant being squirted around like liquid confetti, it was finally mentioned that they were just going to stick a little tube up my arm and into my heart. In fact, these well-qualified, if under-practised, professionals were going to try to do to me what our heroic student Werner Forssmann had done successfully to himself around thirty years before. They were going to try and stick a simple little tube into a vein in my arm and guide it ever so gently into my heart.

To achieve this straightforward end, Werner's heroic Scots counterpart whipped out a scalpel, sharpened it on a leather strap and cut deeply into my arm to expose the largest vein he could find.

'ARRRGH!'

With a yell I jumped upwards, losing contact with the table and almost hitting the ceiling of the operating theatre. At least Forssmann had used his own vein for practice, and whatever pain he'd felt he'd been well prepared for, as you'll see if you read the Endnotes.

While my screams still echoed, someone spoke.

'Damn it! He hasn't had enough anaesthetic!'

'Don't worry, I'll give him a tad more, if you really think – '

'Do it!' said the first voice. 'That screaming of his is putting me off my cheese roll.'

As he spoke, I felt a warm, spreading sensation move over my right arm. This was the blood flowing out of my lacerated vein. It was warning me of its loss, before they could wipe it up and take it away for good.

'Clean that stuff up!' yelled yet another voice, though it might have been the original one become more excited by that time, or possibly changed by a lump of dough with some cheese in it. It spoke to *me* next, and it still sounded excited.

'Did you feel that?' it asked, as I writhed on the table.

'Yes! I did! I thought you said I wouldn't feel any –'

It interrupted.

'You weren't supposed to. Try and be more cooperative.'

I kept quiet; I saw no point in antagonising these people. After all, they were at me with daggers drawn and they didn't seem too competent in their use of them.

'You'll be fine now,' said yet another voice. 'I've given you some more of the local. It's expensive stuff – don't waste it.'

'Thanks,' I murmured gratefully, wishing they'd given me some anaesthetic before they gave me more anaesthetic, if you get my drift; for getting the extra shot was painful too.

All in all, this was fast becoming a nightmare, with me playing the lead role.

Another voice – to me.

'Shit! It won't go in at all now. Shall I give it a harder push?'

'Yeah, go on. Go for it! What's to lose? A bit harder. HARDER, for God's sake! That's it, just a bit more pressure and . . . '

'Oh! That hurts,' I yelped, as a pain shot up my arm that made the male nurse's injection of the previous night seem like relief massage.

Another voice.

'Oh come on . . . it doesn't hurt too much. It isn't all that painful. Now please lie still,' it went on, sounding a bit like Mrs Schiklgruber had years ago – oblivious to pain as long as it was someone else's.

I kept my teeth tightly gritted as the soreness crept up my arm, around the base of my shoulder and across the right-hand side of my upper chest.

'Dammit!' said someone, as someone else clicked the overhead X-ray machine into radioactive action, then ran like Hell to escape the consequences.

There was a sigh of frustration.

'You're not getting it *in* properly. Let me have a try.' I heard what sounded like praying coming from a nurse in a corner. She was fiddling with something in her hands and it looked suspiciously like a set of rosary beads.

'You see, you ease it in just like . . . shit!' It was a voice I'd now come to recognise.

'Where the Hell's it gone now?' it asked. I lay there saying Hail Marys myself, without any rosary or any idea of what they were up to.

'I've no idea where it's gone. It's disappeared – it's a right bloody cock-up.'

There was some sniggering.

'Wait till the chief sees that,' laughed the first voice. 'Shall *I* have another go?' it offered. 'A bit of practice makes perfect, you know.'

'Well, if you really must,' said the other, peevishly. 'But it's his veins messing me up. It's his fault really, not mine. Oh, go on then, have another go at it. What's to lose?' the voice said stuffily, resigned, it seemed, to something less than total success. 'Anyway, we have to get it at least part of the way in before old Thromboclot arrives.'

Suddenly another anonymous voice whispered into my right ear. I felt something being pressed on my lips and I nearly jumped out of whatever skin I had left.

'Don't worry,' it said, 'you're in very capable hands.'

I tried to reply, but couldn't. Someone had stuck a long trail of sticking plaster over my mouth, for reasons unknown. At least it kept me quiet, until someone else ripped it off and proceeded to stick it over the arm I still couldn't see.

'It won't be long now,' someone whispered, sounding more relaxed. 'We generally break for coffee at half-past, so we try to finish before then when we can. If it means cutting corners, well . . . hang on in there.'

I heard the door of the operating theatre slam open and a new voice resounded round the theatre.

'What are you two doing there? I can't leave you alone for a minute! Good God, who did that? Hey! Give that here and I'll do it!'

One of the familiar voices responded.

'Well, it's only our first case, sir, and unfortunately we're nowhere near as gifted as you are at this sort of thing. I'd have managed if the lighting were a bit better. I wonder if a larger candle would help.'

The other, familiar voice sounded piqued.

'I don't think you *would* have managed.'

'I would.'

'Wouldn't.'

'Would.'

'WOULDN'T!'

'WOULD.'

'WOULDN'T!'

'WOULD!'

I heard the sounds of a struggle.

'CUT IT OUT!' shouted Mr Thromboclot. 'No, not that, for Heaven's sake! Good God! Look what you've gone and done now! Damn, shit and budgerigars! I've had enough of this crap. Pull the bloody thing out once and for all,' he screeched.

'That's exactly what I'm trying to do, sir,' said the person I'd decided was an apprentice surgeon, 'but it won't budge a bloody inch!'

'Let me see. Give it here!' I felt a foot on my chest and heard a shout of 'HEAVE TOGETHER, LADS,' then a sharp pain shot down my arm and out like a sudden spurt of blood. There was a moment of silence, followed by a thump on the floor. It sounded ominously like an anaesthetist, a professor of cardiology and an aspiring thoracic surgeon falling in a heap.

'Got the sod at last!' said the boss's voice.

'Always said you were a surgical genius, sir,' fawned the anaesthetist.

'What time is it, anyway?' asked the thoracic surgeon, sounding confused. 'If it's Tuesday at 9.45, then I've got an kutitfastectomy in ten minutes, and it's private too; it'll pay for my healthcare scheme.'

'Those are sods to do,' consoled the boss-man. 'My old chief, Prof. Suture – Joe Mengele's friend – lost a hundred-and-seventy-seven patients trying that one. He got the last one right though, but the uncooperative nincompoop caught pneumonia post-op and pegged it anyway,' he laughed. 'Still, we can't all be perfect, can we?' he added philosophically.

'No, we can't, sir, but you're certainly close,' said the apprentice surgeon, 'and we try to follow, though we'll always be a great many steps behind.'

'That procedure's a piece of cake compared with this fiddly nonsense,' the anaesthetist said. 'I've only lost a dozen myself.'

'Out of?'

'Twelve or so.'

'Not to worry, old boy,' said the boss-man. 'You'll get it right one day. Anyway, we'd better stop nattering and stitch this little blighter up before he bleeds to death. I hate it when they bleed like that. It's so, well . . . messy, frankly. Does anyone have a suture needle handy?'

'Oh! Ooops! I was miles away,' said the surgeon.

'I should have one,' said the anaesthetist. 'At least I did have . . . somewhere. Sorry sir, I'm not quite with it this morning. I went out for a few drinks last night with Nurse Tightskirt. She stayed over and you should have seen the – '

'A suture needle!' demanded Mr Thromboclot.

'Sorry, sir! Now where did I put the blasted thing? It was here just before I bit the twine off.'

'It's here on the floor under all this congealed blood,' said the apprentice surgeon triumphantly. 'The thread's pretty wet and heavy, but it should do as a stopgap.'

'Thanks,' said the boss. 'Now, what do you think, boys? A tacking stitch or a cross-hatch?'

'Well, I like cross-hatch myself,' said the apprentice. 'It's looser, but it leaves a prettier pattern.'

'Then I'll do a tacking stitch,' laughed his boss, and I felt a stabbing sensation in my arm again.

'Oh!' I yelped.

'What's wrong with you?' asked the boss-man sharply.

'I have a bad heart,' I said.

'A right one he is!' said the surgeon.

'A regular comedian,' said the anaesthetist.

'Perhaps we should give him some laughing gas,' sniggered the boss-man and that had them all in various patterns of stitches. I was bundled off the table while the last knot was being tied and dragged onto the trolley, to be wheeled hurriedly back to my room again – to renew my acquaintance with the grape man.

As I rolled along the corridor, another trolley passed and I caught a glimpse of the person lying on it. I gasped. The porter asked me if I needed an oxygen mask, but I ignored him.

'Jason!' I called, sitting up as far as I could with the porter trying to push me back down again. 'Jason!' I called again, for that's whom I'd seen. He was dressed up for surgery and heading for the theatre during coffee break.

'Hi there, Frankie,' he called back, high as a kite on some pre-med or other. 'I'm just off to theatre . . . such high drama!' he added, waving his arm in the air and almost overturning a bottle attached to it via a lead. 'They think a bit of corrective surgery might just do something for me,' he said, before we'd passed one another and were out of mutual sight.

The porter bent over me.

'A friend of yours?'

'Yes. We're at school together.'

He looked at me oddly. Upside-down, he was like some creature with inverted eyes and neither mouth nor nose.

'He must be in a bad way.'

'Why's that?'

'Because he's going in to Doctor Axonkutter. He's a sort of neurosurgeon.'

'A neurosurgeon?' I repeated as we sped along, my arm still hurting with every bump of the trolley's wheels.

'Sort of. Yes. He occasionally takes out bits of brains and things. They reckon he'll become quite famous when he's qualified, like the guys that dealt with you.'

I sat up.

'When he's qualified! Surely he must be qualified before he's allowed to cut people up?'

'Well, you'd think so, yes. You would think that,' said the porter cryptically.

I reflected on the mess they'd made with a simple bore-job on me. Who knew what they might do with something as complicated as a brain?

I spoke.

'Anyway, this is meant to be a hospital for hearts and lungs, not one where they cut out bits of brains.'

The porter sighed.

'I didn't say he cut out bits of brains,' he said casually. 'I said he occasionally *takes out* bits of brains and things.'

'Isn't it the same thing?'

'Not if they come attached to bits of lung,' he said. 'Then you're only taking out bits of lung. If bits of brain happen to be sticking to it . . . ' he shrugged, though upside-down it looked as if he were pulling his stomach in, ' . . . well, that's just too bad.'

I thought about that.

'But Jason doesn't have a lung problem, so what's the point of taking a bit out?'

He sighed again.

'Don't go asking me. I just work here. I suppose they think they can help him. Nothing ventured, you know?'

'Nothing gained,' I said as I wondered what the heck this place really was. If it were the National Health Service I'd have to consider a change of nationality.

'Right!' he said. 'And anyway, where do you think they learn proper skills? They all have to start somewhere. You don't want them screwing up in the private sector. Best to practise in here, get the hours in on less important jobs – like any trade.'

'I suppose so. But Jason's –'

'A sick kid just like you. Now don't get me wrong, but kids like you are giving something back when you volunteer for what will, some day, be state-of-the-art surgery. You're making a contribution to the society that's going to look after you for what's left of your life. Doctor Axonkutter will do his best for your buddy, but if it isn't good enough . . . well, there are genuinely needy cases out there, son, and every bit of practice on kids like you and your friend helps them.'

We fell silent again as the trolley reached my room. The man with the grapes wasn't there and his bed had been stripped down to the mattress.

'Where's he gone?' I asked the porter, who kindly helped me off the trolley and onto my bed.

'You don't want to know, son,' he said, lighting up a cigarette and picking up a solitary grape from the floor. 'Looks a bit like the end of a lung, this,' he said, as he examined it carefully. 'Would you like it?' he asked. 'It might help that dry mouth of yours.'

'No. But would you be kind enough to remove this piece of tubing from my arm?' I asked politely. 'It hurts, and I don't suppose they meant to leave it there.'

'Damn it! They're always doing that!' he complained, as he whipped the offending piece of tubing out of my wound, popped the grape into his mouth and breathed out a plume of cigarette smoke, all at the same time.

'Thanks.'

'No problem,' he said, then pushed the trolley through the door and went off whistling down the corridor, like a lesser form of nightingale.

26

Miss Overprim was firm, but well respected. She was an institution within an institution and she knew all our names, virtually from our first days at school. She'd ruled over our top class for many years, though 'top' in this context didn't allude to excellence. You didn't *get* excellence in our school, where the only streaming we knew of came from places too personal to mention. You reached top class when you actually arrived there and you remained until you were sixteen or more, when – a year older than normal children, and assuming you lasted that long – you were sent out to grass. If you were lucky, you might find a job some place where people didn't mind your highly individualistic background. And as an exceptionally talented kid, there were high hopes for me in that respect. It was suggested I might take up a scientific career: washing test tubes in a sheltered laboratory, for example; and the prospect appealed as much as polio would to a prospective professional footballer.

My first exposure to top class occurred when our own class teacher was off with some ailment of her own. We were distributed between other classes like bits of stale bread in a downmarket aviary and I made top class, along with most of my chums. The morning was routine, but the afternoon was something else again.

There were two or three children at our school who had little or no legs. One was a boy called Wee Jimmy. He was bright but nasty, with an opinion of himself in inverse proportion to his size. In addition to his other talents, which included playing chess more than passably well, Jimmy spoke Italian, as he had an Italian father.

As the Scots say, he had 'a bit o' a tongue in his heed' too, which means he blasphemed, cursed and swore whenever he got the opportunity, which was often enough, as I remember. He'd been allocated to the top class along with the rest of us that day, but he didn't reappear after the lunch break. So I asked Billy where he was.

'Hanging around the cloakroom; he's been in there for ages,' he said, *sotto voce*. 'You'll find him there if you want him. Though I don't see why you would.'

I was genuinely concerned.

'Perhaps I should go and get him? He's in trouble if he's not back here soon. What's he doing hanging around the cloakroom anyway?'

Billy smiled.

'He's hanging on a hook,' he said. 'Someone hung him up and nicked his legs.' It took me a few moments to let this sink in. Jimmy was certainly small enough to hang up, and, knowing what he could be like, I imagined he'd probably deserved to be. But the fact he'd had his legs removed concerned me, so I excused myself from class under the pretext of going to the toilet.

I walked to the cloakroom, which was well concealed from view, and there he was – there was spirited little Jimmy, hanging like a stringless puppet on a coat-hook. He was an animated torso with arms and a head stuck on, and his face was very red and getting redder. I wondered what to do.

I spoke.

'Hello, Jimmy,' I said, unable to think of anything more appropriate.

'Piss off!' he screamed, starting to wriggle harder.

'What are you doing up there?'

'None of your effing business,' he fumed, meeting my eyes with his own and clenching his fists in frustration.

'Would you like me to help you down?'

'I've got no legs to get into, you stupid shit! If you can't see that you're thicker than even *I* took you for. Sod off, you pustule,' he snarled as he waved his clenched fists back and forth like a milkmaid at an unproductive udder.

I tried to be reasonable.

'I could get you a wheelchair.'

He punched the air.

'D'you think I'm an effing cripple? What do I want with a bloody wheelchair? I can walk with the best of you! All I need are my effing legs, just like you need yours – you piece of crap.'

I tried common sense.

'But you don't *have* your legs.'

'Those shits will bring them back,' he said, 'or they won't know what's effing hit them!'

'And who are *they*?' I asked avoiding using any swear words, as I tended to do back then.

'None of your effing business,' said Jimmy, loyally. 'Now sod off and get yourself stuffed while you're at it!' He was redder than a Roman sunset on a warm day.

A man of few but innovative words at the best of times, Jimmy had made his feelings clear. He hadn't taken my help when it had been offered, so I didn't offer it again. He still needed assistance, however, so I returned to my temporary class to find out more about the whole sorry business. In particular I wanted to know where his legs had gone walkies to.

'Who did it?' I whispered to Billy when I got back. Miss Overprim had stuck a map of what Billy thought was 'The World' on the wall and had started talking about it.

'I don't know,' he whispered back. 'Don't worry, someone will find him soon enough.'

And someone did.

Miss Overprim soon spotted Jimmy's absence and asked if anyone knew where he was. No one admitted they did, and although I didn't even shake my head in response to her question, my face felt very red indeed. She left the class to go and look for him and we waited all by ourselves, patiently and expectantly. Twenty minutes or so later, she returned and recommenced our lesson as if nothing had happened. As Billy had guessed correctly, it had indeed been a map of the world and Miss Overprim was now holding a pointer to it. She had a class of devoted, attentive students for once and she'd undoubtedly noted it.

She spoke.

'What do we call an inhabitant of Germany?' she asked, pointing her pointer at some coloured bit on the map.

'A German, Miss,' replied Woody, who'd recently had corrective surgery on his right arm. It was still in plaster and it stuck straight out at a right-angle to his chest.

'Well done, Woody,' said Miss Overprim. 'And what do we call an inhabitant of Italy?' she asked, looking around for answers and adjusting the glasses on her face carefully.

'An Italian, Miss,' said Melissa seriously. Her head moved forwards as she spoke and her voice had an intensity unusual for her. I knew she was as innocent as snow as far as Jimmy was concerned, but she was picking up on the atmosphere.

'And the *capital* of Italy?' asked Miss Overprim.

' "I", Miss.' It was Billy.

Miss Overprim smiled.

'A good try, Billy. The word "Italy" starts with a capital "I", as you say. But by "capital", in this case, I mean the most important city in that country; the country of Italy in this instance,' she explained patiently. 'So you're right, but wrong too. The word "Italy" does indeed start with a capital "I", as you said, but the capital of Italy isn't "I".'

Billy nodded, then sat back and smiled. The rest of us looked at one another.

'It's Rome, Miss' a voice piped up. It was Jean, and there was a clatter of teeth as she completed the word.

'Good! Well done!' said Miss Overprim. 'Now can someone give me another meaning of that word?'

We all looked puzzled, so she wrote 'ROAM' on the blackboard. 'Roam,' she continued, smooth as a razor blade on soap, and every bit as dangerous. '"R-O-A-M",' she spelt out. 'ROAM!'

Melissa spoke quietly.

'To wander about, Miss.'

'And what do we *need* to wander about, as you put it? To roam?' she asked more pointedly.

'Luh . . . Luh . . . Luh . . . Luh . . . '

It was one of the older boys whose stammer had kicked in.

'Legs,' I thought, but kept quiet about it.

'Legs, Miss,' said the stammerer, slapping his thighs with a loud metallic bang. He was another one with none of the natural ones.

'Yes, *legs*,' continued Miss Overprim. She paused and looked round the classroom.

'Now . . . the word "capital" can mean a major city, as we've seen, or it can mean a large letter for a proper noun, as Billy just told us.'

I caught sight of a kid at the front, who'd probably never heard of a proper anything in his life. He looked very worried at this and began to chew at his bottom lips – an awesome task considering he had four of them.

'But it has another meaning,' explained Miss Overprim. 'As in "capital punishment",' she said sharply. 'Can anyone tell me what that is?' she asked, expecting no answer and getting none. 'It's what's dished out when someone is hanged for murder,' she said in a sinister tone too, and I gulped like a drowning goldfish.

Murder, by God! The silence was total – *enceinte*. So Jimmy had died hanging on a cloakroom hook, trousers on perhaps, but legs off.

'So we have "legs",' said Miss Overprim, 'or indeed, *no* legs,' she clarified, 'whereupon we CANNOT ROAM,' she yelled. 'And we have

PUNISHMENT, and a HANGING and an ITALIAN,' she went on, as wails and chatters and screams filled the classroom, like sinners' laments at a roofless Pentecostal Church on a rainy Good Friday.

'Now, do *these* add up to anything?' she asked, as the wailing soared to a pitch and then dropped off again to a guilty, sullen silence.

Billy looked at me in active panic, but the rest of us were very still. We were waiting for something – expecting it. Miss Overprim scanned the class like an assassin. She seemed to sniff the air, seek the scent of prey and try to home in on it.

'Who knew about this?' she demanded. 'Who knew about Jimmy?'

We all looked at one another feigning innocence, and I realised – not for the first time, either – that *everyone* in the class had known before me. Even Melissa had known; I could tell by the droop of her head.

For a moment I felt aggrieved. Yet again I'd been the very last person to know about something! Even after all these years, I *still* wasn't being told things of import. What was the problem here? Were they trying to protect me? Exclude me? Did I need to be protected or excluded? Was I different in some way? I shrugged. I knew now, but the shame I felt at Jimmy's demise soon made me wish I didn't.

Miss Overprim's voice disturbed my thoughts.

'So *you* knew, Woody! You disgraceful, conniving little runt,' she spat. Her anger had at last found a target. 'You ungrateful little scorpion! I'm amazed your parents thought you worth having in the first place!' she raved. Woody looked bemused at this turn of events and began to fret and tug at his chair with his proper hand.

Melissa intervened.

'Woody's arm's in plaster, Miss. He's leaning back in his chair looking up at you. He's not raising it as a sign of guilt – it's stuck in mid-air. He isn't admitting to anything. He didn't know about Jimmy until after it happened. He's innocent.'

Miss Overprim froze in mid-yell.

'I'm sorry, Woody, I forgot!' she said, still pumping adrenaline and still bristling with anger.

She turned her attention to Melissa.

'How did *you* know he didn't know? How did you know he didn't know unless you knew yourself he didn't, which meant you knew when everyone else knew?' she said, puzzling even the brightest of us – me included.

Melissa's head bobbed up and down and I knew she was close to tears. I suffered with her. I was becoming very fond of her and sometimes she looked quite lovely.

'I knew too,' said a voice. '*I* saw him; he told me to "eff off"', but I'd have helped him if he'd asked.'

'My very thoughts,' I thought, and felt stunned at this act of selfless honesty. I looked around to see who'd said it and discovered everyone was looking at me.

Through her tears, Melissa gave me a smile. It had been the first moment of gallantry in my life and I'd been almost unaware of it. Like the other boy's stammer, my testosterone was kicking in at last, but in that gentle, romantic way it begins: poetry at first, not harsh corporeal prose.

'So you knew too, Francis!' said Miss Overprim, sounding as if I shouldn't. 'You could have helped Jimmy but elected not to?'

I felt dreadful.

'He didn't want help. I only saw him hanging there. I'd no idea where his legs were. If I'd lifted him down he'd have, well . . . flopped, I suppose.'

'Yes, he would have "flopped", as you say. But you didn't get help. You just left him there to hang.'

I felt disgraced.

'I'm sorry,' I said quietly. 'I should've done something. I meant to; I just didn't know how to go about it.'

With a snap of her head she turned her attention elsewhere.

'Who else knew about it?'

No one spoke, but I heard some creaking sounds, a few gasps and some sounds like chains trailing over gravel. I raised my eyes to look at the class and saw that every single right arm that was at all raiseable had been raised. Some of the children had lifted the arms of those who couldn't do so for themselves and both of Woody's arms were now in the air.

'We all knew,' said Una.

'Yes, Miss. We all knew,' agreed Melissa.

'Oh, I suppose I knew just a teeny-weeny bit about it myself,' said Jason mildly, preening himself as he did so and self-consciously touching the scar he'd had at the front of his head since his time in hospital.

'I knew too,' said Jean, her teeth dropping with a clack in her mouth, as their supporting hand had been lifted away.

Miss Overprim looked at them all and I thought I could tell what she was thinking. But before I could properly formulate the thought, the door opened and, conditioned by years of such surprises, I looked expectantly for Fatty Spinner or Derek. But both of them had left school a long time ago, though their presence remained stored in my most primitive neural reflexes.

It was Jimmy coming in with a flourish. Our woodwork teacher, Mr Hammerhead, was pushing him in a wheelchair. For a moment I wondered what terrible thing had happened to confine Jimmy to a wheelchair. Then I realised he still hadn't found his legs.

'Where are my effing legs?' he shouted.

The class was deadly silent, with only Miss Overprim composed enough to speak.

'Watch your language, James! We won't have that language in here! Don't dare use it again!'

He clenched his fists.

'*Dove sono le mie gambe del cazzo!*' he snarled.

'I said *watch* your language, not change it,' she yelled. 'Now does anyone here know where James's legs are?' she asked more calmly, and I wondered if Mr Hammerhead could make him another pair. For it was evident from the studied silence that no one knew where his legs actually were, or was willing to admit to that knowledge.

As we all sat in total silence, Mr Hammerhead said something to Jimmy which quietened him down a bit. I imagine he probably said something like: 'There's nothing worse than a legless boy who swears.' For the particular epithet, 'There's nothing worse than . . . ' came to his mouth with the same ease as profanities came to Jimmy's. A brave man I suppose, given he daily watched over ungifted amateurs handling potentially lethal tools, Mr Hammerhead wasn't the most imaginative when it came to addressing us during his woodwork classes, where the frequent cry of, 'I've lost another nail' usually meant the permanent and bloody loss of the cuticle of a deformed finger or something.

I'd also heard Hammerhead shout: 'There's nothing worse than drilling a hole two millimetres short of the intended point,' to some aspiring but jumpy carpenter who could barely shovel food into his mouth without a spirit-level held in front by someone whose hands were steady enough to guide it in.

'There's nothing worse than bending a nail when you're supposed to hammer it right in,' he'd tell some kid, with a mallet and a piece of hard, dense wood, whose reflexes were such that it would have produced better results if he'd used the wood with the nail placed in *it* to batter the mallet.

Overall we never quite knew what to make of Mr Hammerhead, as he was also the only male teacher in the school. It seemed women had a monopoly on the infirm and the disabled, except when it came to woodwork. Perhaps we did need a man in that job, however, for not only did women never qualify to teach such technical subjects in those days, but they were also considered too physically weak to do the ancillary work: such as pulling nails out of a self-crucified hand; forcibly removing a screwdriver from the tightly clenched teeth of an enthusiastic but armless aspiring balsa-wood model maker; or gluing back on wooden feet leisurely sawn off while their owner chatted to some blind kid who sat beside him in a portable bed-bath, twirling screws into sheets of cardboard as a preliminary to attempting the real thing.

Despite all of this, and despite being surrounded on a daily basis by children who suffered from every terrible affliction known to medicine, Mr Hammerhead repeating his mantra of 'There's nothing worse than . . .', doing something quite evidently a great deal *less* worse than the most minor problem any one of these kids had.

But then perhaps he was an optimist of sorts, Mr Hammerhead; or perhaps like most of us he simply used that silly, stupid and usually inappropriate phrase without giving it the common courtesy of even thinking about it.

So whatever Mr Hammerhead had said to Jimmy, I'd no doubt it started with 'There's nothing worse than . . .'

And I didn't mind it at all on this occasion, because it quietened the irascible little creep down, and there was nothing worse than Jimmy when he'd had enough of everyone within cursing distance and decided to give them and the world a good and proper earful at one and the same time.

Mr Hammerhead proceeded to wheel Jimmy over to his desk, where he sat still mumbling in Italian. At least now whatever he said was directed mainly at the desk. On occasion, he'd suddenly rear up like a dog that's lost a fight but doesn't like to admit it. You know the sort of thing; it snarls intermittently and, growling deep and low, bares its teeth in a show of threat, while inside it's really scared witless its foe will resume the attack and start the whole thing off again. 'Retiring with dignity intact', I think it's called, and Jimmy did retire from the fray with dignity intact; snarling and baring his teeth at times, and not without thoughts of retribution, as we were to discover. He sat out that afternoon completely legless and was duly wheeled out to his bus when the time came for him to go home. It seems his mother kept a spare pair of legs in a cupboard, beside his tennis gear. He played the game at county level, according to Billy, who'd seen him play the best of five sets against his brother, in a game his brother won six sets to love.

In due course, however, the janitor, who was the only other male member of staff besides Mr Hammerhead and who sported a 'claw hand' he used to good effect to clear dodgy drains, spotted the legs in the small garden that was part of the school annexe. Someone had planted them toes up, and decorated them with tasteful foliage and an artificial poppy left over from 'poppy day'. A runner of ivy had been draped over the left leg and the right one had been embroidered with pansies.

We never did find out who planted Jimmy's legs, or who'd ripped them off in the first place and hung him up to dry like an old coat. For despite his anger and his loquacious expression of it, he'd never tell. He was respected for that, I have to say, though for little else, perhaps. And it gave him the sort of playground-cred only dreamed of by unpopular, flesh-legged kids in normal schools. I imagine if Jimmy had been embarrassed or ashamed at what had happened it might have been a different story. But he was simply angry, and anger has no need to add to itself the shame of betrayal.

That said, the following week one of the older boys, who was diabetic, found a chocolate mouse in his pocket. We all saw him discover it, so he was obliged to examine it in public. It came with a note:

Don't eat me if you're diabetic. Your insulin might go missing.

Jimmy looked at the boy steadily as he read this, licking a lollipop with his fast little tongue. He had a grim, sharp smile on his face too, when the boy checked his pocket for his syringe and his phial of insulin. When he was certain they were there he threw the mouse and the offending note away and Jimmy nodded with satisfaction. Another boy – a friend of the diabetic, with Kiddie Parkinsonian syndrome and a permanent hand tremor – discovered a gift box in his desk. It contained one of those small, plastic globe-like things with which you're meant to guide a steel ball around a plastic maze and into a hole at the centre. Jimmy stood with his arms out and his hands as steady as a gunfighter's, as he watched the boy lift it up and try to have a steady look at it. It had come with a note too:

You need to be able to get the ball in the hole to get a skilled job.
Otherwise you're destined for a life throwing dice in a casino.

In both cases, the point had been made and the episode was finally put to rest.

27

With that crowning episode, the final remnants of my childhood had more or less gone. Then a miracle occurred at the Special School, in the form of a new teacher called Miss Angelica, who took over top class on Miss Overprim's retirement.

Within a very short time of my being taught by her, she'd both spotted and encouraged my intellectual abilities. I'd graduated to the top class by now and Melissa, Jean and Siggy had been moved up too. Some others, who should have moved with us, were kept back for reasons of 'unsuitability for fast-track education'. Of the four of us, however, only Melissa and I now remained.

Siggy had been carted off to a mental hospital after he'd broken down in class one day, weeping about the fact that as it was language that made everything real, then we'd better watch how we used it. It seemed silly and it reminded me of something my big sister had said once, but that had seemed silly too, at the time. We accepted Siggy's going with equanimity. That sort of thing happened routinely and, compared with progressive blindness, creeping paralysis, idiopathic mortality and that sort of thing, what was going off your rocker? Anyway his persistent insistence that language actually created you and your surroundings – 'So you'd best keep your mouth shut and your thoughts to yourself or else!' – irritated people, so there were a number who weren't all that sorry when Siggy was dragged away screaming in a straitjacket.

For her part, Jean had been taken somewhere to die. They said her teeth had run out of enamel when the bones that held her face together had finally given up on her. Force-feeding hadn't worked either; it just upset her and made her scream with terror when she saw the tube coming. I heard from one third-hand source that she'd been literally begging to die at the end and she finally pegged it in some sort of institution for dying children. Not very quietly either, according to what I heard, but with as much dignity as you'd expect from a great wee girl like Jean under those sorts of quite horrible circumstances.

Una should have moved on with us too, but she was set to join the top class later. In the interim she'd been sent off on some sort of surgical sabbatical, where she was to have her neck broken, or her brace overhauled; possibly both. We were never quite certain what they did to her, but it must have involved a lot of work, as they'd set aside months and months to do it. We'd been told she was going to Lourdes after her sabbatical, which, to be honest, had seemed a bit odd to me. For even then our Health Service was quite a busy institution, and a visit to Lourdes before her surgery might just have saved a few resources.

So with Una away for months, Siggy good and gone – locked up somewhere secure, in a final battle with the demons of his unconscious – and Jean and her teeth disappearing for good in some crematorium or other, it was only Melissa and I who carried the candle in the top class for that bunch of five and six year olds who'd started school some eight or so years before. I still occasionally bumped into Faith and her albino friend, Iris, and though their sight had never improved, it didn't seem to get much worse either. Faith could still read her Braille okay, and her friend could still navigate successfully in the permanent state of twilight that constantly threatened her with total darkness.

We'd now crept into the early 1960s, and the music was beginning to change. We still had the likes of Perry Como and Tony Bennett around, but newer names had come forward, names such as Elvis Presley and Adam Faith and Billy Fury – who had a bad heart just like me – and while some of their music sounded much as it always had, some of it seemed to herald something new in the air, like a novel inert gas with some effervescence about it.

So life was changing, and I'd have liked to have discussed it all with Siggy; but latest reports were he'd become daft as a brush in the place he'd been sent to, and was now insisting everything was created by language – even God! I just hoped they could straighten his bristles out before it was too late for him, too. I'd no idea then, of course, that like the rest of us he had something else lying in wait for him – something so unexpected and dreadful that it's best not to mention it yet.

One afternoon in early summer I brought a piece of paper into schools, covered with lists of chemical formulae I'd copied from the old, two-volume American dictionary we had at home. I used these lists to memorise such formulae as a sort of hobby, and I'd started to do this at lunchtime to help pass away the still-obligatory rest time.

Miss Angelica saw me reading it just before our class started. She came over and leaned over my shoulder.

'What's that, Francis?'

'A list of chemical formulae, Miss,' I said, showing off a bit, I suppose.

She had a closer look.

'Where did you get it from?'

'I copied it from some books we have at home.'

'Chemistry books?'

I felt ashamed.

'No. An American dictionary.'

She came round and faced me.

'Why?' she asked simply, her face looking bright and interested.

'Because I like science.'

She moved directly in front of my desk. I could smell the perfume she wore and I sensed her breasts hovering nearby like custard tartlets. My eyesight blurred for a second and I felt transiently like an albino. I dragged my eyes upward. I felt a strange stirring somewhere – something indefinable, but it was soon overwhelmed by my interest in science.

Miss Angelica spoke again.

'Why don't you become one?'

'One what, Miss?'

'A scientist.'

She was new to the job; she clearly didn't quite understand where we were.

'I don't know how I'd go about that,' I said, wondering if she'd been transferred from the mentally handicapped section.

'It's something to think about,' she said as she walked off, and I was left dealing with some strange and very mixed feelings.

The following day as I left for lunch, she handed me a book.

'You're welcome to borrow this. It might be of interest.'

I looked at it. It was about microscopy and had pictures of pond life and all sorts of things I'd never even dreamed existed. I read it overnight and handed it back next day. I was like a dog with its first bone – and I'd swallowed it in one go.

Over the next few weeks, she gave me a number of books and I read them as quickly and with as much hunger as I had the first one. I continued to copy out formulae and other scientific information from the dictionary, but I started to copy out other things too. Occasionally Miss Angelica would spend five or ten minutes chatting with me about something or other to do with science. More importantly, and very tactfully, she'd ask what *I* thought about the matters she mentioned. While I could have told her the chemical formula for hydrated magnesium sulphate or sodium thiosulphate, I couldn't have told her much else. But the questions she asked were intended to make me think logically; they were phrased to enable me to work things out within the limits of what little knowledge I did have. That was part of her brilliance both as a teacher and a human being, and I'll never ever forget it. She took the time to help one or two of the other kids in a similar manner and they undoubtedly benefited too. But I was only interested in my own progress, and if that seems self-centred – well, try a special school for a decade.

One morning at milk break Miss Angelica suggested I join my local library. I'd never been in the library before, but it sounded a great idea, so I decided to join and looked forward to an endless supply of reading material. I arranged to go along one afternoon after school with a boy who lived a couple of doors along from us. He went to the school where the radio played at dinnertime, a junior secondary school for Protestants. He wasn't a member of the library himself, and he wasn't particularly bright, either. But despite the fact he was jailed for murder some years later, he was as kind and considerate as you could hope for, and that was a fair measure of someone's worth in my book.

I was filled with excitement and anticipation as we entered the building that contained both the local library and the museum. We made our way into the library section and I breathed in deeply when I saw all the shelves of books. I'd never seen anything remotely like it. It was marvellous, but just a bit intimidating too.

I saw a lady standing at the reception desk, so I went over and said I wanted to join. She asked me a few questions – my name, address, that sort of thing – then she asked what school I went to.

'I go to the, eh, Special School,' I said, within earshot of my companion, and just about everyone else in the library it seemed, by the way the place stopped in its tracks and everyone stood stock still waiting for the outcome.

The lady peered down at me.

'Special school? What special school? Are you a gifted child, or something?'

'A gifted what?' I asked, flushing.

'A gifted child,' she repeated. 'Exceptionally clever: a prodigy, a child mathematician, a juvenile chess-master – something like that?'

I frowned.

'I don't think so. I can play a decent game of chess and I'm fairly good at remembering chemical formulae. But I don't think I'm specially gifted or anything. I just like science.'

'I see,' she said, bending her head over and inspecting me more closely. 'So why do you go to a special school?' she asked, observing me as if I were one of the specimens in the microscope book.

'It's a school for children with special requirements,' I said, neutrally. I was determined not to divulge my medical history in public.

'Oh, *that* school,' she said, far too loudly, as my companion eased away and tried to dissociate himself from me. 'I'm afraid we don't have an agreement with *them*, as far as I know,' the librarian continued officiously, as I reddened even further, to the deepest colour I think I'd ever been. 'Let me check in the office, but I don't think we lend books to pupils *there*. I wasn't even sure they could read,' she said. 'But just a moment and I'll check.'

She went off somewhere and I took another look at all the shelves of books. I was torn between them and the certain, complete and utter public humiliation I'd experience if I were refused permission to join. I chose to avoid the humiliation and moved away from the desk. I shuffled slowly to the door and left, with my companion following. He seemed to be keeping his distance, the way I'd done with Martin on my first day at school.

'That was a bit much,' he said, when he finally caught up with me outside. 'Why wouldn't she let you join?'

'Because of my school.'

He looked shocked.

'Just because all those loonies go there?'

'Perhaps,' I said, staring at the ground the way Martin had that first day, too.

'But you're not mad or anything, are you? Just because you go there doesn't mean you're mad. Does it?'

'No,' I agreed. 'I'm not mad.'

'You're just sort of . . . unwell or something. My mum says most of you just have normal problems: slow to learn, fits, sudden tremors, things like that,' he said, mimicking a few of those things for emphasis.

'Yes, something like that,' I agreed, feeling smaller now than the *amoeba proteus* I'd seen in the microscopy book.

'I could join the library for you, if you want,' said the boy. 'But I'm not a gifted child either and I can't read or write too well, so you'd have to fill in the forms.'

'Thanks, but it's OK. I'll arrange it some other way.'

'No problem,' he said, sounding like Billy, and still shaking his head at the injustice conferred on me.

I went home that evening and wept, but I let no one see me do so. Later, I asked my sister if she'd be kind enough to join the library and let me use her card.

She knew something was wrong.

'I'll take you along and you can get one for yourself.'

I shook my head.

'I'd rather use yours.'

'Why?'

'I'd be able to get older kinds of books.'

'You're not old enough for older kinds of books. Anyway, you don't seem to have read many younger kinds of books yet.'

My mother came into the room with my little brother, a surprise addition to the family a few years before.

She'd overheard my sister.

'Oh, he'll be reading more from now on,' she said.

My sister looked at her.

'How come?'

'He joined the library today,' she said proudly. 'This afternoon.'

'Then why does he want a card from me?' asked my sister.

My mum looked at her.

'I've no idea,' she said, switching her gaze to me.

My sister looked at me too.

'I didn't join,' I said.

'Why not?' they asked together.

'They don't have a formal arrangement with my school.'

My sister didn't believe me.

'They don't?'

'No.'

'Then I'll get a card for you on Saturday,' she said, quietly. 'But if they haven't given you one because of the school you go to, or if they've upset you, I'll kick up merry Hell.'

It was one of the few times I'd ever heard my sister say anything remotely profane. It delighted me. She could still be pretty stern at times, but she was a great sister to have on your side.

In due course she got her library card and allowed me to use it, and I got my books at last. So I finally got my hands on an unlimited source of reading material and with my teacher's advice, I was able to be more selective in my reading.

Not long after this, the most important afternoon of my life arrived unheralded, as such times tend to. Immediately before a lesson Miss Angelica took me to the front of the class and, like a decent and upright Mephistopheles, the Three Magi, the Easter Bunny, good Greeks bearing decent gifts and Santa Claus on a spending spree, all rolled into one, told me:

'I've arranged for you to go next door to the Academy to have a look at a proper laboratory.'

The feeling I had was indescribable.

'Thanks, Miss,' I said, inadequately and I felt all weird and wonderful as I said it. But as I turned to go back to my desk, I noticed all the other pupils looking at me. They'd overheard, of course, and noted what she'd said.

I realised that after all these years together, I'd been eased a little bit away from them. I'd been offered an opportunity – albeit only for an hour or so – to attend a normal school and it meant I was leaving them, or so it seemed to me, and evidently, by the looks on their faces, to them too.

Even now I don't know how to describe how I felt at that moment. So I think it's best if I say nothing more about it.

28

Big Bill Penn, principal science teacher at the local Academy, looked like something out of the Wild West, with his prominent nose, wide excited eyes and mass of white flowing hair. As prearranged, he met me at the main door of the Academy, which was quite literally adjacent to my somewhat more modest school. He led me along a maze of corridors to one of the science classrooms, which he'd told me was empty. We stopped outside. He pulled open the door and stood aside to let me look in.

Heaven! No, even better! It was beyond my wildest dreams.

There were test tubes and retorts, conical and volumetric flasks, measuring cylinders, pipettes, beakers and droppers that tapered to perfectly flattened ends. There were real-sized Bunsen burners, jars of chemicals, balances and test-tube racks; there were big brown bottles, rubber tubing, a fume cupboard, wall charts of the Chemical Elements and dark red rubber bungs with glass tubing sitting neatly in holes in their tops. It was perfect – just perfect.

'So what do you think?' asked Big Bill, following me in.

'It's very nice, sir,' I said calmly, understating my feelings as ever.

He stood back.

'Shall we have a good look round?'

'If you don't mind,' I said politely as I walked over to a long, sinewy retort flask and touched its top.

'That's nice too, sir,' I said, and he nodded. I think he'd noticed I was pleased.

Big Bill lit a Bunsen burner and the flame kicked in with a popping sound.

'You adjust it like this,' he explained, moving its thin metal control back and forth with his fingers. The flame grew and shrank and changed colour as he did so.

He put some blue crystals of copper sulphate into a test tube and held it over the flame using a pair of tong-like things I'd never even known existed.

'You should always hold a test tube at an angle to the flame,' he explained, 'and move it about to make sure you get an even spread of heat. That way it won't erupt in your face.' With a hissing sound the crystals had started to turn white.

'Any idea what's happening?'

'It's turning white, sir.'

'Anything else?' he inquired, checking my powers of observation.

'The blue's disappearing and there's moisture forming at the top of the test tube.'

'And why do you think that is?'

I looked at him.

'It's hard to explain in words,' I said. 'I'd really need to write it down, sir.'

He nodded.

'Then on you go.' He pulled a piece of chalk from his impressive black gown and handed it to me. This material sign of academic pedigree was something else I'd never seen before and like everything else in the laboratory, it fascinated me.

'Write it on the blackboard,' he instructed kindly and, seeing my hesitation, gave me some encouragement. 'Go on: you'll never make a decent scientist if you can't use a blackboard every bit as well as a test tube.'

So I did. I wrote out the formula of hydrated copper sulphate, spelling the word "sulfate" with the American 'f'. Siggy would have suggested that my omitting the 'ph' with its special school connotations was a Freudian thing – what he called a 'parapraxis'. It wasn't. My dictionary was American, so I'd no idea how to spell chemical names in the Queen's English.

'That's pretty good,' said Big Bill when he'd seen my efforts, as he laid the test tube down on an asbestos board and turned off the Bunsen. 'Now, what d'you think would happen if we mixed sodium carbonate with hydrochloric acid?'

I scribbled out the formulae for these too, then paused to think for a moment before completing the equation.

'You'd get sodium chloride, water and carbon dioxide gas,' I said, as I proceeded to write the formulae for these out in full too.

'Well done!' he laughed, and I smiled too, pleased and proud to be showing my limited skills in this unique and heady manner.

He became more serious.

'Just one thing. You'd look better with your left hand out of your pocket,' he said, and I immediately pulled out the offending hand. 'Fine! Good! Now, I'd like to bring a couple of the senior boys in to meet you, if that's OK?'

'Of course, sir,' I said, as he went out of the door leaving me alone with this treasure trove.

He returned with four boys from the Sixth Form. He asked if I minded if they put some questions to me. I didn't, and off they went. They were pleasant, smart and sensitive boys who asked question after question on chemical formulae, equations and so forth. They went neither too fast nor too far. They soon assessed the level of my expertise and sensitively kept to it. The only thing they corrected on occasion was my spelling, though even then they were tactful and helpful, being fully aware of my New World dictionary reference source and of my true academic pedigree.

At last we seemed to have reached the end of the session and when I finally put the chalk down and rubbed my hands together to get the dust off, the boys smiled approval among themselves and I felt great. They exchanged approving glances with Big Bill too, and he looked on like a proud father.

The boys were heroic figures in their smart school uniforms, with jackets that had proper badges on their top left-hand pockets. I wished I could be like them, with their dark-blue blazers, grey trousers and knowledge of everything I could ever wish for in terms of a proper education.

Big Bill smiled at them.

'Thanks, boys. You can go now, and thanks again.'

I said 'thanks' too. One of the boys walked towards me.

He shook my hand.

'Thank *you*,' he said. The others followed suit before they made for the door and left us.

Big Bill came and stood beside me. I think my hair was standing on end with sheer exhilaration. Those shakes of the hand were the most welcome touches I'd ever known in my life. For a while, I'd been accepted as a proper schoolboy. A statement of my worth, of that type and degree, had never been made before on my behalf – and it hasn't since either.

Big Bill spoke.

'Any idea what happens when you add a molar solution of potassium permanganate to a molar solution of citric acid?'

I thought about it.

'Sorry, sir. I've no idea.'

'Ah, but you will, son,' said Big Bill, wiping the blackboard clean with a duster. 'Aye, you will, son. I'll see to it personally.'

As we walked back along the corridors of the Academy, past solid-looking doors behind which proper-looking boys were receiving proper lessons from proper teachers dressed in proper academic gowns, Big Bill asked me all sorts of things about my background and my education. I told him lots about the former, but little about the latter; he'd seen most of it anyway, scribbled out in poor American English on a blackboard.

When we reached the main door, he shook hands with me too.

'It's been a pleasure, young Frank,' he said sincerely, using the diminutive form of my name. 'I'll see you again,' he told me finally and I felt as if he meant it.

'Thank you, sir,' I responded, shaking his hand hard, as if it were a lifeline I didn't want to tear myself away from.

'Go on back,' he said finally. 'Get back to your present school for now.'

I wasn't a gifted child, as I've said, nor given the general state of things was I a child athlete, but I ran Hell-for-leather up the driveway of the Academy and headed back to my own school as if I had wings on my feet like Hermes, the god of medical science. 'Get back to your present school *for now*,' Big Bill had said, and his voice and his words echoed loudly as I ran harder and faster than I ever had.

I finally arrived back outside my classroom, puffing and heaving like the grape man had at the hospital. I was tired, excited and confused – and I was loving every single moment of it.

29

For the rest of that afternoon I could barely sit still. I managed to keep my body from fidgeting too much, but my thoughts were fidgeting too and they were less easily controlled. Round and round they flew, re-creating every second of my time in the school lab. I was still tingling with excitement and I could barely wait to get back home and tell my family about it.

Our class had been smaller than usual for almost two weeks. A number of pupils had gone off for a visit to Lourdes at long last, with three or four going from our class, including Una, via her medical sabbatical. Billy, Jason and Woody, still a class down from us, had also gone. I wasn't certain Woody qualified to go on religious grounds, but he went anyway. My family still couldn't afford to send me to Lourdes, but to be perfectly honest I didn't expect any miracles anyway.

My mind was preoccupied with thoughts of science, not religion, as I sat on my return to the classroom ruminating on things chemical and elementary. Miss Angelica had asked briefly how I'd liked my visit and I'd simply said it had been very good. A few of the other children had acknowledged my return and Melissa in particular kept flashing me looks of approval, just as she had on our very first day at school. I was buoyant, happy and elated, and tried unsuccessfully to pay attention to our lesson on how to make anagrams from words of two letters.

Next door, Miss Tartankilty was playing 'Scotland the Brave'. I liked it much better now I wasn't actually in her classroom. It was as if distance made it sound more romantic, much in the way certain aspects of history can seem romantic from the distance given by time, when in fact – as I was finding out from library books – it usually turns out to be very far from it. As I listened to 'Scotland the Brave' scrape round again next door, I was suddenly shaken into the here and now.

'OOG-OO-AH . . .! OOG-OO-AH, O-HAH, O-AAH!'

I almost jumped out of my skin. So did Miss Angelica.

'What's that?' she asked.

'It's just Derek,' said Melissa reassuringly.

'Derek?'

'Yes, Derek, Miss. He's one of our "Old Boys".'

'I don't recall having seen Derek.'

'Oh, he left school a few years ago,' explained Melissa. 'But he went to Lourdes with some of the other children, to assist.'

That puzzled me. I went back in my memory to where I'd been when Derek had appeared at our First Confession.

'But Derek's not Catholic,' I said. 'What's he up to, going to Lourdes? I'm surprised they let him in.'

Melissa spoke.

'You don't have to be a Catholic to help out,' she said, in a remarkably prim voice. 'I imagine he would be made very welcome and benefit both spiritually and physically from such a visit. Anyway, Woody went, and he's hardly a paid-up member of the Vatican State.'

'Perhaps he's become a convert?' I said, still surprised and delighted at Derek's imminent reappearance.

She sighed.

'I don't see why. He's had his crosses to bear too, you know, and I doubt he'd be denied spiritual favours just because of the religion he happened to be born into.'

I wondered about Melissa. Despite my scientific leanings I'd never heard the term 'free thinker' before, but if I had I'd have thought she was becoming one of them.

'Enough!' said Miss Angelica, fully recovered from the shock of hearing Derek for the first time. 'Why don't you all go and greet your friends? After all, it sounds as if you haven't seen them for ages.'

We rose, grabbed the wheelchairs we were responsible for and made for the door. We could hear voices in the corridor: the sound of our returning pilgrims.

I was first to the door, pushing a boy with whom I'd become friendly, in a wheelchair. At thirteen he'd been considered a promising prospect by our local professional football team. A few months later he'd been crippled by polio.

We went into the corridor and I stopped abruptly.

'Hello there, Francis,' said Derek, 'How are you?'

The growing roots of my scientific materialism shrivelled.

'Good to see you, Francis,' said another voice. It was Una. Her head was held as high and as proud as a female giraffe's, and there wasn't a brace in sight. I turned in her general direction. A hand crept forward to meet mine.

'Shake,' said Woody, who was standing to one side with his arms fully and equally extended in welcome.

'Well, you're looking good, Frankie,' said Jason, all macho-looking with an open sports shirt on and boasting the shadow of a beard. He had his arm around the waist of one of the prettier *girls* from the class below us. I looked at them all in amazement.

'What's happened?' I asked, as I saw indisputable evidence of miracle upon miracle right there in front of me.

'What d'you mean?' asked Una, shaking her hair back like some *haute coiffure* model.

'Why, you're all cured!' I said, as I searched for a better way to describe it.

'Cured?' said Woody.

'You're no longer . . . well, eh, handicapped,' I stammered, hating the word but feeling obliged to use it, while searching for Billy. If he'd been cured too, he'd be as white as he'd always wanted to be.

'What *are* you talking about?' asked Miss Angelica, who was standing beside me, holding a tiny girl in her arms who looked as if she could do with a visit to Lourdes, pronto.

'Well they're all, eh, better . . .' I said lamely.

'Better what?'

'Than they were. Cured!'

Derek confused me more than the rest. Despite Melissa's comments and the evidence to the contrary, I still maintained miracles at Lourdes were the provenance of Catholics. I looked at him carefully.

He spoke.

'Ah, I'm not Derek, if that's what you think,' said Derek.

'You're not?'

'I'm Eric,' said Derek. 'Not Derek,' said Eric. And I began to understand.

I looked more carefully.

'*Eric*? You're his identical twin?' I said, horrified that yet another secret had been kept from me. 'Derek and Eric!' That was a hoot.

'Don't be stupid,' said Melissa who was standing beside me protectively. 'They can't be identical twins; they have different voices.'

'Yes,' said Derek-now-Eric. 'I'm four years younger than Derek.'

I tried to work it out as he continued: 'Derek's told me all about you, Francis. Una pointed you out when you came out of your class. Derek's inside listening to "Scotland the Brave".'

'Of course!' I suddenly realised I hadn't seen Derek for years. He'd look older. It was as if until that moment I'd believed people continued to look the way they'd been when you'd last seen them. But it isn't like that, is it?

Una rubbed at her neck.

'This new brace itches. They call it "cosmetic", but it itches something awful. It's hardly worth getting your neck broken for.'

We shook our heads in tacit agreement. I realised she too was no walking miracle, just a neater version of the same thing.

'Gotcha!' screeched Woody, pulling a small pair of scissors from somewhere and sticking them into his arm. 'It's a special prosthetic light wood,' he explained. 'But it works OK and it's hidden by my sleeve.'

I didn't bother asking how they'd managed to put wood in between his proper shoulder and his hand. Instead I looked at Jason and his girlfriend. No doubt there'd be a normal explanation for his deviant behaviour, too.

'She's one of us,' he said proudly, as he looked affectionately at his female companion. 'You won't understand yet, Frankie, but we have similar orientations in opposite directions, if you get my drift.'

I looked from one to the other; at least he seemed happier than usual.

'Excuse the three o'clock shadow,' he went on, 'but I hit adolescence full blown last week. The overnight trip from France was a bit of a rush, so I didn't have time to shave,' he said, as his friend nodded and rubbed her own chin. It gave off a bristling sound and I wondered if she'd been unable to shave too.

'So where's Billy?' I asked. 'I suppose he's as pink and white as the rest of us now?'

There was a deathly silence.

Una shifted her head about uncomfortably.

'He's dead, Francis. I thought you'd know by now. It happened just over a week ago.'

Dead? Billy? No! People like Billy never died!

'He drowned,' said Eric.

'Drowned?' I repeated, wondering what on earth the dark-blue boy had been up to, to go and get himself drowned.

Una squeezed my hand.

'When we arrived at Lourdes he ran off like a hare. Then, shouting, "Sacred bleach here I come!" he dived straight into one of the bathing-pools, fully clothed.'

She paused and looked reflective.

'He never surfaced again. He didn't even float back up. They had to dredge for him with poles until they snagged him and brought him to the surface. When they dragged him out he had a big smile on his face. I saw him, you know, and he looked happier then than I'd ever seen him. He'd become quite white,' she added, 'or anyway, whiter than he'd been up until then.'

I couldn't quite take it in. How could things change like this so suddenly? Once more the movement of time seemed to have altered. But why should things stay the same? I knew they couldn't stay fixed forever; it was just they hadn't seemed to change quite so quickly before. I felt that internal shadow deepen again and began to sob uncontrollably. It wasn't just grief, it was the thought of Billy soaring through the air like Superman. I felt he'd been born for that solitary moment of abandon, that he'd been fated from birth to die like that, flying through the air like a superman, that super boy whom the gods had determined would die all alone, just as he'd lived.

I choked, and wept openly. I missed him. We may not have been bosom buddies any more, but like Al he'd been my early and dear friend. They'd *both* been and they were both gone, and here I was standing weeping in front of all our classmates on the day I'd had the greatest thrill of my own pathetic little life – as a voyeur in an out-of-bounds school a few hundred yards down the road.

Miss Angelica touched my arm.

'He didn't have long to go anyway, Francis. He'd have died within a few months. From what I've heard, it was a better way to go than through heart failure. His condition was inoperable and he'd have gradually faded away from us. He knew that, so maybe he thought it better to go out with a show. He was a young *man* when he died, you know, and no one expected him to attain that. He died like one, too.'

I turned.

'Maybe, but he didn't have a chance from day one. He was born desperately ill, then there was that business with his parents and his brother. But he never gave up . . .' I took a very deep breath. 'It's bloody unfair!' I said, angry and almost breaking down again as I imagined him, in a blur of his hated blue, plunging into that pool and sinking.

'No one said life's dished out in equal doses of fairness,' said Miss Angelica. 'It doesn't work like that, I'm afraid.'

I nodded.

'I suppose it doesn't,' I said.

I heard shuffling sounds and saw the proper, older Derek emerge from the door of the classroom beside us. 'Scotland the Brave' had stopped playing; I looked into the classroom and saw Miss Tartankilty remove it from the gramophone and wipe it clean for the thousandth time. Like everyone else, she looked older to me now: frailer, somehow.

'Time,' I thought, and, for a crazy moment, I thought I heard a breath from somewhere up above me. I looked up; at the ceiling, then out through the window, at the sky. Nothing.

Derek's eyes lit up when he saw me. He got into such a state he made all the movements associated with welcome sounds, but none emerged. I'd been silly to confuse him with his brother, despite the uncanny resemblance. Miracles may well happen on occasion, but not miracles like that one.

I saw an attractive young woman beside him – it was Moira. She'd also grown up; she looked older too. Time was flying by.

'Derek says it's good to see you,' she translated, looking at him with dignity and pride. 'He wants you to know we're engaged. We're going to be married next month' – she put her foot down – 'next month,' she repeated, flushing and failing to translate what Derek had said in response.

I was surprised. I'd never dreamed people at my school would ever really get married.

'Congratulations!' I said, despite myself, wondering already what their children would be like.

'Why, that's lovely,' said Melissa, looking at the two of them and then at me. 'It's good to know romance can blossom in the most unexpected places,' she added, moving away from the group and heading back into the classroom. I followed her back with the rest of them. It was a strange and eventful day.

That night, in one of those moments of great clarity it's impossible to explain to anyone, I suddenly reckoned there had indeed been a miracle at Lourdes. It was the sort of miracle that happens daily and for the most part passes unnoticed. It was Billy's ending his life the way he'd chosen to. That had been a miracle, at least I knew it was then. I understood it all perfectly at the time, but I didn't immediately afterwards – and I certainly don't now.

30

It was around this time that my brother became a full-time member of the rock band. He spent days at a time away from home, touring. And by his own account, and by the far more objective account of the Kodak Brownie snaps he showed me, he led an entertaining and event-filled life.

He'd started taking pills too, on occasion: 'Purple Hearts' they were called – a name that understandably brought Al and Billy to mind. He obtained them privately on a named-patient basis, from someone who sounded suspiciously like a member of his rock band. These pills were in big demand; they seemed to speed up my brother's whole life when he took them. He could go for night after night without sleep, which is brilliant if you don't need sleep much, so they seemed perfectly designed for the rock business. In a less glamorous vein perhaps, they seemed perfect for plumpish women too.

Many of the overweight women in our area began to take these pills and our street became busy with them rushing about at all hours, but especially at night – like rock stars. They didn't seem to need much sleep either. It got so bad at one point they were keeping the rest of us awake by running around all night, ringing doorbells and knocking on doors, telling one another how many pounds they'd lost when they'd weighed themselves for the twenty-fourth time that day, earlier that evening.

It all came to a very abrupt end, however, when a woman who lived three doors along from us went stark raving mad after a record fifteen days and nights of running around in this manner. She went completely off her head and thought she was a giant sausage-roll about to be eaten by all the other hungry women. The men in white coats took her away for a time, removed her Purple Hearts and put her onto another new drug that I, with my specialist knowledge, knew as a benzodiazepine. That done, she improved rapidly and came home a bit embarrassed she'd ever thought her neighbours had wanted to eat her in the first place.

So that had a happy ending. But all the women who'd previously rushed around becoming very thin now started taking this new drug, slowed down and became plump again. I couldn't quite see the point in it all.

In due course, we discovered taking Purple Hearts and the like wasn't the most sensible thing, even to keep yourself going or to shed a pound or two. Fortunately, my brother gave them up very quickly after trying them out, rather than continuing, as some did, to use them to keep himself going.

So that was the drugs bit. On occasion he'd bring friends back at night after a gig, usually at weekends, and they were usually fellow male musicians. On these occasions I'd wake up, get dressed and bring cups of tea and buttered rolls through to his room, to prepare him and his guests for the day ahead. When I did this I'd normally find drum kits, guitars, trombones, saxophones and myriad other instruments sharing a bed with my brother, as their owners slept peacefully on the floor.

Sometimes, however, these fellow 'musicians' were female. Then the procedure was different and everything had to be handled with care, tact and caution. 'They're backing vocalists,' he'd tell my mother, and certainly many of them were highly vocal. I didn't mind any of this and enjoyed being able to do the favour. He'd helped me a lot as a child and now I could return some of those favours in spirit, if not in kind.

On one occasion, however, he pushed his luck too hard. He left one of the 'backing vocalists' behind one Saturday while he went off somewhere, and we had to entertain her. As it turned out, she entertained us with stories about her pet monkey. I'd never dreamed such pets existed, but she assured us they did, and she had one.

In a sense she was also my first date, for my brother still hadn't arrived back by evening, so I took her to see *Demetrius and the Gladiators* at the local cinema. She enjoyed it, she said later while we waited for her bus home. I enjoyed it too, in that sort of minimalist, early-testosterone-induced erotic way you do when adolescence first trickles into you, like an innocent little friend promising to liven your life up a bit – when all the time it's really intent on causing maximum upset in just about every area of life you can think of, for the rest of your days.

When the bus arrived, she lifted her nice long legs onto it, then looked round.

'You know, your brother's a right bast . . . ba,' she said, and 'ba' was fine by me; I was old enough to know what she meant and she didn't have to spell it out.

I was sitting in his room later that night, unravelling and making up balls of wool for my sister, who was knitting some sort of floral cardigan. She paid me to do this, sometimes, so I was gainfully employed and I could hear the click, click, click of her knitting needles in the room adjacent. I heard the outside door close and my brother came into the bedroom. I was angry at the way he'd treated the girl with the monkey, so I put the wool down.

'That young woman was upset. You ought to treat your girlfriends better. None of the rest of us would ever dream of doing that to someone: leaving them behind like that!'

He was in one of his sensitive artistic moods.

'OK, so I'm the black sheep of the family. I don't care.'

I felt sorry for him.

'I didn't say that. I just said you should treat your girlfriends better.'

'Oh, don't try and spare me – I am the black sheep; I've always known it. The rest of you were always the favourites, never me.'

I wondered if he was back on the pills.

'That's not true!'

He was angry and in performance mode.

'Black sheep,' he emphasised, thumping his chest. 'Black sheep!'

I heard my sister's bedroom door open. We'd raised our voices and disturbed her.

I continued to speak, but more quietly. I didn't want her to hear me swearing.

'Your girlfriend called you something – a sort of swear word.'

'What?'

'A "ba", she called you a "ba".'

'A "ba"?'

I nodded.

'Ba!'

He thumped his chest again.

'Black sheep!'

'Have you any wool?' asked my sister as she pushed her way in, looking at us suspiciously. We said nothing. I gave her a ball and she left.

'That was an unfortunate word to use,' said my brother.

'Why's that?' I asked, knowing full well what he meant.

'It reflects on our mother.'

I shook my head.

'No! It reflects on *your* father,' I said, and he stared at me. I had testosterone running into me all right.

I was growing up.

31

One afternoon, I was called to see the headmistress in her office. She ushered me in and asked me to sit down.

'I've been speaking with the headmaster at the Academy,' she said, and I held my breath.

'Subject to approval by the Education Authority and the school doctor, you can attend a chemistry class on a regular basis, to prepare for the Ordinary Grade School Certificate. Most boys do more than one of these, but it's usually when they're older than you and when they're better prepared. If all goes well, you'll start after the summer break. So what do you think of that?'

What did I think about *that*?

'I'd love it Miss. I'll do the very best I can.'

'I'm sure you will,' she said, as a new world opened up before me: one where dreams came true for a while before they turned into a permanent nightmare.

I saw my first Special School football match days later. Unlike most other schools in Scotland, special schools had no official football league. Consequently they had to arrange a league and competitive matches between schools, informally, and these had to take place in playgrounds at lunchtimes.

The gentleman who'd started the Special Schools Handicap League was the former product of a special school himself. His name was Big Jock Tamson and he'd formerly been a supporter of the small, but respected and long-established Scottish football team, Albion Rovers. The 'Wee Rovers', as their supporters know them, were founded in 1882 and entered the Scottish League proper in 1903. They might have been nothing to write home about in Big Jock's day ten years before, but they had a vociferous core of dedicated supporters, as they still have even today. Years before, in the 1919–20 season, they'd helped to attract a crowd of over ninety-six thousand noisy fans to the Scottish Cup final. In the early 1960s, however, such crowds were very definitely a thing of the past and the Wee Rovers were attracting only a few hundred fans. Even so, these stalwarts showed both loyalty and commitment – as did the legendary Big Jock Tamson, which was slightly surprising.

For unlike Jock, most of the other fans could see fairly well. But Big Jock cut a figure at Cliftonhill Stadium, where the Wee Rovers play, because he was easily recognisable with his dark glasses and white stick with the team's colours, red and yellow stripes, on its handle. Big Jock was almost completely blind you see and that's why he'd qualified for his special schooling.

While his compromised eyesight didn't trouble Jock one little bit, it had troubled his former special school team. For when he'd founded it and decided to name it after his more senior favourites, his eyesight had betrayed him. So instead of calling them 'Albion Rovers (Specials)', as intended, he'd called them 'Albino Rovers' instead.

Now this wasn't a bad name for a special school football team, but it was misleading, for most of the players had no sight problems whatsoever, though they did all have *some* type of physical disability, being recruited solely from the ranks of the physically handicapped in the special school Big Jock had attended. Because of their refusal to sign mentally handicapped kids, Albino Rovers had been accused of bigotry. However, Big Jock had pointed out that some of his best friends and enemies were mentally handicapped, which was enough to put such complaints to rest once and for all, certainly among his friends and his enemies.

The opposing team that day, and the one representing *our* school, was called 'Cyanotic City'. It had been founded by eleven former blue babies – unfairly termed 'a bunch of bigoted blue-noses' by their critics – who'd grown up with a philanthropic interest in special schools' soccer. Like me, they'd been unable to play the game themselves when young, so they'd decided to found a team that could by proxy, as it were.

Unlike Albino Rovers under Big Jock, the original founders and the current manager of Cyanotic City didn't confine their choice of players to the P.H. side of our school. They talent-scouted among the M.H. pupils as well, in order to give the side a proper tactical balance and a reputation for equality in terms of who was chosen to play for it. Accordingly, Cyanotic City FC had been well established in special schools' soccer for some years, and was well respected in this admittedly rarefied sporting arena. However, there were still some who claimed that its current players didn't reflect the ethos of its fairly genteel founders, and it was true that the current team was well known for its aggressive approach to winning a football match. In particular, it was claimed some of the mentally handicapped kids had been known to 'lose it' on occasion, though from what I'd heard personally these kids tended to provoke anger, not dish it out, as they were very gifted at playing the game rather than disrupting it.

So it was with a fair bit of apprehension that I stood and watched these teams line up against one another this particular lunchtime, daggers metaphorically drawn and looking like two sets of Hieronymous Boschian gladiators in a recently restored but poorly reconstructed Coliseum.

The centre-forward for the Cyanotics was Rollup Boy, the kid with the hump, who continued to do his equivalent of fifty sit-ups every day while balancing expertly on his back. As I watched, he limbered up by touching his hump with his head, which he moved back and forth and side to side with agility. He looked powerful too, in his specially tailored football gear, despite his small size in relation to the rest of the players.

His opposite number for Albino Rovers was the Headless Boy of Derek-and-his-wheelchair fame. He'd been transferred from Cyanotic City some weeks before, for an unstated fee, though he was still officially a pupil at our school. Given this, he didn't acknowledge a single one of us. He'd grown up too, but you still couldn't see where his head was and he was a sinister-looking figure as he waited in the centre of the park for the game to begin.

Albino Rovers' goalkeeper was a heavy and aggressive boy, who effected his art through masterful use of the crutches he carried covetously, like the personal effects of a refugee. It was said in the appropriate sports columns that he was never without them, which was probably just as well, for otherwise he'd have fallen flat on his face and been no use to anyone, let alone a team as ambitious as Albino Rovers Football Club.

His opposite number was another 'Mr Big' – Big Tam McGowan. Tam was a large, hard, boy from P.H.4, and his particular talent as a goalkeeper lay in utilising the two walking sticks he had. He used these to great effect to batter the ball away whenever it came near him. He was usually well positioned to do so too, as he had two artificial legs with which he could block the fastest-moving ball with equal effectiveness and no discomfort.

The centre-half for Cyanotic City was my wheelchair-bound friend who'd formerly hoped to play football professionally. He was going to do so now, it seemed, if not for money then for something every bit as desirable: self-respect. He'd worked himself up for this game by pounding the wall with his bare fists and I hoped this latent aggression – common to any gifted athlete crippled by polio – would find appropriate outlet during the game. His counterpart was also in a wheelchair, and as they stared one another down along the whole length of the playground, I was reminded of the scene in *Ben Hur* when that very gifted actor Charlton Heston takes on the might of the tricky charioteer Massala.

I'd heard this centre-half was a gifted actor too. He'd had no fewer than four previous adversaries sent off from the field of play for interfering with the spokes in his wheels, which he'd allegedly damaged himself through the discreet use of a knitting needle he kept hidden in the lead of his hearing aid. I hoped my friend wouldn't fall for that one and be sent off the field himself.

So these were the major players, as seen solely from my own perspective. The rest were unknown quantities, and of course I'd never seen any of them play football before.

The referee approached the captains with the ball in his hands and, as is traditional, spoke with them briefly before commencement of action. He did so, however, only when he inhaled. You see, the role of referee was a perfect one for this boy. He'd come from a broken home, and had his nose broken too, as a handicapped baby. It was never reset properly, so when he exhaled a loud whistling sound came out through his nostrils, which was certainly loud enough to stop play on any pitch where he was present, or indeed within a three-mile radius there. He made the captains shake hands, then looked to the linesman to check the time.

The linesman indicated with his left hand that it was time to commence. He too had an authoritative look about him. His fingerless hands were each painted a different colour, one for each team, and he used them like flags to indicate any offence, in the manner of any other linesman with proper flags.

The referee breathed out smartly, the whistling sound caught everyone's attention and as I stood back and positioned myself for the action, the game was on.

'COME ON THE CY-AN-O-TIC CIT-EE!' cried the crowd around me.

'ON YE GO AL-BI-NO!' cried the crowd on the other side of the playground.

The tension was palpable as the players went at it vigorously, and the sound of callipers clashing, wheelchairs whizzing and walking sticks and crutches crunching like makeshift kendo rods filled the air with all the noisy, uninhibited aggression of trench warfare.

'KILL THAT TURD!' shouted Wee Jimmy, with his legs fixed tightly on their stumps as he raised himself high on the back of a boy in front of him.

'CUT HIM DOWN!' yelled Una, forgetting herself for a moment and advocating the sort of violence that was only usually visited on *her* when her neck brace was too tight and had to be adjusted.

I simply stood there watching, enjoying myself immensely, until a sudden shout of 'PENALTY!' hushed our half of the crowd and raised a frenzy of screaming and screeching in the other. My friend in the wheelchair had intentionally used the specially treaded tyres on his wheels to cut someone up in the penalty area and it was a penalty for the Albinos.

It was completely quiet as the Rovers' right-back hobbled up to take it. Our goalkeeper, Big Tam McGowan, perched himself steadily between his walking sticks, making certain as he did so that his wooden legs were digging deep down onto the playground surface. An even deeper hush fell as the Albino right-back moved towards the ball, which had been placed precisely on the penalty spot.

He kicked it . . .

I saw a blurred shape move through the air as Big Tam dived and in so doing left his two wooden legs standing ramrod straight on the centre of the goal line. His arms, which were stretched out from his torso, successfully caught the moving shape: but he noticed immediately, as I did, that what he'd caught wasn't any ball, but yet another leg! In mid-air, he looked at the penalty taker. So did I. We noticed simultaneously that *his* right leg had disappeared. It had been an artificial one too, and Tam had caught it while the ball, in the meantime, headed straight for goal.

'OOOH!' gasped the crowd, as the ball hit Big Tam's detached legs, which still stood solidly on their own on the centre of the goal line. 'AAAH!' they went, as it bounced off and came back out again, hitting Big Tam's head as his torso hit the ground with a thump and his arms enfolded the missing leg of the penalty taker. 'OOOH!' they gasped once more, as the ball was headed away from goal by a brave but very much shrunken Big Tam. Unfortunately for him, however, it went straight back to the penalty taker, who lashed out with his one remaining foot, tumbling as he did so, and connected with the ball before toppling over not too far from where Tam was lying wriggling, trying to get up.

'GOAL!' anticipated the Albino Rovers fans, as the ball headed straight towards the Cyanotic City net once again. But Big Tam, in desperation, threw the leg he was still holding with all the strength of the muscular shoulders his strongly built torso supported.

'HURRAY!' jeered the CCFC fans ironically, as the leg travelled straight as an arrow to hit the ball away for a corner, while Big Tam and the penalty taker lay side by side, with only one leg between them, trying to grab one another by the throat.

'CHEAT! CHEAT! CHEAT!' chanted the Albino Rovers fans, in Big Tam's direction, while the Cyanotic City fans yelled:

'GET INTAE THEM, GET INTAE THEM, THE BABY BLUE BOVVER BOYS!'

It all seemed to be getting a bit out of hand, when the referee sneezed and the whistle blew like a ship's funnel at midnight on Hogmanay. *That* brought the game to a halt, and it brought the atmosphere back to something resembling normality.

'AH DON'T WANT ANY MORE TROUBLE WI' YOU LOT!' inhaled the ref, shouting at us all loudly on the intake. 'OTHERWISE AH'LL CALL THE WHOLE EFFING THING OFF,' he managed, maintaining his silence until he had to breathe out again.

The crowd settled down; they didn't want the game to be stopped.

'FAIR ENOUGH, REF,' shouted a voice from somewhere between my legs.

'GET THE GAME GOIN' AGAIN, REFO, *WE'LL* BEHAVE,' shouted a lesser voice from beneath the first one's legs.

'YOU BUNCH OF VENEREAL CRABHEADS!'

Wee Jimmy was active, shouting at no one in particular, as the ref finally breathed out and with another enormous whistle the game took off again. An Albino player with a curved iron foot smacked the ball towards Cyanotic's goal from the corner flag.

Big Tam, who'd now managed to struggle back into his legs, somehow punched it away with accuracy to the Cyanotic City right-winger. He tapped it with his crutch to a spastic boy, who did a devious feint and rounded the Rovers' centre-half, who tried to ram him with his wheelchair. The spastic boy evaded that challenge, however, and clipped the ball over to a poliomyelitis victim with a fabulous turn of speed. He passed it through to Rollup Boy, who caught it in what seemed like a cavity in his chest, before flicking it upwards over his head. He steadied it for a second at the base of his neck, then thumped it with his hump to the right-winger who'd run in like a sprinter with his callipers falling apart all around him.

'SHOOT!' shouted the Cyanotic City fans.

'GOAL!' they screamed as the winger did and the ball flew by the outstretched crutch of the Albino Rovers' goalie who was lying on his back, smashing his crutches together in frustration and anger as the goal-scoring winger's callipers finally fell completely apart and hit the deck. Devoid of his leather-and-metal supports, he hit the deck with them.

'GOAL! GOAL! GOAL!' cheered the CCFC fans with abandon, as I saw to my horror my friend in the wheelchair propelling it forward in a rage and speeding towards his Albino Rovers' counterpart, who was sitting in his own wheelchair goading him on by making V-shapes with his fingers.

BANG!

The wheelchairs collided with the sound of crunching metal, and as they capsized and scraped along the playground, their occupants grabbed each another by the hair and were soon rolling about on the ground, biting, scratching and thumping one another with their fists and swearing like a couple of really nasty troopers as they did so.

A plastic arm flew onto the pitch from the crowd, and a built-up boot flashed by as I realised the situation was getting ugly again.

'STOP THE GAME, REF!' I shouted, but the ref had no intention of stopping anything; I saw the game had kicked off again and Headless Boy was zooming in on Cyanotic's goal.

'SHOOT!' shouted the Rovers' fans. 'SHOOT, YA BA' HEID,' they yelled, as Headless Boy bore down on the Cyanotic defence like a blunt-headed torpedo. 'SHOOT!' they pleaded as he rounded the left-back and found himself with only Big Tam to beat. He did shoot, and the ball flew by Big Tam and straight into the net for the equaliser.

For a second, Headless Boy's head was almost visible and I stood on tiptoe to try to see it as he raised his arms in a show of triumph.

'Stranger in Paradise', I thought, feeling tearful for some reason and remembering the occasion of my first sight of him pushing Derek's wheelchair on my first day at school. As I acknowledged his moment of glory and fought back the tears, the crowd erupted on every side, with passions flying out of control both on and off the field.

The referee went down to a thrown pump-head valve from an iron lung. The linesman ran to retrieve the ball with his painted, fingerless hands waving about like semaphore flags as he tried to lift it. He couldn't get a grip on the thing, so Headless Boy nicked it from under his grasp and stuck it deep into his shirt, near where his head should have been. He ran off with it, presumably as a memento.

An ageing but aggressive Big Jock entered the field of play then, brandishing his white stick like some medieval lance and threatening one of the home-team players. In response, the three surviving blue-baby founder members of Cyanotic City FC rushed onto the pitch, puffing hard and making a beeline for Big Jock.

'STUFF YOU, YOU BIG ALBINO TOSSER,' they shouted in concert, sounding a bit like The Kingston Trio as they did so. Big Jock turned and set about them with his stick.

The whole place was an inferno of noise, anger and bloodshed, and I watched and listened with horror as the sounds of clashing crutches jarred and the cries of people being impaled by sharpened walking sticks filtered through the afternoon air like those of hope-starved souls in limbo.

In the chaos I saw the linesman trying to strangle the downed referee, but he couldn't get a proper grip on him either. It was potential slaughter everywhere, as former friends ran wheelchairs over one another in an attempt to crush each other senseless and old enemies used pieces of broken calliper to maim their opposite numbers in whichever team had just played against them. It was as if we were on a bloody battlefield during a particularly nasty civil war, and I suppose in a very real sense we were.

'STOPPIT!' I shouted and by some strange miracle it worked. Everything became still and quiet and I found myself the centre of attention.

The captain of Cyanotic City approached me.

'What the Hell's wrong with you?' he asked. 'Who do you think *you're* talking to?'

'Yeah! What's *your* problem?' asked the Albino Rovers captain, who'd joined him and was studying me with equal menace. 'We're only enjoying a quiet game of football,' he said slowly. 'And you're screwing it up for us.'

I stood my ground.

'Why don't you stop the physical stuff?' I said provocatively, wondering where my bravery had come from. 'Play the game as you're supposed to play it – fairly!'

They stared at me.

'Make us!' they said together, as they approached even closer and looked right into my eyes.

'Right! I will!' I shouted, as I threw my first-ever punch in anger and the whole place erupted again.

I went down among them fighting hard, and I knew as I did so that another part of my growing-up process had started. Oddly enough, I was enjoying it too.

An uprooted glass eye hit me on the back of the head and a stray strap from our right-winger's calliper was pulled round my mouth. It was a futile attempt to silence my Thor-like war cry as I fell among them like a thoroughbred Viking warrior.

In the midst of the fray I heard a battle cry: 'FLATTEN THE EFFING WANKERS FRANCIS!' It was Wee Jimmy and I felt very proud of him, as I went about my business as former blue baby turned warrior.

32

My initiation into the world of intra-school physical confrontation, which had thus begun in an institutional football riot, continued apace with a different sort of battle; one that took place just a few weeks later. It came about as a result of my brother's admonition never to allow anyone to call me by the 'ba' word.

Roman Catholic children from normal schools go off now and then on what are disarmingly called 'Religious Retreats'. They do this generally once a year and such retreats take place over a few days, usually at the end of a school term. They're normally run in a purpose-built retreat house, where the priests are dedicated to improving your religious knowledge and your spiritual welfare. In the case of our school, however, we had a part-day retreat once a decade, and it was held in our own town, in a small convent house run by nuns.

Our group of disabled and handicapped Catholics arrived at the convent in a holiday coach, for some reason. It seems the Wee Grey Bus that took us back and forth between home and school wasn't worthy to transport us to a convent. Disembarkation took place, assisted by a flock of nuns. By this time I was feeling progressively more self-conscious about being with my schoolmates, so my start to the day wasn't a good one.

'How are *you*, young man?' asked one of the Sisters, as I struggled out of the front door of the coach carrying a wheelchair.

'I'm fine, thanks, Sister. How are you?'

'How nice of you to ask. Here, let *me* get that,' she said, moving forward and trying to grab the wheelchair. 'We don't want you dropping it. 'We'd have to pool our resources to lift you back into it.'

I was horrified.

'It's not *my* chair,' I said, doing a little jig on the spot to demonstrate my unimpaired mobility. 'It belongs to a colleague,' I told her, I indicating a boy who was almost totally paralysed and salivating on a coach window, leaving a trail that a snail with hypersalivation would be proud of. Someone had called him 'Foam Boy' and the name had stuck.

'Oh – how kind,' she responded. 'What a fine young man you are.'

I beamed.

'I was told to do it by our escort, Mrs Darksole,' I explained. 'But I'd have done it anyway. I like helping these children while I still can. I'm leaving to go to a proper school.'

'Oh! So you're going to go to a proper school?' she said, using the word 'proper' without qualification or comment.

'Yes, the Academy, in a month or so. I'm going to specialise in chemistry.'

'Chemistry! How nice! Well done!' she said. 'I could tell you had the makings of something different the moment I set eyes on you.'

Twenty minutes or so later, the holy little bunch of us followed as the Sisters led us into the main entrance of the convent building. In a room off to the side, tables were laid with cake, soft drinks and all sorts. There was a smell of incense too, and somehow the contrast between that and the beanfeast was incongruous.

But then most things at school were beginning to seem that way – particularly now I knew I'd be getting away from it, at least for a time, and away from everything associated with it, including being treated differently from other kids at retreat houses.

This, of course, was a form of the first deadly sin – pride, and you know what comes before a fall . . . Yes, pride. And as the saying promises, the fall was waiting.

When we'd finally finished our indoor picnic, one of the priests from our parish called in to give us a talk about the ideal family unit: Jesus, Mary and Joseph. We were all encouraged to try to run our own future families with the same degree of sensitivity, care and parental control that Joseph had exerted over his.

'Needless to say, Joseph's boy did very well,' laughed the priest, as Foam Boy drooled in his wheelchair and I wondered just how he'd run *his* family.

When the priest finished, we were released and allowed to wander the convent grounds, though we were asked not to go beyond a sawdust circle near the prefabricated sentry tower they'd set up at the gate. Two of the nuns sat up there with binoculars and one of those anaesthetic dart-guns you hear lots about today, but not back then, if ever.

One of our older boys, who suffered from what he called a 'peach insediment', decided to bisect the diameter of this circle and bumped into me. His speech impediment was an odd one; he made meaningless anagrams of swear words and other slang.

'Sorry,' I said, moving aside.

'Don't worry durst; it's not my fault.'

I widened my arc and moved at a tangent to a tree. For a moment I thought I spotted a nun up there, too, but I continued to widen my arc, in search of what might pass for adventure.

'Sorry,' I repeated as someone bumped me again. It was the same boy: 'Big Bob'.

We Scots have a problem with height, and tend to exaggerate it, either way, but preferably upwards, whenever possible. That's why we have Wee Jimmy, Big Bob, Big Tam and so on, rather than medium-sized Robert, James or Thomas.

'Your fault, cufk you,' he said more forcibly as he wandered off again, leaving me wondering why in the name of God he was wandering about like that.

I went over and asked him.

'Why are you wandering about like that?' I asked, gazing upwards, as he was over six foot tall and I'd only just reached five foot or thereabouts. I was still 'Wee Francis' then.

'Like what, hits?' he said.

'Like this,' I said, looking down at the ground and bisecting a smaller circle.

'Oh, that! I'm looking for a doobly sea serpent,' he said, matter-of-factly.

'A sea serpent in a convent?'

He studied me closely.

'Well, why not, gip-face?'

'Because there's no sea,' I said quietly.

He looked at me through his pentafocals.

'I saw a lady standing on one. In there, kunp,' he said, indicating the room we'd had our picnic in.

I looked back.

'That's the Virgin Mary. It's a picture of the Immaculate Conception.

It has Our Lady standing on a serpent, but I don't think it's a sea serpent.'

'How do you know? Think you're a smart bergug or something? Just because you're going to do chemistry classes at another place, doesn't mean you can try to correct us all.'

I controlled myself. We were on holy ground, as I've said.

'I'm not correcting anything. I'm just saying there are no serpents here, that's all. This place doesn't have serpents. Serpents like that don't exist anyway,' I said, trying to be informative.

'Then what was Our Lady standing on in the picture? You know-all stabard,' he said quickly, before I could fully comprehend him.

Being called a 'stabard' wasn't as bad as the real thing. Even so, it was an attempt at the real thing. So I looked up at him and gave him due caution.

'Call me that again and I'll punch your teeth in.'

'Yea? You and what cufking sea serpent?' he asked, as he walked away.

I decided to ignore him. After all, we were in a convent.

After another five minutes of walking in a circle, we went back inside for more refreshments. The religiously inclined seemed to think the spiritual welfare of disabled people was taken care of by food and not through any spiritual effort by the disabled themselves. Food and drink were adequate, it seemed, for spiritual sustenance of the sickly. No wonder they drew Plimsoll lines amidships on the more indulged members of our school.

Our latest feed finished, we were left alone while the nuns went off to prepare more food and drink. We stood in a small reception area, near a life-sized statue of Saint Anthony of Padua. He was a famous saint and I examined it closely. It was a marvellous piece of religious art, and it towered over me as if in some way its size alone was meant to emphasise the greatness of this most special of saints. Every detail had been carefully crafted to inspire us and make us feel reverential awe in the presence of this celebrated preacher. The statue also happened to tower over a large display cabinet of medals, relics, rosary beads, mini-missals and a number of smaller statues of both greater and lesser saints, which were for sale to proper visitors. Big Bob, who stood beside Saint Anthony too, admiring the top of his pate, glanced down at me and called out to a friend somewhere further down:

'That stabard thinks he knows everything, I was looking for a two-bob bit I'd dropped outside, and that cufrek thought I was looking for a sea serpent.'

The small boy shouted back up.

'A sea serpent? You don't get sea serpents in places like this.' Smiling himself, he looked like an inquisitive tourist at the bottom of the Eiffel Tower.

Big Bob laughed.

'I know, but that daft stabard thinks you do.'

I felt a surge of anger.

'I told you! Don't call me that again.'

I felt like bopping him. On reflection, however, I decided not to resort to violence, whatever provocation he put my way. We were still in a convent after all, and we were being watched over by Saint Anthony of Padua.

'Stabard!' said Big Bob quickly and I jumped over, stood on the tips of my toes and let off a right uppercut. It hit him hard on the chin and like a declining Tower of Babel, or Nelson losing his sea legs in Trafalgar Square, he fell.

At first he fell slowly; then he collapsed like a giant chimneystack. In so doing, he knocked Saint Anthony on the head with one of his flailing arms and as that patron saint of 'all things lost' headed directly into the display cabinet, I think my heart perforated itself with several new holes of localised despair.

Watching this sequence slowly unfold, with Saint Anthony and Big Bob crushing the material and spiritual essences of the display cabinet and its contents, my righteous indignation disappeared and my solitary moment of pugilistic triumph collapsed into a moment of darkness and horror, along with Big Bob of Greater Glasgow and Saint Anthony of Padua. The other pupils formed a circle of despair and disbelief around us and a silence engulfed us, deeper than a mystic's during the dark night of the soul.

'You stupid hearlose,' muttered Big Bob with spirit, as he brushed bits of Saint Anthony, relics of Saint Theresa, plastic bottles of bubble bath from Lourdes and mementos of the miracle at Fatima off his forehead.

I couldn't help but agree.

'Get up!' I said, sharply. 'We have to tidy this mess.' Saint Anthony's face lay in a corner, smiling blissfully at my faith in the impossible.

A door opened.

'What's this? What's happened?' I heard, and I closed my eyes. I prayed fervently it wasn't Mrs Darksole. I opened my eyes and saw one of the Sisters holding a plate of cream buns. She was staring at me as another Sister, with yet another plate of doughnuts, moved near to her. It was the one who'd met me at the coach that morning.

'Don't be hard on him,' she whispered to the Sister with the buns. 'I think he's delusional. He thinks he's going to what he calls "a proper school"; he thinks he's going to become a chemist. Poor mite! I doubt he even knows what a chemist is, except that it's where he gets his prescription.' She put down the plate of doughnuts and fell to her knees before what was left of Saint Anthony and his religious cohorts.

'Come through here,' her colleague said, pointing to an adjacent room, as she assessed the damage on the floor and measured it, I imagine, against her Christian charity. 'We'll say nothing about this,' she added philosophically, like the saint she was. 'Accidents happen.' I embraced her in my head like Mary Magdalene had embraced Jesus' feet at Golgotha.

'Go on!' she urged, as she saved what she could from the wreckage. 'Go on, and don't worry about it.' I began to appreciate the true meaning of a Christian view of things.

'You're still a stabard,' Big Bob whispered, as we fled the scene. 'And if you think sea serpents hang out around here or anywhere else,' he said, 'you haven't a hope in lehl of getting this chemistry certificate you're so proud of at the Academy.'

I realised two things at that moment. Not everyone wishes you well in this life; and nuns, whatever the apparent strangeness of their chosen lives, are saintly.

And I've never forgotten either.

33

I arrived at the main door of the Academy just before ten and made my way to the headmaster's office. I'd been told to report there upon my arrival and I was met at the door by one of the school secretaries.

'Good morning,' she said pleasantly, recognising me though we'd never met. 'It's good to see you.' I felt well and truly welcome, although I was quite aware of the fact I had no uniform on or briefcase in my hands, as proper pupils had. She ushered me towards the corridor. 'I'll take you up to Mr Black's class. The chemistry lesson's starting soon.'

When we reached the classroom, the secretary knocked on the door and the teacher opened it.

'Come in and sit down,' he said, indicating a space that had been made for me at a table at the front of the class. I was to share it with three other boys. So giving them a nod of acknowledgement and feeling every eye in the place upon me, I sat down, took out my pencil, put down my rubber and flattened out my notepad. I was ready for action.

Our first lesson concerned the preparation of oxygen and as it included a proper experiment, I lost myself in this for some time before I really took the trouble to look around. The lab was identical to the one I'd been in during my first visit, and indeed was adjacent to it. The class was larger than I was used to, there being presumably more healthy boys around in 'proper' education than handicapped ones. As I stole a few quick glances, I was left in no doubt that the clientele catered for by the Academy was as different from that of my own school as chalk is from cheese, and then some. The three other boys at my table were probably slightly older than I was, but not by much, and they could even have been the same age. They all wore full-dress uniforms and kept their jackets neatly buttoned and they paid attention to the teacher as he instructed them in the art of heating potassium chlorate.

At first I said nothing to anyone. I simply took notes with the rest of them, as they scribbled with their pens and pencils, turning page after page of their blue school jotters. By now, oxygen was bubbling into an inverted gas jar. Mr Black asked in general terms how we would identify it. I'd read, somewhere, that fortune favoured the brave.

'Place a glowing splint in the jar, sir,' I said into the silence.

'Correct,' said Mr Black, but didn't dwell on it. I felt every eye in the room turn towards me again, to see exactly who and what I was. 'What would happen then?' he asked, turning away from the front and directing his attention towards the back of the classroom.

A boy spoke. I didn't look at him, but I could hear him all right, and I didn't like the sound of him.

'The surplus of free oxygen in the jar relative to that in air will stimulate a glowing splint into an overt, visible plasma combustion: i.e. a flame,' he said. 'Normally the combined preponderance of nitrogen and carbon dioxide – not to mention neon, radon, krypton, xenon and helium – would extinguish it,' he went on, 'but relatively pure oxygen will enable it to ignite.'

'Correct,' said Mr Black. I wondered what dictionary the boy used.

And so it went on. I gave my fair share of answers, as it happened, but they were only a share – and only fair. These boys had a far better grounding in chemistry than me, just as they had in virtually every other subject I'd ever heard of and most of those I hadn't.

When the class broke up, I rushed out of the door as if it were the sole fire exit during a conflagration, but I was pleased enough with the way things had gone. The original idea that I might attend a class every day had been shelved by the Education Department, but I was to go back in a couple of days' time and I would be better prepared by then to deal with it. I now knew the territory and familiarity had bred not the slightest bit of contempt.

On my second day, having knocked on the door and waited for it to be opened before I dared go in, I found a number of school things in my place at the front table. There were a couple of pens, two jotters, a new ruler and one or two other items that would be useful for the class. Most importantly, however, there was a book. It was a textbook on chemistry and it distracted me from everything else around for the very first time. It was the first real school chemistry book I'd ever set eyes on and I'd no intention of taking them off it until I had to.

The boys I sat with acknowledged me a bit more, and they were a great deal more accommodating and helpful than they'd been the first time I'd attended. I understood this, and knew fine well they'd initially perceive me as one of the 'oddballs from the Special', as we were generally known. My first ambition, therefore, was to dismiss that particular idea from their heads, both by my general good conduct and by getting as many chemistry questions right as I possibly could.

By the time we were into the third or fourth week of my first term at the school, I was well ahead in my plans, and through dedicated use both of the book and my God-given wits, I began to make ground at last. One afternoon when classes had finished for the day at the special school, I had almost an hour to wait before going home, during which I had the opportunity to voice my thoughts to Miss Angelica. Though I was now allowed to walk on my own to school via the Academy when I had a lesson there in the morning, I still had to get the Wee Grey Bus there and back when I didn't. That day Miss Angelica supervised us during our wait for the bus. I was sitting beside her and took the opportunity to ask what she really thought about the Academy.

She was thoughtful.

'It's a very good school by any standard. Though as the headmaster once told me succinctly, they "teach both Jesuits and jailbirds". Perhaps they do, but it's a good school and they have a high rate for university entry.'

'So you know the headmaster?'

'Fairly well. I suppose he'd say Jesuit material is in one building and jailbird in another. They divide their pupils by academic ability, so it's segregated just like this school. Some people think any sort of division in education is elitist and a social injustice,' she continued, 'and maybe they're right.'

I thought about that.

'Life's full of injustice anyway,' I said, and I think that was my first grown-up comment on the nature of life.

'It is, but some of our children would benefit considerably from a decent education. And they're not going to get that opportunity until they are seen as equal to everyone else, and not simply worthy of a place in a special school.'

I felt grown up, respected; it was a good feeling.

'So you don't think we should have any special schools?'

'I'm not certain. We'll probably need them until the children here receive integration and proper respect. But if we can achieve that, I'm sure most would do very well in mainstream schools and, most importantly, would benefit in any number of ways from the opportunities a decent education would give them.'

I thought about it some more, took my time, looked around a bit, then spoke like a member of the academic elite.

'We made a toxic gas in the chemistry lab last week,' I said. 'We used a powerful acid, a Bunsen burner, an explosive substance and some corrosive metal.'

'And?' she smiled, looking like sunshine.

'I doubt it would be wise to let *him* loose in there,' I said, nodding gravely in the direction of Foam Boy, who could only communicate by blinking to a carer who noted down what his blinks meant.

'And whatever makes you think he'd want to get up to his elbows in what you handle in a chemistry lab?'

'He'd have to, to get a proper education.'

'He had "proper education" enough as a child,' said Miss Angelica.

'How?'

'He was exposed to much greater danger than you'll find in any school laboratory.'

'Danger?'

'Mortal danger. He's lucky to be alive after being exposed like that.'

I nodded. After all, I was a scientist.

'I suppose a kid like that would be lucky to survive exposed to any sort of infection,' I said sagely.

'Oh, he can handle infection,' said Miss Angelica, 'better than you can, I imagine. No, that wasn't the problem. He was exposed on a hillside directly after his birth.'

'On a hillside!'

'Yes, to see if he were fit enough to live. The Romans used to do it with weak or unwanted children. His parents were from Palermo, close enough to pick up on that sort of tradition. He was lucky; someone found him early the following morning and he survived. But only just.'

'Oh.'

'Anyway, you're correct in saying he couldn't get involved in the practical side of a science lab; however, someone could do the physical bits, while he thought it all through.'

Impressed as I was with Foam Boy's background, I dismissed this.

'You believe he can *think* well enough to do that?'

'I'm certain of it. He has a measured IQ seven points higher than yours,' said Miss Angelica, shocking me rigid.

I composed myself.

'But he's not going to get the chance. Things don't work that way,' I stressed, thinking harder about such issues than I'd ever done, despite my lifelong proximity to them.

'No, they don't,' she agreed, 'but it doesn't mean they can't or shouldn't. Make the most of your chance, Francis,' she said, as the bus arrived and I helped Foam Boy onto it, with a degree of consideration and respect I'd never before accorded him or anyone remotely like him – even though I'd now been cheek-by-jowl with such kids on a daily basis for years.

34

I sat the chemistry exam in May 1963. I did so sitting at a special desk that had been specially placed at the back of the examination room in the Academy. In front sat dozens of boys I didn't know, as they were from the fourth-year classes I hadn't attended. It was the first exam I'd ever taken in my life and I was uncertain how to go about it.

I went into the hall on my own, with the fountain pen Al's mother had given me, and I left on my own after the exam was finished.

Mr Black met me at the door and asked me how I thought I'd done.

'OK, sir . . . I think.'

'You'll have done fine, Frank, don't worry,' he said, and it was the first time he'd used my Christian name since our first meeting. He'd always addressed me by my surname before and I had appreciated that. More than anything else, being addressed by my surname like the other boys made me feel accepted in the Academy. Like school uniforms, surnames made you relatively anonymous, and I thought that very useful at times.

'You'll have passed it,' he reassured me.

'We'll see, sir,' I said.

And, of course, we did.

By the time Parlophone had released the Beatles' *Twist and Shout* EP, I was waiting for the result of my exam – and I had toothache. Toothache had always been as painful for me as it is for everyone else, I imagine, but as an additional burden I had to be treated differently from others for that sort of thing, too. Initially it meant a visit to the dentist and then a further visit to our doctor. Fortunately we'd had the same GP for many years, a gem of a man, the sort where you knew if you could cut that gem, the quality of the others would be flawless too. He'd followed my academic progress with interest, and he asked me how I'd done in my exam.

'I'll know soon enough,' I said, while he gave my chest a thorough examination. 'The results are due next week.'

'And then what?'

'I'd like to do more subjects at the Academy.'

'There's always night school,' he said and my heart stopped mid-beat.

'What about the Academy?'

'They won't let you go,' he said, as he wrote out a prescription. He handed it to me. 'Penicillin,' he said. 'Take it before your extraction.'

I was totally stunned.

'Who won't let me?'

'The Education people. You have a pretty serious heart condition. They don't equate that with a formal secondary education.'

I stopped breathing for a moment and let him worry about it.

'Why ever not?'

'They just don't.'

'And what do you think?'

'I think we do what's best for you,' he said neutrally.

'In my view, that's getting a decent education.'

'Then I don't think you'll get it. I'm sorry.'

I considered this.

'Could *you* do anything about it?'

'Anything I could do might make it impossible for you even to go to night school,' he said, obviously and genuinely concerned. 'I'd have to give a full medical history . . .' He shrugged. 'The kiss of death.'

'Well, that's too bad,' I said, and he nodded. 'I'll go and get my tooth pulled then.'

He spoke quietly.

'You're not a hundred per cent, you know. You never will be. Even something seemingly as simple as getting a tooth pulled could kill you. If you caught an infection . . .'

I looked at him. It was the second and last time that the prospect of death – my death – had been brought up and it didn't scare me one bit.

'It's just a risk like any other.'

'You don't take risks you quite literally can't live with. You've done wonderfully well. You're a credit to yourself and your family.'

I said nothing.

'Oh! One more thing,' he said as I prepared to leave.

'Yes?'

'Are you still getting your sedative? You need it to keep things ticking over smoothly.'

'The school still deals with that,' I answered correctly, though not quite as honestly as it sounded.

'Good. You need it.'

I thanked him and left the consulting room. Then I crumpled up his prescription and tossed it away.

I had a restless night. But the following morning my mother woke me, holding a large, brown, self-addressed envelope. She handed it to me.

'Open it!'

I took my time about it and eased the letter slowly open, pulled out the sheet of paper inside, looked at it and up at her.

'I've got it,' I said calmly.

'Got what?' she asked, pretending she didn't know what I was talking about.

'What d'you think?' I said, toothache all gone, and we fell into one another's arms and hugged each other, as our latest cat looked on in fey, feline bedazzlement.

Within an hour my mother had gone to the nearest telephone box to make some phone calls and arrange visits to my school, to the Academy, to the local Education Authority and to our doctor. She wanted to see what she could do about the advancement of my schooling.

The visits to the headmistress of my school and to our doctor had gone predictably. They wanted to help, but the headmistress said any change of school was a decision for the Education Authority, and the doctor said it was for Solomon – whoever he was. That left the Education Authority and the headmaster of the Academy, whom we arranged to see the following day in his office.

Forbidding in both appearance and manner, he took the time to explain the issue clearly.

'Your son has some knowledge of basic chemistry,' he said as he looked over his glasses. 'But not very much else.'

'Oh, I'm not so sure of that,' said my mum loyally. 'What hasn't he done that the other boys here have?'

The headmaster sighed.

'Physics, maths, biology, English, French, history, geography, arithmetic,

Latin, Greek, applied mechanics, music, technical drawing, metalwork, woodwork, religious instruction, art and art appreciation, Spanish, German, Portuguese, botany, zoology, domestic science and needlepoint for young men.' He took a breath. 'Then there are other aspects of school life to be considered: the Literary and Debating Society, athletics, gymnastics, the school orchestra, the Dramatic Society, the Philatelic Society, the History and Geographic Society, use of the library, homework, the monthly Sodality meeting, the Astronomical Society, compulsory religious studies to a level set by the bishops of Scotland, and the equally compulsory certificate examination thereof.' He paused, breathing hard. 'Not to mention,' he threw in, 'the Duke of Edinburgh Award Scheme, or the annual trips to exotic places in the ship we have at our disposal for such purposes,' he finished, with a look that suggested he could have added even more to his list without great difficulty.

I watched him gasp for breath. When he'd recovered, he looked at me and softened his tone.

'I'll do what I can, but don't build your hopes up. For you haven't a hope – but in Heaven – to start building anything with.'

Our visit to the Education Authority office convinced me finally there was an afterlife and this seemed to be the place its occupants hung out. A large, detached and unremarkable building, many of the staff paid to sit there physically reflected it.

My mother and I waited for an hour to see Mr Noteall, the Chief Education Officer for the region. He was a large, ungainly, confident man, oozing respect and common sense. Unfortunately the respect oozed inwards by way of his self-aggrandisement, and the common sense oozed outwards with equal permanence.

He remained sitting when we went into his office.

'So you want an education, son? Well, I've got one, and it isn't all it's cracked up to be.'

He'd raised my mum's hackles already.

'So you'll appreciate how important an education is for the slow and infirm', she said.

He stared at her vacantly.

'Oh, don't get me wrong. Don't get me wrong,' he repeated. 'I'm not saying education isn't a good thing . . . Just that it isn't the be-all and end-all.'

'Of what?' I asked.

'What of what?'

'Education isn't the be-all and end-all of what?'

He thought about it.

'I've no idea, now I think on it. But it isn't.'

'Isn't what?'

'Isn't what, what?' he asked irritably.

'Education isn't exactly what?'

'All it's cracked up to be.'

I smiled.

'Then you won't mind if I discover that for myself.'

'Pretty smart, aren't you?'

My mum leant forward.

'That's why we're here.'

Mr Noteall looked at his desk, at the wall, through the window, then back at me.

'You're not well enough to be educated.'

'Well, he was well enough to get this!' said my mother, opening her handbag and pulling out my much-abused 'O' Grade Certificate. She banged it onto his desk.

He picked it up.

'It's just a piece of paper,' he said, putting it – and me – down again.

'Well, I'd like to collect some more pieces of paper. But it seems I can't without your consent.'

'Oh, don't get me wrong, I'm Catholic too,' he explained. 'So it isn't anything like *that*.' He meant nepotism based on religion. 'It's not that I don't sympathise, either.'

'Then what is it?'

'You have a hole in your heart. That's not conducive to a proper education.'

I leant forward now too.

'There's nothing *in* holes.'

'A point,' he conceded, rising. 'But not one I can use to assist.' He pointed to the door and we took the hint.

Just before we were physically pushed out my mother turned to have one last attempt.

'The only danger that exists is to my son. If he isn't up to it, he'll suffer and no one else.'

Mr Noteall looked horrified.

'Oh no! No! No! No! No! No! No! No, dear lady! You're very wrong there,' he said and she looked at him, amazed. 'If he drops down dead doing algebra, for example, then it's my responsibility. I could lose my job,' he explained. The creep! His self-interest reminded me of Dr Wink and Bandage Boy.

I turned to face him again.

'I might never even get a job, unless you take that risk.'

'Then the State will look after you for life,' he said, with dreadful conviction, as he pushed us out of his office, closed the door firmly behind us and went back to sleep for the remainder of his life.

35

Outside the Education Office building, a crowd was waiting in silence for us. It consisted of most of the pupils from my school. Some held banners demanding I get natural justice: 'JUSTIS', it read. But I appreciated the sentiment.

Beside them stood a telephone operator from the local exchange. She'd had a call from my Otherbrother, who had long since given up aspirations to the priesthood and joined the Royal Air Force instead. Apparently, the Air Vice-Marshal was standing by somewhere unstated with a squadron of jet fighters to fly to my aid if I needed it.

My sister was there too, with three of her workmates. They'd taken the day off work to support me. It transpired their union representative had wanted to call a general strike in protest at my treatment, but my sister had been against it on ethical grounds and she'd talked him out of it. I agreed they had made the correct decision.

My brother was there as well, looking smart in his mohair suit. He was with a disc jockey from national television, who gave me a flashing smile.

'Hi,' I said, 'good to see you. I've seen you on TV.'

His smile shone again like a sunlit iceberg.

'You have? Who'd believe it? Great! I came to offer my support, young Frank, before I speak record royalty business with your gifted brother.'

'If I *get* any damned royalties,' laughed my brother, as he ushered the disc jockey away for his next TV spot.

'Never forget, we're right behind you,' they called back. And they weren't the only ones either.

At our backs, unnoticed till then, stood Mrs Darksole and Mrs Schiklgruber. The latter had a retinue of her personal guard with her, the M.H. pupils who carried her around town in a sedan chair. She looked good in it, I must say, with her military insignia, her brisk leather whip and her black Doberman.

'I told you you'd never make it,' she said. 'Boys like you don't. You come from the wrong sort of background.'

'We'll support you, Francis!' called a few of her retinue bravely. 'We might not have much up here,' one of them added, touching his head, 'but we could all do that bit better if we had a chance at a more appropriate education ourselves.'

This moved me, and I thanked them. But they were soon beaten into silence with a flick of Schiklgruber's whips, and as it flashed by me, I saw words on its handle:

'This Whip Belongs To Corporal A. Schiklgruber,' it said, It had been written in a compulsive, spidery hand, in what looked like dried blood.

'She must have inherited it from a relative,' I thought.

The next backstabber spoke: Mrs Darksole.

'You're just not good enough to succeed,' she said, as she held out her left hand. 'Kiss it, she said, as he stuck a bejewelled ring into my face. 'It belonged to a bishop called Alphonse Constant. He could perform magic,' she went on. 'Kiss it and we might save you. Well . . . we might save your soul anyway, you sinful, proud, overly ambitious boy.'

I didn't kiss it. Instead, for the first time in my life, I raised two fingers. I offered them to Schiklgruber too. She went pale at the thought. The crowd cheered and applauded, and pledged their support. I gave a little bow and felt tears in my eyes as I did so. I was uncomfortable with praise and approval; I wasn't used to it.

While it all died down, my mind began drifting off onto other things and I had a momentary, crazy feeling that someone I couldn't see was watching me. I felt weak, too, as if I were losing energy. I'd felt that sort of thing before, I realised, but I couldn't remember when. It passed and my mum and I walked away. Our dignity was intact, if nothing else.

As I lay on the floor in my room that evening, I rolled over, hugging my new briefcase and sniffing at its fresh, brown leather. I wore my new school uniform too, and it had a proper badge with a Latin motto – '*fortis fidelis*' – not crutches. They were gifts from family and friends, but no use now, not to me anyway. Instead of a new school, I turned my thoughts to our Special School prom. Like our retreats, it was held only once every decade, and the ten years since the last one were up the following Saturday.

36

The church hall hired for our prom that Saturday evening was a few miles from the town centre. We'd arranged different types of music in order to cater for everyone's tastes. There was a Scottish country-dance band, complete with a Master of Ceremonies, and we had pop-music back-up with an amplified record player and a disc jockey from school whom we fondly called 'Voluble Boy'. We had live rock music too – *pro bono*, whatever that was – from my brother and his band.

The hall had a large central space we could use for dancing and an entrance area, where tickets were collected, that could be seen from the dance floor. There were two rooms off the dance floor, one of which had been converted into a base for the musicians. The other had been transformed from a storage room for altar wine into a cash bar – the word 'bar' meaning it sold orange juice and cola, though there'd been rumours doing the rounds that something stronger might be had on the night.

Most of the staff would attend in due course, but initially the prom was supervised by just four people: Miss Tartankilty, who was to accompany the Scottish country-dance band; Mr Hammerhead, who was to be ticket collector; our claw-handed janitor, who was to act as odd-job man and bouncer, if need be; and our pièce de résistance, Father Mortalsen, who'd also agreed to assist. He'd returned to our parish after some further episode of undefined nervous illness and had offered to take sole charge of the bar, again *pro bono publico*.

I arrived early. Miss Tartankilty and the dance band had already arrived and I saw she was carrying a record. I didn't like to anticipate matters, but I feared it was 'Scotland the Brave' and I doubted the Scottish country-dance band would appreciate that.

The school football team were there too. They'd had a game that day, but had changed from their sports kits into party clothes in their invalid cars on the way to the prom.

I wandered around casually and had a look in the bar, where Father Mortalsen was standing in a corner with his shirtsleeves rolled up. He was sniffing, as if he had an allergy, and examining his arm carefully. It struck me he might have a heart condition himself, and that he'd possibly had a cardiac catheterisation during his absence. That would explain the state of his veins, which from what I could see when he lifted his arm up were in a very bad way indeed. He didn't see me looking, but seemed happy enough as he started to jump in place and shout 'Yeah, Oh Yeah, Oh Yeah!' That reminded me of Al the day we'd had Father Savage sing with us at school, so slightly upset by such memories I moved away without speaking and left him alone with his secrets.

As I went back into the main hall, my brother and his band arrived. They'd all shared my brother's bedroom floor on one occasion or another and had received my tea and buttered rolls accordingly. Despite that, they wandered past me carrying their gear and showing no sign of recognition whatsoever. They just nodded casually saying, 'Hi, man,' as if they didn't know me from Adam. I was totally unimpressed, but said nothing about it. After all they were serious rock stars, and though I was still a walking reference work on popular music, I wasn't really in their league. When my brother walked past and said, 'Hi, man' too, however, I felt right out in the musical wilderness, as well as the educational one, but I let him pass without any comment as well.

I almost bumped into Foam Boy as I went out into the hall. He was being pushed towards the toilet in his wheelchair, which had been decorated with strips of ribbon. He was wearing a black leather cap and under his chin he sported a chequered sequinned bib. He looked very cool indeed, as did his wheelchair pusher; a boy with more muscle than sense, but who looked after Foam Boy as if he were his closest friend.

Una approached me with a smile on her face. She hadn't tried to camouflage her neck brace; instead, she'd decked it out with coloured shells and a combination of intertwined silver and gold chains. She tinkled as she approached and I realised she'd be easy to find if she were needed later on in the evening.

I heard the first few runs of a bass guitar being tuned up somewhere, and Voluble Boy rushed past into a side room carrying his records and other gear. He said 'Hi, man,' too, as he zoomed past to set up his equipment, and I wondered what all these professional musicians said to ladies by way of a decent welcome.

Others arrived thick and fast, including Woody with black leather gloves and a bare, freshly varnished arm on show, and Wee Jimmy, cursing in the reception area already and looking for trouble as he swigged at a bottle labelled 'Rose Hip Syrup', but which was probably his favourite tipple of strong, neat cider.

With the hall fairly full and resounding with chatter and anticipation, I spoke briefly to Jason. He was with his female friend who was called 'Butch', but he had a boyfriend with him too, and he and Jason wore matching pink jackets with small, neatly folded red ribbons pinned in their lapels, something they designed themselves it seems, and though it didn't catch on at the time, it did later. Jason seemed relaxed and happy for once, and as he'd had some pretty bad times recently I hoped that this evening, at least, he'd enjoy himself to the full.

I looked again at the entrance and caught my breath. It was Melissa, and my thoughts became poetic. She looked stunningly beautiful in a white satin dress. She had a circle of freshly cropped bluebells in her hair, her eyes glinted like muted starlight, and her lips glowed red like carmine dewdrops. I felt funny to my tiptoes; the hole in my heart closed over like a rose at nighttime, and I wept inside like the poet Thomas Chatterton had before he'd killed himself, so romantically, aged seventeen.

A voice intruded.

'You uncouth arsehole, what in the name of God are you doing dressed up like that?'

I turned to find Wee Jimmy eyeing me up and laughing, as if the cider had got to him already.

'Like what?' I asked, pulling myself out of my puppy-love thoughts and returning to the world of base reality.

'Like a penguin with the runs,' he laughed, wavering on his artificial legs.

'I'm not like *any* penguin. I'm wearing evening dress,' I explained. 'My brother hired my outfit using royalties he received from a record.'

He tottered.

'You're the only one here wearing any kind of suit,' he giggled, 'never mind a formal one. We all agreed to wear informal dress, but not you – no, not you, you prick. It looks odd, man,' he finished, waddling off unsteadily towards the toilet.

I erupted, but only on the inside. Again! Again! Again! I'd been left out of collective school decisions and turned up looking out of place at my first and only Special School prom.

I decided to get on with it. Anyway, I looked good in my evening wear. My mother had said so before I'd left, while trying to calm my sister, who was on the floor convulsing with laughter at some joke or other – an indelicate one, I imagine, as she was reluctant to share it.

So, despite Jimmy's comments, *I* knew I looked good and that was the main thing.

'Time to go and change, Francis,' whispered Melissa seriously, as she walked past smelling of all the spices, unguents and oils I'd ever heard of. 'The dancing starts soon, and you want to be properly dressed for it.'

With a meaningful but radiant smile, she went off in the general direction of my brother's rock band and in the particular direction of the bass guitarist who was standing at the door.

'Hi, man,' I heard him call to her.

'Hi, man,' she said right back and as I stood in my evening dress feeling like shit-man, a small, wobbly-legged boy walked past me. He had a serene-looking smile on his face, and what appeared to be a fat, messy, self-made cigarette cupped in his hand like some illicit treasure trove.

'You look as if you feel like shit, man,' he said, pausing and studying me. 'Cool it, man, like a penguin on an icecap,' he added, as he stood in front of me puffing and inhaling deeply.

'Want a drag?' he asked, turning to face me, his eyes to my knee as he held out the shaggy, hand-rolled tube for my closer inspection. I shook my head and shooed him on his way. 'Your loss, man,' he said, and disappeared into the crowd, puffing like a steam train. Music was playing in the background; it was a rendition of 'If You've Got To Make A Fool of Somebody', normally sung by Freddie and the Dreamers, but being sung casually at present by the lead guitarist of my brother's band, who was getting things ready for action. Big Bob was standing nearby with a troupe of diverse smaller boys to whom he talked down with fervour and animation. Some were as tall as I was, but they all looked small beside him as he peered down through large, wide, colourful glasses, placed like Chinese lanterns across his eyes. He stared at me coolly and called me a stabard, for kicks. I let him stew. I didn't need a repeat of my fight with him and Saint Anthony, so, stabard or not, he was safe from my fists for the night.

The sound of the bass, still warming up, was supplemented by the piping-hot sounds of the Scottish country-dance band doing the same in the music room. I took a brief look in and saw that the band consisted of an accordionist, a fiddler and a man in full Highland dress, who seemed to be about to play the spoons. This is an old Scottish art, highly effective when performed by an expert, and this man was obviously good at it.

In due course, it was the dance band that kicked off the show. As the Master of Ceremonies took to the stage, anticipation grew, silence fell and he chimed out, in a voice that probably called out bingo numbers for a living, 'Take your partners, folks, for that won-der-ful dance, "The Dashing White Sergeant"!'

There was a rush of activity behind me, and I turned to see six tartan-clad wheelchairs with their equally tartan-clad occupants rolling out smoothly onto the dance floor. On stage, the accordionist played a middle C with gusto and the fiddler hugged his fiddle as if it were an orphaned Stradivarius, while the spoon-man rattled his spoons as if they were gaming-dice with bells on. Then, to Miss Tartankilty's obvious delight and equally obvious excitement, they began to play 'Scotland the Brave' in stirring, live sound – and we were off!

From the centre of the dance floor, where they'd congregated informally in an outward-facing circle, two groups of three wheelchairs rushed to its opposite edges. They then rolled into formal dance-start mode and stood facing one other across the floor, looking still and composed. As the music moved up a pace, they did too and fairly flew towards one another. They met and formed a new circle in the centre, each occupant joining hands with another. In perfect accord with the music, each chair turned to the left, then to the right. They did this eight times in all, I reckoned, as the band played faster and faster and whooped along with them. Sixteen times in total they performed this expertly crafted manoeuvre, and there wasn't a single error of judgement.

As the crowd began to clap and whoop too, the wheelchairs fell back into two groups of three again and the middle member of each group swung round to their right-hand partner and executed three pas de bas by tilting the wheelchairs expertly onto two wheels. As they did so, the left-hand partners clapped their hands in time, along with the crowd and the band. Miss Tartankilty threw her wee tartan bonnet and her prized record of 'Scotland the Brave' into the air, while giving a further wild whoop in a gesture of total musical abandon. That done, the middle wheelchair swung to the left and the whole exercise was repeated.

I stood gaping at their synchrony, as each set of three wheelchairs then executed a perfect figure-of-eight that brought thunderous applause from the crowd. The wheelchairs returned to their original starting positions: two sets of three wheelchairs aligned across the dance floor. Then, in an act of such choreographic audacity it would have made the great Nijinsky seem like a horse, the first set sped like fighter planes on a strafing run, while the occupants of the second set arched up their arms and the first rushed under them to complete the dance with aplomb.

The crowd erupted. Flushed and obviously delighted, the lead guitarist of my brother's band came over to me.

He sighed with professional approval.

'Incredible, man. It's amazing what two sets of cripples can do when they set their minds to it,' he said, just as three of the star turns got up from their wheelchairs, walked over to the ebullient MC and thanked him.

As the lead guitarist looked on in disbelief, two of the other dancers, who'd been stuck permanently in wheelchairs after a brief visit of the polio virus, wheeled themselves gracefully over to where their girlfriends were sitting. They were all beautiful girls, from a girls' school not far from the church hall, and they appropriately rewarded their men for their display of balletic genius by ostentatiously kissing them.

That left my friend, the former aspiring professional footballer, alone in his wheelchair in the centre of the floor. He was in the spotlight, just as he'd once hoped to be, before polio scuppered that dream and crippled him for life into the bargain. He bowed to the crowd in a show of genuine humility, and taking his chance while he had it he milked the applause for all it was worth. He deserved it. He looked as if he'd just received the Scottish FA Cup from King Robert the Bruce himself and I was absolutely delighted for him.

For their next number, the dance band played a swift Scots variant of the popular song 'I Like It'. The spoon-man's spoons flashed like Gerry Marsden's smile and the accordionist's fingers played with the regularity of a cardiac pacemaker. This brought a number of the crowd onto the floor, including Woody and Big Tam, who, with his best new legs on, was already raising his arms and swinging them from side to side in a parody of catching a net-bound football.

Woody, meanwhile, was battering his newly varnished arm with a cola bottle to keep pace with the spoon-man, and to demonstrate that by making his wooden arm obvious it would become less evident – if you get my meaning.

They were all twisting and turning, as 'I Like It' rang out loud and clear; one fit spastic kid even managed to turn his head in a complete circle, as his hips moved in counterpoint and his feet moved counter-clockwise to his head. I felt like applauding at that, but I didn't, since I thought he might be self-conscious about it.

At the bar, I noticed that the janitor was caught up in the atmosphere too. He raised his claw-hand like a pop-song hook each time the phrase 'I Like It' blasted out. I also noticed Foam Boy sitting in his wheelchair in a corner. He was blowing bubbles from a bubble wand his escort held in front of him and by flickering his eyes in his unique form of Morse Code, dictating notes his carer wrote down with his free hand on a piece of paper. I wondered what he was communicating. He stopped blinking and his escort stopped writing and looked at me. Then he walked over and handed me the paper.

'Amazing! He's just worked out that a bubble could invert itself without bursting in this hall,' he said. I studied the paper with interest and disbelief. It was filled with what seemed to be mathematical symbols, but I could make nothing of it.

'Yes, amazing,' I said.

'He wanted you to see it,' he said, and I looked over at Foam Boy, who was staring at me. 'He reckons that if you can invert a bubble without bursting it inside this place, it suggests our reality isn't actually what it seems to be, it –'

I'd had enough. To be honest, I couldn't bear the thought that this drooling boy was cleverer than I was. He looked too grotesque for that. And as for questions of reality – well, they sounded like Siggy's ideas on language and reality, and look where those had got him.

'Yes, he's very gifted,' I interrupted. 'Thank him,' I said, looking over at Foam Boy who blinked, 'but I have to go.'

I walked off, leaving them to their bubbles and advanced mathematics.

As Miss Angelica had said, given the right kind of help, Foam Boy and his counterparts were as able as any of us. But they didn't look the same as the rest of us, and that mattered too.

As 'I Like It' came to an end and the fiddler took a moment to wipe away the sweat from his brow, a slow foxtrot began, and while the crowd changed over to accommodate this, I felt like a black baby turning up at a Ku Klux Klan fancy-dress ball when I saw Melissa walk onto the floor, arm in arm with Voluble Boy. There's no shame in saying I felt slightly upset as they sauntered gently off to the dance band's melodious version of Ray Charles's 'Take These Chains From My Heart'. My own heart was pounding, and neither with joy nor heart disease. I was jealous – heart-jealous, and I hadn't a clue what to do about it.

As they passed me, dancing close and linked like two partners in a crime against humanity, I stood watching in my penguin suit and tried to look cool. But I wasn't! So I grabbed the nearest woman I could get my hands on and dragged her onto the dance floor, as Melissa watched with dreamy eyes and blinked.

I'd grabbed Catriona, the epileptic, the Plimsoll-line-bearing crippled girl. As I embraced her with difficulty, closing my eyes with the effort, I was amazed at the smoothness of her movements and at the softness of her Gaelic voice.

'Yer a great wee dancer, Frank,' she whispered. 'An' I like a man who dresses well,' she said gently, as she fingered the buttons on my waistcoat and pulled me deeper into her, letting me snuggle right in. As I sank in to her soft bits, I realised once again that appearances were deceptive, and they could be so even on a dance floor with a great big girl like the epileptic Catriona.

I took Catriona to the bar and watched proudly as she took her anticonvulsants with a glass of orange juice I'd bought her. Father Mortalsen poured it for us personally. He had a sort of lazy, unattached smile on his face, and the pupils of his eyes were like pinpoints – the result of the bright light in the bar, I assumed. The orange juice came from a carton wrapped in heavy brown paper, for some reason. It was probably watered down. A deal had been done somewhere, I supposed – as they often were in real life, I was learning. I glanced about a bit while Catriona swallowed her pills. For, enchanted as I was by her, I kept hoping for some visual sign of the unfaithful, treacherous and totally immoral Melissa.

After what seemed a very long time, Voluble Boy gave up the delights of Melissa and went back to the job he was there to do. He was playing 'It's My Party', sung shrilly but effectively by Lesley Gore. It had been released the previous month in the US on the Mercury label, but as far as I knew it wasn't available in the UK yet. Despite this, Voluble had got hold of the record from somewhere, and it was probable therefore that he – like Father Mortalsen – was doing shady deals, too. I knew the record had to be a pirated copy or an illegal import and not the law-abiding, genuine article.

I also knew that any deals Father Mortalsen did would be done to help meet his medical expenses. He was a man of the cloth; he wouldn't want simple commercial gain, as Voluble Boy's would.

As I thought about this, it suddenly occurred to me that maybe they were *all* doing deals! Maybe they were *all* making a few bob on the side, every last one of them! They probably held business meetings in the evening for physically disabled and mentally handicapped entrepreneurs, while I'd been wasting my time studying chemistry. I concluded they must have done. I'd been excluded yet again! My mood sank like a stone. I felt panicky too, I have to admit. For Melissa was nowhere in sight. I'd scanned the area for her lovely white dress, while Catriona was dozing beside me in reaction to her epilepsy tablets.

I couldn't see Melissa anywhere. However, as I'd learned the very first day of my chemistry class, fortune favours the brave. So I decided to be brave, tempt fortune – and go look for her.

I tucked Catriona's chin gently onto her chest, using a small, firm portion of her generous left breast to pillow it. Then I went off to see what was doing in the wider realms of the hall, and well beyond it if need be. If fortune did indeed favour the brave I reckoned – wrongly as it turned out – I'd have to get lucky.

37

By the time I'd reached the entrance hall, Voluble Boy was giving his well-prepared preamble to 'Blue Velvet'. I knew about this song from my brother, who now had music contacts in North America – or so he said. I also knew the record wouldn't be formally released there until the following week or so. But here was Voluble Boy playing it openly, and much as I felt privileged to hear it so soon I was still pretty upset.

I was upset too, I suppose, by the fact that its lyrics hinted at an undreamed-of intimacy for me: kissing. I'd never kissed a girl before, and I suppose I wanted to break my duck that way. I suppose too, if I'm to be completely honest, I wanted to break it with Melissa. 'No chance of that,' I thought, as Bobby Vinton sang on and I heard Father Mortalsen saying something about *black* velvet to the janitor, who was standing with his claw-hand round a pint tumbler of black frothy stuff.

I felt I'd had enough of everything and then some. I ran through the entrance hall, past a startled Mr Hammerhead, who shouted, 'There's nothing worse than a boy in evening dress who –'

Outside, I went round to the back of the church hall. For some reason, Foam Boy's undoubted brilliance and seemingly inspired comments on the nature of reality had toppled me from the heights I'd attained with the benefit of my vivid imagination. I'd been a damaged child from a poor, working-class family, who'd sported grand ideas of advancement through education. And here I was, having my very first girlfriend stolen by an imperfect boy, who was playing records at a party for the handicapped – dubbed a school prom – while someone like Foam Boy was addressing the nature of our reality in terms I couldn't even understand, let alone ever hope to emulate. I needed some silence, some time on my own, and I'd get it out here, I was certain.

'It's that big dozy-looking girl from P.H.5,' I heard a voice whisper from round a corner of the building. I listened, despite myself. 'I had my suspicions, you know; oh, I had my suspicions OK. She's on top of that dyke,' it said and I forgot my problems and peered round the corner of the building to steal a quick look at who was speaking.

It was Woody. His varnished wooden arm was pointing towards the small dyke he was referring to. It was a perfect example of its type, with roughly cut, dark-grey stones sealed carefully with roughcast cement, like a life-sized jigsaw. There was no one *on* the dyke at all, and the only people I could see anywhere near it were Jason's ladyfriend, Butch, and another girl I recognised from school. Butch was embracing the other girl; they'd obviously just met this evening after a long separation. I remembered the other girl's name: Clodia. Faith had told me once that a famous Roman poet called Catullus had a ladyfriend called Clodia. For some reason best known to himself, he called her 'Lesbia' instead in his poems.

I looked at Butch and Clodia. I thought about shouting 'Lesbia!' just to see the look on Clodia's face, to see how surprised she'd be – how delighted. But I didn't get the chance, for she'd gone off behind the dyke with Butch – probably to sneak a cigarette; the innocents!

As I crept back round to the other side of the building, I disturbed a boy and a girl in a tangle of iron and plastic bits. They were grunting like Elvis as they tried to sort themselves out, and I had to admit this was a bit more serious than sneaking any cigarette. For a moment I considered putting an end to it by throwing a bucket of water over them, as my sister had done once to a couple of dogs that were 'at it', as she put it, outside our front door. But where would I get a bucket of water from, standing as I was outside a special school prom dance hall?

So I left them to it, and fortunately they didn't know I'd been there. As I left, I heard the girl give out a sort of wailing scream, and I knew she'd done it deliberately to stop whatever had been going on.

Mr Hammerhead rushed past me with a soldering iron and I headed towards a new voice – a louder one, and one I vaguely recognised. It was around yet another corner of the seemingly octagonal building. 'He's a wanker,' said Wee Jimmy, drunkenly. 'Now don't get me wrong, I like him a lot. But that evening wear . . . for Heaven's sake. It's a pisspot pretension to ponce about in that at a proper prom party,' he said, swaying, and enunciating with difficulty. 'I can't see what you see in the puerile prick,' he added, burping a mini-burp as Melissa spoke back, enunciating carefully and drunk on something far more dangerous than cider.

'I love him, Jimmy,' she said. 'Francis is the most wonderful person in the world.'

My mind raced. I didn't want to be seen to be spying, so my body raced too, back round to the entrance, and into the dance hall. Bobby Vinton was finishing his song with a flourish of dark and seductive feeling, and it reflected all the feeling I had inside: soft, gentle, warm – blue velvet.

By the time Voluble Boy's record session had given way to our former linesman standing up on stage singing 'He's Got The Whole World In His Hands', while clapping his fingerless painted hands and accompanying himself by kicking at a tambourine, I'd composed myself. The hall was relatively quiet and the crowd muted, though still chatting away. It felt as if they were waiting for something special to happen. It did – the stage curtain slowly opened and my brother stepped out from behind it with his band.

He was a vocalist, of course, a genuine one; but we saw it wasn't time yet for a song, as the tall, slim, dark-haired saxophonist moved forward with a jump, pulled the saxophone up to his mouth, supported it masterfully with his knee and blasted off into the magical sound of 'Perfidia'.

A cold shiver ran through me and I forgot about everything as I listened with true awe to the loud and inspiring sound of that quite wonderful melody. It blasted my heart and stirred my soul, moving me to the verge of tears that were of happiness, I think, but sadness too. I began to experience yet another first in my life: what live music really meant to those who truly loved it and were gifted enough to play it well. I knew the piece had been released by the Ventures over three years ago, but I hadn't heard it much on the radio, so it was relatively new to me. I captured it in my head, inhaled it into my lungs and as I melted into it completely, I smothered myself in its artistry. I felt I was drowning in it and I was happy to do so – though I surfaced the requisite three times, just to check all was well around me before I went back down under the waves of music again and rested there.

After 'Perfidia', the band's other vocalist gave a rousing rendition of 'Good Golly Miss Molly'. He was no Little Richard to look at, but he was every bit as good to hear, if not better. The drummer's hands flew with the finesse of a concert pianist, evoking the power of a cannon and I realised how the regular backbeat of the drum gave a certain stability to the music in addition to rhythm.

'Shake, Rattle and Roll' followed this, and the place did all of those, as you can imagine, the crowd taking to the dance floor in droves and pounding it close to Hell. Then my brother took the microphone, smiled to the room and said a few kind words of welcome. He changed the mood of it all completely and simply, as he moved effortlessly into the Matt Monro classic 'Softly As I Leave You'.

I felt as proud then as I'd ever felt in my life. He was good, I had to admit. And when he changed over with similar professional ease to 'It's All In The Game', he was so brilliant I almost wept.

Near the end of their session, my brother was encouraging the dancing couples to dance even closer. He was 'flirting the crowd', as he called it, by singing that haunting ballad, 'Our Day Will Come'. As the couples smooched and I watched his eyes smooch with them, they suddenly turned to blue stone. He turned them slowly towards me, gave a look of stark fear and gestured towards the outside door. I understood his concern.

Standing there was his old friend the backing vocalist: the *Demetrius and the Gladiators* lady. She'd obviously come to see my brother, and she'd brought her pet monkey with her! My brother's face was a study in terror, a portrait of grey, Dorian-style. And, as he finished his song and rushed off backstage, I wished Demetrius had been there in the flesh. For my brother would need as much help as he could get, I reflected, with a wild woman and her even wilder pet monkey chasing after him.

38

Meanwhile, back at the bar, there was a problem with Father Mortalsen. As I wondered what to do about my brother, a very small boy in a very big panic rushed up and asked me to go immediately to assist. It had all started, he said, when one of the unbaptised diabetic kids had collapsed midway through a limbo dance and they'd been unable to find a syringe for his insulin. Someone had realised Father Mortalsen was diabetic too, as they'd seen him injecting himself discreetly, hiding down behind the bar to do so, as a man of humility would. When asked, he'd handed his syringe over like a true man of God. Shaking with concern at the diabetic boy's plight, he'd told them to wash it out after use and return it pronto, in case he needed another few units of insulin soon himself. By the time they'd done this, however, he was lying on the ground groaning, flapping his arms around and laughing like a hyena. That's when they'd come to get me. I had an 'O' Grade in chemistry, not a doctorate in medicine, but it was good enough for them.

'He's dropped some acid,' said a thin, pale-faced boy, whom I thought I recognised from somewhere, though I couldn't quite place him at first. Then I could: Spiky Hair – the drug dealer from P.H.1! But it couldn't be him! *Could it?* I bent down to look at Father Mortalsen and the boy slipped away in indecent haste. I searched the floor looking for the acid he'd dropped, but it was as dry as the eggcup full of talcum powder someone had stupidly placed there with a small, silver apostle spoon stuck in it. That must have been some sort of joke. I poured the talcum into a waste-bin full of some other diabetic's used needles, and asked the semi-comatose Father Mortalsen if he'd accidentally swallowed some of the acid before he'd dropped it. As I listened carefully, he gabbled that what he really needed was a line of coke.

There was a table nearby with drinks on it, so I asked some boys to arrange things and, when they'd done so, they dutifully stood in line with Cola bottles at the ready and started to pour it into him one by one.

That did no good at all and, as he coughed it all out in a fountain of fizzy brown froth, he whispered something else: 'Smack! Give me . . . smack! Smack! Me! Give. Me. Smack!' he said, and pointed to his arm with his trembling index finger.

I gave him a good hefty slap across his biceps, but that did no good either, so I slapped his face too and nearly despaired. After all, my brother was stuck with a potentially crazy woman and an even crazier monkey and the last thing I needed was Father Mortalsen pegging it. For if the monkey happened to go for my brother and he needed the last rites, he'd have to receive them from this very distressed priest.

'Hit me with some pot, for God's sake,' he begged. I had to forcibly restrain Big Bob – who was standing watching beside Jason – from doing precisely that.

'He doesn't mean it!' I yelled, as Big Bob wielded an enamel pot in his hand like a mallet while looking at Father Mortalsen's head. 'He's delirious with shock,' I explained. 'Anyway, you'd probably miss him.'

Big Bob adjusted and refocused his bifocals, called me 'a know-all stabard', and walked off.

'A couple of barbs, quick,' cried Father Mortalsen, panicky but slightly more conscious. The recovered diabetic took out two syringes he'd discovered in the priest's back pocket while he'd been searching for his diabetic card, and he stuck them with professional acumen into Father Mortalsen's thigh.

'Arrrgh!' he yelped. 'Some crack! Crack!'

A trainee altar boy from Father Mortalsen's parish had called in and was looking on. He was 'straight off the boat', as we put it in those days, and the boat referred to came from Ireland.

He walked over to the priest.

'Be Jay-zus Father, have ye heard the one about the Scotsman, the Englishman and the Irishman?'

I pushed him aside; I knew what was wrong with our priest now. 'It's "crack" he's after, not *craic!*' I said.

Father Mortalsen looked up pleadingly.

'Well, give me some booze at least!'

A couple of M.H. boys, standing nearby, heard this and tried to help.

'Boo! Boo! Boo!' they chanted. They were good at it, too, and gave it their all – but I fetched a bottle of brandy from the First Aid box the priests always kept full, and poured some straight down his throat.

'Stuff me,' said Father Mortalsen, sitting up a bit and shocking *me* with his language, but attracting the attention of Jason.

'No need to be so disgustingly obvious, Father,' said Jason, with highly evident disapproval and he traipsed slowly away shaking his head. I wondered whatever had become of his well-known sense of compassion.

When the break came at last I went over and spoke to my footballer friend, who was sitting in his wheelchair. With equal measures of amusement and frustration, he'd been watching a fight out at the back of the hall between Wee Jimmy and a couple of M.H. boys who were keen on his girlfriend. I asked him what he thought of the evening so far.

'Let's wait and see what the second half brings.'

'Yes, let's just wait and see what happens,' I said, nodding slowly in agreement.

And of course, we did.

39

As Father Mortalsen recovered from his diabetic coma and Wee Jimmy recovered from the excesses of neat cider, I made my way towards the room where my brother's band was preparing for the main performance. As I did, I passed the country-dance band's spoon-player. He was in a corner, still in full Highland dress, hanging onto a set of bagpipes and surrounded by his plaid.

'Nice set of pipes,' I said, and he swung round in my direction. I saw it wasn't bagpipes at all he was bear-hugging. It was Miss Tartankilty, who had a rare flush of colour on her normally pale, Presbyterian face.

'Ah'm jist having a wee go at his pibroch,' she laughed, and I had the crazy idea she was being *made* to behave this way, as if her personality had been changed by someone – the pibroch player, I supposed. I imagine he'd done it to make her more, well, interesting.

I ignored them, reached the door, pulled it open and went in.

'Way out, man,' said the rhythm guitarist, as he played a melancholic D minor and studied the monkey sitting on my brother's head. 'Yeah, way out,' he repeated, switching to a diminished thirteenth with ease.

'Cut the crap, man, and spare me a hand to cool this boy down,' he added, referring to the monkey, which was now on his lap. 'Help me get him back to the slick chick from the suburbs.' The monkey looked at me and seemed to attempt a look of empathy between us, which I ignored.

'Sure, man,' said the guitarist. He rose from his seat, grabbed the monkey by the neck and dragged it from my brother's lap.

'Gee thanks, man,' said my brother, as the guitarist kicked the monkey in the groin absently – and I wondered once again where my brother had picked up all the cool lingo from. It just wasn't him, or at least it hadn't been. It seemed he was becoming just like the rest of them, an archetypal rock star with no individuality, and silly as it sounds as with Miss Tartankilty, he was being *made* to behave in this manner. But now could that be?

The rhythm guitarist swallowed another of the dark-blue pills he took intermittently, but never offered to anyone else.

He spoke again.

'I reckon that ape-cool-gorilla fancies you stiff, man,' he said to my brother, as the monkey lay outside the door, groaning and cupping its private parts in its hands, reminding me of the night he'd fought with my sister.

'Maybe . . . maybe,' my brother mumbled. 'But I don't fancy *it*!' he shouted, suddenly and with conviction as if he'd suddenly and momentarily lost his mind. The monkey peeked in through the door, groin still cupped in its hairy mitts, and looked on with undisguised adoration.

It did fancy him stiff!

My brother took another look at it, made some sort of decision with a nod of his head, and went off to deal with both it and its owner. He was confident of doing so after taking a couple of the pills which the guitarist had at long last offered him. But he didn't offer me any. As ever, I had been left out. Excluded. But things were looking better. My brother was going to sort things out; Father Mortalsen was going to be fine; Jimmy would be on the mend and off the cider; the prom was going better than I'd expected; and, of course, Melissa had said she loved me.

It may come as a surprise to you, but in addition to my not having been kissed by an attractive young woman before – nor by *any* young woman, for that matter – I'd never been loved by one either. So Melissa's disclosure was as novel to me as monkey-love was to my brother. So I decided I'd better do something about it.

Thus, as Voluble Boy switched records with a seamless but wordy changeover and the voice of Frankie Valli, ably assisted in falsetto by the Four Seasons, blasted out the first echoing cries of 'Walk Like A Man', I did indeed walk like a man, strutting my stuff across the dance floor as I headed towards the entrance hall, where Melissa would be waiting.

'Grrr,' I sounded silently, and a little deaf boy lip-read and signed it with his fingers to his partner. She caught his drift, laughed at me in ASL and signed something back to him. He laughed so loudly his fingers almost fell off with the effort. I ignored them, but I stopped growling anyway and headed for my destiny in total silence.

Melissa was there, as I'd thought. So without hesitation I walked right up to her. As I did, I heard the first few bars of yet another new, US-based and undoubtedly bootlegged record that Voluble Boy had loaded onto his massive and amplified record player. I'd heard it once before and it started with a lyric about dancing, so I took the cue, walked up to Melissa and asked her if she wanted to dance.

She nodded and smiled, but by the time we'd left the entrance hall and found a suitable place on the dance floor, the record had moved on a bit. For a second or so the lights dimmed and the record slowed and stopped. then it started up again, and the lights came back to full brightness and all was back to normal. Now it was The Crystals preparing to sing to us and as we stood near the centre of the dance floor with me trying to be as inconspicuous as possible, their backing group was gently hammering out the first repetitive and seductive beats of that popular R&B marvel, 'Then He Kissed Me'.

I had to clasp Melissa's waist for this one, though I wasn't quite certain how to go about that. So as we stood very close together for the very first time and prepared to dance a free interpretative version of a slow foxtrot, I kept my arms by my side and just stood staring at her. Our eyes remained in contact as the crowd poured onto the floor and we stood unwittingly like two proud lovers in a Shakespearian tragedy, just before the tragic bit entered the plot.

As we prepared to dance, we held onto that look – and our hopes – and I felt what it was like to be loved by a beautiful and incandescent young woman. I was still slightly hesitant and uncertain, however, and my arms were unsure where to put themselves. So Melissa grabbed my left arm and put it firmly around her waist. I managed the other one myself.

Woody was standing beside us, hammering out the refrain of the song on his arm with an ice pick he'd found somewhere, and Wee Jimmy stood beside him, recovered from his fracas and his battle with the cider. He was curled around a very pretty young girl. Jimmy wasn't fully sober yet, but he was trying. No wonder, when you saw his friend. Jason was nearby, too, moving in lissom fashion like a real dancer; he was with his friend, who was equally gifted that way. The boy with the uncertain callipers – the one who'd scored the goal on my one wild day of football – was kicking his heel against the ground, like a racehorse waiting to start, as his partner, a gifted young typist from our one-woman secretarial pool, laughed with him and kicked softly alongside him.

They looked great, I thought. Whether they were on the dance floor waiting for the off, like us, or for one reason or another were obliged to watch it all from the sidelines – as they did life in general – they still looked great, all of them. It was perfect.

The Crystals began and we moved closer together, the music chilling my soul with a melancholy joy. I pulled Melissa close in like the strong young man I was. She snuggled in deep and I felt warm.

As the almost-echoing lyrics unfolded, I saw Jimmy hold on tightly and firmly to his pretty admirer and she to him. Jason was smiling and his partner was holding him close, too. I wondered at this and had my reservations about it, but Melissa poked me in the ribs with a finger and laughed at something I obviously didn't understand. I hugged her even closer and she smelt like fresh lilac.

The atmosphere was still, intimate and charged. I opened my eyes and for one terrible moment I thought Woody was going to charge someone with the ice pick he'd pulled from his arm. But he was merely bowing to a young woman from M.H.3, who'd approached him shyly. He soon stood up again and took her gently by the waist too, being careful not to damage her with his dodgy arm.

The Crystals launched into the chorus, and I felt warm and wanted inside. I thought perhaps I should tell Melissa I wanted to have her baby, but I wasn't certain how you did that, so I said nothing about it. I felt funny and happy, sad and elated all at once. Woody too had a strange, faraway look in his eyes as he danced. He seemed to like it a lot and was close to something blissful himself, I think. I wondered when anyone had last cuddled him like that, and noticed he seemed sad too, in some way, just like the rest of us. The Crystals were coming to the end of their song, so I turned my attention back to them and to my lovely Melissa.

The song finished and I hardly heard it stop. I was in Heaven and Melissa was with me. So were Wee Jimmy, and Jason, and Woody, and the boy with the callipers who played football for kicks. And while Heaven seemed a lovely place to be right then, it seemed a sad place, too. And before Voluble Boy had time to change the record, before the final echoes of that unforgettable song had left me forever, I looked at Melissa and drank in the sight of her. She was shimmering like a rainbow and I glowed inside like a rainbow too and, in a moment of total inner and outer silence, I wanted to act out the words of the song. So I pulled Melissa closer than ever, touched softly at her hair with my fingertips and closed my eyes again as she closed hers.

Reader, I kissed her.

40

Chubby Checker's strident voice broke that particular spell with 'Let's Twist Again'. The place erupted. The dance floor and its surroundings were all in accord, as everyone went for it. They thumped with their feet, thumped with their hands and thumped with every bit of themselves that they could possibly thump with. A couple of good-quality prosthetic hands flew across the room, the leg of a cyborg hit the ceiling and just missed the spotlight, and a boy with wing-like things on his back instead of regular arms tried to fly through a window. He was caught by the claw-hand of the ever-alert janitor before he managed to do so.

As Chubby sang the 'round' bit, wheelchairs spun like carousels, their occupants as enchanting to me as the proud, dignified horses on real carousels are to children. Rollup Boy spun too, revolving around on his back like an upturned gyroscope on an egg top, but with more flair and with a vulnerable human quality that moved me.

Una had rushed onto the floor too and she tapped time with Chubby by knocking her brace with her fist. Then after years of frustration, but in just one single moment of decisiveness, she grabbed at her harness with clenched hands and ripped it off. She tossed it into the crowd with a tinkling sound and she tossed her hair back too, and finally glowed like a starlet. A goodlooking boy from P.H.5 rushed over and grabbed her. They pulled each other close too and as he bent his face down towards hers I discreetly turned away. He kissed her, I imagine, and we lost it completely.

We danced and shook and jumped about and shouted obscenities with Wee Jimmy, as we gave ourselves over to the music in a totality of collective ego-loss. For a few precious minutes it was like the festival of Saturnalia during the reign of the Emperor Domitian. We were all emperors and empresses that evening, and why not? We danced ourselves into an ephemeral ecstasy, as the cares of our known world dissolved all around us and we didn't give a damn. For those few minutes, I felt life was truly great and we'd been placed on this earth to conquer it, not to stand back idly and watch it all pass us by.

And by the time Wee Jimmy finally collapsed from a second overdose of alcohol, Woody had ripped his arm to shreds with the reutilised ice pick and Una had substituted the goodlooker's shoulder for her discarded brace, I was as happy as a narcissistic hermaphrodite that finds itself pregnant, and every bit as confused. Love, it seemed, was a strange and ambiguous thing, and its contrasts of emotion excited me.

I felt a movement beneath me and looked at Melissa in surprise. She frowned again and looked downwards. I followed her look. There was a monkey down there beneath us, and it was excited too.

The monkey ran under my legs and out towards the entrance hall.

'Come back, you little piece of primal shit!' cried my brother, running after it, dropping the 'cool, crazy, way-out scene, man' style of jargon, and returning to the baser stuff I knew him best for. 'Come back, you pissy primate,' he called as he chased after it, and I left Melissa standing in open amusement, to follow them out in the direction of the entrance.

'OOG-OO-AH . . .! OOG-OO-AH, O-HAH, O-AAH.'

I stopped dead in my tracks. My brother disappeared, swearing at the monkey with aplomb.

'Derek?' I thought. I saw a small group of newcomers at the ticket-table beside Mr Hammerhead.

'Hello Francis. Hello Francis,' said Moira, stepping forward and smiling, going down unevenly on one leg before stabilising herself. 'We just dropped in to say a brief hello and to show you the kids.'

'Kids!' I turned and looked at the two smart young men who were standing beside Mr Hammerhead. There was a pram-like thing beside them with two infants in it. They were both sucking at their thumbs and holding packets of sweets.

'Do I know you?' I asked the young men absently, fumbling around in my head as I tried to get some reality back into it, for I was feeling very odd.

'It's Derek and Eric,' said Hammerhead, irritably. 'There's nothing worse than a young man who doesn't welcome his friends.'

I saw someone else standing behind them. I looked closer; I froze. It was Siggy!

Derek and Eric came forward and shook my hand. I felt happy, but . . . afraid.

'What are the children called?' I asked, looking at Moira.

'Cedric and Frederic,' she said proudly.

'Oog-oo-ah . . .! Oog-oo-ah, o-hah, o-aah,' gurgled Cedric or Frederic.

'Oog-oo-ah . . .! Oog-oo-ah, o-hah, o-aah,' gurgled the other one.

By now I'd let go of Derek's hand, but he took mine again and gave it a hard squeeze. He said something that was unclear.

'Derek says we were sorry to hear about your disappointment,' translated Moira. I wondered what he was talking about, as I watched Frederic and Cedric swapping sweets.

'Oh, that's all over,' said Melissa, who'd joined us. 'Francis will finish his education at our own school; then he'll do something scientific with his 'O' Grade.'

I thanked her by smiling graciously, though I thought she was being a bit too optimistic about it all.

'Yes, it's all over,' I said, delighted to see them but still very touchy about my future prospects . . . and still feeling slightly afraid. 'I might study music and team up with my brother. He's a rock musician: professional, handsome and gifted,' I boasted, 'so maybe I'll pen a few lyrics and some music for him.' My brother ran back into the entrance hall – still chasing the monkey and still swearing imaginatively, as Cedric and Frederic looked on in open amazement.

Derek and Eric looked on in amazement too, and Derek – via Eric – said: 'Who's that?' to Melissa.

Melissa smiled.

'It's Francis's brother, the rock star.'

I pushed my way through to Siggy.

He looked dreadful.

'I just dropped in to say goodbye,' he said. I reached for him and he moved back.

'No, it's better not to touch me,' he said. 'I don't want you ending up like me – in some sort of limbo; nowhere really. Better good and gone than here.'

I wasn't certain what to say.

'How did you get here?' I asked him.

His eyes filled with tears.

'I was fitted in. It's that simple,' he said. Then with a brief look and a shake of his head he moved away into the shadows and was gone.

41

I returned to the musicians' room to see how my brother was. His band was there, along with Miss Tartankilty, who'd deserted her pibroch player by now and was playing with the tenor saxophone. I'd heard the term 'groupie' before, but I'd never imagined anything quite as evident as this. Her personality had completely changed; it was almost scary.

'Where's my brother?' I asked, as they all sat looking a bit dazed and confused.

'He's eloped,' said someone.

I was shocked.

'With the backing vocalist?'

'No . . . the monkey,' said one of the guitarists, as the monkey's former owner walked into the room and spotted me.

'Why, hello! You've grown. You look just like your brother!' she said, brightening up immediately and heading towards me, with her long legs leading and her prominent breasts thrust forward like starched pillow-down on the attack.

'Cool, man,' said the lead guitarist, referring to the fact that my brother had eloped with the monkey.

'No shit,' said the drummer.

'Yeah, cool,' agreed the acoustic guitar player.

'Way out,' said the bassist, as I found the way out myself, avoiding the continuing approaches of the monkey woman and heading off into the hall once more to find Melissa and normality.

Things were quieter on the dance floor now and I could see the reason. Most of the remaining staff of the school had turned up as promised, and they were eyeing events with due and judicious concern. A couple of priests and a minister from the local kirk had turned up with them and were moving among the dancing couples, pulling them apart with solid-looking grappling hooks and making them dance together from as far apart as they could reach. I caught sight of Miss Angelica standing in a corner speaking with Melissa, so I ignored the rest and went over to join them.

She smiled.

'Hello, young man. Melissa's been telling me the evening's gone very well,' she said, handing me a large envelope. She made a suggestion. 'Have a look at that sometime; it might focus your attention on certain . . . well . . . issues.'

I took the envelope and had a quick look inside. It was a book. At least *she* wasn't giving up on me, as everyone else seemed to be.

'What is it?' I asked, as I made to take it out and have a look at it there and then. But she gave me a look that cautioned against rushing things.

'Later,' she said. 'Read it later. When you've time to really think about it. And try not to rush to a judgement.'

I was puzzled.

'Thanks,' I said, as I walked over and placed it on a nearby table beside Foam Boy, who'd been sitting there watching us like a camera with no click mechanism.

'Look after this, please, will you?' I asked, and he blinked. I returned to Miss Angelica and Melissa.

'So the evening's gone well?' said Miss Angelica, sounding tired.

I nodded.

'Better than I thought,' I said, cautious as ever with the staff of my school, no matter how approachable, generous or trustworthy they seemed. Cautious too with my favourite teacher, because for a crazy moment she'd seemed a bit less convincing: a bit unreal, as if she *were* losing interest in me, along with everyone else.

Miss Angelica took a deep breath.

'And have you danced much?' she asked, as she gave me an uncertain, almost bored, look and then transferred it, unchanged, over to Melissa.

'Oh, a bit,' I said.

'Well, more than a bit,' said Melissa, looking at me intimately, and my face lit up like a votive candle supplicating the gods of Love.

'You're of an age when you should be dancing,' said Miss Angelica, yawning, as the clerics continued to drag partners apart with the grappling hooks.

Foam Boy, whom I'd noticed earlier showing something to Big Bob, via his cover, was rolled over towards us in his wheelchair and his carer handed Miss Angelica the same piece of paper, I'd seen.

'Oh, so you've finally solved it,' she said almost sadly, looking at the paper absently while he blinked at her cautiously and I felt jealous again, despite his difficulties.

'It's not good to be jealous,' whispered Melissa quietly.

Big Bob passed us.

'You're a jealous stabard and we know things you don't. You still think you know it all. But you don't, not yet! You hypocritical stabard,' he said.

I turned away and fought down the urge to throw a punch again, but decided I'd better speak to him.

'Wait, Bob! Why don't you like me? Tell me what it is about me that upsets you so much.'

He stopped and turned his massive body round to face me.

'You're too flippant,' he said. It surprised me that he even knew the word. 'You make dreadful things seem funny. You've no idea what words can really do. You just want to measure things and test them. You want to describe them in as remote a manner as possible, yet the way we are is the way we're described; can't you see that?' To my amazement, he almost broke down. 'Things don't always benefit from being made fun of, you know, not if you want them to be taken seriously,' he said, suddenly tearful. And that made me think.

'So what do you suggest?' I asked.

He observed me through his large, heavy spectacle frames.

'Change the mood,' he said, slowly. 'Change things before it's too late; no one else can.'

He sighed and wandered off, shoulders bowed, a huge and unlikely philosopher.

'Change the mood, change things,' Big Bob had advised. So I thought about it, and tried to; but it was already far too late.

42

Outside at last and alone with Melissa, I caught a glimpse of my brother and the monkey getting into a taxi and we went over. They snuggled in the back seat. The driver wore a cynical 'I've seen it all now' look on his face, and I wondered if he really had.

My brother wound down the window when I approached.

'We're off,' he said. 'You might think it's crazy, but I'm doing what I've always wanted to.'

'I can see that,' I said. 'Good luck, and thanks for everything.'

Melissa, who'd accompanied me, tightened her grip on my hand. She was looking up at the sky.

She gave a shudder then spoke.

'Oh, it's only a shadow. I thought it was a face, for a moment.'

I knew she was tired and I returned her grip to reassure her, and I had a sudden flood of bizarre memories; of seeing a smiley face in the sky the day I started school; of hearing breathing in the sky; of my sister, like Siggy, once saying language defined the reality of things; of people reappearing in my life when they really shouldn't have; and I wondered if I were going mad – if I *were* mad!

My brother looked at me closely.

'Can I ask you one last thing before we go?' he said, as the monkey snuggled into him: close, harsh, tight and almost bestial.

I nodded.

'Do you really think I'm here in a taxi with a monkey?'

'Of course.'

He shook his head and spoke again, but his voice was different.

'It's time to reassess things; time to stop making fun of them.' He sounded just like Big Bob. 'It's time to stop larking about. We don't only speak and read words, you know,' he said strangely. 'We think them too, and they us. Try to discover the way to sort things out fast.' He looked slightly sinister as he said this and his words puzzled me a great deal.

Through the open window he gave me what was to be his final look, and it was as serious as it possibly could be.

'It's probably too late to say this, but do something while you still can,' he said emphatically, as he closed the window, gave me a final half-hearted wave and went off in the cab with the monkey. He'd already clocked up quite a sum on the meter and they hadn't gone anywhere yet.

'What was that all about?' asked Melissa as they headed off into the distance. I felt tears forming at the great loss I'd just suffered through losing my brother – to a monkey, of all things.

'Tell me what it meant,' she persisted. 'You're the one who's so clever, so tell me what it means: all of it!' I looked at her and I thought on Minerva, the goddess of wisdom and the arts. That worried me. How did I know about her? I'd never even heard of her! Everything was beginning to feel unreal. I felt as if I were there and yet not there – coming and going, a sort of fainting feeling. But I maintained my composure and tried to do what Melissa had asked. And I found I could – as if my thoughts were filled with information I didn't have. As if, instead of thinking them, I was receiving them!

'Well, if I'd written that particular scene,' I began, 'my brother could be taken literally, more or less, or, to be more precise, as literally as I could possibly make him. You see, he thinks language dictates everything. That's one of the reasons he sings and he may be right.' Melissa looked at me lovingly, told me how marvellous I was, then asked me to continue.

'The monkey – a tenacious and pretty primitive individual – could symbolise the less desirable parts of popular culture,' I suggested. 'Its baseness – materialism and sentiment; and its tenacity: the powerful and lasting influence that culture has over us,' I said. She held my hand and we watched the taxi disappear for good.

'The taxi and the driver could represent aspects of time,' I continued, feeling a bit shivery and even more apprehensive. 'The taxi would represent the apparent security of time; the driver, its impersonality and the meter, the high cost of time passing unused,' I said cleverly, while Melissa hugged my shoulder with her head and felt closer to me than ever, and and I had a sudden vague notion I was being watched. I looked round, saw nothing and continued.

'The behaviour of Father Mortalsen, Father Littlegrace and so on, could simply be barbs directed at the cant of quasi-spiritual hopes,' I offered. Melissa nuzzled into me and I felt a wave of tiredness hit me, the way you do when a cloud blocks the warmth of the sun. It was as if the time I'd been given to sum up the story of our lives was already coming to an end and I could somehow feel it. 'Words of inspiration, koans, suggestions of miracles,' I elucidated, 'things like that complicate life for people like us,' I said warmly, but feeling a touch of cold as I did so, as if something warm had just been switched off. 'Things like that can make us place too much faith in what's alleged to be external to us,' I said, believing that with all my heart, 'leading us to have too little faith in ourselves and what is certainly within us.' I still felt that vague feeling someone was not only watching us, but listening too. I swung my arm in a wide arc to include everything in view. 'Everything could be like that!' I exclaimed. 'Everything we've experienced since the first day I met you at school,' I said, unintentionally raising my voice higher than was usual and Melissa giggled nervously as I pointed to the church hall to emphasise everyone in there: the staff, the pupils, the priests – everyone. 'It could all just be a mixture of parable, metaphor, reality and confusion. Like life itself,' I suggested, as I paused a bit and frowned, while from the hall I briefly caught the sound of Mike Berry singing 'Don't You Think It's Time?' and I shuddered.

Don't You Think It's Time?

'For what?' I wondered. 'Time for what?' And for a dreadful moment I felt as if I might topple off the world – simply drop off it and disappear.

I continued to speak to Melissa, though my voice was very shaky, since for some unknown reason I'd begun to wonder what made *me* real, and what enabled *me* to exist from second to second. I still had the feeling of being watched and overheard too, but I continued to ignore it and returned my attention to Melissa, to complete what I was saying.

'If it had been my story, I would have been as honest and as truthful about everything as I possibly could have been,' I assured her. 'Though I have my limitations in terms of expression and recall, like everyone else.' I wondered what gave us duration. Fear gripped me in the heart like a vice, and I wondered again what kept me here from moment to moment and what would happen if whatever it was stopped or went away.

I held Melissa by the waist again and pulled her as close to me as possible, in order to protect her from the world and to reassure myself it was still there. For it all seemed a bit hazy, and I felt a sense of unreality whispering around out there somewhere. I felt a sense of a break in the continuity of things, too, as if I'd once played the central part in something important but that part was gradually being taken away from me. Melissa gently eased away, but kept her fingertips on mine. She faced me and I saw the moonlight reflecting in her eyes, the way a magus would, I imagine, seeing a sympathy there – a correspondence between things separated by distance and time; a continuity between the very near and the very far; her eyes and the moon, reflections of the same, basic thing. She looked beautiful, like a child blessed by the gods on the verge of a marvellous life.

'I see,' she said, as if she meant it.

And I wondered if she really did.

Despite my unease, we remained outside for some time. We studied the sky as it became darker and talked about everything in general and nothing in particular. As we did so, I tried to harbour no illusions of what the future held for us, or for those kids in the hall who'd been designated sick, infirm and hopeless from day one, and who were unlikely to ever amount to much. Kids like myself, who'd been completely written off and forced to spend a life in virtual sleep, or some sort of storybook existence, before they'd even had time to waken up or assert themselves. I wondered what life held for all of them, myself included, and my hopes weren't high. These weren't noble thoughts I had – far from it. They were simply common thoughts addressed to noble and uncommon people. And every few seconds the dark thought ran through my head that time was running out for us all: for me and for them. The sounds of Johnny Kidd and The Pirates singing 'I'll Never Get Over You' filtered out of the dance hall, accompanied by the isolated noises of the outcasts in the church and I wondered if I'd ever get over it all myself – and I doubted it.

I still felt odd, weak and shaky, and I wondered again what was happening to me. I also wondered again whether if whoever or whatever had created me forgot all about me, I would simply cease to exist.

'Let's go back in,' said Melissa, in a worried voice. 'It's too exposed out here, and I feel as if I'm getting lighter.' It was a bizarre turn of phrase, and I realised she was experiencing strange feelings too.

She took my hand again and held it firmly, and we walked quickly back into the hall together as the sky grew darker. We passed Mr Hammerhead and a bunch of similarly puerile staff and hangers-on who were standing talking in excited clichés. They seemed fine; there was no sign of any uneasiness there, though they were preparing to leave. Hammerhead looked at us and said something to one of the others, but we ignored them. The good ones were there too, of course, and we acknowledged them, as they deserved to be acknowledged. We blew each of them a kiss as we passed, and they smiled back warmly and returned the blown kiss with one of their own. They were supportive as ever, but outnumbered.

It became a bit warmer as we entered the front of the dance-hall area itself. Wee Jimmy was standing looking at us, hands on hips.

'Where the Hell have you two been?'

'We went out for a bit, but we're back in for good now,' I smiled, reassuring him. He looked cute, despite being drunk and foul-mouthed as ever, and quite suddenly I realised just how fond of him I really was. He was like a brother – perhaps even closer, and that sudden realisation surprised me, after all these years of disliking him.

'It's bloody freezing out there,' he said. 'And there's talk of wild monkeys running around, too,' he added, suddenly jerking his head round, as if someone had called to him. I thought I might have heard something too, so I looked round as well, but there was no one there and he turned his attention back to us. 'They seem to be causing all sorts of problems, those monkeys.' He staggered in place on his artificial legs.

'I know that,' I said, touching him on the shoulder with affection, just as I felt again that odd sensation you feel when you're being stared at but can't see anyone. I ignored it, but it didn't ignore me. It stayed.

'We saw one of the monkeys,' I told Jimmy, concentrating harder on what was happening around me – fearing the worst, hoping for something less than that. 'But it's gone off, in a taxi.' I laughed forcibly, not elaborating on the circumstances surrounding that particular episode.

We went deeper into the dance area and back to being safe again with all our friends. We sat down at the table near to where Foam Boy still sat in his wheelchair. He was staring into space in all its infinity of possibilities, and I saw the envelope on the table – the one with the book in it I'd left there earlier. I thanked him for looking after it and he blinked an acknowledgement.

'You've done an excellent job,' I said, in order to make him feel part of things, and he blinked again.

'What's that?' asked Jimmy, grabbing the envelope and pulling out the book. It looked impressive. It was a reasonably substantial volume and it seemed brand new. I felt a combination of gratitude and bitterness towards Miss Angelica, and held Melissa's hand while we watched Jimmy scan rapidly through it. My emotions were mixed because, while I knew she would continue to supply me with as much knowledge as she possibly could, I also knew there were others out there who'd never allow me to use it properly.

With a gasp of surprise Jimmy glanced over his shoulder again, as though someone had spoken. He looked quickly over his other shoulder; his neck cringed and his shoulders moved upwards. It was as if he'd become aware of the fact that someone was staring at him too, as if someone was hidden nearby and knew his every move.

'I'm being watched,' he said grimly. 'Someone knows everything I'm doing.' His voice held a certainty I'd never heard from him before.

I looked around myself, and I could feel it too. The base of my neck tingled: it was that feeling of being stared at again – of being studied in minute detail, of some impersonal and secretive dissection being carried out from a distance. I was terrified.

So was Melissa.

'Someone's spying on us,' she whispered, looking pale and very frightened, and causing waves of panic to rise in me, though I tried not to let her see it. 'I can feel it,' she said, bending her large head down, her voice becoming low and faint, getting fainter. 'Someone's spying on us and it's scaring me,' she said finally. I squeezed her hand to try and reassure her, but mine was shaking just as badly as hers and all I did was add to her terror.

'It mentions *me* in here,' said Jimmy, in a flat voice and with resignation, pointing at the book and digging at the page it was open at with his forefinger.

He read on.

'It mentions the rest of us here, too,' he said, with a hard edge to his voice, as he flicked through the pages. 'It mentions us all, for Christ's sake, and it tells everything about us,' he managed to get out, before he broke down with a sob.

I tried to grab the book from him, but he pulled it away as fast as forked lightning, and he looked every bit as fearsome.

'Fuck that,' he said, shaking his head in confusion and throwing the book onto the floor and standing on it.

I looked around and my friends seemed to shrink. We all seemed to shrink, while everything else remained the same size. Jimmy's tiny feet straddled the centre of one of the pages of the book he'd been looking at, then he suddenly fell down into it, tearing a hole through some of the pages, and stood up to his knees in printed paper. Even so, given his diminutive size and his small artificial legs, the book had lifted him up a bit; it had raised him just that little bit higher than usual. The light shone on him briefly; I saw his true condition for a second, and I knew we all could if only we looked, and I felt for him.

Then everything seemed to return to its real size again. Jimmy was still standing on the book, and the extra height it gave him enabled him to look out of the window at the world outside.

'Fuck that sort of thing lying around in here and making us all public property,' he snarled, as he looked down at the book he was standing on, then looked at us and the world outside, and seemed to despair of it all.

I approached him.

'What is that book?' I asked, almost paralysed with fear myself, as I sensed the unknown presence watching me again and knew somehow that when it went, I'd go too, like Al and Billy and all the other friends I'd lost. I'd go when it went, just as suddenly and completely as they had.

'That's a strange thing for you to ask,' said Jimmy slowly, staring at me as though I were an enemy, while Big Bob wandered by, cumbersome as ever but less substantial somehow, as if he were lighter than he'd been earlier. He was looking scared too, but he nodded his head in agreement with Jimmy.

'Bastard!' he said, *properly*. He looked at me, seeming to become even lighter, even less substantial – and my heart raced with fear. 'Yes, bastard,' he repeated. 'No need to disguise things now, is there?'

'And why is that?' I asked, directing my question to Jimmy. 'Why call *me* all sorts of names when you're not exactly spoiled for choice elsewhere in here?' I was terrified but angry, too, as I took a quick look around the hall to discover a more suitable target for his venom. To my horror, I discovered instead that everyone had stopped whatever they'd been doing; and they had all turned towards me, but couldn't make eye contact. Were they ashamed of something? Or were they ashamed of me? They were almost perfectly still, slowly sinking downwards and virtually transparent. There was no longer any music playing; there was barely a sound and nothing moved. There was some light – enough to read by perhaps – but that was fading too. Everything was as still as a graveyard, and all my friends had cowered down now like beaten dogs. I realised they'd been frightened into inactivity, and I knew they too were all aware of something secretly inspecting them – just as we were.

But I didn't give up yet. I had to find out why I'd become the enemy, why Wee Jimmy and Big Bob and presumably the rest of them were viewing me as if I were some sort of traitor.

'So why call me filthy names?' I challenged Jimmy again; my voice could barely be heard, so I wondered if I were dying, and the thought frightened me terribly.

Melissa burst into tears.

'We all knew there was something wrong, Francis – we suspected we weren't real people, not real in any physical way, not like normal people. We've suspected it for years, but we didn't want to tell you about it – we didn't want to worry you any more than we already had. You've got your career to think of; we didn't want you sacrificing that just for us.'

As more memories flooded me of the many hints I'd had, of what was becoming dreadfully obvious but I still didn't want to acknowledge, I grabbed her by the shoulders and shook her hard.

She kept on.

'We've always discussed things when you were resting at dinnertime. We brought Billy and Al up to date in the mornings before you arrived. We discussed things when you went to the Academy too, but we weren't certain. Your family suspected it too, but kept quiet about it. We thought that – '

I turned back to Wee Jimmy, while I tried to take in what she'd said.

'You grab a book intended for me,' I shouted, though it came out as a whisper, while I continued to try and understand what Melissa had meant. Now she was saying she was dissolving. What did that mean? Foam Boy had blinked once slowly then stopped moving completely too. I could see straight through his chest to the far wall, and that seemed to be dissolving also.

'So why am I such a rat?' I shouted at Jimmy, though it was barely audible, and all around us things were disappearing, going away, losing themselves somewhere – just vanishing. 'Why does the book make *me* such a rat?' I yelled soundlessly, as everything seemed to fall apart and disintegrate, as if the universe itself had decided to call it a day and end itself.

'Because you wrote it, you cunt,' said Jimmy slowly, looking at me with a hatred in no way lessened by his gradual understanding of things, while he continued to glance over his shoulder to try to discover what was inspecting him and, at the same time, try to work out where he really was.

'Fuck you,' he said, hating and hurting me with two small words.

We heard a breathing sound above us and felt the familiar moist warmth of someone's breath – and finally we became aware of where we were, and who was looking at us.

Jimmy's head turned upwards towards the source of the breath and he stood on his tiptoes on the printed page he was so precariously perched on. His eyes finally found what they were searching for: the person who was watching him.

'And fuck you, too,' he said slowly, then he took the last breath he'd ever take.

He repeated it twice more, as everything dissolved around us and it all became suddenly dark.

'Fuck you, too,' he said bitterly, in a final show of wilfulness and fading integrity. 'Fuck you, too,' Wee Jimmy repeated defiantly to whomever it was who'd been reading about us and keeping us alive, and then, becoming tired of our story, had closed the book, forgotten about us and caused us all to disappear forever.

When the time came for me to return to school, I didn't go. The school bus arrived and stopped at the bottom of our path as usual, but my mother went out and told the driver I wouldn't be going in that day.

'Or ever again,' I thought, as I stood inside the house, dressed up to the nines in my new school uniform and clutching my briefcase like a treasure map.

I'd decided to bite the bullet, take the bull by the horns, cross the Rubicon, burn my bridges and cast the die all at once. I'd discussed this with my family, of course, and they'd agreed with my decision.

'Yes, just go to the Academy and see what happens,' they'd urged me. 'And if you want any support we'll come with you.'

Well, I was going to the Academy, but I'd no intention of taking anyone with me for support. Not even the living and dead school chums who could have escorted me there, in my head at least, with all the justification in the world. For like most things in life and like most normal people, I was doing this because I wanted to. I wanted to do it very badly indeed and I was doing it for no other reason. I'd decided to force the issue, by and for myself, and you don't need company to do that sort of thing; just guts and a bit of naivety, I suppose, and I had plenty of both back then, if little else.

I left home at ten sharp, when I knew the Academy pupils would be well settled into their first class of the day. I assumed I'd have a better opportunity to argue my case then with whomever one argues such a case with at this late stage.

Accordingly, I was soon walking along the main road to the Academy, the same long road where ten years before I'd stood with my mum on my first day at school, waiting for the selfsame bus that had just been sent on its way by my mother.

We'd moved house twice since then, but, as I passed my former home by the mound, it looked unchanged and familiar. It was someone else's home now, and whatever history I had there, I decided to let it remain. This wasn't the time for reflection, I'd decided, but for action and looking forward. The monument to Marjorie Bruce still stood nearby, and while it was probably riddled with ghosts for me too, I walked past it without encountering any.

I walked past the trees on the road – the apple and cherry blossoms, the oaks, the chestnuts and the elders. There was a monkey-puzzle tree there too, I remember, and stray thoughts flickered within me – spectres and phantoms of other things tempting me to indulge in the past. But I ignored them, and headed for the Academy like a duck to water, but a duck that doesn't know if it will swim or drown when it arrives there.

A bird sang loudly in one of the trees and for a moment I remembered the echo I'd heard all those years ago. For a few seconds it stirred something deep; it reminded me of my dead sister and of Al and Billy and the certain end that waits patiently for us all – while we waste time, and sometimes our whole adult life, trying to make sense of it.

Maybe that perked me up a bit – trickled through to my conscious mind and gave it a nudge. For I was scared witless by now and I needed a nudge from somewhere to keep me walking, to keep me on track towards my crazy and unrealistic hopes and expectations.

I finally arrived at the Academy and went down the long, sloping drive that led to the main door. My stomach churned like a cement mixer with a heavy load and my arms twitched like a puppet in nervy hands. My legs were like treacle – the syrupy sort – and waves of nausea threatened to drown me in the terminal sickness of despair. I knew, however, that I probably looked as cool as frozen cucumber on the outside. For despite everything, I wanted to look that way; for then I might be taken seriously.

When I reached the main door I paused, breathed in deeply and entered. I headed directly for the headmaster's office. He was standing outside it like a sentry with fixed bayonet and he looked every bit as forbidding.

'So you've turned up to force the issue,' he said pleasantly enough, but giving nothing away of his feelings on the matter. 'The Education people still won't allow you to enrol,' he said, as I stood listening, seemingly composed, while my legs shook beneath me like earthquakes.

'I've spoken with them again,' he said. 'I've done all I possibly can to assist. The best we could agree is that you do a few more classes this coming term.'

He spoke with both clarity and meaning, and I heard him.

'Perhaps in maths, if you're up to it; physics too, if they'll allow you.' He finished, looked at me and nodded: firm, stern and totally dependable.

He turned round to stare at some boys who'd arrived late, as I had. They ran off when they saw him and headed for their respective classes. I envied them and felt like running off with them.

'Come into my office for a moment,' he said, not weakening in his resolve one bit, I observed, as I followed him in through the office door and past one of the school secretaries. She smiled at me warmly as we went in to his room and he asked her to get the Chief Education Officer on the telephone. I stood to attention while he sat down at his desk and he ordered me to do the same. The phone rang once; he picked it up and was put through to the appropriate person. He spoke with them for a time and they evidently knew my case.

'So you won't reconsider?' he said, affably, but heading towards the end of the conversation without success. 'Well, he's turned up here wearing a school uniform and carrying a brand-new briefcase,' he said, looking at me as he did so. 'He looks well enough to me.' A look of decisiveness came over his face. 'Then let it be on *my* head,' he snapped, 'I'll be delighted to take all the responsibility. It's about time someone did!' he finished, and slammed the phone into its cradle.

A silence fell over us that spoke of many things and he looked at me, determined, strong and hard.

'Go up to class 3C and tell the teacher I've sent you,' he said calmly. 'On second thoughts, ask the secretary to take you. We don't want you getting lost, do we?' He turned to the papers on his desk and all the other important matters he had to deal with, now he'd finally dealt with me.

'Thanks, sir,' I said simply, feeling I wanted to hug him and take him outside and parade him to the world. 'Thanks, sir,' I said once again as I left his office, feeling as if I'd been touched by a miracle.

I did as he'd advised and the secretary took me upstairs to the class. She knocked at the door and the teacher opened it, looked at us and came out into the corridor. As the door swung closed behind him I caught a glimpse of a couple of dozen boys in there, uniformed and proper-looking. The secretary had a word with the teacher, who introduced himself and told me to come in and join them. I turned to thank her before she left and she had a final supportive word.

'Go on in and get yourself an education, Frank,' she urged, as my teacher stood near the classroom door, watching me with patience and interest and with a very welcoming smile on his face.

'Right,' I said, as I walked right in to that classroom, just as The Rooftop Singers had advised earlier that year in their top ten hit of that name. And as the secretary walked away and her heels echoed loud and clear along the corridor, I did what she'd advised me to do. I took her advice to get myself an education.

And I did.

CHARACTERS AND EVENTS

Unless otherwise stated, all the characters and events in *On the Edge of a Lifetime* are based on real people and real events in a manner congruent with the comments made in the Preface.

FAMILY

The characterisations of my immediate family are only accurate in part.

My sick sister is a composite character and the description of the events surrounding her death refers to two family bereavements that occurred when I was a young child. As with many families then, tuberculosis was an ever-present worry and concern. The one member of our family who contracted it survived.

My eldest brother was singing semi-professionally in his early teens.

My sister attended our local convent school, which was a few minutes' walk from our home.

My elder brother went off to train for the priesthood as a youngster. He left well before ordination. The allusions to my Otherbrother's bizarre behaviour are quite unrelated to my brother. They are allusions to teachings of, and practices in, the Church that many found difficult and punitive, including me. The medically acknowledged spectre of 'masturbatory insanity', and of its prevention by eating cornflakes referred to in this section of the book, is described by J.D. Weinrich in: *The Oldest Obsession: Scientific American: Triumph of Discovery* (Helicon, UK, 1995), p 206, from which this account is taken.

THE SCHOOLS

My special school was the Sandyford Special School for Physically and Mentally Handicapped Children; it was also commonly called the 'Special School'. It had an annexe, the Mary Russell Institute, where children with Down's syndrome were educated. On one side of our school we had Abercorn Junior Secondary School, on the other, Saint Mirin's Academy: the school I ultimately attended. My sister attended Saint Margaret's Convent School for girls. All these schools were on the same road: Renfrew Road, Paisley.

THE MONUMENT

The monument to Robert Bruce's daughter, Marjorie, remains to this day.

ON THE EDGE OF A LIFETIME

The incident at the mound with my father happened more or less as described. The mound was situated directly outside a neighbour's window: the late Scots folk singer, entertainer and radio DJ, Danny Kyle. It was Danny who alerted my family to my presence at the mound.

LITERARY QUOTES

'The horror! The horror!' with due acknowledgement to Joseph Conrad. 'Like some unlikely character in a novel, the woman in white. . .' with due acknowledgement to Wilkie Collins. 'Reader, I kissed her' with due acknowledgement to Charlotte Brontë.

DR WINK AND MEDICAL CONSULTATIONS

The description of the first medical consultation is based on accounts later obtained from family members. The second is partly based on memory. My abiding memory of Dr Wink is of enormous eyes behind – presumably strong – spectacle lenses. Whatever the circumstances, I left with the impression I'd made the decision concerning which school I should attend.

BANDAGE BOY

While there was no Bandage Boy, private schools did, and probably still do, accept pupils with forms of handicap that would have sent them into state special schools. Indeed children with problems of the sort seen in special schools sometimes went to normal state schools. So 'bums on seats' may well have been a factor in special education.

WERNER FORSSMANN

Werner Forssmann and his work are still discussed in medical circles with great admiration and respect. A German surgeon who knew him told me Herr Forssmann had fortified himself appropriately the night he took the scalpel to himself.

A brief account of the pioneers of cardiac surgery can be found in Roy Porter's *The Greatest Benefit to Mankind* (HarperCollins, London, 1997), Chapter XIX; pp 614–18 from which this account is taken.

SURGERY

During a cardiac catheterisation, when my arm was cut for insertion of the catheter, I felt the cut, I yelled, felt the blood spread, and almost hit the ceiling of the operating theatre. As intimated, this was many years after Forrsmann had managed to carry out the procedure on himself. It was only a few years ago that a proper diagnosis was made concerning my heart condition. It was – and is – a relatively minor problem improperly diagnosed from the outset. If I'd known this earlier, I would have pursued a career in clinical medicine. But, had I done that, I would almost certainly have had few of the experiences I now view as having been of immense value in other respects.

THE PUPILS

Derek
My first dubious memories of school are of the school bus, and of Derek, a boy probably in his teens then who was badly handicapped and whom I saw being incontinent on my first day at school.

Martin
Martin and his mother were very much as described, though, to the best of my knowledge, Martin never did speak.

Al and Billy
The early characterisations of Al and Billy are accurate from my point of view as a five year old. We had many discussions in the Rest Room and in the playground, many of which revolved around why we were actually there. I met Al's mother a few times over the years. She seemed a devoted caring mother and, while not as eclectic as depicted in her search for a cure for her son, would undoubtedly have done anything she could have to assist him.

Al was less forthcoming and more reflective than Billy, who wasn't quite as boastful as portrayed. Billy's secret wasn't literally true. However, over the years, I learned things about my fellow pupils' backgrounds that were usually surprising and often distressing. Many had more than one cross to bear in life, and few mentioned it.

I don't remember the circumstances of Al's death, though I do remember speaking with him shortly before he left school for the last time. His mum thanked me some time later for being his friend. I have no recollection of the circumstances surrounding Billy's death either.

Jean
Jean was an extremely bright, charming and eloquent little girl, despite the fact she was a very sick little girl too.

Siggy
Siggy is based on a reflective, clever and well-informed boy I met in hospital, who ultimately died after unsuccessful cardiac surgery.

Jason
Jason is a composite character of two boys at school, though I've never personally met a gay five year old.

Drug Dealer
There was no drug-dealer in P.H.1, but there was a precocious extortionist who succeeded in obtaining toy cars from kids who hadn't finished drinking their school-milk and were afraid of being 'told on'. This boy blackmailed me for weeks until I grassed on him.

Melissa
Melissa was a kind, practical and very bright young woman whom I was extremely fond of up until I left the Special School permanently. If I'd stayed on there and we'd become 'an item', I would have been very fortunate indeed.

Wee Jimmy
The episode in the cloakroom with Wee Jimmy happened, though I didn't see him *in situ* on the coat hook. I'm uncertain to this day whether his legs were really nicked, though he certainly arrived back at the classroom in a wheelchair.

'*Dove sono le…*' I obtained this quote from a friend. I believe it's extremely, graphic Sicilian Italian, though it wasn't translated for me.

Big Bob
The incident in the convent with Saint Anthony and Big Bob occurred exactly as described and for the reasons described. Mrs Darksole was with us, but she never did find out.

Faith
I became very fond of Faith, who had albinism. She was a fabulous young woman with a drive and enthusiasm for life I've rarely seen in others.

Una
Una was much as depicted and a good friend.

Woody
Woody is a composite character, but I'm certain his anger is very real indeed.

Other pupils
As indicated, the other pupils are based on real people.

THE TEACHERS

Miss Goldenheart and Miss Trulygood
Our first two teachers were saints, and, if I recall correctly, sisters.

Mrs Schiklgruber
Mrs Schiklgruber existed OK. I sat in with her religious instruction class on occasion. On Monday mornings, she cross-examined her mentally handicapped charges concerning the colour of the vestments worn by the priest the previous day. I never saw her physically harm anybody, but I doubt I ever saw anyone more ill-suited to teaching of any sort. For all I know she may well have been related to Adolf Hitler's grandmother: Mana Schicklgruber . . .

Mrs Darksole
'Her sharp little fists. . .' Corporal punishment, though officially forbidden, was dished out at the special school. Mrs Darksole was confronted with this in the presence of our headmistress and my mother. She denied punching me on the head frequently, but when the pupils were asked about it they honestly, collectively and bravely said she did so, and not only to me.

Miss Angelica
Miss Angelica was a gem! I often had serious chats with her, while I waited for the school bus to take me the few hundred yards back home. She was an inspiration. I did indeed perceive the badly handicapped as being less worthy of an education than I was, until she enabled me to see the many fallacies in this line of reasoning.

Miss Tartankilty
Miss Tartankilty was from the north of Scotland and proud of it. She was a relatively severe lady, but not unkind.

Mr Hammerhead
Mr Hammerhead was our woodwork teacher. But he was a calm, casual man, and the only male teacher in the school.

Miss Overprim
Miss Overprim was an excellent teacher who stood no nonsense and treated us like normal young adults.

RACIAL PREJUDICE
Black people were not a common sight in the Glasgow area in the 1950s. I grew up referring to them as 'Darkies' and obtained most of my information about them from children's books and the Church's 'Black Baby' system. I have it from a personal source that, in Africa in the 1950s, there was a 'White Baby' system run by the Church.

FREE DINNERS
'Socratic wisdom' is an awareness of one's ignorance. Socrates requested free meals for life from the court that sentenced him to death. I don't know if it was a feature of normal schools, but the 'free dinner' queue we had in the Special School – whereby those children whose parents couldn't afford the 'dinner money' were made to queue up in isolation from the rest of the class – was, in my view, iniquitous.

FIRST CONFESSION
We had our First Confession at school in a specially prepared classroom much as described, though there was no wood panelling put up for it.

CLERGY
The attitude of some clergy, and some religiously inclined lay people, to handicapped kids was often unhelpful. Some tended to patronise them, and they were frequently treated as if they possessed some elusive spiritual quality that would benefit anyone who was nice to them.

Father Mortalsen
Father Mortalsen is a composite character. I was very fond of the priest who took my First Confession. Years later, I heard him make fun of the Special School in public, when he addressed the class I was in at my new school.

Father Savage
We did have a black missionary talk to us at school; and the questions asked were almost certainly similar to those depicted.

EXORCISM
There was a fairly spirited Caucasian White Father around our family at

that time, and he carried out an exorcism on a relatively close member of my family. To the best of my knowledge there was no genuine religious, or any other, reason for him doing so. We were having domestic problems at the time, of the financial sort. He'd spent many years in Africa, where, according to him, this was common practice. The words depicted are copied verbatim from the ritual he used.

SCOTS TEMPERAMENT

The Roman historian Tacitus comments on the Scots' internecine squabbles in *The Agricola and the Germania* section 12, page 62, of the revised translation by S.A. Handford in the 1970 edition published by Penguin, London.

THE MAGNET

The incident with the magnet is based on an event where my production of a magnet in the classroom coincided with sudden twitching in a girl who sat directly in front of me. She wore two callipers and, for a few seconds, I thought the two incidents were related. My godfather was killed as indicated, when an ambulance collided head-on with his motorcycle.

THE LIBRARY AND SOCIAL BACKGROUND

The incident at the library happened as described, and my barely literate friend offered to help out as described too. In any situation where school was discussed, the fact that you went to the Special School evoked an unpredictable response in people. In consequence, any talk about school was a source of anxiety to me.

The neighbour mentioned wasn't convicted of murder – that was another one. The area I was brought up in was a mixed, working-class, council estate. You tended to keep to your own street, and in the one we lived in latterly there was a mix of people and professions. To the best of my recollection, they included a future priest, nun, prostitute, murderer and at least one murder victim. They were all pleasant enough people to me.

LOURDES

The scene of the returning pilgrims from Lourdes is based on fact, but no one died during it nor were there any miracles.

SPECIAL SCHOOLS' FOOTBALL

The account of the football match is based on regular soccer matches that were, often ingeniously, played in the school playground. Tempers often became heated during these games, and there were occasional fights. On one occasion when we had a P.H. versus M.H. match, the M.H. side of the school hammered us. I once asked a boy at the Academy to watch one of these games and give me critical comment. He did. He went on to become an international footballer.

SEX, DRUGS AND ROCK 'N' ROLL

I had an active interest in popular music for many years, mainly through my brother's association with it. In the early 1960s my eldest brother toured with a rock band, members of which frequently stayed over at our home. 'Uppers' and 'downers' were popular at this time and used as 'pick-me-ups', slimming pills and sedatives. 'Purple Hearts' (amphetamines) were soon discovered to produce a form of psychosis.

The incident with my brother's girlfriend and the monkey is accurate; as, in great part, is the 'ba-ba-black sheep' occurrence.

The scene at the prom with my brother and the rock band 'The Alex Harvey Big Soul Band' is taken from a magnificent performance of the musical piece 'Perfidia' they gave at my sister's wedding. Both Alex and his younger brother Les, who used to demonstrate his brilliant guitar-playing in our living-room, died prematurely in unfortunate circumstances.

STUDY OF CHEMISTRY AND THE ACADEMY

The events described with the chemical formulae are quite exact. The incident where Miss Angelica mentioned my prospective visit to the school-lab happened as described. Big Bill was very real, as was his lab demonstration and the behaviour of the senior pupils towards me. I have no doubt whatsoever that this episode fired me with the will to obtain a proper education.

My first day part-time at the Academy was much as described. In retrospect, it must have been difficult at times for both the teacher and the boys to have an outsider sitting in their class observing them and how they behaved.

Most of the pupils at the Academy were welcoming, few openly critical.

I sat the chemistry exam in 1963 as described. In terms of academic achievement, it was my finest hour.

FULL-TIME EDUCATION

Like the other children at my school, I was considered unsuitable for a formal full-time education for health reasons, and, I suspect, bureaucratic reasons too.

The discussion with the headmaster of the Academy happened as described.

The attitude of everyone involved in deciding my scholastic future was probably understandable; and, while there was no specific Mr Noteall, the intransigence of the Education Authority did seem extreme at the time. My eventual entry to the Academy happened almost exactly as described.

THE PROM

We had no Special School prom, but we did have a number of well-attended social occasions for adolescents. We played rock music, danced, messed around and did everything else other kids did. On occasions like this our problems were indeed in the spotlight if anyone cared to look.

ORGANISATIONS

If any reader is interested in actively pursuing any aspect of the issues raised in *On the Edge of a Lifetime*, there are many local and national agencies, in both the voluntary and public sectors, involved with discharging and improving the educational and social welfare of children with what these days many choose to term 'special needs'.

FINAL COMMENT

On my first full day at the Academy full time, another late-starter (a boy from a junior secondary school) accompanied me into class. He shared my birthday and his mother had known mine well in childhood. He wore a calliper.